PASSION FOR THE HEIST

ALSO BY K'WAN

PASSION
FOR THE
HEIST

K'WAN

TOR PUBLISHING GROUP
NEW YORK

PASSION FOR THE HEIST

Copyright © 2024 by K'wan Foye

A Forge Book
Published by Tom Doherty Associates / Tor Publishing Group
120 Broadway
New York, NY 10271

www.torpublishinggroup.com

Forge® is a registered trademark of Macmillan Publishing Group, LLC.

The Library of Congress Cataloging-in-Publication Data is available upon request.

ISBN 978-1-250-83489-8 (trade paperback)
ISBN 978-1-250-83490-4 (ebook)

Our books may be purchased in bulk for promotional, educational, or business use. Please contact your local bookseller or the Macmillan Corporate and Premium Sales Department at 1-800-221-7945, extension 5442, or by email at MacmillanSpecialMarkets@macmillan.com.

First Edition: 2024

Printed in the United States of America

0 9 8 7 6 5 4 3 2 1

PASSION FOR THE HEIST

PROLOGUE

Rush hour was just starting as Ruth Tolbert descended the stairs of the Columbus Circle subway station on 59th Street. She wore a dark-colored wool dress that was threatening to swallow her petite frame. She had borrowed it from one of her "cousins" who happened to be a little thicker than Ruth's size-four body. It was short notice. Ruth didn't have anything clean to wear to her appointment that afternoon and wanted to make sure she looked presentable. The material was light, but you'd have thought it was made of lead instead of wool if you judged by her stooped shoulders. This had not been one of Ruth's finest days.

Ruth found herself sucked into the crowd of people moving through the subway station, most just getting off work and in a hurry to get home. She was jostled this way and that as people bumped, pushed, shoved—and in one instance she was pretty sure someone groped her—as she moved toward the platform where the northbound A train would arrive. When she finally made it to the platform she found an unoccupied pillar and placed her back against it. She could've fallen asleep right there. Ruth was exhausted, but her fatigue was more spiritual than physical. She was so tired.

Her eyes drifted to an ad that was slapped on one of the subway's white tile walls. It was a poster depicting an image of a bearded white man who bore a striking resemblance to Jesus Christ. The only difference was that instead of a robe, the man in the picture was wearing a suit. His image levitated over a small group of people who seemed to be offering praises to the knock-off Jesus in the cheap suit. His hands were outstretched as if he was about to bestow a blessing upon them. Printed across the bottom of the poster in Gothic letters was the slogan, PUT YOUR FAITH IN TOD, followed by an 800 number where you could contact the law firm of Tod Leibowitz, Esq.

Ruth wasn't sure why, but the borderline blasphemous advertisement made her laugh. It started out as a chuckle, but built to a maddened cackle that caused the few people who had been standing near Ruth to take a cautious step back. She could only imagine what they were thinking, and there had been a time when she would obsess over other people's opinions of her. Ruth had never been the most attractive girl, rail-thin with a pointy nose and big feet. This made her the last picked by boys at functions where guys and girls usually paired up, and her subpar wardrobe didn't earn her any points with the fly girls. She had spent most of her youth trying to crack the glass floor of social acceptance, beholden to other people's opinions of her. That day, she couldn't bring herself to care.

Something moist splashed on the back of her hand. She looked down and found a droplet of water rolling over her knuckle. It was shortly joined by another. She hadn't even realized that she was crying. Her tear-stained hand drew her attention to the sheet of paper clutched in it. She smoothed it out and scanned over it again for the fifth or sixth time, as if it would somehow read differently than the first. It didn't. It was a grim reminder that her entire life had been altered by the few strokes of a stranger's keyboard.

"Are you okay?" Ruth heard a small voice ask. She looked up to find a boy of about ten or eleven giving her a concerned look. It was an innocent-enough question, but it cut her like a knife.

"No, I don't think I am," Ruth said, trying to keep her voice from shaking.

"Malik, what did I tell you about talking to strangers?" A woman appeared behind the boy. From the resemblance, Ruth assumed that it was his mother.

"But she's crying, Mama." Malik confirmed Ruth's assumption.

"Which is none of your concern." The woman snatched her son away and ushered him farther down the platform. Before departing she cast a pitying look over her shoulder at Ruth.

"Fuck your opinion," Ruth mumbled under her breath.

In the distance she saw the approaching lights of the A train coming through the tunnel. This was the signal for everyone who had been waiting on the platform to move forward so as to ensure they were able to board the likely already-crowded train in hopes of finding a seat or somewhere to stand. Ruth pushed off the pillar and stood with her toes touching the yellow caution line that ran along the edge of the platform. The train was getting closer. She cast one last glance at the advertisement on the wall. Put your faith in Tod. *What a fucking joke,* was her last thought before stepping off the edge of the platform and into the path of the approaching train.

The subway station was filled with the sounds of the train's brakes grinding against the metal tracks as the conductor attempted to bring the train to a complete stop, followed by screams. Little Malik found himself knocked to the ground as the crowd surged forward, toward what was sure to be a gruesome scene. He lost sight of his mom and barely managed to scramble out of the way to avoid being trampled by the stampede. In his quest to find cover, he spied a crumpled piece of paper lying on the ground near where the crying girl had been standing. He wasn't sure what made him pick it up. Malik read over the paper. Most of it read like Chinese arithmetic, but he did understand two words: *HIV* and *reactive*.

PART I
TWILIGHT

CHAPTER 1

Percy Wells, known to those who had found themselves on the wrong end of his skill set as Pain, was no stranger to violence. In fact, his earliest memories of life had been born of violence. One that stood out to him was when his father had laid his mother out with a short right hook. Seeing his father lay hands on his mother wasn't an unusual thing. The few times he could ever remember his father sparing enough time to come around his mother, they were either fighting, getting high, or fucking. Sometimes all three in one visit.

Pain would've been lying if he told you that he could remember what had prompted his father to strike his mother that particular time. What made this situation remarkable was the speed of the strike and the amount of blood it drew. It was akin to watching a rattlesnake tag an unsuspecting rodent. The gash opened by the punch was a small one, but it bled like his father had hit an artery in his mother's head. That day was one of only three or four times Pain could remember ever seeing the man who creamed in his mother and passed on not only his name, but the generational curse he carried. Pain was born into and had lived with violence all his life, but none of it was quite like what he currently found himself in the middle of.

There were over a dozen men clustered into the common area shared by the unit of the prison Pain had occupied for the last eight months of his four-year stretch. He used the word *occupied* instead of *resided* because the latter would've implied he could even fathom the thought of ever looking at prison as somewhere he'd gotten comfortable enough to make a home of. As far as he was concerned the few correctional facilities he'd passed through during his bid were simply temporary stops on the road he found himself on. Now that he'd traveled it once, he knew where the potholes were and would be able to avoid them if, God forbid, he ever had the misfortune of coming that way again.

Fists flew while homemade blades flashed in the dim yellow lights that hung from the ceiling of the unit. A good portion of the men who were in the common area that day were engaged in a hellish battle that teetered along the lines of becoming a riot, had the numbers been greater. Those who weren't getting into it did their best to try and avoid being mistaken for an enemy of one of the opposing sides and attacked by accident, or try to keep from being splashed by the blood that seemed to be flying everywhere. It was no easy task for the neutral parties because as far as the active combatants were concerned, anybody that wasn't on one of their sides was fair game. When the stakes you were playing for were life and death, there were no gray areas.

To Pain's right, a man yowled. Pain turned in time to see his belly being ripped open with a jagged screwdriver that was wielded by another inmate. The wails of the wounded were deafening in his ears, and twice he almost slipped in the blood that was rapidly coating the floors. If he had to describe the situation in a word it would've been *chaos*. What made it worse was that this was a chaos of his own making. Pain had been the match that ignited this powder keg.

A shadow descended over Pain, cast by a man who stood around six-five with a body mass that easily tipped the scales at three hundred pounds. His ugly face was one that was familiar to Pain. He had never bothered to learn the man's Christian name, but he was known to inmates and guards alike as Brute. The moniker spoke to his character because for all intents and purposes that's just what he was, a brute. In every facility he'd been a guest of, he survived by preying on both the weak and the strong. He wasn't particular about whose food he ate, so long as he went to bed full every night. In Brute's hand was a length of shaved pipe that had been pried from a bathroom sink, flattened on one end and sharpened to a razor's edge. The homemade weapon dripped with the blood of the inmates Brute had carved through during the battle to be granted a private audience with Pain. The men who he had cut down were little more than collateral damage, but his beef with Pain was personal. The hateful glare Brute leveled at him said as much.

Had it been a movie this would've been the part where the hero and villain exchange some well-scripted banter about what had brought them to that point, but this wasn't an action film. It was real life. There were only five words spoken, all by Brute, but they carried the weight of everything that was going on around them: "You owe me a kiss." Then it was lit!

Brute moved with a speed that should've been impossible for a man his size. Pain barely avoided the strike from the pipe/spear that was thrust at his face. The blow had been meant to blind him, but missed its mark. A coolness settled in Pain's cheek, just below his left eye. Then the burning kicked in. Pain knew that he was cut, but didn't have the chance to assess the damage before Brute was back at him. This time he went for Pain's gut in an attempt to impale him. The spear met with some resistance when it contacted the body armor under Pain's shirt. The armor was comprised of nothing more than duct tape and the jackets of a few hardcover books Pain had stolen from the prison library. The book covers kept Brute's spear from emptying Pain's insides, but didn't stop the point from piercing the fat of Pain's stomach.

Brute smirked triumphantly before driving his weight at Pain, forcing him against the nearest wall. The more pressure he applied, the deeper Pain could feel the spear pushing into his gut. There was no question that he was about to become another notch on Brute's belt. As his wound leaked, his life began to flash before his eyes. He thought of all the things he had done, as well as the things he would never do and the people he would never see again. His eyes latched onto an image of his grandma reaching out to him. He'd never have a chance to thank her for all she'd done for him. No . . . he couldn't go out . . . not like this.

As if by an act of sorcery, a weapon appeared in Pain's hand. It was a bedspring that had been hammered as straight as it could be and sharpened into a needle-like point. The end was wrapped in toilet tissue and held to the spring by layers of heavy tape, which allowed a more secure grip. Pain studied it for a brief moment as if trying to figure out what it was and where it had come from. Then the homemade weapon spoke a single word that would make everything clear to Pain: *Live.*

Moving as if animated by some unseen force, Pain raised his hand and drove the bedspring into Brute's neck. The bigger man paused as if trying to determine if he had just been stung by a bee or a mosquito. Pain didn't leave him long to wonder. He ripped the coil from Brute's neck and hit him again. This time it was in the forearm, which got him to slacken his grip on the spear. Pain ignored the fire in his belly and cheek and went into survival mode. He hit Brute over and over with the coil, striking him in the face, chest, arms, whichever parts of his body he could get to. Brute was so flustered he abandoned his spear and rushed at Pain. He managed to grab Pain around the throat and began choking him, sending them both falling to the ground. The whole way down, Pain kept hitting him with the bed spring. There was so much blood that there was no way of telling where Pain's injuries began and Brute's ended.

He couldn't remember how it had happened, but somehow Pain found himself on top of Brute, straddling his chest. Fighting was going on all around him, but Pain shut it out. His focus was locked on Brute. The big man's once-white T-shirt was now stained deep red. He was bleeding from the wounds gifted him. Brute was broken and probably not long for the world unless he received immediate medical attention. The king of the cellblock had finally been dethroned. It was done.

There was a moment of hesitation on Pain's part until his eyes met Brute's. Even on the threshold of death, there was still defiance in his predatory glare. Pain's brain was suddenly flooded with the memories of the injustices he and so many others had suffered at the hands of the bully. There was only one way to purge his brand of evil from the world. Pain raised the hand holding the bed coil, poised for the killing blow, and struck with everything he had. Had his blow rung true it would've punctured Brute's brain and ended him for all time, but this was not to be.

An unseen hand grabbed Pain by the wrist and pulled him from the giant just before the blade contacted his skull. Pain landed on his back and before he could right himself, the body of a fallen combatant landed on top of him. This was followed by another and then another and so on, to the point where Pain found himself trapped under the weight of the men. It was suddenly very hard to breathe, and for a time Pain experienced what it must've felt like to drown. Only he wasn't drowning in water, but in blood. There was a sliver of light at the end of the dark tunnel of flesh that he was trapped in. An outstretched hand beckoned to him. Without thought, Pain grabbed the hand and held on for dear life. Slowly, he found himself being pulled free, and when he broke the surface of bodies he inhaled the precious life-giving air. Pain was thankful to whichever angel of mercy had pulled him free and was about to tell him as much, when he found himself pulled into a reverse choke hold. He struggled but could not budge the muscular arm that was crushing his windpipe. With some effort he managed to turn his head enough to get a glimpse of whomever was strangling him. Who he saw was no angel of mercy, but a demon.

Brute stood behind him wearing a sinister grin and flashing a mouth full of bloodied teeth. He leaned in and pressed his blood-stained cheek against Pain's, his breath hot and foul. He ran his course tongue over Pain's ear before whispering into it: "Now, about that kiss."

Pain was awakened by the sounds of his own screams ringing in his ears. He instinctively leapt to his feet, ready to continue the fight for life or death that he had been locked in. Yet when he looked around he didn't find Brute, as he was expecting, but an older man wearing a bus driver's uniform.

"Take it easy, buddy. I was just trying to tell you that this was the last stop." The bus driver finally found his voice. He was no longer touching Pain's arm, and had moved himself to a safer distance.

The words came out like gibberish to Pain, as the sleep fog was only slowly rolling back from his brain, but his survival instincts were moving much faster. Near-feral eyes flashed to a point just beyond the bus driver. A woman had paused in her exiting of the bus to see what would become of the crazed man in the back seat. She wasn't alone. There were at least a dozen pairs of eyes on him with looks that ranged from confusion to fear. Two young girls seated near the front of the bus were even recording him with their camera phones while trading snickers. Pain felt like an animal on display.

"Did you hear what I said?" the bus driver asked calmly.

Pain didn't answer right away. He was still half expecting the mirage of being on a bus to fade and to discover that he was still behind the wall. His gaze went beyond the bus driver and focused on the road-stained windshield of the bus. Just outside, above the thickening traffic, the sun was just rising over a skyline that Pain knew all too well. "No more locked doors," was all Pain offered in way of a response.

Pain brushed past the startled driver and through the gawking people toward the exit. He almost twisted his ankle and fell in his haste to get off the bus. The smells and sounds of the hectic city seemed to assault him all at once, making him feel like he was suffering from sensory overload. He had been caged so long that feeling the cool pre-dawn air on his face felt like an extension of the nightmare he had been having on the bus. "No more locked doors," he repeated like a mantra. When Pain looked up and saw the night sky had begun to fade, and the sun was just about to announce its presence, he felt his eyes moisten in joy. It wasn't a nightmare, but a dream. After years of incarceration, Pain was really home.

CHAPTER 2

Passion arose at roughly the same time as she had every morning for the last few years, right before dawn. She never needed to set an alarm to wake at that hour; it was just something that her body had been programed to do. Even before she had adopted the predawn rising ritual, Passion never slept longer than she needed to. That was something her mother had instilled in her. "Tomorrow isn't promised to anyone. Life can be snatched from us at any moment without rhyme or reason, and every day that we wake up is a gift from God. Never waste a moment of it." Her mother could be really heavy into God and the church. Sometimes too heavy for Passion's tastes. Back then she couldn't really understand what her mother was trying to teach her, but as she got older and suffered a bit more, she received the message. They were all living on borrowed time.

She gave her joints a good stretch before swinging her long legs over the edge of her twin-size bed. She expected to feel the rough threads of her area rug under her bare soles, but instead her feet sank into something lumpy and warm. Cuddled up on the floor next to her bed were her cousin Claire and a light-skinned boy that Passion recognized from the neighborhood. Ramel was his name, if she recalled correctly. She didn't know him well and the only reason he was even remotely on her radar was because she had peeped him sniffing around Claire for the past few weeks. Passion had tried to warn Claire about the slick-talking youngster and his intentions, but the fact that the two of them were likely naked beneath the cheap sheet said that Claire hadn't listened.

Passion gave Claire a nudge with her foot, but it failed to stir the girl. So, she tapped her shoulder blade with the heel of her foot. It wasn't necessarily a kick, but it had the same desired effect. Claire sat bolt upright and looked around nervously like she was under attack. When her eyes landed on Passion they narrowed to slits.

"Bitch, I know you didn't just kick me like I'm some dog," Claire snapped. Her skull was still heavy with sleep and she couldn't understand why Passion was coming at her.

"You rather I kick your simple ass to bring you back to reality, or watch you get your shit cracked when Uncle comes in here and catches you being a ho?" Passion looked at Ramel, who hadn't so much as paused his snoring.

Claire looked at Ramel as if she was just noticing him. About then is when the fog released its grip on her brain and flashes of the night before began coming to her. She had let the liquor carry her out of pocket. "Shit!"

Passion watched from her bed as Claire tossed the sheets, frantically looking for something swallowed in them. In doing so, she exposed Ramel's sleeping and naked form. Passion blinked twice, zeroing in on his midsection. She felt herself staring now, and hadn't meant to, but Ramel had one of the biggest penises that she had ever seen. Even with him unconscious and his dick half flaccid, she could tell that the young man was capable of inflicting some serious damage with it. She smacked her lips unconsciously while her brain drifted to a nasty place in the corner of her mind. "I might have been in a coma, too, if I'd spent half the night trying to take all that." She hadn't meant to say it out loud, but had.

"What kind of beating my pussy can stand up to ain't none of your concern," Claire said defensively. She hadn't missed Passion staring at Ramel's penis as if she was trying to decide if it would taste better with hot sauce or ketchup.

"It becomes my concern when one of you little hot-in-the-ass broads does something that can affect what goes on with the rest of us," Passion informed her.

"Whatever, Passion." Claire sucked her teeth and went back to searching through the sheets for whatever she was looking for. A few beats later she dug her cell phone from the sheets. She tapped the screen, but it remained dark. It was dead. "That's why my alarm didn't go off," she said more to herself than anyone else.

"Your alarm might not have gone off, but you know he's going to go more than off if he comes in here and catches you being freakish with some random boy," Passion warned. The color draining from Claire's face said that she didn't have to expound on who she meant by *he*.

"Wake up!" Claire began shaking Ramel. When he was slow to

respond, Claire grabbed the plastic cup of water that Passion always kept at her bedside and threw it in his face. That got his attention.

"Mama . . . I'm drowning!" Ramel called for his mother, while his arms flailed like he was trying to swim up from the deep end of a pool.

"Put your clothes on." Claire ignored his confusion, shoving his jeans and sweatshirt into his lap.

"Let me get five more minutes." Ramel sucked his teeth and attempted to lay back down. Passion stopped him.

"Shorty, that extra five minutes ain't worth the rest of your life. Because ain't no question in my mind that if my uncle comes in here and catches you, you're surely going to die," Passion told him.

It was then that Ramel remembered where he was and why he had been skeptical about coming in the first place. "Oh, hell nah!" He jumped up and began hurriedly dressing. He had wanted to fuck Claire in the staircase, which was their norm, but she picked that night to suddenly develop morals and insisted that the only way she was going to give the pussy up was under someone's roof. Ramel's mom was home, and didn't play those kinds of games, so they couldn't go there. This was when Claire suggested that they go back to her place. He knew what time it was with her uncle, and entering that apartment would've been a bad idea when he was at home, but crossing that threshold while he wasn't there was borderline suicide. Still, Claire's phat ass looked so good in the tight pink boy shorts, and the pussy print in the front was calling his name. Against his better judgment he went for it, and now he found himself moving like a man just highlighted on *America's Most Wanted* and trying to get out of the apartment before the marshals kicked the door in.

"You ain't got time for all that." Claire pulled him to his feet as he was trying to put his boots on.

"Hold on with all that. You acting like I stole the pussy, knowing damn well we always negotiate in good faith. I ain't really feeling how you're treating me, considering," Ramel said, not feeling the way he was being rushed out like some type of sneak thief. He had taken Claire to BBQ's and bought her a bottle of liquor before coming back to the apartment with her, and felt like he deserved a little more courtesy than he was being shown.

"Bruh-bruh, we can discuss that at another time. Right now, I need you to get the wind beneath your feet and fly." Claire ushered him out of the bedroom and to the front door.

Passion sat on the bed for a time longer, listening to the arguing couple's voices as they receded through the living room and finally out the front door. Ramel clearly wasn't happy with the treatment he was receiving from his temporary bedmate, but getting him out of the house when she did should've been looked upon as a gift, considering the alternative. He didn't know it, but Claire had just done him a solid.

After making sure there were no more bodies to step on, Passion headed to the bathroom. She sat on the toilet and relieved herself while going through a mental checklist of the things that she needed to do that day. Next, she moved to the bathroom mirror where she proceeded to brush her teeth. Standing in front of the mirror she took inventory of herself: clear pecan-colored skin, twinkling brown eyes, and an infectious smile when she allowed herself to do so. She pulled free of the colorful bonnet that she slept with to hold her hair in place and shook her dreadlocks loose. She pinched the end of one of them between her green-painted fingers and pulled it to its limit. Her hair was just past her shoulders now. A far cry from when she had started. A few years ago, Passion had done the Big Chop, cutting the long brown hair she had been growing since birth down to an Afro. When her family witnessed what she had done, everyone just assumed she was having a mental breakdown due to everything that she had just gone through. It wasn't a breakdown though, but a rebuild. The things she had held most dear in life had been stripped from her, so she decided that the superficial should go as well: no heat to her hair, no weaves, and no makeup, save for the occasional coat of lipstick. She wasn't making a statement with the act, or trying to fit into any group or trend like some girls did when making such extreme changes. It was just something Passion felt like she needed to do to reset her wounded soul. Everything that she had been taught or told to that point was burned down, and from the ashes rose a phoenix crafted in the image in which God had made her: all natural. She was still no expert at flying, but the more she healed the higher she soared.

As Passion was toying with her hair, the long sleeve of the shirt she had slept in fell back. Along her forearm, stopping just short of her wrist, were remnants of scars old and new. Those scars told a two-sided story, one that both beat her down and lifted her up. When people who saw the scars asked Passion about them she would never offer more than some fabricated story about a childhood injury, or for those who hadn't known her that long, something along the lines of being clumsy at school. The truth behind the scars was something more intimate, and she had only found one person she trusted enough to be that candid with. The collection of scars was her cross to bear.

She applied a bit of cocoa butter to some of the more recent scars and fixed her sleeves. As she was brushing her teeth she considered jumping in the shower, but decided against it. Any other morning Passion would've taken advantage of being the first one in the bathroom, and not having to wait to wash her ass or brush her teeth, but not this one. The time she had spent dealing with Claire's mess had put her behind schedule. She had precious few minutes to spare or run the risk of missing her regularly scheduled meeting. The shower could wait.

While Passion was washing her face, her eyes went to her neck in the reflection of the mirror. She felt her heart skip when she found it bare. She dropped the rag and her hands instinctively went to her throat as if the image was playing tricks on her. She then began shaking the shirt she wore, which doubled as a nightgown. She looked to the floor hopefully, but nothing fell out. With terror gripping her chest, Passion bolted back into the bedroom. She ripped both pillows and sheets from her bed, frantically searching. When the sheets yielded nothing, her mind immediately started playing out the worst-case scenarios. There was no way she could've been careless enough to lose it. Not something so precious. Someone in the house had to have stolen it. It wouldn't have been the first time they'd helped themselves to something or hers, and most of the time she let it go, but not this. All the girls in the house had at least a touch of larceny in them, so this made it hard to say for sure exactly which one had done it, but Passion planned to take her time in finding out.

She was fishing around under her mattress, in search of the scalpel that she kept tucked there to keep the bad dreams away, when she caught a glint of something in her periphery. It sat in the nook between the head of her bed and the closest window. Had the light of dawn not been creeping through her window at just that angle at just that time, Passion would've probably never noticed it. But there it was in all its sparkling glory. She dropped to her knees and snatched it up, keeping it cupped in her hands like an ember she was trying to keep from going out. It was a thin white gold chain with two twin heart-shaped pendants hanging from the end of it. To the casual observer, neither the fourteen-karat chain nor its diamond-flaked hearts would've earned more than a second look, but it was the most valuable thing that Passion owned. It was as much of a reminder of a bad yesterday as it was a beacon of hope for a better tomorrow.

Claire had yet to return to the bedroom, and the third girl they bunked with was still asleep. This would allow Passion a few rare moments of privacy, which she was thankful for. The waking hour, as she called it, was an intimate time for her and she hated sharing it when she could avoid it.

The sky outside the bedroom window had just started to burn a pale pink, but orange tendrils were beginning to snake their way through. Blue skies wouldn't be far behind. Passion grabbed the lone pillow from the twin-size bed she slept in and laid it over the top of the radiator under the window. It took her a minute to find a comfortable-enough position to where the radiator's ridges wouldn't cut into her ass through the worn feathers and thin fabric of the pillow.

From the nook of the windowsill, Passion grabbed a loose cigarette. She generally kept one or two stashed there so as to make sure she had at least one for herself every morning. Most of the girls who lived in the house smoked, so between them bumming for cigarettes or asking for bust-downs on ones already being smoked, packs didn't last long. Of all the smokers in the house, she was the only one who bought more than a few loose cigarettes at a time, so she often found herself as the go-to when one of the girls was out and craving nicotine. Passion didn't mind sharing with her cousins, but with the price of Newports constantly rising in the city, their begging could at times be bothersome. Whenever she bought a pack, Passion would always set a few to the side for herself before letting it be known that she was holding.

Passion lit the cigarette with a lighter she had found on the floor. Her cousins may never have had any smokes, but they always had lights. Bics fell randomly out of their pockets and purses when the girls stripped for the night, so she could always find one abandoned or lost on the floor or under one of the beds. She sparked the cigarette and held the smoke in her lungs, letting it tickle around to the parts of her that may have still been asleep. When she exhaled the smoke, she caught a slight head rush. Nothing like smoking a blunt, but enough to pull her brain from whatever happened the day before and into the now. She was officially awake.

After taking a few good tokes from the cigarette and making sure it was burning properly, she turned her attention back to the skyline. Light poured between the tall buildings in the distance. She could feel her heart start to race. Though it was a regular morning ritual for her, it always felt like the first time. Finally, the sun came into view with all the flair of an opening scene from an Oscar-worthy film. As the light made its way through her window, she closed her eyes and let the warmth wash over her face. It was a simple thing, but to her it was like the gentle caress of a loved one and a reminder of better days.

Passion's love of the sunrise was born on a family trip to the West Coast. Her mom had a friend who she knew through her job, who had relocated to the West Coast, where he purchased a beautiful house in Malibu. Her old coworker had invited Passion's family out west for a visit. Her dad hadn't been up to the trip, but her mother insisted, so he had no choice. Passion's dad always deferred to the whims of her mother and she could never remember him having won an argument. He usually just caved to whatever it was that she wanted. Watching her walk on him all those times bothered Passion. She had always seen her father as such a strong man. He was her invincible hero . . . except when it came to her mother. She was the one person who could tear away the mask of invincibility and make her husband seem like less of a man. This would leave invisible scars on her daughter that would affect how she dealt with the opposite sex later in life. Passion wasn't sure who she resented more, her mother for breaking her father or him for allowing it. What Passion couldn't comprehend at the time was that it wasn't that her father was a weak man, her mother just held power over him. It was a power that Passion wouldn't fully understand until she later inherited it.

Passion and her mom wanted to fly to California, but her father didn't. He'd had a friend who died in a plane crash, and ever since he had refused to set foot on one of the metal birds. Passion's mother was pissed, but her father wouldn't budge. It was the one thing that Passion could remember him finding enough of his voice to stand up to her mother on. So, as a compromise, they borrowed an RV from the church they attended and made it into a road trip. Passion, like her mother, hadn't been thrilled at the prospect of driving nearly three thousand miles over a few days when they could've simply flown and been there in a few hours, but by the time they had made it as far as Ohio she found that she was actually having a good time.

People who didn't have the opportunities to travel outside of what was familiar to them had no idea how big and beautiful the rest of the world was, and therefore they would not be motivated to go and explore it. Passion was fascinated by the towns and cities they passed through and the people she saw. To her, they were so different. Leaving New York was like visiting another country. Passion made her dad stop in just about every state they crossed to grab some small trinket to remind her of their passing through. The frequent stops added an additional nine hours to their trip, which Passion's mother complained about the whole time, but her dad didn't care. He knew that taking this trip and showing his daughter the country would create memories that would live with her forever. That alone was worth the price of admission.

Watching the sunrise had been her mother's idea. She had always been a night owl, which was why she worked nights at her job. Even on nights her mother didn't have to work, Passion would sometimes wake up to use the bathroom and find her awake, sitting in the window, smoking cigarettes and staring out into the darkness. It was as if she were looking for something, though what? Passion never found out.

In every port that they would spend the night in, Passion's mother would wake her up shortly before dawn to watch the sun come up. Some might think that one sunrise was no different than the next, but this wasn't true. At least not for Passion. To her, each sunrise over every city was unique in its own way. From the East Coast through the Midwest, each sunrise offered Passion something uniquely beautiful, but none of them compared to the first time she had seen the sun rising on the Pacific Coast.

It had happened during the last leg of their family trip out west. It was just before dawn and her father was pushing the RV along the Pacific Coast Highway. This was one of the few mornings that Passion's mother had slept through their sunrise ritual. She'd had a few drinks at a local bar the night before and was sleeping it off. Passion was awake, though. She was sitting in the passenger seat of the RV, holding a map and playing navigator for her dad. Not that he needed directions now that they were so close, but it made Passion feel helpful. She had gotten bored with the map and was looking out the window at the passing ocean when the first rays of the morning sun hit it. The light made the water sparkle like there were diamonds under the surface. In California the sun didn't take its time as it had done creeping over the rooftops in New York, or having to peel through the gray skies of Ohio. No, Cali sun showed up without invitation, hesitation, or interruption to blanket the coastline, signaling the beginning of a new day. It was the first and last time she had ever seen something so beautiful, and the memory of it would be forever burned into her young mind. Ever since beholding that first sunrise on the California coast, Passion had made it a habit to wake up early enough to watch the sun rise. She had seen over one thousand sunrises since then, but none quite like the one she had seen hitting the Pacific Ocean.

The daydream brought Passion's hand to the twin heart lockets she wore. She ran her thumb over the engravings on the back of each heart: GEORGE and EDNA. Those had been her parents' names. The bit of ashes inside the lockets and the ritual of watching the sunrise were all that remained of the loving souls who had brought Passion into the world. One was her joy and the other . . . her pain.

CHAPTER 3

"I don't know how y'all can smoke them things." A voice intruded on Passion's moment. She turned and found a pair of big, doe-like eyes staring at her from beneath the blanket covering the daybed on the other side of the room. The third occupant of the bedroom was now awake.

"My fault, Birdie. Is the smoke fucking with your asthma?" Passion stubbed the cigarette on the wall outside the window before flicking what was left of it to the wind.

"Nah, you good." Birdie came out from under the blanket and sat up. She was a young girl; slender of build with long arms and legs and a nose that was slightly too large for her small face. Her features were how she earned the nickname Birdie, because of her close resemblance to an ostrich.

"Go back to sleep. You still have another hour or so before we gotta start getting ready for school," Passion told her.

"You know when I'm up, I'm up." Birdie slid from the bed and came to stand next to Passion. For a few seconds she didn't say anything else, just stared out the window and tried to see what Passion saw that pulled her from sleep each morning. "You think it's gonna rain today?" she asked, looking to break the awkward silence.

"Feels like we get hit by a storm every day, even when the ground ain't wet," Passion told her before peeling herself away from the window. She moved to the small hope chest next to her bed, which held her few meager belongings. From it she selected her outfit for the day, which consisted of her favorite USC sweatshirt and a pair of worn jeans. It had always been her dream to one day attend the University of Southern California, but somewhere along the line her dream was derailed.

"You think Claire is okay out there?" Birdie moved closer to Passion. She didn't invite herself to a seat on the bed, she just hovered over it until Passion nodded that it was okay to sit.

"Claire has been getting herself in and out of shit for as long as I've known her. She'll be fine. Ramel is a thirst bucket, but he ain't no ass-kicker. Even if he was, ain't nobody swifter with a blade than Claire."

Birdie chuckled. "Her blade work is impeccable. From what I saw, her mouth game needs a little work, though. Too much teeth and not enough spit." She jabbed her thumb at her mouth and flicked her tongue into her cheek to mimic a blow job.

Passion gave Birdie a shocked look. "Was your little nasty ass watching them freak off?"

"With all the noise they were making, how did you expect me not to?" Birdie questioned. "Ramel had that girl in here calling on all the saints while he was giving it to her. I'm surprised it didn't wake you up, too, considering they were damn near under your bed getting busy. Oh, I forgot, you can sleep through a nuclear blast and wouldn't budge," she joked.

"Sleep is my only refuge these days. It's my escape," Passion said seriously.

A brief quiet slipped between them.

"I wish I had that," Birdie broke the silence. "An escape from the bullshit."

Passion turned to Birdie and really looked at her. She recognized the misty eyes and slight quiver of the lip as early warning signs that Birdie was about to go there. She was about to crawl down a psychological black hole. Passion had pulled her out of many such funks, but that morning she wasn't sure that she had it in her to do so. But she would try. Passion stroked Birdie's hair, which was pulled into a short ponytail, and pushed a smile to her lips. "You got an escape, Bird, and it'll be the greatest escape than any of us raised in this bullshit can ever hope for. You're going to graduate high school and fly up out of this bird's cage. When you march down that aisle and receive your diploma, you better keep going and don't you dare look back."

"But you looked back," Birdie pointed out. There was a brief period when Passion had run away, but she soon found how cold the world was, especially when you didn't have a pot to piss in. So she eventually came back.

"And like Lot's wife, I turned to salt." Passion looked around the room she shared with two other girls. "Now, go take advantage of the fact that the bathroom is free and shower before Claire comes back to wash that whore's stink off her."

Birdie smiled and went off to get herself ready. While Birdie showered, Passion went about the task of straightening their shared bedroom. She picked up dirty socks, bras, and underwear, which she deposited in the laundry hamper to be washed. It pissed Passion off to have to pick up behind her roommates as if they were children. Besides Birdie, Passion was the youngest in the house, but from the way she was forced to mother all of them you'd have thought that she was the eldest. Sometimes she was tempted to leave the messes the girls made, but they would likely just step over the clothes as if they weren't there until they began to pile up. This would create a bigger mess than anything in the bedroom. One of the rules of their uncle's apartment was to keep it tidy at all times. It was a rule he enforced with an iron fist.

When Birdie returned from her shower, Passion grabbed her towel and toiletries so she could have her turn before any of the other girls beat her to the bathroom. In the hallway she met Claire, who was just coming back into the apartment. She was just about to enter the bathroom when Passion cut her off. "I had dibs."

"C'mon, Passion. I just want to grab a quick shower. I'm all sticky." Claire motioned toward her lower regions.

"That ain't my problem. And I know you weren't dumb enough to let that boy hit it raw?" Passion questioned. When Claire averted her eyes, Passion had her answer. "Claire, what do I always tell y'all about protecting yourselves?"

"Ramel ain't got nothing." Claire rolled her eyes.

"How do you know? Last time I checked, people with STDs didn't walk around with signs on their foreheads advertising that they're burning. Let's say for the sake of argument that he is clean, what about pregnancy? You can barely take care of yourself, let alone a baby," Passion scolded her.

"You act like if Ramel did get me pregnant he wouldn't help me out. Ain't like he's broke," Claire defended him.

Passion gave her a disbelieving look. "Claire, are you really going to stand here and try to make sense out of getting pregnant by a dude who sells dime bags of weed in the projects and fucks you in stairwells?" she laughed.

"You gonna let me go in the shower first or not?" Claire asked with an attitude.

"Not," Passion said before going into the bathroom and slamming the door in Claire's face.

Passion took a long, hot shower. While she was in there she washed and conditioned her hair. It had been a while. She worked her fingers through her roots, creating an almost orgasmic feeling. The shower was one of the few places in the apartment where Passion could find privacy. At any given time, there was a half dozen people or more living under that roof and only four bedrooms. The adults in the house had their own rooms, and Passion roomed with Claire and Birdie, but everyone else who happened to be crashing there had to get in where they fit. There had been plenty of mornings when Passion found herself having to step over bodies on the floor in order to get to the kitchen.

The water had started to cool. She must've been in there longer than she had thought. It was so easy to get lost under the warm spray, especially living in a place that could be so cold. Daring to prolong her moment of serenity, Passion turned the water up higher, hoping to bleed what little heat was left while she finished washing herself. Generally, she might've tried to save at least a little hot water, knowing Claire needed a shower more than any of them, but that morning she allowed herself a rare act of selfishness. After the week she'd had she deserved the tender mercy of a long shower.

Passion took her time while lathering her body: neck, legs, arms. The rough green loofah felt liberating moving in circular motions over her skin. When she went to wash her breasts, she found that her nipples were swollen. This meant that her period would be arriving soon. This meant cramps that would only add to the aches and pains her body was already feeling from running around almost nonstop for the last couple of days.

She'd started out just rubbing her thumbs over her nipples to test the tenderness. She wasn't even sure when her index fingers had joined the party, but before she realized it she was gently massaging her nipples between the two digits. The she cupped one of her breasts and began to knead it like she was working the knots out of a tense shoulder. It felt good and she wanted to feel better. Passion's hand slipped between her legs and began playing with her sex. She used two fingers to hold her lips open to let the steadily cooling shower water pepper them. Her toes curled against the rubber shower mat as she continued to work herself. Holding onto the shower bar, she placed one foot on the side of the tub so that her legs were spread wide, and dipped a finger inside herself. She was so wet that you couldn't tell where the shower water ended and her juices began. One finger turned into two, and finally Passion was jacking three of her fingers to the knuckles, in and out of her God-given lake. The low panting she'd started out with had dipped to grunts and curses muttered under her breath as she felt herself going there. Passion wasn't sure if it was the fact her period was so close, or all the stress she had been under lately, but this nut felt different. It was the answer to everything going wrong in her life. With eyes closed and head thrown back, Passion finger-fucked herself into a release of atomic proportions.

The water had gone completely cold. It felt amazing against her skin, which felt like it was on fire. Her forehead was pressed against the shower tiles, and her shoulders rose and fell with her heavy breathing. She stood like that for a good little while because she didn't trust that her legs would support her if she tried to step out of the shower right then. No sooner than she had finished the deed did she start to feel the first hints of embarrassment. It wasn't that Passion thought there was anything wrong with masturbation, but she was always teasing the girls about it because they were so open about doing it. In front of them Passion pretended not to be into it like that, but behind closed doors her fingers could play her pussy like a baby grand piano. "Damn, I needed that," she breathed into the wall.

"Looks like you needed that and then some." A masculine voice scared the daylights out of Passion.

A short, roundish man with a clean-shaven head and lips too big for his face stood in the cramped bathroom with Passion. She could've sworn that she had locked the bathroom door, but the fact that he was in there with her said that she hadn't. Over the fresh smell of her body and hair, she could still smell the stench of liquor and cigarettes coming off him. Bloodshot eyes roamed openly over Passion's naked body. "Damn," his lips mouthed while his hand tugged at his crotch.

It only took a second before the initial shock wore off, and Passion snatched a towel off the rack. She covered herself as best she could. "D'fuck? Who are you and what the hell are you doing in here?"

"Up until a second ago, enjoying the show," the man said with a sly grin.

Passion pulled the towel tighter around her. "Weird-ass nigga! What are you, some kind of pervert? You get off on looking at little girls?" She stepped from the shower so that if the creepy man tried something she'd have a better chance of defending herself on dry ground.

"Nah, it ain't like that, baby. I'm a friend of the family," he told her.

"I only came to find somewhere I could take a piss. Running into you has been an unexpected bonus, I wasn't expecting no show. I'll be out of your way in a minute." He turned to the toilet and began undoing his pants.

"What do you think you're doing?" Passion asked in disbelief.

"I told you, I gotta take a piss." He pulled his dick out and began relieving himself into the toilet. It was thick and traced with veins leading up to a swollen, mushroom-shaped head. He caught Passion's eyes lingering on his dick longer than they should've. "What's the matter? You're acting like you've never seen a cock before. Living in this house I find that hard to believe. Bet you ain't never seen one as pretty as this, though." He gave it a little shake and some of the excess pee dripped onto Passion's foot. "You can touch it if you want."

Passion felt her vision shift, followed by a ball of ice starting to form in her stomach. This was the first hint that she was slipping into what her therapist used to call "the darkness." That was the place where Passion's mind would retreat to when her body was being put through something traumatic. The little voice in the back of her mind would assault her with whispers of worthlessness and self-loathing. Believing that she was deserving of what was happening, she would retreat to the furthest corners of her mind and relinquish control of her body to the darkness. From her hiding place, she would watch as a mental spectator while her physical body was punished. This was something that had begun to manifest before her parents died, triggered by an event that had been the subject of a few whispered conversations within her family.

When she first started showing signs that something might've been going on with her mentally, her father was concerned, but her mother dismissed it as her just acting out. She blamed him for spoiling her so much. Her mother, like so many other parents, treated mental health like a taboo subject. Something to sweep under the rug or ignore rather than face and run the risk of a stigma being attached to them. She was more concerned about how it would look in their social circles, especially the busybodies at the church their father made them attend. There were sure to be untold amounts of gossip if it ever got out that they had a child that was mentally unwell. It wasn't until Passion started cutting herself that they were forced to seek help. Ironically, they ended up finding help for her amongst the same people they were trying to hide it from, the church. There was a member of the congregation who her parents trusted, a psychiatrist who had a private practice. He offered to treat Passion at a discounted rate, and discreetly so that it wouldn't get out. Her father was suspicious, but her mother was okay with it, so Passion was given over to the doctor's care. Her mother had only wanted to help her baby girl, but ended up unknowingly making the problem worse.

After only a few weeks of treatment, Passion's sessions were brought to an abrupt halt. The psychiatrist unexpectedly closed down his practice and moved out of state. The official story that had been given to the church was that he had been offered a position at a prestigious clinic somewhere down south, but there were rumors that suggested otherwise. It was sometime later when the same psychiatrist made headlines in a Louisiana newspaper. Several young girls he had been treating came forward with allegations about him and his "private" practice. It made for quite the scandal and was the talk of the congregation up north. The police questioned all of the young girls who the psychiatrist had previously treated, including Passion. In their lone interview, Passion denied ever having been assaulted by the man. That was good enough for them. Had anyone taken the time to peel back enough layers of that onion then they would've seen that it was really a scallion. The writing was on the wall, but no one bothered to read it.

Something warm and sticky dripped onto one of Passion's bare feet, bringing her back from wherever she had been. The man must've taken her stunned silence as an invitation. His penis was in her hand and he was working her wrist so that it was moving back and forth. Pre-cum was beginning to ooze over her fingers and drip across her knuckles. He was smiling at her while he forced her to jack him, as if he was doing Passion a favor by violating her. His glare put her in the mind of an episode of *Law & Order: SVU* she had seen. In his eyes was the same malice as a suspected serial rapist who had spent a good chunk of the episode trying to convince detectives Benson and Stabler that he wasn't a predator. This was right before he went out and claimed his next victim. The ball of ice that had been in her stomach melted away, and in its place was a burning fire.

"See, ain't no thing, baby," he whispered while continuing to use her hand to pleasure himself. "Let me just stick the head in."

"How bad do you want some of this tender, underage pussy?" Passion asked in a sultry voice that sounded nothing like her own.

She moved her hand and let the towel fall away so that he could get a good look at her. She could feel his cock swell in her hand. It was fat with blood, like it would explode with the right amount of pressure.

"Bad enough to pay you to keep quiet about it," he offered. He reached into his pocket and pulled out his bankroll. The way she was stroking his dick he was worried that he wouldn't even make it to the pussy before blowing his load.

"Keep your money. This one is on me," Passion told him before snatching the soap dish from the sink and cracking him upside the head with it.

"You dirty bitch!" the man snapped, clutching the spot on his skull where Passion had clocked him. The blow would likely leave a knot, but it hadn't broken the skin. He reached for her, only to calm the girl, and things went from bad to worse.

"Don't touch me!" Passion's voice struck the pervert right before her fist did. He stumbled, more from the shock of her stealing on him than the blow actually doing any damage. She attacked him like a wild woman, kicking, punching, and scratching. Her naked breasts swinging and her snatch exposed, but she was beyond the point of embarrassment. She was an animal backed into a corner.

The fight spilled out of the bathroom and into the hallway, nearly knocking the door off its hinges along the way. The man managed to get a hold of Passion's wrists and prevent her from punching him anymore, but little did he know his problems were just starting. The commotion had woken everyone in the house and probably a few of the neighbors as well. The man forced Passion to the ground and straddled her, pinning her under his weight so that she couldn't move. She continued to fight, even managing to bite his thigh. This is when things got ugly, and he slapped her across the face. He raised his hand for a second slap and it was about then that he felt something cold and sharp at his throat.

"You got one more swing, and that'll be the end of your days in this world," a female voice whispered in his ear. "Try me, nigga. I dare you!"

The man was strong, but his flesh was tender and the knife was sharp. He released Passion's wrists and held his hands above his head like in an old Western when the sheriff got the drop on the bad guys. The woman, still with the knife to his throat, helped him off Passion and to his feet. When he was standing and Passion was safe and out of the way, the woman kicked him in the ass and sent him to the ground, chin first. The man rolled over, sat on his ass, and glared up at the woman who had kicked him.

"Bo, you must've lost your last mind treating me like you don't know who I am and what I do!" he snapped. Ted was his name. He was a petty criminal who owned a used car lot which provided all the young dope boys with cars and no-questions-asked paperwork. Ted also laundered money through this dealership for some of the players in the game. This put his services in high demand, so it gave Ted an inflated sense of self-importance

"Yeah, Ted. I'm hip to both, which is why you just a little shook up instead of cut up," the woman called Bo replied. She was an older broad with skin the color of curdled cream and hips so wide she had to turn sideways to enter some rooms. Bo was the den mother and triple OG of the house. Her word was the closest thing to law that they had under that roof. Next to the man they all called Uncle, she had the most authority in the house. "What you doing in my house?"

"I invited him." Another voice joined the conversation. At the sound of it, the temperature in the room felt like it had dropped ten degrees.

Standing in the doorway was the man of the house and resident living nightmare to all who resided under that roof. Joseph Green, called Uncle Joe by the girls in the house and pretty much everyone else, was a large man, standing at about six-three and tipping the scale somewhere north of two hundred and fifty pounds. He had coal black eyes and a wide nose that was slightly crooked along the bridge from being broken several times. His lips were thick, with the bottom one having a pinkish strip cutting across it as if it had been scorched. Bo called it the "drunk lip," but never to his face. Uncle Joe was wearing a white shirt under his three-quarter-length leather jacket. The top four buttons of the shirt were undone so you could see the three gold chains that were almost lost in the foliage of his hairy chest.

He wasn't alone. The newest girl in the house, Zeta, was shoved halfway up Uncle Joe's ass. That was her usual station, underfoot. Zeta went out of her way to please Uncle Joe whenever she could. Of all the girls in the house, she was the least liked. Not just because she was a notorious kiss-ass, but because she was also drop-dead gorgeous. She was a five-nine, cream-colored bombshell who resembled a younger version of Bo, only she was taller and didn't have the hips. Zeta may not have carried an ass as heavy as Bo's, but what she lacked in her rear end she made up for with her 38D cup, and a head game that was said to be out of this world.

From Zeta's confident pose while hovering in Uncle Joe's shadow, you could tell that she thought she was killing it. She was wearing the gift Uncle Joe had tossed her to go along with her promotion: a blue faux fur with the collar and cuffs dyed snow white. It was something that Joe had claimed from the spoils of a low-stakes robbery as payment for a debt owed by the robber. The coat wasn't worth much, but Zeta treated it like it was a shroud of freshly spun gold. Underneath the cheap jacket she wore a white latex dress that was so short you could almost see the lips of her vagina peeking out.

The cream-colored dream looked over the squabbling trio in the hallway with judgmental eyes. Eyes that said she wouldn't squirt a drop of piss on either one of them if they were on fire. Zeta was not only the newest girl, but also Uncle Joe's current favorite. Knowing that she had Joe's nose open made Zeta feel like her shit didn't stink, and she was always peacocking around the apartment while looking down her nose at the rest of the girls who lived there. She'd even challenged Bo's authority on more than a few occasions, and Bo had been with Uncle Joe the longest. Everyone knew that Bo was Joe's right hand, but instead of Zeta playing her position as his left, she wanted to be his only. She made no secret of this either. The only reason Bo hadn't yet tried to kill her in her sleep was for fear of how Uncle Joe might take it. It wouldn't have been the first time Bo had tightened one of Uncle Joe's random thots for jumping out of pocket. There were rarely any repercussions because of Bo's status, but Zeta was a different case. Bo had been running with Joe long enough to know when his nose was open off a new piece of pussy. It fucked with his vision and sometimes his judgment, so Bo had to handle Zeta differently.

Joe stood there, bloodshot eyes sweeping over everyone in the room as if he was waiting for someone to explain what he had just walked in on. None of them seemed to be able to find their voices. Even Ted, who had been slick at the mouth toward Passion and Bo, couldn't do much more than avert his eyes. Uncle Joe was a man who hated to have to ask a question twice, and most times the second ask was followed by a violent act. Those who knew him well recognized the look on Uncle Joe's face. He was "picking a Herb." That meant that he was searching for one person to turn his displeasure upon. When no one spoke up, Uncle Joe put himself in the mind to choose violence. He'd just decided whose face he needed to slap for making him repeat himself. Thankfully, they were all spared by a simple truth.

"Your drunk-ass friend almost got the last shave of his life." Bo's admission stayed the potential execution. She was probably the only person in the room who knew just when the fuse would reach the powder keg.

"I told him he could come up to use the bathroom," Uncle Joe informed her. "I was looking for a parking spot, but apparently Ted has the bladder of damn child and kept threatening to piss himself in the back seat of my new Benz, which his ass had overcharged me for when he sold it to me. I gave him the keys and told him it was cool to come up ahead of us to handle his business."

"Well maybe you should've called ahead and told me? Joe, you know how you get with men being in here when you ain't around. You don't play it. That's law. So, imagine my surprise when I get up to put your coffee on, like I'd know you'd want when you came in, and I find this fool out here putting his hands where they didn't belong." Bo nodded in Passion's direction.

When Uncle Joe looked to Passion, it was as if he was only noticing her for the first time. She was standing just behind Bo, who was between her and Ted. The towel she had retrieved from the bathroom floor was barely covering her breasts. When Uncle Joe saw the hateful look she was shooting at Ted, a roughly drawn, stick-figure animation of what may have just transpired played in his head. Uncle Joe stalked across the room like a jungle cat, eyes locked on Passion. From the tension in his movements you'd have thought he was about to slap her down, but instead he took her delicate chin in one of his large hands. For a few beats he said nothing, only studied Passion as if she was an exquisite piece of art that had just been put on display. When he was done with his examination he put a question in the air: "You touch what's mine, Ted?"

"This ain't none of what it looks like, Joe." Ted shuffled uncomfortably in place.

"That ain't what I asked. You know how I feel about having to ask the same shit twice, so do the right thing with your next statement," Uncle Joe warned.

"Joe," Ted began calmly, "it was a misunderstanding. I walked in

the bathroom without knocking first and just scared the girl a bit."
He downplayed it.

"Is that what happened, Passion? You misunderstand Mr. Ted's intentions?" Uncle Joe asked her.

Passion thought on the question before answering. She knew with just a shake of her head she could have the perverted old man pushed from this world. The terrified look in his eyes said that he knew this as well. The power she held over Ted at that moment made her lower regions hum, almost as intensely as when she had been playing with herself in the bathroom. Imagining Ted's blood on the walls made her almost giddy, and for an instant she toyed with the idea of letting Uncle Joe finish. She wondered if watching one man take the life of another over her could make her cum as hard as she had when she was in the shower? Then she caught herself. That was the darkness speaking, not her. Passion nodded her head in agreement with Ted's story, and stayed his execution.

Uncle Joe let his eyes linger on Passion for a bit longer, as if he didn't fully buy her story, but wasn't going to press the issue. "That's a good thing." He let his finger slide softly down Passion's cheek before turning his attention to Ted. "We been friends for a long time, but I'm awfully protective over my niece. I'd hate to have a miscommunication ruin our friendship."

"You ain't gotta worry about that, Joe. I'd never sample a meal you didn't invite me to," Ted told him.

"That's one meal you'll never sit down at the table to taste, so I guess we ain't gonna have no issues," Uncle Joe said. He looked at Passion, who was still standing there with nothing but a towel covering herself. "Go put some fucking clothes in before you find yourself the motive behind me doing something stupid."

As Passion was entering the bedroom, Birdie was coming out. She had a nervous look in her eyes and a box cutter cuffed in her hand. Passion knew the look and what Birdie had intended to do, but she stopped her by grabbing her about the arm and pulling her into the room behind her and slamming the door.

"You okay? That nigga do something to you?" Birdie fired off questions.

"I'm fine. Grab your stuff so we can get to school on time," Passion answered, and began quickly dressing.

"I heard you yelling and when I looked out the door I saw you wrestling with that man. I was about to get it shaking." Birdie brandished the box cutter as if Passion hadn't seen it already. She was a ball of nervous energy.

Passion took Birdie by the shoulders and looked her in the eyes. When she spoke, her tone was the most serious that Birdie had ever heard it. "The day any one of these no-account men that keep company with Uncle Joe give me anything that I didn't ask for, is the day I'm going to become property of the state for the rest of my life."

Birdie nodded that she understood just what Passion was insinuating. "I wish I was strong like you."

"You are, Birdie. Even if you don't know it yet." Passion hugged the younger girl. "If don't nobody in this place have my back, I know you do," she cut her eyes at Claire, who was lying across her daybed, scrolling through her phone. She was pretending to be oblivious as to what had been happening on the other side of their bedroom door. Claire had just pulled a sucker move and she knew it. Passion always rose to the defense of the girls in the house. She looked at them as family, even Zeta. The fact that Claire had been willing to leave her for dead stung. It was a slight she wouldn't soon forget.

Passion finished dressing before grabbing her knapsack and tossing Birdie's to her. She steered the young girl toward the bathroom door so they could head to school, but before leaving Passion had some parting words for the coward Claire. "The same hand you call yourself biting to be spiteful, might be the same hand you need to pull yourself out of the deep end. When and if that time comes, you better pray to God that I ain't the one who has to keep you from drowning."

Passion reemerged from the bedroom and Uncle Joe and Ted were sitting at the kitchen table, passing a joint between them and sipping from plastic cups. Zeta had come out of her fur jacket and was standing in the kitchen washing the dishes that Claire was supposed to do the night before. Bo was on the couch counting and separating bills of various denominations. Zeta might've been Uncle Joe's new flavor of the month, but Bo was the only one he trusted to count his money.

"Y'all headed out for school without eating no breakfast?" Bo paused her counting to address the girls. "I made some grits and eggs. Get you some before you leave."

"No time. We don't want to be late." Passion spoke for both of them. She cut her eyes at Ted, who was at the table with Uncle Joe, eyeballing her and Birdie.

"You know it's hard to concentrate on school when your ribs are touching," Uncle Joe spoke up. "Bo, break Passion off fifty out of that scratch you counting up. I can't have her going to school hungry and not being able to focus."

"It's okay, Uncle Joe. I get paid tomorrow," Passion told him. She didn't like taking money from Uncle Joe, because she knew that it usually came with a catch. She had seen him rope countless girls in that way.

"Nonsense," Uncle Joe waved her off. "I know that diner you insist on slaving at after school don't hardly pay shit. You take this money and get something to eat. You're going to be this family's young scholar, so all you should be worrying about is your grades and not where your next meal is coming from."

"Shit, Joe. I been keeping time with yours all night getting that bankroll together, and you ain't offered me nothing more than a drink and some chicken wings," Zeta whined.

"If your shit-for-brains ass had stayed in school, instead of trying to get out onto the fast track, you might be the one getting lunch money instead of whore money, yet here we are." Uncle Joe chuckled, as did Ted. Even Bo laughed at that one.

"Thanks, Uncle Joe," Passion said in a tone sweeter than she'd have normally taken. This was to irritate Zeta. From the hard look the girl was shooting her, it was working.

"No thanks needed for as long as you keep me happy, Passion. Be a good girl, and listen to your uncle. That's all I ask," Uncle Joe said, giving Passion a look, which made some in the room uncomfortable.

"Say, Joe . . . I hate to break up your little thang, or whatever, but I came here with a purpose. My pocket's feeling a little heavy and could stand to lose some weight." Ted found the courage to swing the dialogue back to why he had come here in the first place. He was trying to get his dick wet.

"Square biz." Uncle Joe got back into business mode. "You know my rates and my rules."

Before Ted could enter into negotiations with Joe, Zeta's thirsty ass abandoned her dishes and sashayed into the living room. She perched herself on the edge of the dining room table, leg slightly spread so that her thigh was exposed. "Honey, you know I'm the only one in this crummy place who speaks your language. This is where you need to be spending your coins tonight."

The move Zeta had attempted to pull was some real cutthroat shit. Everybody caught it, but none really absorbed it except for Uncle Joe. She had jumped off the porch too early and too eager and he couldn't stand a thirsty bitch. His fist balled, and he was about to push himself to his feet when once again Bo interjected.

"Hot-in-the-ass young bitch! You know that ain't how we do things. Joe puts the plays and the players in motion, while we stay ready in case he decides to call one of our numbers!" Bo scolded her. From the way Zeta rolled her eyes at Bo, it was clear that she felt like she was being played, but Bo was actually trying to save her from getting her lip split. Uncle Joe hated to be challenged or back-talked to, especially in front of company. Zeta mumbled something under her breath and fell back, but only slightly.

"No offense, Z, but you ain't what I got a taste for this evening. I find myself in the mood for a meal that's a bit more tender." He looked at Birdie. She was kind of on the homely side, but he would make it work. Ted had a thing for girls who were a little less developed.

Birdie felt like every eye in the room had turned to her. That was probably because they had. All of the girls who lived in the house, with the exception of Passion, had to put in work at some point. For the most part, Birdie always managed to slip through the cracks. She'd done things that she wasn't proud of a time or three, but the majority of the men who came through to solicit the service of Uncle Joe's girls rarely gave her a second look. She didn't have much to offer in the way of a body, and she wasn't the most attractive thing, so more often than not she was dismissed as the funny-looking girl that nobody wanted to pay for.

"Nah, you don't want none of that." Bo came to the table. "She ain't but a child . . . mostly skin and bones. Why don't you let me go see if Claire is up? She'll get you right." Bo made to walk toward the bedroom, but was stopped when Uncle Joe grabbed her about the wrist. He didn't have to say a word because the cold look he was giving her said it all. "Joe, let one of the other girls handle it. Let her be," she pleaded.

PASSION FOR THE HEIST | 37

"Ain't like she's no virgin. She been fucking off with that boy Junior from the next building for the last few months," Zeta interjected. She was bitter about being shooed away in favor of one of the other girls and wanted to stir the pot of trouble that was cooking.

"I ain't been fucking off with nobody. Junior is my boyfriend!" Birdie argued, not realizing that she was digging the hole deeper for herself.

"See, since she's already broke in you ain't got to worry about me hurting her none," Ted said. "What do you say, darling? You wanna make yourself a little money to buy your fella something nice?"

Birdie looked uncertain, so Uncle Joe decided to give her a not-so-subtle push in the right direction. "Birdie, when your mama went to prison for killing that John and you found yourself sleeping in stairwells and on park benches, trying to keep from freezing to death, who took you in?"

"You did, Uncle Joe," Birdie answered.

"And when your grandma was taking the SSD checks that were coming from your dead daddy, and letting you and your siblings go hungry, who fed you?"

"You did, Uncle Joe," she repeated.

"And when you asked me why I did all those things for you without you even having to ask, what was my answer?"

"You said because we were family. What makes a strong family is doing what one of its members needs before they even have to ask," Birdie said, reciting from memory. She knew where Uncle Joe was about to go with this.

Uncle Joe leaned forward and took one of Birdie's frail hands in his larger one. "Now, if this ain't something you're up for, I understand. I won't lie and say I won't be disappointed. You know how much your Uncle Joe hates to be disappointed." He gave her hand a small squeeze. "It makes me start to second-guess some folks, and their appreciation of my generosities."

Birdie glanced at Passion, who looked like she was on the verge of exploding. Passion slowly shook her head no, letting Birdie know that she didn't have to. If Birdie decided to buck against this, Passion would stand with her on her decision. She was hopeful that for once Birdie would stand up for herself, but knew it wasn't to be when she kept her eyes locked to the ground and said, "Passion, I'll catch up with you in school."

"Birdie . . ." Passion began, but was cut off by Uncle Joe.

"You better get going so you won't be late," Uncle Joe told her. His tone was even, but his facial expression said that the subject was no longer up for debate without someone in the room getting hurt.

Passion felt her eyes well, but the tears never fell. She turned to Bo, who was trying to keep her game face, but she could tell that the older woman felt just as powerless as she was. She was the one ally Passion felt like she had in the whole room, and Bo had folded, same as Birdie. Passion's hands were tied. She couldn't fight for someone who wasn't willing to fight for themselves. That was a lesson she had learned a few years back. Taking a deep breath, and thrusting her chin up, Passion left them to their devices.

––––––––––––

By the time Passion reached the elevator in the hallway, she was on fire. Her finger jabbed the button angrily and she tried to will the car to hurry up. She was livid about what had just taken place.

Passion was no dummy. She had learned a long time ago what kinds of games her Uncle Joe played with the women he provided shelter to. Outside of Passion, there wasn't a piece of pussy that passed under that roof that Joe didn't sample at some point. Uncle Joe was Passion's mother's brother, but she had to admit that there had been times when he looked at her like he was oblivious to their genetic bond. Occasional hungry looks aside, Uncle Joe had never disrespected Passion like he did the others girls and she guessed that's what made it so easy for her to tolerate what went on under that roof. Still, it didn't make her feel any less the coward for turning a blind eye.

She was in her second round of angrily jabbing the elevator button when the apartment door opened. Her breath caught in her throat as she anticipated seeing Ted and Birdie on their way to their romp, or worse, Uncle Joe. Passion needed to put some distance between herself and the toxic-ass environment she resided in before she snapped. For as much as she hated school, that morning she would be thankful for the seven-hour distraction. Who stepped from the apartment was neither Joe nor Ted, but Zeta. She was once again wearing her fur jacket, but she had traded the heels she was wearing when she walked in that morning for a pair of worn brown Uggs. She ambled up to Passion, and glared at her over folded arms.

"If he sent you to make sure I'm actually going to school and not planning on doubling back to plead Birdie's case, I can save you the trouble. I'm cool on all that bullshit y'all got going on," Passion said in an easy tone. In her mind she was genuinely working to convince herself that she was done coming between the girls in the house and whatever dangers faced them in the world. It was a thin line, but a starting point for her to convince herself to stick to it.

"Spoken like a true princess in this kingdom of shit!" Zeta chuckled. "Ain't nobody stunting you, Passion. Joe needed a pack of smokes, so he sent me to get them from the store."

The elevator finally came and the girls stepped on.

"Don't you mean, *Uncle* Joe?" Passion continued the conversation as they descended. Her tone was heavy with sarcasm. All the girls, with the exception of Bo, called him Uncle Joe, even the ones he shared no blood with.

Zeta let out a hearty chuckle. "*Uncle?* Girl, that Uncle shit went out the window first time him and tree-trunk dick crawled into my bed. You and Birdie's dizzy ass are probably the only ones in the house still jacking that middle school shit, but you're gonna get with the program eventually."

"And what's that supposed to mean?" Passion asked defensively.

"What it means is, the only reason your precious little pussy ain't been played with is because you ain't eighteen yet, and Joe ain't got no taste for the penitentiary. However, the way I hear it, you have a birthday coming up. You'll be eighteen in a few weeks, right?"

"Yeah, and? The arrangement between you chicks and my uncle don't apply to me. I'm his sister's kid."

Zeta laughed as she stepped off the elevator out into the lobby. "Girl, you too smart to be so stupid. Normally, I'd stick around, burst your bubble, but *Uncle* Joe needs his smokes. See you soon, birthday girl." She sashayed out of the lobby.

CHAPTER 4

The train ride back uptown proved to be equally as bumpy for Pain as the nightmare-filled bus ride from upstate had been. The first hiccup he'd run into was when he tried to pay his fare for the train. The city had long ago done away with subway tokens and switched to Metro-Cards. Pain hadn't been gone long enough not to be familiar. Where he ran into trouble was purchasing a card. Usually he'd just approach the token clerk in the booth to buy a card, but the city had done away with a large number of the clerks and replaced them with kiosks. The machine kept rejecting the crumpled bills he was trying to insert and he didn't have a credit card. Pain had to wait until he came across a Good Samaritan who was willing to swipe him through the turn-stile with her MetroCard. He tried to pay the older white woman, but she refused, claiming that she was happy to help those less fortunate whenever she could. She had basically mistaken Pain for a beggar. Looking at his reflection in one of the store windows he passed, he couldn't say that he blamed her.

Since being sent to prison Pain had gained about twenty pounds, which meant that the clothes he had gotten locked up in no longer fit. He dressed out in an off-brand gray sweat suit, a green army jacket that had seen better days, and an Afro that looked like it hadn't seen a comb in ages. He was also sporting the beginnings of a beard that could use a trim. The only sign of the man who Pain had once been were the Top-Five Air Jordans on his feet. He looked a mess, and hoped that he didn't run into anyone he knew when he hit the block.

When Pain got on the northbound subway he noticed that almost everyone was wearing masks. It was the new mandate. Pain had seen the horror stories on the news, same as everyone else, about how the deadly virus was washing over the planet. He knew of a few cats in the prison who had contracted Covid, but this was his first time being dropped in the thick of it as a free man. Watching the news and listening to misinformed stories about the virus in prison could not have prepared him for the world he had come back to. Everyone on the subway seemed to be on edge. Pain had made the mistake of sneezing and damn near everyone at that end of the subway car put distance between themselves and him.

It had been years since Pain had been on the subway, but the same rules applied. His head was on swivel the whole time. He knew too well the number of cuckoo birds and people up to no good who frequented the New York City subways. The crime rate underground in New York was almost as bad as it was aboveground. There weren't many empty seats, just the little double numbers near the door and an empty space between two people on the benches. Pain opted for the middle seat on the bench. The double seats near the door were a setup. In his day, Pain had caught plenty of people sleeping who took the seats near the door. He would wait until just before the doors closed before booking his unsuspecting victim and escaping before they even knew what was happening. At that point there was never much they could do about it, because the train would be back in motion. He chuckled thinking back on some of his less-than-civilized days and the things he would do for a dollar.

At the next stop, more people got on and filled out the remaining seats, including the ones by the door. The unlucky occupant was a young female. She had shoulder-length hair, which she wore in neat dreadlocks. She was wearing a mask, so Pain couldn't see her face outside of her beautiful brown eyes, but he could see the rest of her just fine. She had a Coke-bottle shape: thin waist with a round ass that seemed to dance under jeans when she moved to take the seat. She flipped her hair back and Pain caught a glimpse of the necklace with two lockets hanging from her neck. It wasn't anything spectacular, a simple chain with two white gold hearts hanging from it. The only reason Pain even gave it a second look was because his mother and grandmother had owned similar pieces. His grandfather had passed after a nasty fight with brain cancer. Between the chemo and the disease eating away at him, there wasn't a lot left of the man they remembered, so they decided to cremate him. After the funeral the family was able to order jewelry pieces that held the ashes of their loved ones. His mother and grandmother were the only two who opted to have the pieces made. The rest of the family was more concerned about how much money would come back from the life insurance policy than carrying about a piece of their patriarch with them.

The girl must've felt Pain watching her because she looked across the train at him. It was an awkward moment for him, so he tried to flash her a friendly smile. In response she rolled her eyes at him and shifted her body. If Pain's luck with women continued like this during his homecoming, the only way he was going to get any pussy was if he paid for it. He was definitely out of the loop and it would take some work to get him back in.

From her knapsack she pulled out a book and busied herself with it. From the tattered cover and dog-eared pages, he knew this wasn't her first time reading the book. If he had to judge by the condition it was in he'd say it was one of her favorites. His eyes went to the title on the jacket: *Road Dawgz*. Pain was familiar with the book. He had read it while he was locked up. His cellmate had been trying to get him to read it for months, but Pain refused. The dudes on the cover looked soft and the synopsis didn't sound that interesting. The only reason he had relented and picked the book up was because he had run through just about everything they had in the prison library and didn't have anything to read at the time. When he was done, he was glad that he picked the book up. It was one of the best novels that he'd ever read. After *Road Dawgz*, Pain tracked down more titles by the author, as well as others on the publishing roster. Pain had so many Triple Crown books that they started overrunning his cell and he had to start mailing some of them home.

Pain tried to busy himself with anything but the reading girl. His eyes traveled up and down the subway car over the faces of people, wondering what their stories were. It was a game he and his mom used to play, called "people watching." They would ride the subway or buses and study the passengers, and try to guess what the real stories of their lives might've read like. At the far end of the car there was a man leaning against the door with a brown pizza box under one arm. It wasn't the first time Pain had seen someone with food on the subway, but there was the lack of grease stains on the bottom and the care with which he held the box that made Pain guess that there was something more valuable than his breakfast in the box.

On the opposite side of the car there was a young girl who couldn't have been a day over twenty, if even that old. Sitting on the seat beside her was a boy of maybe two or three, and she had a newborn strapped to her chest. She was scrolling through her phone, likely on social media catching glimpses of the life she could've been living had she not let a man make a promise that he couldn't keep not once, but twice. She loved her kids, that was apparent in how she was so on point with them; from the toddler randomly jumping from his seat, to the bottle expertly balanced in the mouth of the infant on her chest. Life had dealt her a lot, and she was handling it, but her eyes spoke of how tired she was.

At the next stop a cluster of young men spilled into the car. They were about high school age, but from the bottle they were not so discreetly passing amongst each other it was doubtful that they were on their way to anyone's educational institution. The fact that it wasn't even 9 AM and they were drinking told Pain all that he needed to know about them: Whatever they had been seeking the night before they still hadn't found, and the fact that they were still on bullshit the next morning said that whatever it was had been important to them. Pain knew his kind when he saw them. They spread themselves throughout the car, which let Pain know they were on bullshit. He'd done the same thing with his crew back in the day, spread out through a car and make your moves all at once. Pain didn't have a weapon on him at the time, but he had the foresight to know what they were up to, so it gave him one up.

There were at least a half dozen stories that Pain had been able to pull from his people watching. They were all interesting in an imaginary way, but he couldn't help but find his attention turned back to the reading girl. From the speed with which she was flipping through the pages of her book, he knew that she was just skimming through the best parts and not digesting the story. That was a clear sign of a busy mind. Her eyes were on the pages of the book, but her mind was elsewhere. He tried to get a read on her . . . to piece together a story of what her life was like outside the steel and concrete confines of the subway car. What was her personal heaven or hell? Hell showed up ten seconds after he'd had the thought.

The train pulled into the station and the doors slid open. People were coming on as well as getting off, including the boys Pain had spied. Just as the doors were about to close, one of them made their move and grabbed for the reading girl's knapsack. To her credit, she put up one hell of a fight, socking one of them in the chin while still holding onto her knapsack. Deciding that the bag was too much trouble, one of the boys snatched her necklace and slid from the train just as the doors snapped closed. She pounded the doors futilely as the train pulled out of the station. When she turned back to Pain and he saw the broken look in her eyes, it did something to him. The young dude who had snatched her jewelry had looked at the necklace as something that would put enough money in his pocket to eat for the night, but to the girl it represented something that was irreplaceable. And he felt that.

A few people who had seen what had happened used the time between that stop and the next to fake concern and question the girl about the experience. A few less than tasteful characters had even pulled out their phones to record her reaction to the robbery. The whole display was disgusting to Pain. Not just because people were more interested in posting this girl's pain to their social media pages than helping her, but because in a past life Pain had been the one snatching jewelry in subway cars. The reading girl got off at the next stop. She pretended to be okay, but Pain saw the truth in her eyes. She hadn't just been robbed. She had been violated. She cast a glance back at Pain, and if he lived to be one hundred he'd never forget the look in her eyes. For as much as he wished he could've assuaged her hurt, realistically there was nothing he could do. He was fresh home from prison and barely in a position to help himself, let alone anyone else. Having to eat that tasted like shit in his mouth, and it wasn't a flavor he planned on getting used to.

It was still early when Pain came up out of the subway station on 103rd and Central Park West. He expected to be greeted by the mix of addicts and corner boys coming out to start their morning shift, but instead found himself confronted with a bunch of unfamiliar faces. Most were European white kids who were likely staying at the hostel on the corner. They milled back and forth with the ease and carefree natures of people who lived off Riverside Drive. They obviously had no clue what kind of shithole block they had chosen as their temporary residence while in the states. The neighborhood had clearly changed, but so had Pain.

He pulled the hood of his sweatshirt over his head and began walking up the block, toward his building. He kept his head down, but his eyes up. Pain knew that at some point he would have to make his rounds, but he didn't want to see anyone just yet. All that would come once he had gotten himself settled. Right then, all he wanted to do was get home, hug his granny, and take a shower.

Seeing the girl get robbed on the subway was renting space in his head for free. He didn't know her from a can of paint, and couldn't figure out why he cared so much. Maybe because he had a grandma and had once had a mother who could've easily fallen victim to the young punks. Pain was all for getting it how you lived, because that's how he had come up, but what happened to the rule? He and his crew ran the streets like a pack of wild dogs, but there were certain lines that even they wouldn't cross. Anybody could find themselves food if Pain was hungry enough, but women, elders, and children were never on his dinner menu. He had even physically disciplined members of his crew who violated that unspoken rule. He was a thief, but an honorable one, if that made sense. While he was away, he had heard more than a few stories about how the next generations of crooks were built differently than he had come up, but these lil niggas had no morals that he could tell. Fitting into this new world was definitely going to be an adjustment.

Before going to see his granny, Pain decided to make a quick stop at the small convenience store which sat between the blocks. Back when he was still on the streets trapping, he would never start his day without getting his grandmother a cup of coffee and a newspaper. It was their thing. He figured that it would bring a smile to her face when she saw that after his years away he still hadn't forgotten their tradition.

Lingering in front of the store was a dude who Pain felt like he had seen around before but couldn't quite place. He was short with pecan skin and ears that stuck out from the side of his head. His eyes were red, but not like the tint of someone who smoked weed. More like the eyes of a man who had just come off a drinking bender. He took slow drags from his Newport, watching Pain approach. It wasn't a malicious look, more like one of anticipation. Like you'd just bumped into someone you hadn't seen in a while and were waiting for them to recognize you and speak. The stare Pain gave him in return was a hard one. In prison if a man stared at you that long they were either trying to fight or fuck. Pain would happily give him the former if that's where his head was at. He had years of pent-up aggression inside him, and didn't much care who it spilled over on. The staring contest between them ended when a group of kids came out of the store, holding the snacks they had gotten for school. Pain stepped to the side and allowed them to pass. When he again turned to the man, he had wisely found something else to focus his attention on other than Pain.

When Pain went inside the convenience store, it was like stepping through a time warp. He and his little friends had been coming to that store every day for as long as he could remember. Sometimes it was to buy things with whatever coins they had scraped together that day, and other times it was to steal. Whether with good or bad intentions, they found a reason to visit Rahman's store at least twice per day. The kids fucked with Rahman, because even when he caught them stealing he would never call the police or tell their parents what they had been up to. He'd just do things like make them sweep out the storeroom for a week or stack boxes in the back to work off their debts. The kids all thought Rahman was soft for how he handled the little thieves, but it wouldn't be until Pain was older that he would really understand why Rahman took it so easy on them. He understood their struggles.

Instead of Rahman behind the counter, it was his son Joey. His actual name was something that Pain could never pronounce correctly, so everyone called him by his middle name: Joseph, or Joey for short. Joey had been working in his father's store since before he was big enough to see over the counter. He was a few years younger than Pain, but had always carried himself like a young man far beyond his years. Joey came up under Pain and his gang like one of the lil homies from the block, but his father always kept a tight enough leash on him to where he couldn't get caught up in the bullshit like Pain and the other kids had.

Joey was manning his post behind the register, engaged in a conversation with a young girl who was wearing a skirt that barely covered her ass. Pain had to do a double take when he looked at her face. It was Wendy, a chick from his building. The last time Pain had seen her, she was running around skipping rope and begging the dope boys for dollars to buy candy, but judging from her outfit Wendy wasn't into skipping rope anymore.

"C'mon, Joey. Run it again for me," Wendy was pleading. In her hand was an EBT card.

"Wendy, I ran it twice and there's no money on it. I can let you slide for the sandwich, but not the cigarettes and beer. Technically you know I'm not even supposed to let you buy alcohol and tobacco with food stamps," Joey reminded her.

"Man, you and your dad been letting us buy whatever we need with stamps since the beginning of time," Wendy argued.

"I know, and that's when there's money in the card. Yours has only got a dollar-twenty on it. I can't do it," Joey said.

"Maybe we can work something out?" Wendy batted her eyes suggestively.

"Wendy, I've known you and your mom too long to ever think about going there with you. Don't come at me like that," Joey checked her. He was about to continue his chastising of the fresh young girl when he spotted Pain. "Oh shit! I know that ain't who I think it is?" he exclaimed, coming from behind the counter to greet him.

"What's good, Joey?" Pain embraced him.

"All is well. I see they finally let the bird out of the cage. You look good, Pain," Joey beamed. Pain had always held a special place in Joey's heart because he never let the other kids pick on him when he was hanging in the projects.

"I feel good, too, now that I'm free," Pain told him. He looked at Wendy, who was eyeing him. "What up, lil mama? You can't speak?"

"Hey, Pain. Welcome home." Wendy gave him a hug, which lasted a little longer than Pain was comfortable with. Wendy always had a crush on Pain, but she was too young for him to entertain.

"Thanks. Why you in here causing trouble?" Pain asked playfully.

"I'm not causing anything. I'm trying to get ya man Joey to do me a solid, but he's acting funny." Wendy said, rolling her eyes at Joey.

"Wendy, you know I look out for you any time you or your mom needs something, so stop it. You just mad because I won't let you cop cigarettes and beer for that fake-ass pimp you've taken to running with." Joey's eyes went to the door, where the guy who had been staring at Pain was trying to pretend that he wasn't peeking in.

"He ain't my pimp, he's my man," Wendy said indignantly.

"Then tell your *man* to come out his pocket with some cash or go somewhere else. Bum-ass dude trying to send a little girl to do his dirty work!" Joey spat.

"You know what? Fuck you, Joey!" Wendy cursed and stormed out of the store.

"Damn, lil Wendy out here selling pussy now?" Pain asked Joey, but his eyes were on Wendy and the dude who had been outside waiting for her. They were having a heated conversation, and he clearly didn't take the news well that she had been turned away.

"Wendy is into all kinds of stuff that she has no business in. But it isn't just her, it's all the young ones out here. They growing up too fast with no guidance, which is why I always thank Allah for my dad and solid dudes like you who never let me stray out of my lane when I was growing up," Joey said sincerely.

"I wasn't doing nothing for you that I only wished somebody had done for me."

"I know, P. Your heart has always been purer than most."

Pain laughed. "I wouldn't say all that, but I do have a moral compass."

"So, now that you're home, what are your plans? You hooking up with your old crew?" Joey was curious. He like everyone else knew that Pain's star was on the rise before he took his fall, and was curious to see if he planned on picking up where he'd left off.

"I ain't on that type of time no more, Joey. I'm a few hours released from prison, so right now the only thing I'm focused on is seeing my grandmother again after so long. I just wanted to pop in to get something for her before I go upstairs."

"Tall coffee, light and sweet, and a copy of the *Daily News*?" Joey remembered.

"Yes, sir."

"Got you. Go ahead and grab the paper while I get you right." Joey climbed back behind the counter to prepare the coffee.

Pain went to the rack near the door and began sifting through the newspapers. Through the glass he could see Wendy and her dude still arguing. Wendy looked like she was pleading with him about something, but he wasn't trying to hear it. For the first time Pain really took a good look at the dude. He was rocking a dusty Versace hoodie, baggy jeans, and Prada sneakers that looked like he'd copped them from Canal Street instead of the store. If the dude was a pimp, as Joey had accused, Pain couldn't tell. He struck him as the type of man that would jump into a new outfit without washing his ass. How a girl with as much potential as Wendy had allowed herself to get hooked up with a dude like that was beyond Pain's understanding and above his pay grade to care enough about to try and figure out.

He turned his attention back to the newspapers and picked up a copy of the *Daily News*. On the front page was a headline about the opioid epidemic that had been sweeping through the country the last couple of years. Pain had never really danced with anything harder than weed or liquor, but he'd heard quite a bit about the new fad of popping pills that had gotten so popular while he had been away.

"Coffee is ready," Joey announced.

"My man." Pain placed the newspaper on the counter and dug into his pocket, but Joey stopped him.

"Don't insult me like that. Your money ain't no good," Joey told him.

"Man, you know I ain't never been no charity case."

"It ain't like that, Pain. I know you're just coming home. If you feel that strongly about it, spin back and take care of your tab once you're on your feet." Joey pushed the coffee across the counter.

"You a good dude, Joey." Pain gave him dap.

"You're a better one. Give Ms. Pearl my love when you see her."

———

Pain was in a better mood when he came out of the store than when he went in. It had felt good to see a friendly face in Joey, and even better to feel that he was still loved in the streets. For as much as Pain had done for people when he had been a free man, it hadn't been reciprocated when he had taken his fall. Outside of his grandmother, no one really wrote him or put a dime on his books. Things like that would have driven some men to come home bitter, and feeling like the world owed them something, but Pain had never felt like that. He knew from the day he was sentenced that all he would have to depend on through his bid would be himself. He had adopted this mentality from his time running around with an older cat named War, who had become like a mentor to him. "You can have a hundred soldiers backing you when you're on the streets, but the minute the judge bangs that gavel you'll find yourself an army of one," the old timer had schooled him. He'd been right, too. Pain had found himself truly alone on an island while in prison, and it had taught him to appreciate his own company.

"How you fuck up on something as simple as a pack of cigarettes and a twenty-two ounce of St. Ides? I swear, you gotta be the squarest whore I ever dealt with." The pimp was yelling at Wendy when Pain was coming out of the store.

"Mud, that ain't on me. It's your own fault for sending me in the store with a card that was shot!" Wendy countered. "And besides, who the fuck wakes up to St. Ides? That's some real 1996 shit."

"Bitch, you know I got an old soul. You said that was your people and he'd let you slide. Now I'm gonna have to walk up on the ave and see if they'll let me swipe my card for a few loose cigarettes until later on," Mud fumed.

"Why are you even trying to use your EBT for a pack of cigarettes anyway, when we should have some cash. I made three hundred at the club last night," Wendy reminded him.

"That bread went to overhead. How you think I keep your dizzy ass in crab legs and tampons? As a matter of fact, why you even questioning a real nigga? You out of pocket right now, whore!" Mud was agitated. She had indeed made money shaking her ass the night before, but Mud had tricked most of it off that morning. Before he met back up with Wendy he had taken another chick he was trying to recruit on a small shopping spree at Rainbow. Of course he wasn't going to tell Wendy that, though.

"No, I'm not out of pocket. I'm out of my mind for fucking with your lame ass. Me and you done, Mud," Wendy told him. She had only been with Mud for a few weeks. He filled her ear with empty promises about making her his bottom bitch and all the money they were going to make together, but so far all Wendy had gotten for her troubles was a sore pussy and a purse that stayed on E. She turned to walk away from Mud, but he grabbed her arm roughly.

"Bitch, don't you ever give me your back!" Mud shook her.

"Get off! You're hurting me!" Wendy jerked her arm free. When she did so, Mud lost his balance and fell onto a trash bag that was sitting on the curb. Seeing him flat on his ass made Wendy chuckle and Mud didn't like it.

"Oh, you think I'm a joke?" Mud was instantly back on his feet. He drew his hand back and slapped the fire out of Wendy. She stumbled, tripping backward down the stairs that led to the store's entrance. She would've surely fallen and cracked her head open had it not been for Pain catching her.

"Yo, you good?" Pain asked Wendy. Her lip was bleeding, and she had lost a shoe when she fell.

"Fuck no! This nigga put his hands on me!" Wendy tried to charge at Mud, but Pain restrained her. "Chill, ma."

"That bitch ain't crazy. Let her go, so I can kill her ass out her!" Mud threatened.

"My man, it ain't that serious. Why doesn't everybody just calm down?" Pain suggested. "Wendy, I'm gonna walk you to the building so you can go upstairs and clean yourself up."

"That bitch ain't going nowhere, unless I say. Homie, I don't know who you are and what your connection to Wendy is, but you might wanna mind your business before we have an issue," Mud threatened.

Pain wanted to laugh. He didn't know Mud, but he was fairly certain that he could whip his ass without even trying. A part of him wanted to bust Mud's shit just off principal, but he made it a rule not to involve himself in domestic situations. "My guy, whatever you and Wendy got going on ain't my concern, but I can't in good conscience stand by and let you lay hands on her. Y'all wanna scrap? That's your business. All I ask is that you don't do it while I'm around."

Mud gave Pain a comical look. "Who is you? Captain Save-A-Ho? That's my bitch and I'll do with her as I please. Now bring your ass on, Wendy!" He reached for the girl, but Pain grabbed his wrist.

"Now, I've been trying to be civil about this, but you're about to make me come out of character," Pain said calmly. The kid was really testing him.

"Fuck your character!" Mud jerked away from Pain. He pulled a knife from somewhere in his hoodie and brandished it.

Seeing the knife gave Pain pause. "You know what? You got it, big dawg." He took a cautionary step back.

"I know I do, pussy. Now fuck up outta here and stay outta grown folk's business." Mud was feeling himself, seeing that Pain didn't want the smoke.

Pain made to step away, before turning and throwing the cup of hot coffee in Mud's face. Mud let out a high-pitched scream, hand going to his face. Pain moved in, secured the hand holding the knife, and brought it down over his knee, causing Mud to drop it.

"Chill, you got it . . ." Mud pleaded. His face was on fire and his wrist felt like it might've been broken.

"Nah, I'm about to give you just what you're asking for," Pain announced, before firing a vicious right cross. Mud went down in a heap. "Get it, nigga!" he growled, but Mud just laid there, curled in a ball. He was about to stomp Mud for good measure when something quite unexpected happened.

"Leave him!" Wendy cried, before throwing herself on top of Mud protectively.

"What the fuck?" was all Pain could think to say because the situation had him dumbfounded.

"Just leave him be, Pain. You didn't have to hit him! You okay, baby?" Wendy cradled Mud in her arms.

All Pain could do was shake his head in disgust. A few seconds ago, Mud had been whipping her ass and now she was protecting him? This was too much. "This is just why I don't get involved in domestic shit." Pain shook his head and walked off, leaving the whore to her pimp.

The situation between Mud and Wendy had darkened Pain's mood. He hadn't been out of prison twenty-four hours and was already involved in some shit that could've sent him back. All he wanted to do was go home and see his grandmother and stay out of the way.

He was crossing Manhattan Avenue when a silver Jeep Cherokee came zipping through the intersection and almost clipped him. "Stupid muthafucka!" he shouted, flipping the driver the middle finger. Much to his dismay, the driver of the SUV slammed on the brakes and put the vehicle in reverse. This was the last thing Pain needed, a confrontation over some road rage shit less than twelve hours after being released from prison. He was trying to be low-key and this was only going to make him hot. He started to keep walking in order to avoid the conflict, but there was something about trying to avoid a fight in his own hood that made him feel like a sucker. So, against his better judgment, he stood his ground.

Pain's hand slipped into his pocket and clutched an old No. 2 pencil that he had found on the bus earlier. He wasn't sure why he had picked the writing instrument up, but was glad that he had. His time in prison had taught him some very creative tricks in turning even the most basic items into weapons. He would try his best to de-escalate the situation, but if the driver was unwilling to reason with him, Pain would get his point across another way . . . pun intended.

The driver hopped out of the car and started toward Pain, who was still standing in the spot where he had almost been mowed down. He was a short man with a stocky build. From the aggressive strides he was making toward Pain, there would be no reasoning with him. He wanted action, and Pain had it for him. As the driver neared, something about him rang familiar to Pain. He sported a full beard and dark glasses covered his face, but there was something about the way that he moved that Pain recognized. It wasn't until they were almost face-to-face that it struck Pain.

"Fuck is good, my nigga? We got a problem?" The driver moved in on Pain, fist balled and spoiling to hit something.

"That all depends. Are you finally going to tell the truth about you fucking shorty with the prosthetic leg back in middle school?" Pain asked with a smirk.

The driver snatched off his sunglasses and gave Pain a quizzical look. It took a few seconds for him to realize who he was talking to. When he did, his big pink lips spread into a grin wide enough to show off all thirty-two of his teeth. "Holy shit? I know that ain't my nigga?"

Pain removed his hood so that his face was fully revealed. "What it do, Case?"

"Oh shit! My guy is home!" Case grabbed Pain in a bear hug and spun him around like he was Dorothy Hamill. "Damn kid, I thought I was gonna have to tighten me a nigga up this morning."

"Same old Case. Always ready to throw hands." Pain gave him a knowing smirk. Charlie, as his mom had named him, was one of Pain's closest comrades. They had been friends since grade school and crime partners almost as long. Charlie was given the name Case because of his notoriety for finding himself on the wrong side of the law. At any given time, he would be in somebody's lockup fighting a case or on the streets trying to catch one. He was a career criminal and made no apologies for it.

"Shit, these days I throw iron." Case lifted his shirt so that Pain could see the butt of the gun shoved down the front of his jeans. "But fuck all that. What you doing out here walking around looking like one of the damn fiends?" He gave Pain's outfit the once-over.

"I just got out. I'm coming from the train station," Pain told him.

"Train? Man, when we spoke last week I told you that I would come and pick you up from the prison when you got released on Thursday. What happened? They spring you early?"

"Today *is* Thursday," Pain informed him. "I waited around for about an hour, before I finally jumped on the bus. I didn't want to be anywhere near that jail for longer than I had to."

"My fault. When you're hustling twenty-four seven the days start to run into each other," Case said apologetically.

"From the looks of your whip, business must be pretty good." Pain admired the Jeep.

"That ain't mine. It belongs to one of my little bitches. She lets me push it when I'm out here running around. She be at work all day, so she don't need it," Case said. "As a matter of fact, why don't you jump in and take a ride with me real quick? I can fill you in on what's been going on in the hood."

"I kinda just wanted to go see my grandmother and take a shower before I jump back into the mix," Pain said. He knew that once he and Case hooked up it was possible that it would be a few hours before he made it back.

"Stop acting like that. Your shower can wait, and Ms. Pearl ain't home anyhow," Case told him.

"How do you know?"

"Because I saw her coming out of the building about twenty minutes ago. She said she was on her way to a doctor's appointment. I offered to drive her, but she wasn't trying to hear it."

"Do you blame her after what happened last time?" Pain asked. A few years prior he and his grandmother had been in the car with Case, on their way to the fish market. Case saw someone who owed him money in traffic and decided to hawk him down for it. Ms. Pearl was pissed and vowed never to ride with Case again.

"Wasn't my fault, dawg." Case recited his most famous line. He never accepted responsibility for his bullshit.

"It never is, Case . . . it never is."

"So, you gonna make this ride with me or not?" Case pressed.

"The last time someone asked me that I ended up in prison," Pain reminded him.

"Man, you know I'd never put you in a cross like that ho-ass nigga did. Don't even joke with me like that. It ain't that kind of ride, P. I just wanna shoot uptown and grab these sneakers right quick. They just came in and dude is holding them for me since yesterday. I don't want him thinking I changed my mind and let 'em go. I'll have you back like half hour. No longer than forty-five minutes. I'll even let you drive." He tossed Pain the keys.

Pain stood there for a time looking down at the key fob in his hand. His good sense told him to decline and catch Case another time, because he knew they could never go from point A to B as planned. This was likely to turn into an adventure. Still, it had been a long time since he'd ridden in anything except a bus, and longer still since he'd been behind the wheel. Against his better judgment, he agreed and got into the car with Case.

CHAPTER 5

"Yo, you know you can go a little faster, right?" Case asked from the passenger seat. He was breaking weed up into a cigar husk, and watching cars zip past.

"I'm going the speed limit. I'm on parole and your ass is rolling a blunt. I ain't trying to get pulled over," Pain told him. He had both hands on the wheel and was laser focused on the traffic. You could tell that it had been a while since he had driven in New York traffic.

"Bruh, they legalized this shit while you were gone. Stop being all scary and give this bitch some gas!" Case insisted.

Pain pushed the car to forty mph, but was careful not to go a mile over.

"This nigga here," Case said under his breath while he finished rolling the blunt. He fished a lighter from his pocket and fired the weed up. The car was immediately filled with a sweet-smelling cloud. Of course, Pain cracked the window, which irritated Case. "What is your problem?"

"I told you, I'm on parole. I don't want that shit in my system and end up pissing dirty," Pain said.

"Homie, you ain't getting high. I am! And besides, it ain't like they're going to find no hard shit in your system. This is just a little weed. Everybody smokes now. Even the crackheads have put down the pipes and picked up the blunt." He held the rolled cigar up for emphasis.

"Whatever, man. I'm just not trying to jam myself up and end up back behind the wall."

Case sat up and gave Pain a look. He knew that his partner was dead serious. "Let me find out that little souvenir you brought home from prison got you walking on eggshells." He went to touch the now healed-over scar on Pain's face, but Pain slapped his hand away.

"Don't," Pain said seriously.

"My fault, I didn't mean no disrespect. I heard how you was giving it up in prison," Case said with a smirk.

"What's that supposed to mean?" Pain asked defensively.

"Nothing, just that you was holding it down on some real gladiator shit," Case explained. "Heard you even clipped a few dudes inside."

Pain spared him a glance and turned his attention back to the road without replying.

"Pain, what's going on with you, man? I expected you to be a little rigid, just coming home an all, but you been uptight since I picked you up. You act like we strangers or something," Case said.

"Case, it ain't like that. You're my brother, never doubt that. I been through some shit over the last couple of years. Shit that would've broken most dudes, but I'm still standing. When you've seen and done the kind of things I had to get accustomed to doing, it leaves mental residue. You can't wipe away that kind of stain in just a few hours or with a change of scenery. I just need some time to decompress, that's all," Pain told him.

"I feel you. Take all the time you need, my guy. I'm just here to help make your transition back into the world as smooth as possible. That's why while you were away I've been out here chasing this bag so hard. I wanted to make sure that when you touched down I had a position for you to slide into." Case reached into his glove box and pulled out a small baggie filled with pink pills bearing Transformer emblems.

"Fuck is that?" Pain asked, looking at the pills as if they were something alien.

"The future." Case plucked the bag, jarring the pills a bit.

"That ain't new. White boys and club kids been popping pills since way before I went to prison."

"I know, but it ain't just limited to white folks and club kids anymore. This designer shit is all over the place now: Ecstasy, Mollies, Perks, Zannies . . . the landscape of the drug game has changed and we have rap music to thank for it," Case joked.

"You dumb as hell," Pain laughed.

"But I'm serious, though. Parents too busy working and doing other shit to raise their kids, so the internet is doing their jobs for them. Between these weird-ass songs that are constantly spinning on the radio and social media, it's the blind leading the blind and the smart reaping the benefits."

"That's cold."

"That's the new world. Pain, these days I make more money off my phone than I ever did on a street corner, and I'm gonna show you how to get it the same way," Case promised.

"So, you telling me this internet shit has made you hang up your gloves?" Pain asked.

"Not entirely. You know this is just like any other business and I need capital to keep it going. The power of the pistol is still the fastest way I know to raise money, but at some point, we're going to move away from this shit entirely."

"How does Queen feel about this new direction you're moving in?" Pain asked.

"This ain't got nothing to do with her," Case said in an irritated tone and busied himself looking out the window.

"You know the crows don't fly without her charting the flight pattern," Pain reminded him.

Case turned to him. There was a look on his face that said he wanted to say something, but wasn't quite sure how to word it. "Pain, quite a bit has changed since you been gone. Most of it has been for the better, but not all of it."

"Is there something I need to know?" Pain asked. He had known Case long enough to know when he was keeping something from him.

"Nah, man. Nothing for you to worry yourself about right now. You're fresh home. Let me deal with the headaches and you just focus on getting your feet back under you."

Case directed Pain to a sneaker store up in Washington Heights. Pain circled the block twice, but couldn't find a parking spot. He was going to wait in the car while Case picked up his sneakers, but his friend insisted that he double-park and come inside with him. Pain was concerned with the car being ticketed, but Case didn't seem too worried. It wasn't one of the big-brand stores, but a boutique shop where they primarily carried specialty items; kicks that you weren't likely to find in a major retail spot. Case went off to speak with one of the workers and left Pain to look around the store.

Pain drifted up and down the walls of sneakers; more browsing than actually being interested in their inventory. Most of the sneakers that lined the shelves were loud, or just downright ugly. Hardly Pain's speed. He picked up one shoe, a halfway decent–looking blue and orange number, and out of curiosity peeked inside at the price tag. He damn near dropped the shoe when he saw that they ran seven hundred and fifty dollars. Pain had paid handsomely for sneakers before, but he refused to kick out what some people spent on their rent in the projects for a pair of shoes that he would likely wear twice before getting bored with them or they were no longer in style.

"Y'all got those in a size five?" a voice came from behind Pain. He turned and found himself in the presence of a butterscotch beauty, dressed in a Louis-trimmed track suit that hugged her body as if it had been made for it. Pain struggled to find his voice. He just stood there like an idiot staring into a pair of beautiful brown eyes. It had been a long time since he had been in the presence of a beautiful woman and it showed in his reaction.

"Hello?" The girl cocked her head as if she was trying to figure out if he were deaf or possibly mute.

"Huh?" Pain discovered his tongue.

"I asked if you have those in a size five?" she repeated, and pointed one of her pink manicured fingers at the sneaker Pain was holding.

"Oh . . . um . . . I don't work here." Pain placed the shoe back in its place on the shelf.

"Sorry, I saw the sweat suit and thought . . ."

For the first time since he'd entered the store, Pain noticed that everyone in its employ was wearing similar gray sweat suits, only theirs bore Nike logos on the chest and his was bare. "Honest enough mistake." He tried to hide his embarrassment. "So . . . um . . . you shop here a lot?" he tried to make small talk.

"Excuse me." The beauty brushed past him and went in search of someone who could actually help her with her purchase.

"I gotta get my shit together," Pain said to himself while looking down at his outfit.

After picking his face up off the ground, Pain found himself a seat on one of the benches that were reserved for customers trying on shoes. He continued to watch Ms. Louis as she chatted up one of the workers about the sneakers she and Pain had been looking at. He watched her as she slid one of her dainty feet from the Nike she was wearing and placed it into the orange and blue sneaker. He couldn't help but notice the curve of her foot. It was almost perfect. He even studied her socks for lumps but found none, which meant she probably had nice feet. He imagined what they might look like once they had come out of those socks and were propped on his shoulders. He found his mind taking him to a place where he had no business going as a free man and felt a tinge of embarrassment.

Ms. Louis was making her way to the register to pay for her purchase about the same time Case was coming out of the back room carrying two sneaker boxes. He saw the mischievous grin spring to his friend's lips and knew that he was about to try his hand with Ms. Louis. He hoped that Chase had better luck than he had. To Pain's surprise, Ms. Louis didn't give Chase the cold shoulder like she had with him. She actually gave him a few words. From the respectable distance they kept from each other while holding conversation, Pain didn't feel like it was a flirtatious exchange. More like one of familiarity. Case knew her, and maybe, just maybe, there would still be some hope for Pain somewhere down the road.

"Have a nice day," Pain said to Ms. Louis as she was leaving the store. She never even gave him a second look.

"Can I help you find something?" A young Latino man wearing the store's signature sweat suit approached Pain.

"Nah, I'm good," Pain told him. That should've been the young man's cue to leave, yet he lingered. He obviously had more to say.

"A'ight, it's just that you've been sitting here for a while. This ain't a hangout spot, so if you ain't shopping I'm gonna need you to leave," the young man told him. From his tone Pain could tell that he was really just trying to do his job and it wasn't personal.

"I hear you, shorty. As soon as my man gets done I'll be out your way," Pain said. Again, he expected the young man to move on but he continued standing there.

"Yo, J.J., fuck you over there doing? Starting trouble as usual?" Case called from the other side of the store. He was trying to get his foot into one of the sneakers he had come to pick up and seemed to be having some difficulties. Standing over him, holding a sneaker box, was an older Spanish man who resembled the younger one.

"I got this. I'm just trying to tell my man right here that we don't allow no loitering in this store, but I don't think he's hearing me," J.J. said, trying to sound more like an enforcer than a sneaker store employee.

Case paused from trying on his sneakers and walked over to where Pain and J.J. were. "Oh, so that's how you on it, huh? Making sure ain't no broke niggas just loitering around in your dad's spot?"

"C'mon, Case. You know we cater to exclusive clientele. We got a rep to protect," J.J. capped, looking down his nose at Pain. Now that Case was in the audience he felt like he had to put on an extra show of it. "I was trying to be cool about it, but my man is acting like we ain't speaking the same language."

The irritation on Pain's face was clear. He had tried to be poised about it, but J.J. was getting on his nerves and Case gassing him up wasn't helping. Chase had always been the instigator of the crew and he was working on walking young J.J. into a smack. Pain decided to put an end to Chase's little game. "Shorty," he began in an even yet firm tone, "you about to let this nigga walk you smooth into a wall."

"What's that supposed to mean?" J.J. asked, looking like he was poised for a fight.

"It means that if you don't remove yourself from my personal space, I'm going to bounce you off of every shelf in this spot," Pain said flatly.

J.J. wasn't quite sure how to respond to the threat. The man in the tight sweat suit didn't look like a sucker at all. In fact, if it hadn't been for Case gassing him from the sidelines he probably wouldn't have pressed the issue. Now, with not only Case, but his dad watching as well, he would have to stand on what he wasn't putting out there.

Case watched the two of them with an amused smirk on his face. J.J. looked like he was thinking about taking a swing, and Pain was inviting him to do just that. For the first time, Case could see all those years of pent-up aggression rolling down his friend's face like a death mask. He was struggling to keep himself together, but the more J.J. hovered over him in defiance, the more Pain's resolve began to slip. Case let the rage continue to build until the moment he saw Pain's shoulders tense. That was his tell. The thing that put you on alert right before Pain did something biblically violent. Case waited until the moment just before Pain exploded to dead it.

"At ease, soldier." Case placed a calming hand on Pain's shoulder. He could feel the anger rolling off of him in scorching waves. His friend looked up at him, eyes ablaze and wide. Pain was ready to hurt something, but with just a shake of his head, Case calmed the beast. Not there, not that day.

"You know this guy?" J.J. asked, relieved that he didn't have to end up fighting him.

"Do I? This dude has been my partner in crime since you were still swimming in your dad's nuts! Not only do I know him, but so does the rest of the city. He's a living legend. I'm actually a little disappointed that you don't know him. And here I thought you were a student of the game." Case shook his head in disappointment at J.J.

The youth looked to his dad, Julio, who had quietly positioned himself at Pain's blind side while he was having words with his son. There was a question in his eyes.

"They call him Pain," Julio said in a tone that was neither warm nor cold. It was as if he was simply stating a fact.

"The Blackbird!" J.J. gasped. His stomach lurched as he realized that he had almost tried to sucker punch a very dangerous man.

Blackbird, the title echoed in Pain's skull. Blackbird, sometimes referred to as the Bird of Prey, was a name that he had not been called by in a long time. Someone he cared for very much had gifted him that moniker. It had come from the Nina Simone song "Blackbird." She said that it reminded her of him when she listened to it—an angry little bird lost in the world who was never meant to fly. *"Your mama's name was Lonely, and your daddy's name is Pain,"* she would sing to him, before planting a soft kiss on his forehead. It was she who helped him to find his wings and his way. A fledgling no more, he would be her bird of prey . . . her Blackbird. Pain had done things in his old life that he had worked very hard to forget about while he was away. Hearing the old nickname brought every dark deed rushing back to the surface.

"Yo, I meant no disrespect. I thought you were just some random dude who had wandered in here to window-shop. I had no idea I was talking to the Queen's executioner," J.J. said apologetically.

"I'm just a man, kid. Nothing more," Pain said modestly.

"Bullshit!" J.J. challenged. "I once heard a story about you hijacking a city bus and taking that shit on a robbing spree all over the city."

"It was a box truck, and we only hit an appliance store. Stop listening to everything you hear on the streets," Pain told J.J. in a tone that said he didn't want to talk about it.

"Sorry, I didn't mean to be all up in your mix," J.J. said apologetically.

"Listen to this guy. Always the modest one." Case threw his arm around Pain. "You've gotta excuse him, J.J. He's only been back in the world for a few hours, so he ain't quite warmed up yet. But don't let my friend's shabby appearance fool you. In his day Pain was one of the greatest heist men to ever slip on a pair of gloves and jack a nigga for their shit. I can't tell you how many times he's saved my ass or how much money he's put into my pockets. Don't feel no type of way about giving this guy his flowers. He deserves them, even if he doesn't think so."

"Definitely. Man, your name has been ringing in these streets since I was in grade school. I can't believe I'm meeting you in the flesh!" J.J. said, doing a poor job of hiding his excitement.

"J.J., if you're done having your fanboy moment, there are some boxes in the storeroom that could use your attention," Julio cut in. He didn't care for the way his son was gushing over Pain. J.J. had only heard the stories, but Julio knew exactly who and what Pain was.

"Okay, Papi," J.J. relented. He wanted to stay and pick Pain's brain some more, but he could tell from his father's tone of voice that this wasn't something up for debate. He gave nods to the two gangsters and disappeared into the storeroom.

"Some kid you got there, Julio," Pain remarked.

"J.J. can be a knucklehead, same as any other eighteen-year-old, but he's a good kid. I keep him close so he can stay that way," Julio said. There was an underlying message in his statement. It was a warning to stay clear. "Case, you need anything else?" he shifted the conversation.

"I think I'm straight. I wanna get a few pieces for my man, though." Case patted Pain on the back.

"You ain't gotta do that, Case," Pain told him.

"Like hell I don't. Pain," he lowered his voice so that Julio wouldn't overhear, "you fresh out of the joint. I know you haven't had a chance to start getting your bankroll together yet. I wanna help you get started. Buying you a few pieces is the least I can do."

"You know how I feel about handouts," Pain said. For as bad as he wanted some new clothes, he didn't want to impose on his friend. Pain was used to having his own and not depending on the mercies of others to meet his needs.

"This ain't no handout, this is me doing what I'm supposed to do for my brother," Case said sincerely. "Besides, ain't no way you're going to be riding around with me sporting them prison rags. I got a reputation to uphold."

"Fuck you." Pain shoved him playfully.

"But on the real, get anything you want from out of here. Julio, hook my boy up and put that shit on my tab!" Case held up a credit card.

"You got it, Case," Julio agreed. "So, Pain . . . anything in particular catch your eye?"

Pain thought on it for a minute. His mind went back to Ms. Louis and how she had looked at him. "Yeah, let me see the blue and orange joints in a size thirteen."

CHAPTER 6

When Pain walked out of the store he looked like a totally different person. In addition to Case hooking him up with two pairs of sneakers, he also got a few new outfits. The one he was currently wearing was a royal blue Izod sweat suit and a crisp New York Knicks hat, and of course the infamous sneakers. Generally, they weren't something that Pain would've worn. They weren't his style. The only reason he was moved to get them was because they had caught Ms. Louis's eye. The sneakers spoke a language that only a certain class of people understood, and Pain was aiming to place himself in that number.

Pain and Case carried their bags out to the double-parked Jeep, laughing and talking just like old times. Pain felt like a different person in fresh clothes. There was even a little more spring in his step when he came off the curb to open the hatch. He was tossing his bags into the back when he heard Case curse. "Everything good?" He peeked around the back of the car.

"Thirsty-ass niggas got me." Case held up the orange parking ticket that had been waiting for him on the windshield.

"I tried to tell you we should've parked," Pain reminded him.

"Greedy-ass city." Case balled up the ticket and tossed it on the ground before jumping behind the wheel. "So, yo . . . I gotta pull up on my man on the other side of town for a quick second. I got some light business to conduct."

"See, here you go with the bullshit. I told you that I wasn't trying to be outside all day. I need to check in at the crib," Pain said.

"Stop crying, it ain't gonna take long at all. It's not even noon. We still got enough time to see my man, bend a few corners, and still get you home before Ms. Pearl gets back from her appointment. Shake out for a while and show off your new drip." Case elbowed him lightly. They were back out in traffic and headed east before Pain could protest.

"Oh, I meant to ask you earlier. Who was that bad muthafucka you was talking to back at the sneaker store?" Pain asked. He still had Ms. Louis fresh on the brain.

"You mean Lolo? I've been knowing her for a few years since she moved out here from Chicago. She ain't nobody," Case said dismissively.

"She looked like somebody to me. That bitch was beautiful!" Pain exclaimed. "I tried to chat her up at the spot, but she played me like some bum-ass nigga."

"The way you were dressed, can you blame her? But on some G shit, Lolo is one of them chicks that are about a dollar. She don't wallow in the mud with us soldiers."

"Then it's a good thing mud is the last place I'm thinking about wallowing. I'm trying to get next to shorty," Pain told him.

"At your own risk, my nigga. Lolo comes with a whole bunch of bullshit, namely her dude. He's a cat who goes by the name of Lee. He's getting a little money up on 153rd."

Pain searched his mental Rolodex and couldn't find the name. "Doesn't sound familiar. Do I know him?"

"You might or you might not. Lee was doing his thing while we were still out here running, but his star didn't really start rising until you went away. Him and his crew clipped a few heavyweight dudes and called themselves building a monopoly out of the territories. It don't stretch but a few blocks in every direction, but I'll be damned if it doesn't feel like it's growing a little bit more every day," Case gave him the rundown.

"He about that life?" Pain asked curiously.

"You didn't hear me when I said him and his boys have killed a few dudes?" Case gave Pain a look. "For the most part, Lee and his crew keep to themselves, but he's been known to jump off the porch if he feels strongly enough about something. Much like what you're planning."

"Who says I'm planning anything?"

"You did. I could see the wheels turning in that devious little brain of yours when you started asking about Lolo. I know you, Pain. That's a nut you don't need to be trying to crack," Case warned.

"I'm trying to get my dick out the dirt," Pain said, trying to remember the last time he had a shot of good pussy. He was knocking down one of the female corrections officers in his previous prison, but she was a dead lay. She liked to bend over the maintenance sink and let him plow into it, with very little effort on her part. The only thing she was really good for was making sure he had access to contraband.

"I'm gonna make sure you get laid, but it'll be by a bitch you won't have to shed blood over. Now enough about pussy. What's up with this paper? I know after busting your nut, getting your pockets right will be the immediate order of business."

"Fosho," Pain agreed. "I met a dude while I was locked up, who has a cousin out here that can plug me in with this construction gig. Until that comes through, my new PO is supposed to get me into this job program."

Case looked at Pain as if he had just cursed at him. "Man, save that bullshit you spinning for your parole officer. This is me, P. I'm talking about real money, not just holding a job so you don't get violated and sent back. This drug thing is really just getting off the ground for me, so it'll be a while before I can really afford to feed the troops off that. I got some other stuff lined up that I can pull you in on, though."

"I don't know, Case. I just spent a long time behind the wall and the thought of going right back ain't too appealing. I was thinking I'd take things slow and try the legit route. At least for right now."

This made Case laugh. "Pain, this is me you're talking to. We're cut from the same cloth, so I know you like your money the same way I do, long and fast. You'd go crazy in the first week trying to work a nine-to-five. Look, I know your legs ain't quite back under you yet, so we can start you off slow. You ain't gotta touch no iron. I'll put you behind the wheel or doing something else and still give you an equal split of whatever we rip off. I need my right hand with me in these streets!"

"I hear you, Case, but I'm gonna have to pass. If it's all the same to you, I'd like to enjoy my freedom for a little while before I risk throwing it away again," Pain said honestly. He'd be lying if he said he hadn't thought about going back to his old life on more than a few occasions while he was away, but he knew he couldn't go that route again. Not if he wanted to keep the promise he had made.

"If that's what you gotta tell yourself to sleep at night, that's cool." Case knew that Pain meant what he said, but he also knew his friend's nature. Pain was a wolf and there was only but so long that he could pretend to be a sheep.

Twenty minutes after leaving the sneaker store, Pain found himself following Case into a building on 112th Street and Park Avenue.

There were a few dudes huddled in front of the building who looked like they were plotting when the two of them walked up. Pain immediately got on point and kept the dudes in his line of vision, but Case strode by them as if they were invisible.

"Loosen up, dawg. We good over here," Case said, picking up on his friend's tension. They were in the lobby waiting for the elevator. He impatiently kept jabbing his finger at the button as if that would make it come any faster.

"Excuse me if I don't share in your confidence, but the last time I checked this was enemy territory," Pain reminded him.

The summer before Pain had gone to prison their crew had been into it with some dudes from Carver Houses. It stemmed from an incident that had occurred at a hole-in-the-wall lounge that damn near everybody in Harlem frequented. Pain and his crew were in there thick, drinking and living it up. A regular Saturday night. One of Pain's partners, a guy named Mo, had been watering some random chicken head with Hennessey for half the night. She was sloppy drunk and all over Mo. It was looking like she was ready to slide off and let him defile her in some dark corner until her boyfriend showed up. Instead of the dude checking his lady, he took issue with Mo. He started barking in Mo's face and talking all crazy like Mo was some kind of sucker. He found out the error of his ways when Mo smashed a bottle over his head. The night ended with the crew stomping the dude out. If Pain recalled, somebody even punched his broad in the face for good measure. It was a nasty situation. It didn't take long for word to get out that it had been members of Pain's crew who whipped the dude out. The kid who had taken the beating came through Pain's projects and shot it up one night, hitting a random person who hadn't had anything to do with the conflict. In retaliation, a few of Pain's boys went across town and shot some dudes in Carver.

This went on back and forth for months. Eventually some older, reputable dudes from their respective hoods got the hotheads together and negotiated a cease-fire. There would be no more random shootings in each other's neighborhoods, but there had been the occasional incidents if one side got caught out-of-bounds in or around the other's projects. As far as Pain knew, the same rules of engagement still applied.

"Man, all that old shit is dead, P," Case said as they boarded the elevator. "Half the dudes we were into it with are dead or locked up, and the other half don't want no smoke. We moving strong out here these days."

"Sounds like the Crows got shit all sewed up," Pain said with a hint of pride.

"Something like that," Case offered flatly.

They got off the elevator on the fourth floor, where Case led them to an apartment at the end of the hall. Music was playing inside and beneath it you could hear voices. Case rapped on the door in a pattern and waited. The peephole rattled seconds before the locks came undone. When the door swung open, Pain was pleasantly surprised at who he found standing behind it.

He was a tall, light-skinned youth of about sixteen or seventeen, with sleepy brown eyes. His hair was faded at the sides and long on top, with short dreads that tickled the tips of his ears. Dark brown eyes stared out from beneath hooded lids that were threatening to snap shut at any moment. He was slightly older than Pain had remembered him and his cheeks sported the very beginnings of a five-o'clock shadow, but for the most part his face hadn't changed. When his eyes landed on Pain, he saw recognition flash in them.

"I know that ain't who I think it is?" the light-skinned youth beamed.

"Sup, Riq?" Pain extended his fist.

"Fuck all that. Show me some real love!" Tyriq pulled Pain into a warm embrace. He was like a child who had just been reunited with a lost parent. In a sense, Pain had been that to him.

Riq, which was short for Tyriq, had been under Pain's wing since he was about eleven years old. He was the little brother of a girl who Pain used to finger-bang behind the bleachers in middle school. For as long as he could remember, Tyriq had been one of those little badass kids who loved trouble. He was always doing something: fighting, cursing, stealing. The kid had no home training to speak of. One of his favorite little licks to pull was watching where the dealers in the neighborhood stashed their drugs, which he would steal and resell to dealers in other neighborhoods at a discount. He got away with it until he had the misfortune of stealing a package that belonged to Mo. Mo was no one that you wanted to fuck with in general, but over his money he could turn into a real beast. When Mo found out who had pinched his drugs, he threw Tyriq a good beating and was about to break one of his hands for good measure.

This was when Pain stepped in on his behalf. Had Pain not been there at the time he probably wouldn't have given a shit what happened to the little thief, but because of his relationship with Tyriq's sister he couldn't just stand by and watch while Mo did him dirty. It took some doing, but Pain managed to convince Mo to let Tyriq keep his digits, provided that he worked off the debt. As it turned out, Tyriq was even better at selling drugs than he was at stealing them. He was quite the little salesman. They ended up keeping him around as the unofficial crew mascot. When Mo got locked up on a parole violation and the drug spot dried up, Pain began teaching Tyriq the tools of a slightly different trade.

"Damn, kid. It's good to see you!" Pain said sincerely. Next to Case he probably missed Tyriq most of all. "You getting big on a nigga out here." He held Tyriq and looked him over. It was then that Pain noticed a familiar marking just under Tyriq's right eye. It was of a blackbird with its wings spread. Pain knew the mark well because he had it tattooed in several places on his body. It was the mark of the beast. "It's like that?" He didn't bother to hide his disappointment.

"Babies don't stay babies forever." Tyriq broke the embrace. "So, when did you touch down?" he changed the subject.

"Just this morning," Pain told him.

"Case, why didn't you tell me you were going to pick big bro up? I'd have rode with you," Tyriq complained.

"That's because he never made it to pick me up. I ended up riding the bus back to the city," Pain filled him in.

Tyriq gave Case a sour look. "How you gonna have the Blackbird fly back to the nest on a goose? That's all kinds of wrong."

"Blame it on my head and not my heart." Case placed his hands over his chest. "I know I fucked up, but I plan to make it up to him at his welcome-home party tonight!"

"Bruh, you know even before I went up north I wasn't the party-type dude. I'm even more to the chest with it now. The last way I want to spend my first night out is surrounded by a bunch of fake-ass niggas showing fake-ass love, knowing damn well the only reason most of them will even show up is to take pictures and say that they were in the building. I ain't for all that dick-sucking if it ain't coming from a bitch," Pain said.

"You know I know better than that. I got a homegirl who's the manager at a little lounge-type joint downtown. I'm thinking we grab some of the homies, a few pretty bitches, and grab a table or something. We ain't gotta do it too big," Case assured him.

"Let me think about it."

"Don't think too long. If we're gonna do it I need to get on some phone calls while it's early," Case told him.

After a bit of small talk, the trio made their way into the living room. Seated at the dining room table was an older man with salt-and-pepper hair. His thick glasses kept sliding down the bridge of his nose every time he leaned in to squint at something on the screen of the laptop in front of him. His fingers flashed across keys as they entered another line of information. On the table were also two printers and a piece of equipment that Pain couldn't identify. The machines hummed softly in rhythm with his typing. Stacked neatly in a box beside him were a few dozen drugstore gift cards.

On the sofa across the room, a thin girl sat cross-legged watching something on the oversized television that took up most of the wall in the small living room. She absently twirled a strand of her honey blonde weave around her finger while taking slow drags off a long blunt. She pulled her eyes from the television long enough to spare them a glance before going back to her program. She was so high, whether she even realized they were there was anyone's guess.

"She okay?" Pain asked.

"That's my girl, Patrice. She just a little zooted," Tyriq explained. "Trice, look alive girl. You see we got company."

Patrice hit the blunt and let a cloud of smoke ooze from her nostrils before answering. "I'm high, not blind."

"Then act like it, and at least try and be a good hostess. We got a special guest," Tyriq informed her.

"Case ain't nobody. He's here damn near every other day," Patrice said. She was more interested in her blunt and her show than anything Tyriq had to say.

"There you go with that smart-ass mouth. I'm not talking about, Case. This here is my big brother. The one I'm always telling you about, Blackbird."

This did get Patrice's attention. She had known who Pain was since before she had hooked up with Tyriq. Not personally, but by reputation. Older chicks in her neighborhood would always swoon when they told stories about the Queen and her Blackbird. Legend had it that he was the Queen's concubine, as well as her vengeance. She'd heard all kinds of tall tales about the man who was said to be the slayer of the Queen's pussy and her enemies alike. Most of them were probably bullshit, but nonetheless entertaining.

"Nice to finally meet you, Blackbird." Patrice paused her smoking long enough to sit up and extend her hand to Pain.

"Pain," he corrected her before shaking her hand. The more he heard the name, the more it irritated him. When he shook Patrice's hand he found it to be rougher than he had expected. She was no stranger to work. Unlike Ms. Louis, this one would wallow in the mud with the soldiers. Whether that was a good or bad thing, it was still too early to tell.

"From all the stories I've heard about you from Riq, I feel like we know each other already," Patrice said.

"Well, I hope he hasn't already soured you on me before I get a chance to do it myself?" Pain joked.

"No, Riq actually speaks really highly of you. He said you helped him through some real rough times."

"Riq is family. I'd do anything for that cat," Pain said.

"And I'd do anything for you," Tyriq chimed in. "Trice, do me a favor and go grab them roll-ups off your nightstand."

"There are roll-ups right here." Patrice gestured toward the assortment of rolling papers and cigars on the coffee table.

"I want the ones from the bedroom," Tyriq insisted. Patrice finally read between the lines and got off the couch. "Space cadet," he mumbled once she had left the room.

"How long you been with her?" Pain asked Tyriq.

"Almost a year now. I met her one day when I was down at the Department of Probation checking in," Tyriq explained.

"She on paper, too?" Pain asked.

"Nah, she was my PO."

"Get the fuck outta here!" Pain laughed.

"Dead ass. Shorty was feeling a young nigga's style. One thing led to another and the next thing you know, she got steady access to this dick and I got a license to steal!" Tyriq boasted.

"I taught you well, grasshopper." Pain rubbed Tyriq's head playfully.

"Yeah, you did. Oh, and speaking of stealing . . ." Tyriq grabbed a box from the coffee table. When he flipped the lid open it revealed assorted pieces of jewelry. It reminded Pain of a miniature leprechaun's hoard. From the box Tyriq pulled a beautiful gold chain. From the end of it dangled a piece of black onyx fashioned to resemble a bird, trimmed in gold. "I scraped a few pennies together and got you a little welcome-home gift."

Pain admired the pendant. Even in its simplicity it was beautiful . . . thoughtful even on Tyriq's part. Beautiful and all, Pain didn't miss what the piece symbolized. "I can't accept that, Riq."

"You don't have a choice. Since it was custom-made I can't sell it back without taking a loss, and you know Case don't pay a nigga shit," he laughed. "Please, I want you to have it." Tyriq held the chain up.

Pain was hesitant, but he dipped his head and allowed Tyriq to slip the chain over it. When the metal touched his skin, it sent waves of cool through his neck, settling in his shoulders. He felt the gentle pull from the bird pendant as it swayed softly, looking to get settled. It had been a long time since Pain had rocked a chain of any kind. There was always a small surge of confidence when he put on a new piece of jewelry, but the custom piece nearly made Pain feel like his old self again. Slowly but surely the broken pieces of him were being put back together.

"I know shit is different now with the team, but you'll always be the Blackbird to me," Tyriq explained.

"I love you, my nigga." Pain hugged him.

"I love you too, big homie. Now that you're home we about to start putting shit back in order, starting with a little piece of unfinished business. Me and Case got—"

"A transaction to conduct," Case cut him off before he could finish his statement. "That piece you set me out with was hitting." He held up the credit card he had used in the sneaker store. "Those numbers are good, but who knows for how long? Let's run them up while we still can."

"Nigga, you had me out shopping with you with a fraudulent card?" Pain asked angrily. Pain was a street dude, accustomed to selling drugs and pulling robberies, but fraud opened you up to a different kind of charge.

"Calm down, Pain. I had the situation under control and Julio was in on it, so nothing could've gone wrong," Case told him.

"I was locked up with a dude who felt the same way until the feds picked his case up and they shipped him from state prison to some shithole in Iowa. They hit that boy with wire fraud and I think he's sitting on ten years because of it. I don't fuck with the federal govern-ment and neither should you. Them boys play different," Pain warned.

"Chill, big homie. We got a whole system in place that spares us those kinds of headaches, thanks to modern technology. We buy the profiles from the web, which gives us access to names, dates of birth, socials, and some more shit. Once we got that, ol' Vinnie works his magic on the computer and with the pressers and makes us duplicate cards. That old head is so good that his cards can fool any chip reader or security system that a store has in place," Tyriq explained as if he was teaching a course on credit card fraud.

Pain looked to the old man at the computer, who still hadn't so much as looked up from his work. "And what happens if that old-timer gets caught up? He doesn't look like he's got enough years left in him to do whatever time they'll probably throw at him."

"Vinnie is the last person we ever have to worry about talking," Tyriq said confidently.

"What makes you so sure?" Pain asked.

"Because he's deaf and mute," Tyriq said with a smile. That ex-plained why the old man barely acknowledged their presences and why Case and Tyriq spoke so freely in front of him.

"I leave behind a crew of some of the most qualified heist men in the city and come back to find out y'all have traded in your pistols for plastic." Pain plucked the credit card from Case's hand and examined it. He was familiar with scamming, but it had never been his thing. He liked to get it the old-fashioned way, with iron.

"Being a gangster ain't about how you get it, but making sure you keep getting it." Case snatched the card back. "I don't know why you're worried about it anyhow, considering you're on some square shit now." Then to Tyriq: "Our boy has hung up his guns in favor of a paycheck."

"Get the fuck out of here," Tyriq said in disbelief. He looked to Pain to deny Case's claim, but his big homie said nothing. "Pain, you schooled half of us on how to hit licks. You trying to say you ain't with the shits no more?"

"It ain't like that, Riq. It's just that I got this parole shit hanging over my head and I ain't trying to go back to the pen for no dumb shit. My grandmother is getting old and I wanna spend whatever years she has left on this earth as a free man," Pain explained.

"I can respect that, Pain. I wish I had someone out here who I needed to be around for, but I don't. It's just me so I live how I live. I could give a fuck about tomorrow, as long as I'm having fun today, feel me?" Tyriq asked.

"I feel you, Riq. I ain't knocking nobody's hustle, I'm just speaking for me. I gotta fall back for a minute," Pain said.

"I hear you talking, square nigga," Case capped before flopping on the couch. "Let's see how long you stay in the background when them ribs start touching."

CHAPTER 7

Passion sat in the back of her psychology class, trying her best to sit still and focus on the work. She was anxious for it to be over. It wasn't that she didn't enjoy the class. Psychology was one of her favorite subjects. She was even fond of the professor who taught the course. Professor Higgins had been an around-the-way girl back in her day, so she wasn't as square as some of the other instructors. She was down-to-earth and easy to talk to, and she always made it her business to check in with Passion to see how she was doing. Professor Higgins didn't know Passion's whole story, but she had a pretty good idea of what things were like in her house. She had gone to school with Uncle Joe.

She'd first learned of Professor Higgins's relationship with Uncle Joe the previous semester. Passion wasn't in her class yet, but she was fortunate enough to be one of a group of girls selected to be a part of her mentorship program. It was something that Professor Higgins had put together in conjunction with the school for the benefit of young girls. It wasn't anything too heavy. She taught them stuff like résumé building, filling out college applications, and for those who needed it, feminine hygiene. You'd have thought that young women ranging from the ages of seventeen to twenty would've known how to take care of their bodies, but many didn't. In addition to what was outlined in the mentorship program, Professor Higgins would often have deep talks with the girls about life in general. She understood that some of them lacked strong female representation in their homes, so she tried to set the best example that she could for them. Talking to Professor Higgins was more like talking to a big sister or auntie; she was by no means perfect, but she was real and that's why the girls took to her the way they did, especially Passion.

Before becoming a part of Professor Higgins's mentorship program, Passion hadn't had any interest in psychology. Her original course of study when she'd signed herself up for community college was business management. She saw herself one day going on to become some big-time executive at some random corporation, but Professor Higgins had tapped into something deeper. Passion admired Professor Higgins a great deal. She would always be the first one to show up to the program and the last to leave. She was always hanging around Professor Higgins and trying to drink from the well of information that was her brain.

It was after one of these sessions that Passion learned of Professor Higgins's relationship with Uncle Joe. Passion had stayed behind after the program had ended, which wasn't unusual, but this particular evening they had gotten so caught up chatting that time got away from them and it was late. Passion was fine taking the train back uptown, but Professor Higgins offered to drive her. She was headed to Harlem anyhow, so it wasn't out of her way. When they arrived on Passion's block, Uncle Joe was sitting outside with some of his minions. He was all teeth when he saw that it was Professor Higgins driving the car that brought Passion home. She, however, didn't return the enthusiasm he showed in seeing an old friend. She was cordial, likely for the sake of not wanting to offend Passion, but it was obvious that she didn't have a lot of love for Uncle Joe. Back then, Passion didn't know Professor Higgins well enough to pry into her business, but she had asked Uncle Joe about it. The cagey gangster smiled as if he was reliving some carnal memory and only offered: "Letti and me got history."

It took several weeks of attending Professor Higgins's program before Passion began to warm up to her enough to let her in on her personal life. In return, Professor Higgins did the same. Passion learned that at one time Professor Higgins had really been out there playing in the streets. As a youth she sold drugs and had even been arrested. It was due to some guy she had been dumb enough to sell drugs for who she wouldn't name. Passion couldn't be certain, but if she had to guess she would've said the guy was Uncle Joe. She had gotten probation instead of jail time. Almost going to prison was the turning point in her life. She got her shit together and put her focus back on school.

After graduation she enlisted in the military, where she served two tours overseas. During that time, she had been a part of a unit that had been personally responsible for the recovery of at least a dozen girls who were being trafficked throughout parts of Africa and the Middle East. It was her time spent liberating those poor girls that planted the seeds for the initiatives to help young women that she would start later in life. By the end of her final tour she had received her master's degree. Shortly after arriving back in the states she continued her education, studying for her PhD while working a job in law enforcement. Though through all their talks, Passion could never remember her saying which branch. She would usually dance around the subject whenever it came up. After earning her PhD, Professor Higgins decided her skill set was better suited for education instead of incarceration, so she moved back to New York and accepted a teaching position being offered by BMCC. Passion had once asked her why she chose a community college instead of one of the more prestigious schools that had also been chasing her, and Professor Higgins replied: "Because I wanted to make a difference." And that she had, at least in Passion. Professor Higgins had done something for the young girl that not even her parents had been able to do: dare her to dream. Passion went from admiring Professor Higgins to wanting to walk a mile in her shoes. This is what had inspired Passion to sign up for the psychology course.

But as much as Passion loved Professor Higgins and her class, school was the last place she wanted to be that day. It had been a struggle all day long for her to concentrate on her work because she had been thinking about Birdie. She hadn't heard from her since she left her at the apartment that morning, which wasn't like her. Ever since Passion had gifted her a cell phone, it seemed like Birdie spent all of her time on it. From the time she woke up until the time she went to bed, that phone was glued to her palm. She always texted Passion throughout the day while she was in school, but that day . . . nothing.

She was tempted to call Birdie's school and find out if she had showed up that morning, but decided against it. That could possibly raise a red flag. All the girls who were underage and staying with Uncle Joe were on shaky ground when it came to child protective services. Uncle Joe and his connections had been able to keep them all under the radar so far, but all it would take was a reason and child protective services would be at their door. As she thought on it, that may not have been such a bad thing. She was almost eighteen so there wouldn't be much they could do with her, but what about the other girls? What about Birdie? No, Passion would just have to suffer through her anxieties until her last class was over.

At 1:30 on the dot, Passion was out of her seat and headed for the classroom exit. She was thankful that it was her last class for that day, because she had been itching to hit the streets. She needed to get a line on Birdie ASAP. She figured if she hurried she could make it uptown to check the house, and if she wasn't there, make it over to her high school before the students were dismissed for the day. She was about to slip out when Professor Higgins stopped her.

"Passion, could I speak with you for a minute?"

Passion sighed and made a U-turn. "Hey Professor Higgins, what's up?" she smiled, trying to hide her mounting anxieties.

"I was hoping you could tell me." Professor Higgins perched herself on the edge of her desk and took off her glasses. She was an attractive woman with skin of deep caramel and eyes of the same hue. Her long, salt-and-pepper dreadlocks were pulled into a neat ponytail and tied in the back with a yellow and green-striped ribbon.

"How do you mean?" Passion faked ignorance.

"I mean, why weren't you in my class today?"

Passion didn't understand the question. "What do you mean? I was sitting in the same seat I sit in every Monday, Wednesday, and Friday."

"I saw your body in your seat, but you were clearly mentally checked out. Is everything okay?" Professor Higgins asked.

Passion considered the question. She and Professor Higgins had the kind of relationship where Passion could tell her anything and never worry about it being repeated, but this was different. For as cool as Professor Higgins was, there was no doubt in Passion's mind what she would do if she found out what was going on with the girls in Uncle Joe's house. She'd burn the whole thing down with Uncle Joe in it. She didn't want to lie, so she opted for a half-truth.

"I got robbed earlier," Passion told her, reluctantly.

"Oh, my God! Are you okay? Where did it happen? Did they hurt you?" Professor Higgins rattled off questions while checking Passion for injuries.

"I'm fine. They just roughed me up a little and snatched my necklace," Passion told her.

"Thank God. The important thing is that you're unharmed. The piece of jewelry they snatched can be easily replaced," Professor Higgins told her.

"This wasn't just some piece of jewelry. It was the lockets with my parents' ashes in it. It was the only piece of them that I had left." Passion tried to hold them back, but she couldn't stop the tears from falling.

"I'm so sorry that this happened to you." Professor Higgins embraced her. "This city gets crazier and crazier every year. Ain't safe for decent folks to ride the subways anymore. Tell you what, I've got some friends in the police department. I can reach out to them and maybe someone can get a lead on your necklace."

"Don't bother. The police don't give a shit about what happens to people in the hood. It'd be a waste of your time because they probably won't even look, let alone find it. Fuck the police!"

"Passion, I hear you. Lord knows I had my fair share of issues with the law when I was coming up, but all cops ain't bad," Professor Higgins said as a matter of fact. She retrieved a box of tissues from her desk and handed it to Passion.

"Thanks." Passion plucked three sheets from the box and wiped her eyes and nose.

"Does your uncle know what happened to you?" Professor Higgins asked.

"Joe? God, no! That fool would likely go ballistic."

"Yeah, Joe always has been extra as hell," Professor Higgins laughed. "Now, you stop that crying. You don't wanna get crow's feet at the corners of your eyes and start looking like a washed-up old hag like me," she joked.

"Knock it off, Professor. You look better than girls I know who are half your age," Passion said honestly.

"I guess I've held up okay over the years. You should've seen me when I was your age. I didn't quite have all this," she pinched Passion's hip, "but I was nice to look at. I swear, I don't know what they're putting in the food you kids are eating these days that has you developing so quickly. Uncle Joe had better keep his eyes open and his pistol ready to protect you from them young boys, who I'm sure are sniffing around you."

It ain't the boys I'm worried about. It's the old men, Passion wanted to say, but kept it to herself.

"Did you hear what I asked?" Professor Higgins questioned.

"Huh?" Passion had checked out momentarily so she hadn't realized the professor was still talking.

"I asked how the job is working out for you?" Professor Higgins said. One day it had come up in conversation that Passion was looking for a way to make a little extra money. Professor Higgins called in a favor and got her a job waiting tables at a diner downtown. One of the managers had been a student of the professor's two semesters prior. The job didn't pay a lot, but it would keep Passion from having to depend solely on the mercies of Joe. It would also make for good life experience, and would get her in the habit of earning her way through life.

"It's okay, I guess," Passion shrugged. "I just wish I could get in more hours."

"If you did, you'd probably be even less focused on school than you are now. And speaking of which, when are you going to come by so we can finish going over those college applications?"

"I'll get around to it, I guess," Passion said unenthusiastically.

"You *guess?*" Professor Higgins gave her a quizzical look. "Passion, only last week you couldn't stop talking about the list of schools you want to apply to, and now it's you *guess?* Come better than that, little girl."

"I didn't mean it like it sounded, Professor Higgins. It's just that I got a lot on my plate right now," Passion told her.

"Tough shit, we all have a lot on our plates in this thing called life. And I have a news flash for you: The more successful we become, the more that will be dumped on our plates. You're hitting your stride, Passion. Don't start slacking on your education now."

"I'm not slacking, Professor Higgins. You see me in class every day applying myself," Passion said.

"You're right. You come in here every day and do the work. I can't take that from you. But now it's time to move onto something more challenging than a few courses a week at the local community college. This isn't to say that there's anything wrong with attending a community college. Hell, I clap for kids who stick with it long enough to bother graduating high school, so you know I'm singing from the rooftops for anyone continuing their education on the collegiate level. What I'm saying is, you"—she pointed at Passion—"are capable of so much more."

"These days, I'm not so sure anymore." Passion said in a defeated tone.

"Hey . . . hey, you know I don't even play all that self-pity business so knock it off," Professor Higgins said sternly. "Now, I get it. Your life has been a bit more complicated than the average girl your age, with what happened with your parents and you having to be raised up by Joe's ass; that ain't no excuse to quit. I've seen your high school transcripts and for the first three years your grades were more than good enough to get into USC or any other university of your choice. But for whatever your reasons, you damn near flushed your entire senior year down the toilet and took yourself out of the running. That had to have been a tough pill to swallow, but you didn't let it stop you. You came down here on your own and enrolled in school, so I know the want is still there, but want isn't always good enough. Our lives are fueled by passion, no pun intended. I'm passionate about what I do, which is why I get up and do my job every day whether I feel like it or not. Some mornings I find it hard to get out of bed, but I do. You wanna know why? Because I'm passionate about helping kids like you become something more than what society tells you that you can be. You've got to use that same passion to push yourself over the hump so you can get into USC."

"But what if I do all that you say and realize it was for nothing?" Passion questioned. "What if I come in here, bust my ass to try and get back on track, and still can't get into USC?"

"Then you pick another university. Or another, or another, until you can pull yourself up to the next level. You have to program yourself to believe that failure is not an option. I see you in class when we're doing our hypothetical case studies and you deep-dive into some of these people's heads. I also see you in our program, uplifting some of these other girls when they sink to places where I can't reach them. You have a natural gift for making people believe when they're in doubt. Now, I just need you to transfer that same energy into yourself. Stop with all this self-doubt foolishness and recognize your greatness. I tell you girls all the time that you are queens, and queens don't settle, we rule!"

"You're absolutely right." Passion said with conviction. Whenever Passion heard Professor Higgins speak, it always spoke to more than just her ears. She felt the words in her soul. Since she left the house that morning, Passion had felt like there had been a dark cloud hanging over her head, but all it took was a conversation with Professor Higgins to bring the sun back out.

"I know I am, which is why you're going to come see me tomorrow so we can finally finish going over this stuff for your next round of college applications," Professor Higgins said in a matter-of-fact tone.

"I got you, Professor Higgins."

"Don't have me, have *you*! I'm serious, Passion."

"And so am I. I'm gonna come see you," Passion assured her.

"Then let's seal the deal." Professor Higgins extended her hand. When Passion shook her hand the professor noticed two Band-Aids on the inside of Passion's forearm. "What's this?" She raised Passion's arm to get a better look.

"Nothing." Passion snatched her arm back and pulled her sleeve back down.

"Are we really going to do this again?" Professor Higgins folded her arms and glared at Passion. The girl dipped her head, but she wasn't getting off that easy. Using her finger, she tipped Passion's chin up so that she had to meet her gaze. She found the corners of Passion's eyes moist. "What's going on?"

"Nothing, just some stuff I'm dealing with right now. It's not that deep." Passion tried to downplay it.

"But it's deep enough for you to start cutting yourself again?"

Professor Higgins was one of the few people who knew one of Passion's darkest secrets. She was a cutter. It was something that she did when she was stressed. It had started not too long before her parents died. It was part of the reason she had ended up in therapy, and a direct result of the trauma she had suffered. Back then it was bad, and a few times Passion had cut herself deep enough to require stitches. Her parents had thought that she was trying to commit suicide, but she had just accidentally gone too deep with the razor. As she got older she got more skilled with the cutting, and even better at hiding the marks it left behind. It wasn't something she did often, only when she was under extreme stress. The bloodletting was one of the only things that seemed to even her out when she felt like she was dancing too close to the edge of her sanity. Pain was good. Pain was what helped her determine what was real and what was in her head. It was her way of keeping herself grounded. It had been a while since she had last cut herself, and then the business with Birdie happened. Before Passion knew it, she was sitting in the corner in the back of the bus gently dragging a thin razor across her skin.

"Passion, are you still taking the medication that the doctor prescribed you?" Professor Higgins asked.

"No, I told you that they were making me fat and sleepy. I can't be running around like no overweight zombie." Passion rolled her eyes.

"Then maybe they could've looked into lowering your dosage. I thought the medicine was doing good with keeping you balanced?"

"I don't need no pills to keep me balanced. I got this," Passion told her.

"You know how many times I've heard people say that before something bad happened? Passion, I know you're not big on talking to a therapist, but maybe speaking with someone will help you work through all this."

"No . . . fucking . . . shrinks!" She gritted each word out. The professor had hit a sore spot, which is what triggered Passion to respond so harshly. She hadn't meant to, but that's how it came out. "Sorry, but you know . . ."

"No need to apologize, Passion. That one was on me." Professor Higgins knew how Passion felt about therapists. "I'm just saying that sometimes it helps to talk about it versus holding it in."

"I hear you, Professor Higgins, and thank you for always worrying over me, but I promise I've got things under control," Passion said with more confidence than she actually felt.

"Okay, I'm going to take your word for it. I know you're a strong young woman, but even the mightiest of us have our moments of weakness. As someone who cares about you very much, I want to do everything I can to help you work through whatever is going on with you, even if it means sometimes turning a blind eye. On the flip side of that, as a mental health professional, I'd be breaking my oath if I felt that someone was a danger to themselves or others and didn't say anything. That being said, should I be worried about you, Passion?"

The weight of the question sat on Passion's shoulders like two acrobatic midgets using her like a circus prop. "No," she responded before her spirit had a chance to convince her to be honest about the fact that her life was in shambles.

CHAPTER 8

By the time Passion emerged from the train station on 125th Street, she felt like she had just worked all night slinging boxes in a warehouse. She was tired, not just physically, but mentally as well. Professor Higgins always knew which knobs to turn when it came to Passion. She had a gift for drawing raw emotions from her no matter how deep Passion buried them. Passion sometimes wondered if the psychologist kept a profile on her, or did her pain just speak so loudly that everyone could hear it, too? For as tired as she was, there would be no time to rest. She still hadn't heard from Birdie.

She found her attention turned by the loud thud of music bumping from a car speaker. It was so thunderous that it rattled the windows of several parked cars. The speakers, and the noise, was courtesy of a lime green Audi that was double-parked outside of Popeyes. It might've been cute had it not been for the thick gold rims it was fitted with. The license plate might've said New York, but the car screamed "Country Nigga."

Standing near the car was her best friend Juju's older brother, Jay. Juju was a hustler, but Jay was a gangster and everybody in the neighborhood knew it. The quiet Asian boy wasn't to be fucked with. Passion usually tried to avoid him when she could. It wasn't that Jay had ever done anything to her outright. It was just subtle things that he did and said that always made Passion think he felt some type of way about his sister being best friends with a Black girl.

At the moment Jay had his back to Passion. He was speaking with a young kid, who was leaning against the loud Audi. He was short and dressed in baggy jeans that hung off his ass and a plain black sweatshirt with a gold chain. A black bandanna was pulled tightly around his braided hair. He reminded Passion of "Tha Carter II" Lil Wayne. Shorty must've felt Passion staring, because the next thing she knew, both he and Jay were looking in her direction. Passion lowered her eyes and tried to keep walking, but shorty was on her heels.

"Sup, lil ma? Where you off to?" Shorty fell in step with her.

"For you to find somebody else's parents to play with, young man," Passion said dismissively and kept it pushing. She was still technically a teen herself, but he looked like a high school freshman. She thought her response was cute and tasteful, but he didn't.

"Damn, it's like that? Well, fuck you too, bitch!" Shorty called after her.

Being called out of her name gave Passion pause. Passion could've kept walking. She should've kept walking, but after the day she'd had, it wouldn't sit right with her spirit to go to sleep that night letting that little boy disrespect her. She'd been stepped on enough in the last twelve hours, and she'd be damned if she let him add to the footprints on her back.

"Fuck me?" Passion turned abruptly. "Fuck ya mama! That's the problem with you young boys, instead of accepting rejection, your natural instinct is to resort to disrespect. You don't know who I am or who I might know around here that might come see you about that disrespect." It wasn't a threat. More of a fact.

This amused shorty. "I'm Lil Sorrow, shorty. Ain't shit I fear but God," he boasted.

"At the rate you're out here going, you'll probably meet him sooner than later," Passion capped.

"Be cool, that's one of my sister's lil friends," Jay finally stepped in. He looked at Passion like she had been the one who started it.

"A'ight, you get a pass since you fam and all," Lil Sorrow said playfully.

"Bye bye!" Passion flipped him off and kept on about her evening. She didn't have to turn around to know the little boy's eyes were still on her. He was cute, but far too young and abrasive as shit. Passion was attracted to bad boys, but that kid had a prison number written across his forehead and she didn't have time. Passion had too much going on in her life to be putting money on some young nigga's books.

Her building was only a five-minute walk from the train station, but Passion did it in about three and a half. For the entire walk she kept getting this weird feeling in the pit of her gut. It wasn't like the ball of ice that impregnated her when she was about to slip into the dark place. This felt more like eating food that had been left sitting out all night. Something wasn't right.

When she reached the building, she found the Unusual Suspects loitering in front of the store connected to her building. She called them this because they were the most unusual bunch of halfway hustlers that she had ever met. There were three of them that day. With them, the rotation could change depending on what day of the week it was, but the core trio were rarely absent in part or whole. In these three poor souls, Passion saw a cautionary tale every time she passed them.

"What up, Passion?" Ed, who was the oldest of the bunch, greeted her. He was a chubby brown-skinned dude who always came outside looking like he had just rolled out of bed. You could catch Ed at four in the afternoon and he still might have cole in his eyes like he just woke up. For the most part Ed was harmless, but he had a con game that most people would never see coming. That's how he made his bread, trimming suckers. Even the ones he saw every day.

"I'm good, Ed. How you?" Passion replied.

"G-mackin," Ed capped back. He was one of those old heads who still tried to carry himself like he was young, but usually butchered any slang that had been invented after 2005.

"Y'all seen Birdie out here today?" Passion asked.

"I'm just coming out," Ed told her.

"What about you two?" she addressed his boys. "Either of you seen Birdie today?"

"Not since last night. She slid through and copped some smoke from Mud," a short, brown-skinned man named Paul told her. Paul was probably the coolest of the three. He was the neighborhood hustle man. One of those dudes who could get you just about anything, from jumbo cases of toilet paper to weave bundles. If you needed it, he could get it for you at below-average costs.

"I could've sworn I asked you not to sell weed to that girl?" Passion addressed Mud.

Mud chugged the last of the dollar nip of Bacardi he'd been sipping from before answering. "Man, that girl grown. Her money spends just like everybody else."

"She's sixteen, you damn degenerate!" Passion fumed. Mud was her least favorite of the trio. He was both a drunk and a troublemaker. From sun up to sun down Mud hung on the block, drinking, harassing females, and telling stories that nobody wanted to hear. Let him tell it; at one time he was the crown prince of Harlem, but you'd be hard-pressed to find anyone who could validate his claim.

"Shit, I was doing more than that when I was sixteen!" Mud laughed, and when he did it made Passion cringe. The laugh sounded like a cough that couldn't quite come out. It probably wouldn't have been so bad if he wasn't always laughing. Everything was a joke to Mud, which was part of the reason he was a joke to everyone else.

"Playing like that is probably what got your ass tightened up," Ed joked.

Passion hadn't noticed at first, but Mud had a bruise under his eye and one side of his face looked swollen. "What happened to you?"

"He got hit by a bird," Paul answered for him, which made Ed laugh.

Passion didn't get the inside joke. "Y'all niggas weird."

"Dare to be different, baby." Mud turned the situation into a joke. "I got a better question, though: Where you coming from looking all sexy and shit? You'd look even better with a nigga like me by your side." He invaded her space.

Passion took a step back. She could smell the liquor coming off him in waves and it was threatening to make her nose run. "Knock it off, Mud. We already had this conversation."

"I believe it ended with her telling you that she wouldn't piss on you if you were on fire," Ed reminded him.

This had happened the previous summer. Somebody from the neighborhood had passed, so there were some heads outside drinking and telling stories about the departed. Mud of course had had one too many. He spent the majority of the night downing nips that seemed to endlessly appear from his pocket like magic. And all the while he kept professing his undying love to Passion. She knew that he had been drunk and tried to keep it cute, but Mud had started getting real aggressive. They exchanged words, and it even got to a point where Mud had gotten into Passion's face like he was going to hit her. Unfortunately for him, he did it just as Bo was walking up. She put that big .45 under Mud's chin and walked him around the block while they had a conversation about the importance of respecting women. That was the first and last problem Passion ever had out of Mud.

"I dead-ass thought Bo was going to shoot you," Paul recalled.

"Me, too. I'm kind of mad she didn't. If anybody out here gonna put a bullet in me, it'd have been an honor for it to have been a gangsta of Bo's caliber. I'd have died a legend!" Mud proclaimed.

"Something is wrong with you." Paul shook his head sadly.

Passion was about to say her goodbyes and go upstairs to check on Birdie when her best friend Juju came out of the store. Her hair was done up in thick green braids, streaked in purple here and there, and tied at the top of her head so that they spilled around her round face. She was wearing a gold Lakers warm-up suit with the matching yellow, white, and gold Magic Johnson Converse. She had her head down, working a quarter against a scratch-off, so she didn't see Passion right off. When she finally looked up and spotted her friend, she flashed a smile, showing off the gold teeth across the bottom of her mouth.

"What's up, bitch!" Juju greeted Passion with a warm hug. Outside of the residents of Uncle Joe's apartment, Juju was the closest thing to family that Passion had. She was the first friend Passion made when she moved to the neighborhood and the chemistry between them was instant. They were both outcasts who had lost a lot and knew how to keep secrets.

"Just coming from school. What's up with you?"

"Shit, about to spark up." Juju pulled a pack of Backwoods from her pocket for Passion to see. "You trying to get high right quick?"

"I wish, but not right this second. You see Birdie?" Passion asked.

"Nah, not today. Everything good?" Juju loved Birdie almost as much as Passion did.

"Should be, but I just wanna make sure. You never know, fucking with this place." Passion looked up at the building with sadness in her eyes.

"Say less. I'm gonna roll with you. Let me just give scrams what I need to give him right quick." Juju jerked her head in Ed's direction. Ed was standing there, trying to pretend that he wasn't watching the girls. There was an anxious look in his eyes.

"Handle your business," Passion told her.

Juju waved Ed over. She gave a cautious look around to make sure that no one was watching, before dipping her hand into the crotch of her warm-up pants. She came up holding a tightly wound paper bag. Passion knew what was in it. Not just because she knew that Juju was the neighborhood weed girl, but because she could smell it. The shit Juju sold was straight gas, but it wasn't for everyone. Juju kept her sales to people she knew around the neighborhood. She had the access and connections to where she could've expanded if she chose, but she kept her business low-key.

"Sup, Jujitsu?" Ed greeted her jokingly. It was what he would call Juju when he wanted to get under her skin.

"Do you know how racist that sounds? And after all these years, why do I have to keep telling you that I'm Korean, not Japanese, dick!" Juju shoved the bag into his chest.

Juju's ethnicity was the running joke of the block. If you spoke to her over the phone or saw her in the right light, you might mistake Juju for being a light-skinned Black girl or maybe Puerto Rican, but she was one hundred percent Korean. She had moved to New York with her family when she was five years old. They settled in Harlem, smack in the middle of the hood. People gave Juju shit all the time, claiming that Juju was just another culture vulture, but she wasn't. What you saw with Juju was really who she was. Her family lived and owned businesses in the neighborhood, so Juju had grown up around nothing but Black and Brown kids for her entire life. It was natural that theirs was the culture she wound up embracing. Juju was aware of and respected her Korean roots, but she identified with the people she had been raised with.

"Chinese, Japanese, Korean . . . don't make me no never mind as long as you keep coming through with the fire-ass flowers!" Ed told her.

"That ain't never gonna change. But you, I gotta slide with my girl real quick. I'll catch you when I spin back," Juju gave him dap and walked with Passion into the building.

———

On the ride up on the elevator, Passion gave Juju the rundown on how she had bumped into her brother and the disrespectful kid who called himself Lil Sorrow.

"Yeah, that one is a handful," Juju confirmed. "I don't know him like that, outside of seeing him here and there with Jay, but his name is definitely one that's out there ringing."

"But he looks like a baby!" Passion said.

"He young, but he runs with dudes that got old blood on their hands. These kids growing up way too fast, ma." Juju shook her head.

"Don't I know it," Passion said, thinking of her own troubles. "Ju, I wanna tell you something, but you can't let it go no further than us."

"Bitch, you don't even gotta add the disclaimer. You know how we rock," Juju said, and she was right. They had often been each other's crying shoulders, and voices of reason when they were on the verge of doing something stupid. There would also be no judgment from Juju either, since her family weren't the most law-abiding business people in their neighborhood. So Passion confided in her the events of the day.

"Damn," was all Juju could say. There was more in her heart that she wanted to let out, but she knew that wasn't what her friend needed right then. So, she reserved judgment. Juju knew what time it was with Uncle Joe. Her parents did business with him, but always warned her never to go into his apartment. Back then she didn't really understand why. Uncle Joe was always nice to her when she was growing up. Even when she went through her phase of being hot-in-the-ass and flirting with men way older than her, Joe never crossed that line. It could've been because he respected her parents, or knew that her brother would try and kill him if he found out. It was a line Joe just never crossed with her. It wasn't until she was a little older and playing in the streets herself that she began to understand the nature of Uncle Joe's business and the reason for her parents' warnings.

Passion feared the worse when she stuck her head in the door. To her surprise, the apartment was quiet. In fact, she even smelled something cooking in the kitchen. That was a sure sign that something was wrong, because nobody in the house really cooked like that except Passion and sometimes Rose, and nobody had seen Rose since she robbed Uncle Joe and ran off. She was "the one that got away." Uncle Joe always promised to murder her if she ever set foot in New York again. They all knew that she was somewhere in Maryland, and with Uncle Joe's connections he likely could've tracked her down if he wanted to, but he didn't. It had even been suggested that he send men down to bring her back, but he never did. Uncle Joe was a vengeful son of a bitch by nature, so Passion couldn't understand his reluctance when it came to hunting Rose down. It was as if he would rather her stay missing than confront her. Rose being MIA eliminated her from being the one in the kitchen cooking. Further confirmation that something was off was the fact that the apartment was spotless. It had been a mess when she left, but someone had done a thorough cleanup job while she was at school. What had happened there to warrant such a thorough cleaning?

With Juju on her heels, Passion entered the apartment and headed for the kitchen. It was there that the plot thickened even more. Bo was moving around the kitchen, checking pots. Three of the four burners were going and there was also something in the oven. Bo could cook her ass off, but she hardly bothered. The only time you would find her in the kitchen cooking like this was when she was stressed out or sad. Passion's heart suddenly filled with dread. What had her extended family done?

When Bo turned and saw Passion and Juju standing in the doorway, she jumped like she had just been caught with her hand in the cookie jar. "Oh, hey girls. I didn't see y'all standing there."

"Hey, Ms. Bo. How you living?" Juju greeted her.

"Barely above the poverty line," Bo joked. "Passion, what are you doing back home so early? Something happen at school?"

"Where's Birdie?" Passion got straight to the point.

"In the bedroom. She wasn't feeling well so I let her stay home from school today," Bo explained. There was something about the way Passion was looking at her that she didn't like. "What's wrong with you?"

Passion didn't answer. She turned and marched to the bedroom. Both girls breathed collective sighs of relief when they walked in the shared room and found Birdie in bed asleep. Passion sat on the edge of the bed, careful not to wake her. She lifted the blanket and checked the girl. She'd stripped off the clothes she had been wearing earlier and was now wearing a nightgown that Passion didn't recognize. It was sheer and trimmed in fur around the bottom. She noticed a small tear at the shoulder. Gently, she brushed Birdie's hair from her face. She still had traces of lipstick smeared over her lips. Birdie never wore makeup. Passion didn't have to guess what had happened and it made her blood boil.

Birdie must've felt Passion's presence because her eyes fluttered open. She looked confused at first, but once she realized who had disturbed her slumber, her lips formed a weak smile. "Hi Passion."

"Hey, little girl. How are you feeling?" Passion smiled back at her.

"I'm okay. Just a little out of it," Birdie told her. She propped on her elbow and rubbed the sleep from one of her eyes. It looked like she was having a hard time keeping her balance. It was then that Passion noticed three bruises on her arm that were shaped like fingers.

"Are you okay? Did somebody hurt you?" Passion asked, examining the bruises. Someone had to have grabbed her arm pretty roughly to bruise her so.

"I'm fine. Ted got a little carried away, but Uncle Joe straightened him out. He showed Ted how he should be doing it to me and after that we got along fine," Birdie said groggily. It was as if she still wasn't fully awake.

Passion had already been disgusted at the thought of Ted having sex with Birdie, but hearing that Uncle Joe had played a role of any kind during the act made her want to vomit. She spared a glance at Juju who looked like she was trying her best not to cry.

"I'm so sorry that happened to you, Birdie," Passion said emotionally.

"Wasn't your fault, Passion. Wasn't nobody's fault. I know I gotta pull my weight to stay in Uncle Joe's house," Birdie said, as if it were simply a fact of life. "What time is it?"

Passion wiped the lone tear from her cheek and looked at the digital clock across the room. "Just after three."

"My goodness. I've slept the whole day away. Let me get up." Birdie made to sit up, but the room began so spin so she laid back down.

"Don't get up, Bird. Just lay here and rest for a time. I'll wake you when it's time to eat," Passion told her, fighting back her anger. Bo had claimed that Birdie wasn't feeling well, but in truth, she was drunk. Passion could smell whatever they had given her to drink coming out of her pores.

"You know Uncle Joe don't like it when we sleep all day. I got chores to do." Birdie tried to rise again, but Passion forced her back down.

"You've given this house more than your share today, Birdie. Don't you worry about no chores. Get some rest, and let me worry about Uncle Joe." Passion brushed her forehead tenderly.

Birdie gave her a dopey smile. "You know? I been thinking about something lately, Passion," her words slurred slightly.

"And what's that?" Passion asked.

"Our plan. How we always talk about escaping this place once we get our money right."

"Soon, baby," Passion assured her.

"Why not now? You know Uncle Joe got a stash? We can rip him off and go wherever we want," Birdie said.

"Girl, Uncle Joe ain't got enough worth stealing. Besides, even if he did, Bo keeps it under lock and key. I'd rather wrestle a bear than tangle with her," Passion joked.

"I ain't talking about what he keeps in that old safe in the back of the closet. I'm talking about a secret stash," Birdie whispered. "After him and Ted had their way with me, I heard them talking. They thought I was sleeping." Her eyes darted around nervously like she was afraid Uncle Joe would pop up from beneath one of the beds. "Ted asked Joe when he was gonna come get that, because it was making him uncomfortable sitting on his car lot."

"Birdie, they could've been talking about anything. That doesn't mean Joe has Ted hiding money for him," Passion told her.

"Then why didn't they want Bo to hear?" Birdie questioned. "You know the only time Joe get all secretive is when he got extra money he don't want Bo to know about. We can steal one of Joe's pistols and run down on Ted bitch-ass like," she made her fingers into the shape of a gun, "this is a muthafuckin stick up." She popped up and waved her finger-gun drunkenly. Passion caught her as she almost fell out of the bed.

"Birdie, you are drunk and need to sleep it off." Passion coaxed her back down.

Birdie lay back on the pillow and her eyes began to droop. "That's why I love you, Passion. You always take such good care of me. You always gonna take care of me?"

"Always," Passion promised her. She was smiling, but inside she was sobbing. "You rest now, Birdie . . . go on and rest."

When Passion stormed back into the kitchen she damn near had smoke coming from her ears. Juju had kept her trapped in the bedroom for an additional ten minutes in an attempt to calm her down. She was upset about what had happened to Birdie and rightfully so. After making Passion give her word that she wouldn't do anything stupid, she let her out of the room. The minute she did, Passion shot out like a bullet. She needed answers.

When she arrived in the kitchen she found Bo applying a coat of butter to the biscuits she had just taken out of the oven. She wasn't alone this time. Zeta leaned against the kitchen counter, chomping on a piece of fried chicken. She had retired her clothes from earlier and was now dressed in a pair of sweat pants and a T-shirt. Out of the tight clothes and with the layers of makeup wiped away, Zeta looked less like a street walker and more like the young twenty-two-year-old girl that she was. Two sets of eyes turned to Passion, who stood in the kitchen doorway, nostrils flaring.

"Birdie still back there sleeping?" Bo asked.

"Yeah, she's still sleeping. I guess I would be too if I spent all morning getting pumped full of liquor," Passion spat.

"Ain't nobody gave that girl no liquor. All she had was half a beer with Uncle Joe earlier. You know that girl ain't got no head for drink." Bo downplayed it. It was a weak lie. She knew it and so did Passion.

"I can't imagine there are too many sixteen-year-old kids who can hold a drink, since they've got no business drinking in the first place. How could you let them get Birdie drunk, Bo?" Passion asked emotionally.

"Ain't nobody made that girl take that beer. She asked for it. And since when do any of you girls listen to me these days? Y'all think you're grown now and gonna do what you wanna do, so I just stay out the way and let you be," Bo said. She moved from her buttering of the biscuits and busied herself with the few dishes in the sink.

Passion walked over and turned the water off. "Is that what you're telling yourself so you don't feel no guilt behind letting a grown-ass man run up in a child? Last time I checked, the state pays you to protect us!"

The whole kitchen got quiet. Even the pots cooking on the stove seemed to go quiet. No one was naïve enough where they didn't know what kind of operation Uncle Joe was running, but none would dare say it out loud. Especially in front of someone who wasn't a part of Uncle Joe's family. Passion had just thrown down a gauntlet that not even Zeta's defiant ass would've had the balls to.

Bo took her time drying her hands with the dishcloth before folding it neatly and hanging it over the faucet. She turned to Passion and gave her a look that could've only been described as cautionary. "I understand that you might be feeling in a way right now and I can't blame you for that, but you might dull that sharp tongue of yours a bit when speaking to me. This is Joe's house, but never forget who's running it."

"I know Bo, and I'd never disrespect, but even you gotta see the wrong in what went down," Passion said.

"That was some bullshit, to be sure," Bo agreed. "Birdie ain't built for what the rest of us signed up for, but ain't none of you naïve about how the bills get paid around here."

"I don't even know why you're all bent out of shape about Birdie having sex," Zeta chimed in between bites.

"Because she's a kid and don't need to be fucking on no grown-ass men!" Passion barked.

Zeta rolled her eyes. "Girl, bye! Birdie ain't hardly no virgin. She ain't do nothing in here with Ted this morning than she was doing to support her junkie mama's habits. Or did you forget how our little bird came to occupy this cage?"

Birdie had come to Uncle Joe's about a year or so after Passion had moved in. She was a familiar face in their neighborhood because her mother, Betty, often dragged the child with her when she came to buy her drugs. Betty wasn't one of those functional crackheads. She was the vicious type that had no boundaries on what she was willing to do to get high. Passion had once heard a story about Betty letting five or six of the dudes from the next building gangbang her for three ten-dollar rocks. One of them had even gassed her to let him shove his pet snake into her pussy. It was all fun and games until the damn snake bit Betty and she ended up in the hospital. Thankfully, it wasn't poisonous and she would live to smoke again.

Uncle Joe knew Betty from back in the day and had somewhat of a soft spot for her, or so he always claimed. Because of their relationship he would sometimes allow her to get drugs from his workers on credit. Betty ended up playing on his kindness and running up a tab that she had no hopes of paying. Of course, Uncle Joe wasn't happy, and no one wanted to be on the wrong end of him. Since he and Betty had history, Uncle Joe decided that instead of harming Betty he would let her work off the debt. As a part of the deal her daughter, Birdie, would have to move into the house with the other girls. This was not only to keep Betty honest, but because Betty wouldn't have to worry about a babysitter. Uncle Joe could work Betty twenty-four seven selling drug and pussy. Bo told him that he was crazy for putting drugs into a junkie's hands and expecting them to come back with straight money, but Uncle Joe insisted. Betty lasted for less than two weeks before temptation got the best of her. She ran off with two thousand dollars' worth of drugs and some cash. They crazy part was that when he found out, he didn't even seem mad. When Passion got older and became more familiar with the beast that she was dealing with, she realized that his interests had never truly been in Betty in the first place.

"That still don't make it right," Passion addressed Zeta.

"I'll tell you what, if you feel that strongly about it, why don't you march into the bedroom and wake Uncle Joe up so you can tell him about himself," Zeta challenged.

Passion grew quiet. Nothing she could say or do short of taking Birdie and fleeing would help either of them. Even if she did go that route, there would be no place they could hide where Uncle Joe couldn't find them. He had contacts everywhere. "I'm going out." Passion turned on her heels.

"Where you going? Dinner will be ready in an hour so," Bo told her.

"I'm good. I don't have much of an appetite right now." Passion left the kitchen and the apartment.

Juju stood there for a time longer, giving Bo and Zeta a look that bordered on disgust. Zeta rolled her eyes, clearly not giving a fuck one way or another, but not Bo. She had managed to keep her game face in Passion's presence, but once she was gone the mask slipped and Juju saw what was hidden beneath: helplessness.

Juju came outside to find Passion in front of the building pacing back and forth. She hadn't waited for Juju to come out of the apartment before jumping on the elevator and taking off because she didn't trust herself not to do something stupid, like lay hands on Bo. It was likely that she would get her ass kicked for her troubles, but it would feel better than just standing around doing nothing.

They didn't speak. They didn't have to in order to convey what Passion was feeling. Juju started walking and Passion fell in step behind her. They ended up across the street from their building and sitting on one of the benches that ran along Morningside Park. Passion continued to sit there and brood while Juju rolled the weed into a Backwoods. She let Passion do the honor of sparking it as she obviously needed it more.

"Breathe, girl . . . just breathe." Juju rubbed Passion's back while Passion hit the weed. She knew her friend well enough to know that she was about to slip into a very dark place.

"This is so fucked up, Ju." Passion expelled the weed through her nose. She immediately felt the tickle and her eyelids gained weight. Juju definitely had some bomb shit, but it only worked to dull Passion's pain instead of taking it away.

"Tell me about it. That shit is low, even for Joe. I mean I ain't trying to knock nobody's hustle. We gotta get it how we live, but Birdie?" Juju shook her head for lack of anything else that would properly convey her disappointment. She had lost respect for Uncle Joe. She had known for years that he sold pussy, but she had always figured that he at least had some type of boundaries, but apparently he didn't. A thought entered Juju's mind. It was one that she'd had before, but this would be the first time she ever gave voice to it. "You and Uncle Joe . . . he's never . . ."

"God no! He's a depraved muthafucka, but he's still my uncle. He wouldn't go there," Passion assured her.

"After hearing about him tossing lil Birdie up, I don't put shit past him. Your uncle is a foul dude," Juju said seriously.

Passion didn't disagree. He was her mother's brother, but he didn't possess any of the qualities she had come to recognize when it came to the maternal side of her family. Her mother didn't have much family, but the few cousins and great aunts twice removed that she had met here and there over the years were decent, hardworking people. Not saints, but not Uncle Joe either. He was a straight-up gangster, and you didn't have to look very deep to find the wickedness in him. It was as if he had been cut from a totally different cloth. She reasoned that Uncle Joe being so corrupt was why he and her mother had been estranged. She could only remember meeting him once prior to her parents' deaths, and that meeting had been a brief one: a few words passed between siblings when they had run into each other on the street one day. Outside of that, her mother never really talked about her brother. Passion had only ended up in Uncle Joe's care because he was the last living relative that either of her parents had who was willing to take her in. It was either move in with him, or go into the system until she turned eighteen. He was a stranger to her, but also the lesser of two evils, or so she had thought until after living with him for a while. In hindsight, the foster care system might've been the better choice when measured against what was going on at Uncle Joe's.

This took her back to the remark that Zeta had made that morning, in response to Passion saying that since she was Joe's sister's kid the same rules of the house didn't apply. He'd never try her. Zeta had called her stupid, but why? Was she trying to suggest that Uncle Joe would try and sleep with his own niece? Uncle Joe had proven to be a man who was morally bankrupt, but not even he would attempt something so disgusting as to force himself on his sister's daughter. Then Passion thought about little Birdie. Joe used to treat her like family too, but now she was laid up half drunk, and broken by two grown men. All for a few dollars and a cheap thrill. The more she thought about it, the more uncertain she became of what Joe was or wasn't capable of.

"What do you make of the stuff Birdie was saying about Joe having a stash nobody knows about?" Juju asked.

"That girl was drunk. If Joe did have a stash that Bo didn't find out about, he sure as hell wouldn't trust Ted's larcenous ass to keep it safe. He'd rob Joe blind the first chance he got. It would serve him right, though. After the bullshit today, I could give a fuck what happens to Uncle Joe or anybody else in that house except Birdie. Shit, it might be a blessing in disguise if something happened to Joe. At least me and Birdie would finally be free."

"Maybe we should kill him?" Juju joked, while looking off into space.

"That might not be such a bad idea."

Juju looked at Passion, who was wearing a serious expression. "You know I was only fucking around, right?"

Passion didn't respond.

"Check it, baby girl." Juju got serious. "I won't even sit here and try to pretend that I can imagine what it's like to live in that house of horrors. That shit needs to be saged and then burned to the fucking ground. I know you tried to emancipate yourself before, but Uncle Joe blocked it, but you'll be eighteen soon. Once you cross that finish line you can get the fuck out of there and not Uncle Joe or anyone else will be able to stop you! You can finally go back west and watch that sunrise on the Pacific Coast like you've been dreaming about." Juju was one of the few people Passion had shared her dream of getting back to the West Coast with. She wanted it more than anything. "Who knows? Maybe I can come out too, and me and you can run through Cali on some Thelma and Louise shit."

"Wouldn't that be something?" Passion laughed. She could see them now: her and Juju cruising up the Pacific Coast Highway in a drop-top, hair blowing in the warm breeze and good weed in their lungs. It would be amazing. Just the thought of it made Passion smile, and then reality set in. "I can't. If I leave, who will look after Birdie?" She had thought of running away from Uncle Joe's house of horrors on more than one occasion, but the thought of leaving Birdie behind always stopped her. Being in the house she was able to provide Birdie with at least some small measure of protection, but if she left there was no one to stop Birdie from being victimized by Joe's other girls, or worse, Joe himself. He had now tasted her goodies and Passion feared that he might develop an appetite for the teenage girl.

"Passion, you know I'm the only one besides you who loves that girl, so I can understand how you feel about having to leave her behind, but you can't save the next person if your shit ain't together. Get on your feet first then reach back for your people. Did you start saving up money like I told you to?"

"I've got a few dollars tucked away. I picked up some extra shifts at the diner, but you know they don't hardly pay shit. I mostly depend on tips to get me through. I got an income tax check coming too, but for the little bit of money they pay me it ain't gonna be more than fifteen hundred, if that," Passion told her. Between what she had saved over the last couple of months and the tax return she guesstimated she'd be sitting on just a little under three grand. It was a decent sum, but hardly enough for a fresh start.

"I got some bread put away that you can have. It ain't but a few grand, but it's yours," Juju offered.

"Ju, I can't take your money. You're out here every day risking your freedom for that bread. I can't," Passion refused.

"Stop that. I still live with my parents, I don't have any kids, and the only habits I have are weed and the occasional drink. I basically don't have any real bills, so most of what I make off hustling is profit. As far as the weed, it's legal now so I think my freedom will remain intact."

Passion wasn't used to people paying kindnesses on her without wanting something in return, so she wasn't quite sure how to receive what Juju was willing to do for her. Her eyes misted, but she didn't cry. "I love you, Juju." She hugged her best friend warmly.

"I love you, too." Juju rubbed her back. "Now cut it out before you have me out here crying. It took me an hour to do this makeup."

The two went back to their smoking and people watching on the side of Morningside Park. They had smoked a whole blunt and were half through the next one. Neither of the girls was feeling any pain. The problems that would be awaiting Passion when she got back home were still lingering in her mind, but they were no longer at the forefront. The good weed and the comfort of a great friend eased some of the hurt she had spent the whole day carrying.

"I got an idea." Juju suddenly perked up.

"What's up?" Passion asked curiously.

"What if I told you that I had a way to turn that fifteen-hundred-dollar income tax check into a few thousand?" Juju asked. She was just recalling a conversation that she had overheard her brother having that could be just the thing to solve Passion's problems and put a few dollars in her pocket at the same time.

"Juju, you know I ain't about to be out here selling drugs with you. I'm too pretty for jail," Passion said seriously.

"Nah, nothing that extreme. Look, I got some place that I need to be in a little while. Why don't you change your clothes and come with me and I can fill you in along the way?"

"What kind of spot?" Passion was suspicious. Juju was her girl, but sometimes she found herself hanging out in questionable places.

"Stop being so damn scary. Just some place to let our hair down. My brother and some of his partners are getting together for drinks. Somebody they know is just getting out of jail and you know every time somebody comes home from a bid these fools find a reason to celebrate. I hear there's going to be plenty of bottle popping, and a few free drinks are just what you and me need tonight."

"Na, Ju, I don't know about spending my night hanging around a bunch of drunk gangsters. I could stay home for all that," Passion joked.

"Since when?" Juju gave her a challenging look. "Passion, save that goodie-goodie shit for Professor Higgins, or those other muthafuckas who don't know how you can get when you let your hair down. All you attract is gangsters. As a matter of fact, didn't that one dude you were running around with last summer recently get locked up for shooting a bitch?"

"Allegedly," Passion corrected her. Passion had briefly dated a young dude named Jason who was up-and-coming in the streets. Jason was rough around the edges, with no home training to speak of, and wasn't very smart, but the sex was amazing. She had fucked with him off and on over the course of a summer. Things were good until he started showing signs of being clingy. He always wanted to be up under her and was obsessed with knowing her comings and goings. They weren't exclusive, and she knew Jason did his thing, but whenever she tried to do hers he started clowning. When she tried to break things off, Jason acted like he wanted to get physical. She didn't think that he was dumb enough to put his hands on one of Uncle Joe's girls, but why tempt fate? When it became obvious that he wasn't going to leave her alone willingly, she decided to get creative.

Two weeks following her breakup with Jason, Passion learned that he had been arrested for attempted murder. The way the streets told the story, the mother of his child had busted him cheating and they ended up getting into a fight. During the fight she stabbed him several times, and in response he shot at her. No one was sure if he was actually trying to hit her, but in a twist of dumb luck the bullet ricocheted off a pipe and hit her in the face. She lived, and Jason went to prison. It was a tragic tale, but Passion didn't lose any sleep over it.

Passion couldn't help but to chuckle at how well her friend knew her. It was true, she did attract bad boys. Thug wasn't a part of her regular diet, just something she indulged in when she had a taste for it. This was usually during periods when the darkness was on her heavily. When she was smothered by feelings of inadequacy and could find no relief in cutting herself. She wouldn't admit it, but there was a part of her that got a thrill from dealing with dangerous men. Sure, she attracted more than her fair share of young men on the right track, but there was just something about flirting with danger that turned her on.

Since she was a child, Passion had always known that there was power in pussy. Her father allowing her mother to dog was proof of that. That had been her first glimpse at the power, but it wouldn't be until she was a little older that she would get her first taste of it. Sometimes when men who did business with Uncle Joe came around, Passion would flirt. Never anything too heavy; a suggestive look here, a passing touch there. It was never an outright invitation, only enough to make sure they noticed her. Sometimes a second look was all it took to cause a man to get beside himself. Passion didn't do this because she was actually attracted to any of the men. She just wanted to see how far she could push the envelope. One boy, in his adolescent eagerness, had tried to steal a kiss from Passion when they thought that no one was watching. Unfortunately for him, Uncle Joe had eyes everywhere. He beat that boy so bad that he ended up in the hospital. It was after that incident that Passion realized what her mother had known all along, and her father found out the hard way: Pussy wasn't just power, it was a weapon!

"You know my brother's crowd ain't really my crowd either," Juju picked up. "Half those guys are killers and the other half thieves, but they all spend money. I'm trying to see if I can get a few ounces of this weed off and put that money toward our trip out west." She gave Passion a wink.

"Bullshit, you're just using that to guilt me into going with you. That's petty as hell, Juju."

"Then don't make me go there. Just say you'll come with me. We won't be out late, only long enough to have a drink . . . probably two, while I'm hustling this bud, and we out." Juju had a way of making things sound like they would be just that simple, but they rarely were.

Passion thought on it. She didn't have anything else to do that night and she didn't have class in the morning. She couldn't remember the last time she had been anywhere where she could vibe out and have some adult conversation. Then she thought about it. "I'm not really trying to go back upstairs to Joe's house to change right now. No telling what I might try and do to that fool. Do you think they'll let me in wearing this?" She motioned to her sweatshirt and jeans.

"Girl, they ain't about to let you in nowhere but a homeless shelter wearing that," Juju laughed. "Come with me back to my crib. You've got way more hips and ass than I do, but I think I got some shit that you might be able to squeeze into."

CHAPTER 9

It was well after sunset when Case and Tyriq dropped Pain back off in the projects. Just as he had suspected, Case's quick run uptown ended up turning into an all-day affair. They ended up riding with Tyriq and Patrice to her homegirl's house. Patrice's friend was a girl named Sheila who did hair out of her crib. Sheila was a little on the chubby side, but she had a pretty face and an angelic smile. Pain would find out that they had lured him over there so that Sheila could do his hair. He started to protest, but couldn't argue with the fact that with his Afro in such a state of disarray and unkempt knots he looked like a homeless person in a new outfit.

Pain was skeptical because he didn't know Sheila, and he was funny about who he let play in his hair. After a while he gave in and took a seat in the chair. A few hours later his fears were put to rest when Sheila handed him the mirror. Sheila had braided his hair in neat, slanted braids that rolled across his head almost like a wave. Sheila was so nice with it that Pain even allowed her to bust out the clippers and give him a shape-up. When she was done he looked five years younger than he had when he walked into the joint.

While Pain was getting his hair braided, Case, Patrice, Tyriq, and Sheila passed weed around, drank, and told stories. Pain sat contently listening to them talk shit, adding his two cents to the narrative as needed. Being around his closest friends in a room full of beautiful women made it feel just like old times. Pain was so deep in the moment that he had to stop himself twice from taking the blunt when it swung past him. He didn't smoke any of the weed because he didn't want to have an issue with his PO, but he did allow himself two glasses of champagne.

At some point Sheila had lured Pain into a back bedroom where she gave him a proper welcome home. He couldn't remember stripping, only finding himself propped on his elbows on a queen-size bed missing his shirt and pants. At the foot of the bed stood Sheila. She watched him from under hooded eyes while undoing her pants. She stepped out of them while simultaneously pulling her shirt over her head. Her arms unfolded from her bra, letting it fall to the floor as she came to stand before Pain.

Pain took a minute to take her in. It had been some time since he had laid eyes on a naked woman outside the corners of his mind. He wanted to drink in the moment. Sheila's body was much tighter than he had assumed when she was still fully dressed. She had a bit of a stomach and stretch marks crept up her thighs and hips, but Sheila wasn't badly put together. Unconsciously he smacked his lips, while he tried to think of which end of Sheila he wanted to start from.

Sheila sensed his hesitance so she took the initiative. She took him by the wrists and placed his hands over her breasts. His palms were rough and callused so they scraped against her large caramel nipples. She wasn't mad at the sensation. Sheila pressed his fingers closed around her breasts and massaged herself with his hands. Once he caught on and picked up on the rhythm of what she liked, she left him to his devices.

He felt it when her nipples hardened between his kneading fingers. When Pain heard her moan softly it stirred something in him. He could feel his dick wake up in his boxers. Pain laid his face against Sheila's stomach and let the heat from her body spill into his. He then began planting soft kisses on her stomach and up her sides. Her hands ran firmly down the back of his head, threatening to ruin the braids she had just spent the last couple of hours doing. Pain let the long fingers of his left hand trace a map down Sheila's body, until it found the X that marked the spot.

Sheila gasped when she felt Pain's finger slide inside her. His digits were long and his nails were rough and chipped from not being clipped in a while. She suffered through it and let him find his way. Once she was good and wet it wasn't so bad anymore. Her breath caught when he slipped two fingers in and then a third. She spread her legs and lowered herself down so far onto his fingers that her fupa was resting in the palm of his hand. Sheila rocked back and forth on his fingers in a steady rhythm while Pain took her there.

Pain wasn't sure what had come over him but he suddenly found himself very, very horny. He had already been horny when Sheila took him into the room, but now there was a little extra sauce on it. The anticipation of being about to get his dick out of the dirt made him hungry for what she had. He scooped Sheila about the waist with his free arm and, with his fingers still in her, stood and spun Sheila onto her back on the bed. He made sure to look her square in the eyes when he removed his fingers from her and began to suck on them. Pain knew that if his boys knew the kinds of things he was about to engage in behind that closed door they would never let him live it down. He would be branded a simp and probably the butt of personal jokes amongst the crew for at least the next two summers. He was well aware of how they would view it, but at that moment he didn't give one good damn. If this was to be the first piece of ass he got since coming home from prison, he was going to enjoy it as if it would be his last. Sheila didn't know it, but her ass was about to set the bar for Pain and his dick on their comeback tour.

If Sheila hadn't been shocked by Pain licking her juices off his fingers three hours after meeting her, she was sure to be by his next trick. Pain shoved her back onto the bed and spread her knees apart. He knelt over her, glaring down like the conquering hero. The next thing she knew he had his face buried between her thighs. Pain had to have been half-python because she could've sworn that she felt his jaw unhinge when his entire mouth enveloped her pussy. When his tongue rolled out of his skull it damn near tickled her asshole. When Sheila had invited Pain into the back room it had been with the intent to be the first chick to put her pussy on the infamous Blackbird upon his return to the world. He had been gone for a while and once he got a taste of what she was working with he was sure to be turned out. Unfortunately for her, the tables appeared to have been turned.

Pain could feel his dick swell with blood while he was eating Sheila's pussy. She tasted clean and sweet like she knew how to take care of herself. He suckled at her snatch like a juicy peach, holding her by her thighs so that she couldn't squirm out of his reach. His manhood was now bloated, and swollen to the point he feared it might explode if he didn't release what he was holding back. He pulled his face from between her thighs and positioned himself to enter her missionary. Sheila, however, had other ideas.

Sheila never thought she would ever say that she was happy to have a man stop eating her pussy, but Pain was the exception. He had licked, sucked, and poked her to the point where she started seeing spots. Her body was so awash with waves of pleasure that it took her a minute to realize that he was no longer eating her out. Pain hovered over her, long black dick standing strong and erect for the killing blow. She wanted to feel him inside her. If his dick was half as good as his head game she was gonna move this nigga in and give him her Social Security number. Yes, she wanted badly to feel his dick, but first she needed to taste it.

When Sheila's lips closed around Pain's dick he felt his leg shake. It was like her mouth created a vacuum seal around his shaft, and the only thing he could feel was the heat radiating from her tongue. Pain tried to maintain his cool as she slipped him farther and farther into her mouth. Pain knew that he was a well-hung cat, but this girl had already made half his dick vanish into her mouth and showed no signs of slowing down. Pain felt himself hit her tonsils and reasoned that she had to be done, until she opened up what felt like a trap door in the back of her throat. It was over.

Sheila gagged when she felt the warm, thick spray of semen fill her mouth. It coated her tongue and dripped down the back of her throat as Pain came prematurely. When she pulled his dick free of her mouth, she caught another blast of semen to her face. She cursed herself for giving him some of her five-star head before letting him fuck. Dudes who were out getting pussy on the regular were no match for her top-notch top, so she couldn't fault the convict for coming up short.

Pain looked down at the girl, still kneeing between his legs. There was cum on her chin, and some smeared up the side of her face. Seeing her painted with his cream reminded him of an episode of *The Three Stooges*. There was a big food fight at a dinner the Stooges had crashed, and during the fight Moe had hit Larry in the face with a custard pie. The comparison made Pain giggle. The giggle grew into laughter and eventually led to Pain doubled over, laughing hysterically.

"What the fuck is so funny?" Sheila asked defensively.

Pain tried to compose himself enough to offer an answer, but couldn't. He just couldn't stop thinking about the damn custard pie. Needless to say, Sheila was both embarrassed and pissed, so she kicked Pain and his gang out. Pain couldn't even be mad at her for reacting that way. He was mad at himself for not at least getting the pussy, but the good laugh and bomb head made it worth the price of admission.

CHAPTER 10

Pain was riding up on the elevator in his building, replaying the events of what had turned out to be a very full day. Case and Tyriq had been talking about hooking up with some of the old gang at a lounge later that night. They tried to get Pain to come along, but he declined. Between running with them all day and Sheila sucking his entire soul out, Pain was drained. He wasn't fit to do much other than hug his granny, eat, and get some sleep. He'd had his fun for the day, but tomorrow he was going to have to get on his grind and start looking for a job. He had a few leads that he needed to follow up on and wanted to get an early start.

The elevator arrived at his floor and the door slid open. Pain was so engrossed with trying to figure out how to operate the new cell phone that Case had insisted on buying him that he wasn't paying attention to where he was walking. He slammed into what felt like a wall, jarring him and causing him to drop one of the shopping bags he was carrying. When Pain finally did look up he realized that it wasn't a wall he had walked into, but a man.

The man/wall stood about an inch or two taller than Pain, but was heavier. He had broad shoulders that anchored thick arms and hairy knuckles like a gorilla's. His face was hard and strong with a long chin that made him resemble a half moon when he faced a certain way. At one time he might've been considered handsome with his curly hair, light skin, and hazel eyes, but time and poor habits were starting to catch up with him. His skin had lost its shine after years of hard drinking, and those curls that had once made women want to have his babies were now starting to thin on top. Wearing jeans that were a bit too snug for Pain's tastes, a faded flannel shirt, and worn work boots, he looked like one of those male models that you might find in a JCPenny Big & Tall clothing ad. Only JCPenny models didn't walk around with Glocks strapped to their hips. Pain had been ducking the law long enough to know a cop when he saw one. Especially this cop.

"Ain't this a surprise. My man Percy Wells." The cop flashed a phony smile.

"Marshall." Pain greeted him in a clipped tone.

"Damn, I haven't seen you in, what, six or seven years? And you greet me like I kicked your dog." Marshall faked hurt.

"Because you *did* kick my fucking dog," Pain reminded him.

Marshall Goodwin, sometimes called Goodie by those who knew him well enough, was no stranger to Pain. They had a history that stretched back probably longer than his relationship with Case. Like Pain, Goodie had grown up in that neighborhood. He was from the west side of the projects while Pain hailed from the east side. They wouldn't have run in the same circles either way because Goodie was sixteen years Pain's senior.

Goodie had always been a semi-square dude who loved to sniff around people he wasn't cut out to be in the company of. Such was the case with Pain's mother, Lizzie. Goodie had been sweet on Lizzie since they were kids, but could never worm his way out of the friend zone. He would often hang around her and her friends, tricking off the money he made at his after-school job, buying them liquor and weed. All for the privilege of being up under Lizzie. A time or three he had even professed his love to her, but Lizzie never took him seriously. She liked bad boys and Goodie didn't have quite enough dog in him to qualify. The nail in his coffin came when Lizzie had fallen for Pain's dad and ended up pregnant by him.

While Goodie went off to college to continue his education and chase his dreams, Lizzie found herself stuck in the projects learning how to be a teen mom. Their lives went in two different directions, with Goodie finishing school and enrolling in the police academy while Lizzie struggled to raise her son, hustling to make ends meet. Over the years, Goodie would pop up at Ms. Pearl's apartment from time to time to check on Lizzie and her mom. He claimed he was just trying to be a good friend, but everyone knew that with every visit there was always some hope that Lizzie would change her mind and finally give him a chance. It became obvious after a while that Lizzie would never want Goodie the way he wanted her, and it caused him to develop a resentment toward her. He loved Lizzie far too much to ever take his anger out on her, but had no such reservations when it came to her son.

Around this time, Pain was starting to grow up and out into his own, so he was becoming a constant fixture on the block with the rest of the knuckleheads. Goodie had worked his way up from beat walker and had become a young detective. Whenever he rode through the block and saw Pain on the scene he was on his ass. Goodie would roust Pain or whoever he happened to be with at the time. It got to the point where some of the older kids stopped wanting Pain hanging around because he was making them hot with the cops. Pain had gone to his mother in an attempt to get Goodie off his back, but the cop had sweet-talked her into believing that he was only staying on top of Pain to keep him on the straight and narrow. In truth, Goodie couldn't stand Pain. Every time he saw Lizzie's son it served as a grim reminder of something that he felt like had been stolen from him.

After Lizzie's death, no one in the neighborhood saw much of Goodie anymore. Rumor had it that he had taken her death so hard that he couldn't stand living in the city anymore and had been reassigned to a police department in Indianapolis or some other Midwestern city. As far as Pain was concerned, he hoped that Goodie would stay gone forever. But here he was.

"I only kicked your dog because you set him on me," Goodie pointed out.

"I didn't set him on you. You tried to swing on me and that's why he bit your ass!" Pain reminded him.

"Could've been worse. I could've shot him. And you," he added as an afterthought.

"You might as well have. They euthanized my dog behind that bullshit," Pain recalled. And it still hurt when he thought about the pit bull mutt he'd owned as a teen. Just about everybody hated that mean-ass dog, but Pain loved him. It had been one of his closest friends. "I heard you had been reassigned and were giving out parking tickets somewhere in Indianapolis or some shit?" he said, changing the subject.

"Yeah, the NYPD started to feel a bit small to me after a while so I decided to broaden my horizons. I can assure you that I wasn't handing out parking tickets, though." Goodie pulled out his wallet and flipped it open so that Pain could see the contents. There was a gold badge pinned to the inside.

"So, you're a detective now? Big fucking deal. Why don't you go back to the Midwest and harass them niggas out there? You got no authority in this city anymore," Pain dismissed him.

"See, if you had stayed in school then maybe your dumb ass would know the difference between a city badge and a federal one." Goodie tapped the eagle on his badge. "This here says I can harass punk-ass niggas like you in any one of these good United States that I catch you wrong in. I'm a U.S. Marshal now, not some local cop anymore."

"Marshall the marshal!" Pain laughed.

"Little fucks like you always laugh until I got my knee in their backs, slapping those bracelets on and dragging them in front of a federal judge. You ever been in front of a federal judge, Percy?" Goodie didn't wait for Pain to answer. "Of course you haven't. You ain't reached that rung on the criminal ladder yet, but at the rate you're going I suspect you will before long."

"Fuck you and that badge, Goodie. What the hell are you doing skulking around in my hallway, man?" Pain was tiring of the game.

"Your job," Goodie capped. "Your grandmother had a doctor's appointment and some other errands to run today. Seeing how she didn't have anybody reliable around to help her out, I stepped up. You know it's a sad thing when I see how some of our elders have been left out here to fend for themselves. Especially when they have kids and grandkids they raised who should be here to make sure their needs are taken care of."

"In case you haven't heard, I've been out of the loop," Pain said sarcastically.

"Yeah, I know all about your little vacation. Drug possession, right?" Goodie asked. "You know, I always pegged you to be smarter than to ride around in a dirty vehicle. That story never sat right with me, but I guess since you never spoke to the contrary those really were your drugs, huh?"

"Since you've always acted like such a know-it-all, why don't you tell me?" Pain challenged.

"I don't know everything, but what I do know would make for an interesting story," Goodie told him.

"Fuck is that supposed to mean?"

"It means that I kept tabs on you while you were away. I hear that you had a very colorful stay behind the wall. They tell me that your stay in prison was an eventful one, Jack. Isn't that what they had taken to calling you after you killed Brute? Jack the Giant Slayer."

"I ain't killed nobody," Pain lied.

"You ain't gotta lie to me, Pain. Hell, from the kind of man I hear Brute was, you did the world a favor by taking him out. I should be shaking your hand." He extended his hand, but Pain ignored it. "Right, the Giant Killer don't like to be touched. I guess that's what put you and Brute on the outs. Real touchy son of a bitch from the way I heard it. They say his thing was targeting the young guys in the prison who had the biggest reputations on the streets and sticking his dick in them. I heard he was like the Wilt Chamberlain of the prison system. Tell me something, Percy. Did Brute ever try and make you a part of his harem?"

"I don't play them kind of games, chump," Pain checked him.

"You sure?" Goodie narrowed his eyes at Pain. "A young dude as handsome as you? I'll bet there was no shortage of big dick perverts lined up to do you all kinds of favors."

"Goodie, if you're trying to get a rise out of me, you're going about it all wrong. You and them deviant-ass fantasies of yours can get the fuck on somewhere and out my mix."

"And what are you going to do if I don't?" Goodie moved to stand toe to toe with Pain. "What if I said that there was nowhere else I'd rather be than up in your fucking mix?"

Pain's set his bags on the floor and looked the taller man in the eyes. "Get out my face, Goodie."

Goodie's eyes went from Pain's clenched fists back to his face. "What? You feeling like a gangsta? Do something. I dare you, convict."

The word *convict* brought Pain back to his senses. Goodie was a stone-cold sucker, but he was still law enforcement. Knocking him out less than twenty-four hours after Pain had been released from prison would certainly lead to a trip back. With this in mind, Pain took a step back.

"That's what the fuck I thought, lil nigga. Save that hard-rock talk for somebody who ain't seen your medicals," Goodie laughed and blew Pain a kiss.

Pain couldn't remember the exact moment that the protective wall he had put between his rage and his good sense cracked, but it did. One moment he was watching Goodie's chapped lips pucker and the next he had a hand full of the man's shirt and was ramming his fist into his face. He'd struck him twice before his brain registered what he was doing.

He caught the older man off guard, which worked to his advantage in the beginning. Pain was known for his solid right cross, but years of Goodie getting punched in the face had added a strength to his jaw that kept him standing. Pain paused for only a second after the second blow, but that was all the window Goodie needed to turn things around. He cracked Pain across the chin with his elbow, snapping his head to one side. He had expected it to be enough to drop the young thug, but much like his, Pain's chin was stronger than he had anticipated.

Pain had to admit, he was pleasantly surprised that Goodie was actually willing to scrap. He always took him for the type to take a good pop to the mouth and curl into the fetal position. No, Goodie was trying to prove something. His mother's ex-stalker was scrappy, catching Pain a nice shot to the gut. He followed up with a knee that, had he not telegraphed it so that Pain had time to see it coming, would've probably broken his nose. Instead, Pain grabbed his leg behind the knee, holding him off-balance and at his mercy. He could've knocked Goodie out twice if he wanted to, but his punches were reserved for men. To him Goodie was a bitch, so he treated him like one and slapped him in the mouth. Goodie spun like a cartoon character, and wheeled back around into a second slap. In the beginning, Pain hadn't wanted to put his hands on Goodie because of his badge, but by that point he didn't care about the consequences that would come of this. He wanted blood. "You was a bitch then and you a bitch now!" he shouted when Goodie went down to one knee. Pain was thinking about kicking him in his face just on principle, but before he could decide Goodie pulled his service weapon. The line had officially been crossed.

"You little fucking punk! You know who the fuck I am? I'll put a hole in your ass for laying hands on me!" Goodie shoved Pain against the wall and dug the barrel of his gun into his forehead. His lip and nose were bloody and his eyes had a wild look about them.

"You got it, Goodie," Pain said, forcing calm into his tone. Goodie was a coward, not a killer, but Pain had heard too many stories about frightened men pulling triggers by accident.

"That's *Marshal* Gooden to you, lil nigga!" Goodie screamed, raining spittle on Pain's top lip.

"Marshal Gooden," Pain corrected himself.

"I can't believe you had the balls to raise up on me." Goodie wiped the blood from his lip with his shirtsleeve. "Only reason I ain't gonna put a hole in your head is because of that sweet old woman in that apartment down there. You probably too cheap to have insurance and

I ain't trying to leave her with another bill to struggle with. But don't think I don't wanna end you."

"Do what the fuck you do, nigga!" Pain spat defiantly. His eyes burned to the point where he felt like they might tear. Not because Goodie had hurt him physically, but his handling of Pain was damaging to his manhood. Pain felt helpless and it burned him.

"Oh, trust me. I intend to. See, you think you slick, running around playing the reformed convict, but I know better. You think my ear ain't to the streets? Like I don't know what your sticky little fingers are in? I ain't gonna squash you like the roach you are in this project hallway. All I gotta do is wait, and I gun you down when I catch you in the act. A righteous kill. The minute Blackbird spreads those wings, I'm gonna clip 'em!"

"I wouldn't hold my breath," Pain sneered.

"I'll bet my pension on you ending up dead or in prison in under thirty days. It's in your nature, Percy. Your daddy was a fuckup who got murdered in the street and I expect the same outcome for your evil ass."

Gun be damned, Pain was about to swing on Goodie again and worry about the consequences later, when the door at the end of the hall opened up. Both Pain and Goodie froze. Standing at the end of the hall, glaring at them over the rims of her glasses, was Pain's grandmother, Ms. Pearl.

"Who all out here making that damn noise?" Ms. Pearl questioned. Even with her glasses, her vision wasn't the best so she had to strain to see over distance. It took her a minute, but when she recognized her grandson her eyes went wide. "Percy?"

"Hi, Granny," Pain greeted her.

"What y'all doing? Marshall, why you got that gun on my grandson?" Ms. Pearl questioned.

Goodie was stuck. He had been caught red-handed and he'd be hard-pressed to have to explain to a woman he loved like his own grandma why he was about to shoot her last living relative.

"Wasn't about nothing, Granny," Pain spoke up. "Goodie was just showing me the gun they give him at his new job. You know he's a security guard now, right?"

"Well, y'all come in out of the hallway and quit horsing around. I don't want nobody calling Housing on me about all the noise you're keeping," Ms. Pearl told them.

"Actually, Goodie was just leaving. He's got a bullet to catch." Pain slapped Goodie on the back with enough force to make him stumble.

"A what?" Ms. Pearl was confused. "You know I can't keep up with the slang you kids use. Just come in out of the hallway." She went back in the apartment.

"Once again, Granny to the rescue. Only so long you're going to keep hiding behind her skirts," Goodie warned Pain.

"Nigga, I ain't hiding. You know how the fuck I give it up," Pain shot back.

"Oh, I know just how you give it up. That's why when I come I don't plan on asking any questions." Goodie shaped his fingers like a gun and pointed them at Pain. "See you soon." He slid into the elevator and left.

Pain continued to stand in the hallway after Goodie had gone. He had to compose himself before going into the apartment and talking to his grandmother. They hadn't seen each other in years and he didn't want to still be covered in negative energy the first time they shared an embrace. Goodie had him heated. If he hadn't pulled that gun, there was no telling what Pain might've done to him. It had been a long time since Pain had felt the helplessness that came with being unarmed and at the wrong end of a gun. He promised himself that it was the last time he would ever allow himself to be caught lackin' in the streets.

CHAPTER 11

Ms. Pearl lived in a three-bedroom apartment in the hood. She had been there almost as long as the projects themselves. At one time every room in the apartment had been alive with activity; kids playing or adults listening to records and sneaking tokes of grass whenever Ms. Pearl would go to the store. At one time her apartment had been the gathering spot in the hood, alive with activity, and some wayward soul always occupying one of the spare bedrooms or crashing on the couch, but now all but one of the rooms were empty, and the house quiet.

The minute Pain stepped into the living room he felt like he had been transported back in time. Almost everything in the apartment was as he remembered it: glass coffee table, cast-iron dinette set. Every piece brought back memories of his childhood. The only thing that had changed about the living room was that Ms. Pearl had finally taken the plastic off her burgundy velvet living room set, and gotten rid of the outdated television that was almost as old as Pain and replaced it with a newer model. There was a fifty-two-inch flat-screen mounted on the wall that hadn't been there when Pain first went away. Pain had been on her for years about a new television, but she had been adamant about her old one working just fine. Apparently she had changed her mind, but knowing his grandmother was on a fixed budget he wondered where she had gotten it from.

"Goodie give me that," Ms. Pearl said, noticing Pain staring at the television. She was wearing her favorite floral nightgown and house shoes. Her long silver hair was braided into two plaits that hung down her back. Ms. Pearl sat in her favorite armchair with a snack tray set up next to it. On the tray was a glass ashtray and a can of Pabst Blue Ribbon beer.

"All the years I tried to buy you a new television you never let me. You even made me take the forty-inch that I got you back to the store," Pain reminded her.

"You know your money ain't no good in here." Ms. Pearl waved him off.

"But Goodie's is?" Pain raised an eyebrow.

"Goodie's money comes from a bank. Yours out a shoebox," Ms. Pearl told him. She picked up the remote and turned on the television. A 4K image of a white game show host came on the screen. "Move out the way. You're blocking the screen and you know I need to watch my quiz show."

"Granny, you're more interested in that cracker than showing your one and only grandson some love?" Pain spread his arms dramatically, purposely blocking the television.

"Well, you're sure as heck not gonna get it unless you come over here, because you know I sure ain't about to get back up," Ms. Pearl told him.

"I missed you, Grandma." Pain hugged her as tight as he dared. She felt thinner than he remembered. Beneath the gown he could feel her bones and was nervous that he might break her. When had she gotten so frail?

"I missed you too, Percy. Why didn't you tell me that they were letting you out today?" Ms. Pearl asked, peering around him to see her game show.

Pain shrugged. "I wanted to surprise you."

"You would've been the one in for a surprise had I caught you sneaking in my house and shot you," Ms. Pearl told him.

"With what? That old .38 you keep claiming to have that none of us have ever seen?" Pain teased.

"Hmpf, my pistol like Jesus. Just because you ain't never seen it don't mean it ain't real. The day somebody try me I'm gonna provide them with a front row seat to the resurrection!" Ms. Pearl declared.

"You crazy, Granny," Pain laughed and took a seat on the arm of her chair.

"Boy, you ain't been gone that long. You know I don't play about people messing up my good furniture. Move," she shooed him.

Pain knew that she'd had that furniture since hip-hop was invented, but Ms. Pearl didn't play about her furniture, so he moved from the arm of the chair to the loveseat. When he rested back on the cushion, he felt papers crunching beneath him. Pain reached down into the loveseat and came up holding some old envelopes.

They appeared to be bills. Before he could really investigate, Ms. Pearl snatched the envelopes from his hand. "What are those?"

"My business," Ms. Pearl told him before dropping the mail on her snack tray. "I wish I had known that you were getting out today. I would've fixed you something to eat."

"It's cool, Granny. I had a little something earlier. If I get hungry I know how to go in there and fix myself something," Pain assured her.

"Right, my baby the chef. You're the only living soul who knows all my recipes. You could've really done something with that if you had stuck with it," Ms. Pearl said. One thing she always made sure of was that the children who lived under her roof knew how to cook. Lizzie was the best, next to Ms. Pearl, and Pain came in a close third. The boy could burn some pots.

"The universe chose a different path for me."

"Right, pistols over pots," Ms. Pearl chuckled.

"Ha ha, very funny, Granny. We can talk about me later. How have you been?" Pain wisely steered the conversation in a different direction. He was well aware of how his grandmother felt about his lifestyle choices and wasn't up for hearing about it just then.

"I can't complain," Ms. Pearl said with a shrug. "My hip's been giving me a little trouble, but other than that I'm okay. I'm here to see another day, so I'm thankful for that." She produced a pack of cigarettes from the pocket of her duster and plucked one into her mouth before she began patting her other pockets for her lighter.

"I thought you quit?"

"I did. Then I started back," Ms. Pearl told him. She finally found her lighter and got her cigarette going. She tried to take a deep pull, but ended up sending herself into a coughing fit.

"See." Pain plucked the cigarette from her lips and stubbed it out in the ashtray. "The doctor keeps telling you that you need to give these things up."

"Doctor keeps telling me lots of things. That don't make him right." Ms. Pearl produced another cigarette. Pain snatched that one, too.

"I'm gonna need you to start listening to what your doctors tell you to do and stop giving them a hard time. I wanna have you around for a lot more years, young lady," Pain teased her.

"Percy, only y'all young folks stress yourselves out over when you're going to die. When you get to my age you've already seen and done pretty much everything you'll do in this life. I know God ain't gonna take me before I'm ready, and he ain't gonna leave me here no longer than need be," Ms. Pearl said confidently.

"All the same. No need to tempt fate or speed up the process with you chain-smoking those Kools."

"Percy, you ain't been back in my house but for five minutes and you already getting on my nerves."

"And I'm going to keep getting on your nerves until you start doing the right thing," Pain told her. And he meant it. "Granny, I know things have been rough on you for the last couple of years, with me being always in trouble and all."

"You ain't never lied about that," Ms. Pearl said with a reflective chuckle. "You've been into mischief since you was a little boy. Even when you weren't looking for it, it always seemed to find you. Do you remember that time when you were about seven or eight, and we were all at that house party? You had gotten into a fight with that older boy. What was his name?" She tapped her chin in thought.

"Juice," Pain recalled. Just the mention of the name made his jaw hurt.

It had been a party for some little girl in the building. Pain and the girl weren't even friends, but because their mothers and aunts were tight, he was forced to go. Pain had overdosed on Kool-Aid and found that he had to pee something fierce. By the time he made it to the bathroom he felt like he was on the verge of pissing himself. Unfortunately for him, there was a dice game going on in the lone bathroom of the apartment. There were about four boys crammed into the small space, throwing three green dice against the bathtub. Pain tried to explain his situation, but the boys didn't pay him any mind. They were more concerned with the loose dollars they were gambling for than the little boy holding himself and doing the pee dance in the doorway. Seeing that being polite was getting him nowhere, Pain changed his tactic. In the toughest voice his still-developing vocal cords could project, he informed the boys that if they didn't let him use the bathroom he was going to piss on the floor and that would be the end of their game. The others boys moved aside so that Pain could use the toilet, but Juice had to be a dick about it.

"Lil nigga, take your ass to the stairwell and handle your business," Juice dismissed him. He was a rough-looking kid who sported his hair in an uncombed Afro. Juice fancied himself something of the neighborhood bully, but he only targeted kids that were smaller than him.

"I don't think I'm going to make it that far. It's going to be the toilet or the floor," Pain informed him. He wasn't trying to be a smart-ass, only trying to get the older boy to be sympathetic to his plight.

"Juice, let the little dude use the bathroom! We can move this to the hallway," one of the boys urged. He just wanted to get back to the game.

"Damn that. I'm up three dollars. This bathroom is my lucky spot, and I ain't moving until I finish taking you sucker's money!" Juice capped, scooping the dice and shaking them in preparation for his next roll.

Pain stood there filled with uncertainty. He had to use the bathroom really bad, but it was obvious that Juice wouldn't let him. He could've done as Juice had ordered and gone out to the stairwell, but that would present him with another set of problems. For one, he doubted that he would make it that far. Doing as Juice said would've made him look like a punk in front of the other kids who had gathered to watch the exchange. Not that any of them would've been in a position to judge him. Juice had kicked most of their asses already at one time or another. His biggest concern though, was the fact that he knew if he pissed himself his mother was going to whip his ass. It was at that moment he decided that he feared his mother more than he feared Juice. Right there, for all in attendance to see, Pain whipped his adolescent dick out and relieved himself over Juice's shoes, and the dice money.

"That boy beat the hell out of you," Ms. Pearl recalled. The worried look on her face said that she was reliving the moment.

"Yeah, Juice got me good."

"I was hollering for somebody to get him off you, but Lonely wouldn't let anyone interfere." Lonely was Lizzie's childhood nickname. Granny called her this because she was always by herself. "She just stood there and watched you get whipped. I'll give it to you though, every time he knocked you down you got back up," Ms. Pearl said proudly.

"Because I was afraid that if I didn't he might get to stomping me too, instead of just punching me," Pain laughed. He was serious, though.

"At first, I was mad at your mama. What kind of person lets their child get whipped on like that?" Mr. Pearl shook her head. "Then I came to understand her logic . . . why she stood by and let you take that beating."

"She was preparing me for the world," Pain filled in the blank. "Mom taught me two valuable lessons that day. The first one was respect. I had no business pulling my thing out and peeing on that boy. That was disrespectful and he was right to slug me. The second lesson I learned was never to back down. No matter how big my opponent was, I would face them head-on regardless of the outcome."

Juice never tried to pick on Pain again after that day. In fact, the beating he took had earned him the respect of the older boys. He'd lost the fight, but he never stopped coming at Juice. This showed everyone watching that the boy had heart. Not long after that, Juice and his crew had started to let Pain hang around with them. It was running with Juice and his crew that Pain first learned the art of the stickup.

"So, now that you're home, what do you plan on doing with yourself?" Ms. Pearl asked.

Pain pondered the question before responding. "Get a job, I guess," he said with a shrug. "My new PO has some leads for me to follow up, probably mostly manual labor, like factories, maybe some janitorial work."

Ms. Pearl laughed.

"What's so funny, Granny?"

"Nothing, I'm wondering how much you having a job is going to cost me this time? The last job I can remember you having was when you were fifteen and working at Legman's butcher shop, and I'm sure I don't have to remind you how that turned out?"

She didn't, because Pain could remember like it had happened yesterday. His grandmother had managed to pull some strings and get Pain a job working for the local butcher, Mr. Legman. Everyone from the neighborhood shopped there and Ms. Pearl and Mr. Legman had a decent enough relationship. Pain was to be hired to come in after school and help out at the shop. It was back-breaking work, like unloading trucks of meat, for shit pay, but it made Pain's grandmother happy so Pain thugged it out.

Working for Legman was no walk in the park. He was a mean old bastard who was constantly chewing on a nasty brown cigar. The constant smoking had browned and rotted his front teeth and his breath always smelled like shit. In addition to all this, Legman was also a closet racist. Sure, he smiled at and played nice with the Black women who came into his shop to spend their money, and they loved him for it. But Pain doubted if they would still praise the old Jew if they knew what went on behind closed doors. Legman segregated his meat. He saved the fresh cuts for his white customers, but sold the Black and Brown customers old meat. He'd even once saw him drop a Puerto Rican woman's chopped meat on the floor in the back and still pack it up to sell to her without so much as rinsing it. When Pain saw how Legman was playing, he decided to teach him a lesson.

One night, just before the end of his shift, Pain rigged the lock on the bathroom window. After Legman closed shop for the night, Pain doubled back with Juice, Case, and a few others from their gang and robbed the place. Using Juice's mother's van, the robbers made off with a few dozen pounds of meat and some cash that had been left in the register. Case had wanted to sell the meat, but Pain wanted to give it away, so Juice came up with a compromise. They pulled up to a pantry in the hood and gave away half the meat to some of the less fortunate. The other half they sold to a kid Juice knew named Jay and his family. They owned a restaurant uptown and didn't care about the meat being stolen.

Pain and his crew likely would've gotten away with the heist had it not been for the cameras. Pain hadn't been working there long enough to know about them. Legman had cameras all over the store. Still, their faces had been hidden during the robbery. What had gotten them caught was the camera that Mr. Legman had secretly placed in the bathroom. This was so that he could make recordings of women when they asked to use the bathroom in the store. When he went back and watched the tape, he saw that it was Pain who had tampered with the window that the thieves had entered through.

Ms. Pearl had to go to Legman damn near on her hands and knees and beg him not to press charges. He agreed on the condition that he was paid for the meat and cash that had been snatched by the youngsters. Ms. Pearl had to work double shifts at her housekeeping gig for a month to pay off the debt. In hindsight, she probably shouldn't have given Legman a damn dime. True, Pain would've been in deep trouble had Legman gone to the police, but then he would've also had to explain the camera in the bathroom.

"Yes, trouble has followed you for your entire life," Ms. Pearl repeated.

"Well, those days are behind me, Granny. You've got my word on that. I'm going to get myself a job and do the right thing so I can take care of you," Pain promised.

"I can take care of myself, baby. Whatever you do, should be for you. No need to worry about me, the lord takes care of his faithful," Ms. Pearl said.

"Well, even the lord can use a little help sometime."

"I'm glad you came home with your head screwed on straight this time, Percy. You know prison ain't nothing but a revolving door once you get caught up in that cycle of in and out. You're still young, and got your whole life ahead of you. Don't waste it, Percy."

"I won't, Granny. I won't."

Ms. Pearl's eyes went to the bags Pain had set on the floor near the door when he walked in. "What's all that?" she asked suspiciously.

"Just a few pieces I picked up today. Since I put on some weight while I was away, my old clothes didn't fit too well," Pain told her.

Ms. Pearl gave him a look. "Boy, you fresh out the cooler so I know you ain't got no job and no money. Where you get that stuff from? You out boosting on your first day home? And here you were just talking about how you were gonna fly straight an be out here to take care of me!"

"Calm down, Granny. I didn't boost anything. Some of the guys put together a small pot for me and bought me a few pieces," Pain explained. He opted not to tell her that it came from Case, because she knew where Case got his money and likely wouldn't approve.

"You be careful who you accept gifts from, Percy. Never know what they'll ask of you in return," Ms. Pearl warned.

"Nah, Granny. It ain't like that. Those are my brothers," Pain defended.

"How many of those so-called brothers came to see you while you were in prison?" Ms. Pearl asked.

Pain couldn't answer right off. Case had come to see him twice while he was on Rikers Island, but hadn't made the trip when he landed upstate. Tyriq had tried to visit him once, but was turned away by the prison. He was underage and without having an adult with him they couldn't let the boy in. Outside of that, Pain's list of visitors was damn near nonexistent.

"Your silence proves my point," Ms. Pearl continued. "Listen, Percy. I know you been gone a long time and are anxious to see some of the people you left behind to catch up. I can't begrudge you that, but what I will tell you is, for the most part them boys are doing the same thing today that they were doing when you left. You ain't missed nothing except whatever trouble they managed to get themselves into while you were gone. Stay clear of people who don't believe in progress. You get me?"

"Yes, Granny."

"Good, now get them bags out of my hallway and let me watch the last bit of my show in peace." Ms. Pearl picked up the remote and increased the volume on the television.

Much like the living room, Pain's bedroom was like stepping through a wormhole into the past. Granny had cleaned up his bedroom, but outside of that she left everything as it was. The same posters hung on the walls, his sneakers were stacked neatly in boxes in the corner, and his basketball trophies still lined the shelf on the wall over his bed. Once upon a time, Pain had been a pretty good athlete. He played baseball, basketball, and had even run track for a while. Basketball was his true love, though. He was good at it, too. Not good enough to where he had delusions of going to the NBA, but still good enough to make a Division I team . . . maybe DII.

Resting against one of the trophies was a photograph that Pain hadn't seen in years. The last time he saw the picture it had been taped inside one of Granny's old photo albums. Now it rested inside a gold frame with birds carved into it. It was a picture of a much younger Pain and his mother, Lizzie. People always said that Pain resembled his father, but that was until they saw him standing next to his mother. They had the same thick lips, rich black hair, and dark eyes. The only major difference between them was that Pain had his father's wide nose. Pain ran his finger over the photograph of him and Lizzie standing in front of the Ferris wheel at Coney Island. It had to have been Easter because Lizzie was wearing a nice dress and Pain a cheesy powder blue suit with white shoes. She had made him suffer through church that morning, but his reward was her taking him to Coney Island and letting him get on almost every ride and gorge himself on cotton candy until he was sick. That day was one of the best memories he had of his mom. It was a time before their lives began to spiral.

Placing the picture back on the shelf, Pain moved to his closet. Inside were some winter coats, which were probably outdated by now, a few sports jerseys, and a line of baseball caps across the top shelf. Without looking, he started tossing his shopping bags into the closet. When he tossed the one with the sneaker boxes inside into the closet, he heard something break. Curiously, he dug through the bags and way in the back of the closet he felt something solid wrapped in a large plastic shopping bag. Pain pulled it from the closet and set in the bed. Using his fingernails, he ripped through the plastic. What was inside gave him mixed emotions.

From the bag he pulled out a large plaque. Behind the cracked glass were two replica gold records. They had been presented to a rap group called Bad Blood to certify that their single "Slap Ya Self" had sold more than five hundred thousand copies. Lizzie had been so proud of that plaque that you would've thought she had been a part of the group who earned it rather than the mother of one of its member's baby.

This was before Pain had been born. As he'd heard it, his mom and dad met after one of Bad Blood's concerts. She and one of her friends had been lucky enough to get invited to an after-party the group was having at some hotel in Midtown. Pain's father, also called Pain, was on Lizzie minutes after she walked in the room. He was the bad boy of Bad Blood. He wasn't as handsome as their leader, True, or as witty as another member of the crew that they called Lex, but he had an undeniable swag about him. Lizzie didn't spend that night with him, but they did one night during the following week. One night turned into ten when Pain invited Lizzie to go on a short tour of the Northeast that the group was heading out on.

That week and a half was like a whirlwind romance for Lizzie. Pain didn't trick off on her like the other group members did with the girls they had travel with them, or met in different cities. Pain was a notorious cheapskate, but what he lacked in financial affections he made up for in emotional. Pain was kind and attentive when it came to Lizzie. Even when the groupies stepped out of place, he was quick to put them back in. He and Lizzie had only known each other for a few days and he was treating her like she was his girl. Lizzie couldn't front, she loved the feeling.

Granny had been against Lizzie seeing Pain. She believed that all musicians were in league with Satan. That was probably largely due to a failed marriage she'd had to a bass player back in Memphis. It probably didn't help that some of the group members were still actively involved in the things that they rapped about, especially Pain. He was in the streets way heavier than the others and sometimes his two worlds overlapped. Ms. Pearl had condemned their relationship. She believed that the group was cursed and was afraid of whatever evil they attracted landing on Lizzie. Ms. Pearl was only trying to look out for her daughter, but Lizzie had stars in her eyes. To seal the pact of their relationship, Pain had presented Lizzie with the plaque from their single going gold. She was on top of the world, until the bottom fell out.

Three months into the relationship, Lizzie found herself pregnant. It was her second time getting pregnant by Pain, but he'd made her abort the first pregnancy. He claimed that his career was too hectic to focus on a kid. He was trying to get to a bag. His two other babies' mothers must not have gotten that memo. Only Lizzie. Pain wanted her to have another abortion, but Ms. Pearl stepped in. She'd sat by and allowed Pain to snatch one life from her daughter and wasn't going for it a second time.

True to her nickname, Lizzie had a lonely pregnancy. All she really had was Ms. Pearl to lean on for the entire thirty-three weeks. Pain didn't want a baby, but promised that he would at least be around to make sure that Lizzie and the baby were good. Of course, that was a lie. Every time Lizzie had an appointment, Pain always claimed to have a studio session or some other label business to attend to. It was Ms. Pearl who took her to all her appointments and ran her errands when she had to go on bed rest for the last two months of her pregnancy. To Pain's credit, he did manage to find his way to the delivery room when his son was born. He stayed long enough to hold him for the record label's photographer to get a few pictures and then he was gone again.

This on-and-off game played out between Lizzie and her child's father for the first few years of Pain's life. The rapper would blow in and out of town from time to time and pop in on Lizzie and his son. Mostly when he wanted some pussy. Over time, Lizzie began noticing small changes in Pain. He was a dude who loved jewelry to the point where he couldn't even go to the store without at least one of his chains on, but Pain seemed to be wearing less and less jewelry every time she saw him. The last few times, he wasn't wearing any at all.

That was around the time when Lizzie started hearing whispers about her baby daddy. Seemed that he had been getting a little too caught up with the industry lifestyle and it was starting to show. The one time Lizzie tried to talk to him about it, it went bad. She approached him from a place of love, but he took it as her disrespecting him, so he punched her in the mouth. That was the first and last time she had ever approached him about it. A month later the father of her child was gone.

Pain and several members of the group Bad Blood were murdered in what was reported to be a drug-related shooting. Knowing Pain, it was twice as likely that he had crossed the wrong person and the devil had come to claim his due. Not only was Pain gunned down, but he took several members of his group down with him. They had the misfortune of being with him when his ticket got punched. Not long after, the member of the group who had survived, True, was also gunned down. His murder wasn't about drugs, but karma. In the end, Granny's theory about the group being cursed came to fruition.

Lizzie loved that plaque. It hung over her bed like a shrine to a man who had treated her like shit and left her with a kid she would have to bust her ass to try and raise. In Lizzie's mind, the plaque represented a part of her former lover that was good. That was how she always wanted to remember him. That plaque would hang on Lizzie's wall until after she died. Ms. Pearl had offered it to Pain, but he declined. Unlike his mother who still found parts of a wicked man to love, Pain couldn't see it. He didn't hate, nor did he love, his sperm donor. He simply didn't know him well enough to have an opinion one way or another.

After putting the plaque back and his clothes away, Pain made his way to the kitchen. The snack box he'd eaten earlier was starting to wear off and he was hungry. He knew Ms. Pearl probably had some left-overs in the fridge. It was Monday, so he knew he'd find some scraps from whatever Sunday dinner she'd fixed. It had been some years since he'd had his grandmother's cooking and his mouth watered at the prospect.

Rubbing his hands together in anticipation like a fat kid, Pain snatched open the refrigerator. There were not only no leftovers, but not much of anything at all. There were a few scrapings of tuna in a

bowl, and a half pitcher of Kool-Aid, but outside of that the refrigerator was empty. He pulled the freezer open and found that it too was
bare. For as long as Pain could remember, Ms. Pearl always kept a refrigerator stocked with food. No matter how lean times got, you could
always find something to quiet that hunger in Ms. Pearl's kitchen. To
find it empty was unheard of.

Seeing no food in her house bothered him. He knew that his grandmother lived on a fixed income, but from the looks of her kitchen she
was hurting way more than he could've ever imagined. He headed into
the living room, intent on discussing her finances, but found her sleeping. She had dozed off in her armchair as she had done so many nights
when he was growing up. The talk could wait. As gently as he could, so
as not to wake her, he covered his grandmother with one of the knitted
blankets from the couch. As he was doing so, one of the envelopes he
had discovered earlier fell from the snack table. Curiously, Pain picked
it up and read over the contents. It was a past-due bill for her cable.
They were scheduled to disrupt her service within the next three days.
The past due was four hundred. It would be tough, but not impossible,
for Pain to hustle up and keep his granny's cable on. The next one was
a bit steeper. It was a medical bill to the sum of eighteen thousand dollars that had gone into collections. The amount almost stumbled Pain.
What could she have had done that cost so much? And why didn't her
insurance cover it? What the hell was going on with his grandmother?

Pain spent the next thirty minutes or so hunting down his grandmother's mail from around the house and going through it. In his
sorting of coupons, magazine subscriptions, and ignored bills he was
able to piece together the last few years of Granny's life. Most of her
debt was medical expenses. He came across some forms from her insurance company that Granny was supposed to fill out and return,
but the old woman must've forgotten. Therefore, her coverage had
been reduced and insurance was now only paying a fraction of her
medical costs. What insurance didn't cover she had to pay for out-of-
pocket. When her savings had been bled dry, his grandmother had to
rely on her credit cards to keep up with her medical costs. It felt like
with each piece of mail that Pain opened, the further down the rabbit
hole he slid, but what finally threw the dirt over him was the last piece
of random mail he discovered. He'd almost dismissed it as another
pamphlet advertising something that his grandmother had bought or
was planning to buy. That was until he opened it.

It was an aftercare summary that outlined a course of treatment for stage-three breast cancer. Pain had to read it again to make sure his eyes weren't playing tricks on him. They weren't. His legs betrayed him and buckled. Had it not been for him bracing himself against the edge of the dining room table, he'd have probably fallen and split his head open. This was why his grandmother had so many medical bills . . . she was dying.

For the next twenty minutes, Pain sat on the arm of the loveseat and watched his grandmother sleep. Her brows were knotted and her lips twitched like she was having an argument in her dreams. She was just as feisty in her dreams as she was in her waking. His beloved granny. She was the one person who had always been there to love him, guide him, and even protect him. How could he survive without her? He couldn't, nor did he plan to. Pain made up his mind right then and there that he would not accept that this sweet old bird was going to die. He was no doctor, but he knew that stage-three cancer wasn't as bad as stage four. This meant that his granny still had a shot, provided he was able to get her the proper treatment. To do this he would need money, and depending on how far Granny's cancer had progressed, he was going to need it in a hurry. He grabbed his new cell phone and hit one of the two saved numbers in the device. "Yo, text me the address of the spot y'all at. I'm about to pull up."

PART II
DAWN

CHAPTER 12

When Juju told Passion she had some stuff that she might be able to squeeze into, she had been speaking quite literally. Her closet was mostly full of streetwear and sneakers, but Juju did have some killer pieces in the cut. High-end dresses and blouses that her mom was always buying her in hopes that she would one day break out of her tomboy phase and wear. Too bad none of those fit Passion, who was at least two or three sizes bigger than Juju. She managed to find Passion a nice-fitting green silk blouse with a pair of slip-on Gucci shoes that covered her toes, but left her heels out. She didn't like her feet out and it wasn't summertime, but those were the only pair of shoes that Juju had that Passion could get her feet into. She was just thankful that she had applied ample lotion to her feet that day, because people loved to talk about an ashy heel. The top and the shoes were easy to put together, but it was when they were trying to find her some bottoms that they ran into trouble. Juju always bought her jeans two sizes too big because she liked them baggy, but Passion still had some difficulties pulling them over her ass. It took the combined efforts of both her and Juju to get the jeans all the way on and fastened. Passion felt like she could barely breathe, but at least she looked cute.

When the girls arrived at their destination in the Bronx, Passion found herself surprised by two things. The first was that the gathering wasn't being held at a club, lounge, or even a bar for that matter. It was at an auto repair shop. At least that's what it appeared to be. The building was two stories tall, with three large garage bays taking up most of the first floor. It was after hours and the doors were pulled down, but you could see shadows moving around behind the small smoked window. From the pungent smell of weed coming from inside, Passion doubted that whoever was in there was working on cars. Hanging above the entrance was a sign that read STONE & CO. AUTO REPAIR, but when Passion had last visited the place it went by a different name.

It had been maybe two or three years prior, and Passion was still new to Uncle Joe's little family. Something had gone wrong with Bo's car so she needed to take it in for repairs. Of course, Passion tagged along. Back then she used to stay glued to Bo's hip. At the time, Bo had been one of the only people in the house who didn't look at Passion like a piece of meat or a threat. She was kind to Passion, and she made those early years tolerable.

Uncle Joe instructed her to take the car down the street to a buddy of his, but instead Bo took it all the way to the Bronx. When Passion asked why, Bo told her because she had a rapport with the owner and would get a better deal on the parts. The shop they arrived at was the same one Passion found herself standing on the doorstep of with Juju. Back then it wasn't called Stone & Co., but Brakes by the Pound. It was owned by a young man named Alonzo. Passion remembered seeing him for the first time and thinking how handsome he was with his pecan skin and bright smile. Bo's old thirsty ass was on him from the time they walked in, flirting and letting herself brush against him every time she passed. The whole time Alonzo politely blocked her advances, but something in their body language suggested that at one time there had been something there. Passion left that day thinking Alonzo was nothing more than a cute mechanic. It wouldn't be until a few months later when Bo received the news that Alonzo had been murdered that the truth would come out about who Alonzo, aka Zo, really was, and it wasn't a mechanic.

Juju's walk as they approached the entrance was one of confidence. Passion's, not so much. There were some very unsavory-looking characters loitering out front, all looking at Passion like she was fresh meat. Juju hardly paid them any mind as she marched in the direction of the man assigned to the door. He was very average looking, medium height with an unremarkable face. He couldn't have been more than one hundred and seventy-five pounds, and that was being generous. Passion could remember thinking that at his size there wouldn't be much he could do to stop them if someone tried to bum-rush the joint. That was until he stood up from the stool he'd been sitting on and she saw the gun shoved down the front of his jeans. Living with Uncle Joe had taught Passion a thing or two about guns. She couldn't be totally sure what caliber weapon he was armed with, but she could tell it had been modified by the incredibly long clip jutting from the butt. She reasoned it held at least fifty shots. More than enough to deter troublemakers and underage girls alike.

"I don't know about this shit," Passion whispered to her friend.

"Girl, shut the hell up and stop acting like a square. I got us," Juju said through gritted teeth as she summoned up a phony smile for the doorman. "What's good?"

"Shit, not a damn thing for y'all underage asses," was his reply.

"Underage?" Juju flashed him an indignant look. "First of all, I'm twenty-two. Second, since when do you need ID to hang in a garage? Boy, stop playing with me." She tried to step by him, but the doorman blocked her path.

"Little girl, ain't nobody got time to be fooling with you. Go find a mall or something to hang out at. This is a grown folks gathering, so I suggest y'all take that bullshit somewhere else before something bad happens to you," the doorman warned.

"I wouldn't worry too much about that. I don't think any of the jokers hanging in there want the kind of problems that come with fucking with Jay's sister," Juju capped.

"Wait, you're J.K.'s sister?" The doorman used her brother's nickname.

"His *favorite* sister," Juju said, as if they had another sibling.

The doorman weighed it. The girl could've been bullshitting, but how many other Asians did he know that hung in a spot that was lousy with Black and Brown killers? If the kid raised a stink because he turned her away and made a big deal of it to her brother, he could find himself with a problem he didn't need. "Fuck it," he relented. "I'm gonna let you two girls in, but if I catch y'all young asses anywhere near the bar, I'm bouncing you both out and it ain't gonna matter whose sister you are."

"Thank you, sweetie." Juju batted her eyes before walking across the threshold. Once they were inside she turned to Passion. "Told you I had us. Now let's go find the Hennessey!"

Pain hadn't had any expectations when he left his granny's apartment that night. He just knew that he needed to get out. Both his mind and his heart were heavy from what he had uncovered about his grandmother's situation, and the longer he sat there amongst her mounting bills and medical records, the more space his grandmother's diagnosis took up in his head. He needed to move around and come up with some kind of plan, and that's what brought him to The Yard, also known as Stone & Co. Auto Repair.

Pain had never been to The Yard, but he'd heard a little chatter about it while he was locked up. During the day it really functioned as an auto repair shop, but on nights when the weather was nice enough the owners would host gatherings in the huge lot behind the shop. That's why they had nicknamed it The Yard. The gatherings weren't much more than some gambling, drinking, and on a good night a little food, but the attendees were always exclusive. The crowds were generally made up of personally invited guests, but it also hosted certain people whose names carried enough weight on the streets to get them past the doorman. Pain fell into the latter category.

When Pain had called Case to tell him that he was pulling up, the plan had been for Pain to stay long enough to have a drink or two and maybe get some advice from his boys about how to best tackle his grandmother's situation, but of course it didn't go like that. Case had called damn near everyone he rocked with and had them pull up to The Yard, and the next thing he knew, Pain's easy night had turned into a welcome-home party. He hadn't wanted the attention, but he'd be lying if he said that it hadn't felt good. He must've hugged at least twenty people and slapped the palms of probably twice that number as people poured in. More than a few of them had sprinkled themselves in to dick ride the notorious Blackbird, but for the most part it was genuine love. Pain was overwhelmed. He had spent so many years being a nobody in prison, he had almost forgotten that at one time he had been a big deal. Being back in the limelight felt right, even if only for the night.

"Air been smelling like shit the last couple of days. I should've known it meant that sucka nigga was back in town," Case spat. Pain had just given him the rundown on what had happened between him and Goodie back at his grandmother's. Case was probably the one person who wanted Goodie gone more than Pain did, but for different reasons.

"That marshal's badge they pinned to his chest must've gave that pussy some heart, because he was talking crazy. He thinks I'm still in the game, and claiming to know what I'm up to, but I ain't on shit! I been clean since I touched down and I plan to stay that way."

"You think he was skulking around the projects because he knew you were home and wanted to bust your balls, or you think it's something else?" Case fished.

Pain shrugged. "Fuck if I know."

"Umm," was Case's response as he thought on it. He had heard some chatter through the grapevine about the city organizing some kind of new gang task force to slow the little knuckleheads down from killing each other. The difference between this task force and the one currently deployed by the NYPD was that the new one would not be confined to the city limits. These guys were federal, which meant that they could still chase you if you crossed state lines. That was a rumor that had every nigga in the hood on pins and needles. He should've know it would've only been a matter of time before Goodie showed up, all things considered. His timing was just terrible. Shit had just gone from bad to worse. "Look, just stay away from that dude."

"You act like I was out looking for this joker. He popped up on me like some stalker shit," Pain told him. "This dude has got a real hard-on to catch me slipping, so y'all might wanna be on your toes, too."

"I ain't worried about Goodie. That dickhead couldn't keep up with me on my worse day," Case boasted.

"Still, I wouldn't want what y'all got going on to be compromised because this nigga is on me. Maybe I should fall back from the gang for a while?" Pain suggested.

"It ain't that serious, P. If I know Goodie the way I do, this is about you and not the crew. Still, I'll put somebody on him and try to find out if he's working some kind of angle. It'll be fine," Case assured him.

"I hope so, fam. I got too much going on in my life right now to have to deal with that dude pressing me. I'm still trying to wrap my head around what I'm going to do about this situation with my grandmother," Pain continued.

"Yeah, that's some heavy shit. Everything going on with Ms. Pearl and all. You good?" Case asked.

"Honestly? I don't even know, my nigga. I don't think it's really hit me yet," Pain said. "All them years I sat up in the joint I went through different stages and phases. In the beginning, I was on some bitter shit—mad at the people who claimed to have love for me in the world, but hardly wrote me and never visited."

Case's face couldn't hide the fact that Pain's admission had stung. "Bro, you know I would've gotten up there, but—"

"You ain't gotta say it," Pain cut him off. "It bothered me a little bit, but I understand. You were out here living from one day to the next, dealing with shit of your own. This ain't about that, though. So, just let me finish. There was the bitterness and then came the impatience. Most days felt like they were dripping by like molasses. Ain't nothing like feeling like you've been locked up for years and look at the calendar to realize it's only been a few months. Finally, I got to the point where I was hopeful. As my time got shorter, I started planning for all the things I wanted to do and the people I needed to get at. In all this, I never considered my grandmother. I mean, she didn't visit but we spoke regularly because she kept money on the phone and she sent packages when he could. Granny had me and I knew that from the day I walked in that muthafucka. If nobody else was going to hold me down, I knew Granny would make sure I was straight. In all of that not once did I stop to think what she might be going through out here without me. People like her always seem like they're good and we start getting so used to the idea that they are, we never consider that they might not be. Like, why the fuck is my seventy-something-year-old grandmother spending her money to make sure I got food packages and fresh underwear instead of me taking care of her?"

"Pain, you're being too hard on yourself. When you were out here and getting money with the team, you always made sure Granny had a few dollars in her purse and the refrigerator was stocked," Case reminded him.

"That ain't enough!" Pain countered. "If I was really taking care of my grandmother then I would've been out here with her and on top of her business. Maybe if I had been they could've caught that cancer shit before it got so far gone." His voice was heavy with emotion. Pain wouldn't dare cry in a room full of criminals, but he could feel his eyes stinging a little.

Case was quiet for a time, but when he next opened his mouth he said something profound. "Time is the one thing that we can't get back," he began. "It's behind us, so no sense in looking over our shoulders and stressing over it. What you need to be focused on is the future. You're home now, so you'll get to make up for what you missed out on. As far as the money, that shit is gonna come. We'll see to that."

"Oh, so you got ten or fifteen grand laying around? Because that's about what it's going to take just to start clearing her debt," Pain informed him. He hadn't meant to sound insensitive or ungrateful, but he was stressed out.

"No, but I got a way for us to get it. Like I was telling you earlier, there's still only one way I know to get money in a hurry." Case made his fingers into the shape of a gun. "Me and the guys got a few licks lined up. We always got room for an extra man."

"I told you, I ain't trying to—"

"I know, get back in the life because you on some square shit now," Case cut him off. "Pain, I respect the fact that you trying to fly straight, but I can't think of no nine-to-five that's going to get you the amount of bread you need in the time that you need it. Now, you can keep standing on that soapbox shouting about reform and shit, or you can get back in these streets and do what you gotta do for your old bird."

"I wanna stay straight," Pain said softly. He was trying to convince himself more than Case.

"I get that, and I'm not knocking it." Case draped his arm around Pain. "Bro, you're fucked up in the pockets right now. Come on one job with us, and if you still feel like flying straight then this is a dead issue. Worse case, you can go out on those job interviews with some money in your pocket instead of lint. One and done, Pain. One and done."

Pain wanted to argue with Case, but he couldn't. His friend had pointed out something that Pain already knew, but was reluctant to accept. He could work three jobs and it could still take years for him to dig his grandmother out of debt. If Case and the crew were still getting to it like they had been before he went to prison, he'd be able to settle his granny's tab in a fraction of that time. What he needed was literally there for the taking. All he had to do was reach out and snatch it, but what about his promise to his grandmother? It wouldn't have been the first time he had vowed to her that he would go straight only to turn around and get arrested again, but this time had been different. His last bid had really taken a toll on him and he wasn't sure that he had any more years left in him to give the state, and there was a fifty-fifty chance that more prison time awaited him on the other side of that door Case was tempting him to walk back through. Still, it was only one job, right?

"Man, why y'all over here all huddled up like a football team instead of enjoying this party?" Tyriq interrupted their conversation. There was a blunt tucked behind his ear and one dangling between his lips. From his low-hung eyes, you could see that the young man was already faded, but the beer in one hand and shot glass in the other said he had no plans on slowing down. "Pain, you get on some new pussy yet? Or ol' girl wore you out before she kicked us out?" he asked louder than necessary. When he draped his arm around Pain, he reeked of liquor.

"Your ass is drunk." Pain shrugged him off and fanned the stench.

"And you should be, too!" Tyriq countered. "This is your coming-home party, baby boy! We gonna drink good, fuck some bitches, and blow a bag in your honor. Then we'll hit you with your welcome-home gift."

"What gift?" Pain asked suspiciously. Tyriq opened his mouth to answer, but Case cut him off.

"A surprise. Nothing too crazy, just something me and bro felt that you deserved for all you've been put through these last few years," Case said with a sly grin.

"C'mon, man. Y'all have already done enough. Some new clothes, a few dollars in my pocket, and good drink in my liver. I'm good, fam. Really."

"If you say so," Case said and left it at that.

"There this fool go." Jay walked up on them. His hair was freshly spiked and dyed a shade of green so dark that it almost looked black. A thick gold chain hung from his neck, swaying back and forth across the broad chest of his fitted black T-shirt. Tattoos covered just about every inch of his exposed arms, telling the story of his life and his struggles. "Riq, how you gonna spin off with my blunt and then cuff yours?"

Tyriq plucked what was left of the blunt from his mouth and looked at it as if he was seeing it for the first time. "My fault, Jay. I was trying to check on my man and got caught up in the moment. Yo, this is big bro that we been telling you about, the homie Pain."

"What up? They call me JK-47." Jay extended his hand.

"Is that right?" Pain gave the Asian kid the once-over. He talked like a rapper, but looked like a K-pop artist. Pain was always cautious of new faces—some old ones, too—and as far as he knew, Jay was a new face.

"Word life. My name is ringing off out here a lil something, but nowhere near as loud as the Blackbird." Jay flipped his hands, thumbs hooked and fingers spread to mimic a bird with its wings spread. He meant it as a sign of respect, but it wasn't taken that way.

"Homie, your feet ever leave the ground?" Pain asked. It was an odd question, but only to those who didn't know the correct answer.

"Huh?" Jay looked from Pain to Case in confusion.

"Meaning you with the shit you representing?" Pain looked at Jay's hands. "You a Crow?"

"Crow?" Jay asked with an amused smirk. Pain's face remained cold. Jay looked to Case, who wore an uneasy expression. "Nah, I'm just a business man."

Pain didn't like Jay's response. The dismissive chuckle irritated him more than the fact that Jay was playing with something that he clearly had no understanding of. He also caught the exchange between Jay and Case when he asked if the boy was a Crow. There was something there that he couldn't see yet, but he would.

"J.K.'s people have the line on hardware. He hits us with some real friendly numbers when we need to tool up. That's why we call him JK-47," Case explained.

"True indeed. I got shit for all occasions, Glocks, 9's, rifles. Shit, I can even get you a slingshot if that's your weapon of choice," Jay joked. He was trying to lighten the mood between him and Pain, but fell short. Seeing that making nice with the Blackbird was pointless, he turned his attention to Case. "Yo, I need to get in your ear about that thing you asked me about." He paused, waiting for Case to say it was okay to speak in front of Pain.

"That's my brother. Whatever is said here will never leave this circle," Case assured him.

"Nah, it's cool. I'm about to see about the bar. I probably don't wanna hear whatever else ya man has to say out his mouth anyhow," Pain told them and walked off.

Case waited until Pain was out of earshot before turning to Tyriq. "What the fuck is wrong with you? How many times do I have to tell you about running your damn mouth all the time!"

"Case, stop that bullshit man. You know I ain't never had no filter and I ain't gonna grow one overnight. That's just that," Tyriq said flatly. "And why the fuck is it all of a sudden a secret? He's gonna find out at some point."

"And that point ain't until I deem it so!" Case snapped.

Tyriq saw where this was going with Case. For the briefest of moments, he had considered entertaining his big homie's bullshit and blaming it on the liquor later, but instead he took the high road. "Whatever you say." He walked off.

"Damn, Case. It seems like all your people overdosed on testosterone tonight. I'm picking up on a lot of hostility, especially from that Blackbird joker. From the way y'all been chatting him up the last few years, I expected something different. Someone who is less of an asshole, feel me?" Jay had picked up on the shade Pain was throwing his way. Had it been anybody else he'd have popped on them. He was hardly a sucker, and not used to people coming at him sideways without a little bloodshed.

"Don't read too deep into it. Pain just crawled up out of a hole, so it's gonna take him a minute to re-sharpen his social skills. He'll come around, though. What's good?" Case turned the conversation back to business.

"I spoke to my guys, and they'll be able to provide most of the stuff from your list. At least the major shit," Jay told him.

"Bet, what's the number looking like?" Case was already working out the figures in his head.

"For everything? I got the number down to twenty grand even. Half on delivery, the other half when you get right."

"Since when did we have to start making deposits on orders instead of settling the tab after the score, same as always?" The change in their normal terms threw Case.

"Since word started getting around that you might be living on borrowed time," Jay told him. "Told you trying to burn that sour old man was a bad idea."

Indeed, Jay had warned him, but it hadn't stopped Case from putting himself between a rock and a hard place anyway. Case had done a transaction with some older joker from Harlem for some pills. His regular connect was out of town, so he went to this dude he had been turned on to through a friend of a friend. He was a chili pimp, but he also had a line on some pills that were supposed to be pretty good. The old head was one of those arrogant cats who always tried to talk down on young gangsters like Case. Had Case not been in a bind he'd had never fucked with him. The drugs ended up being high-powered, so Case went to cop from him again. This time the old head tried to put points on the price. He hit Case with a line of bullshit about inflation, but Case knew that he was only playing with the numbers because he thought that because Case had come to him twice that he was his only source. Case made three more transactions with the old head and always came with straight money, so he got comfortable. On Case's last order he tripled down, agreeing to give the old man half up-front and pay the rest in a couple of days. Of course the old man added points on that order too, because it was on consignment. Case paid his asking price with no problem, because he knew that he was getting over on the old-timer with the funny money. As it turned out, Case had just bitten the hook that the old-timer had been baiting for weeks. He had been a small fish who set Case up to be eaten by a shark. Because of Case's greed, he was now caught in a dangerous web and the only way out of it would be to compromise his morals, or find a way to kill the man who was currently holding his feet to the fire. That had seemed an impossible task, until recently. Pain being back in the fold might've been just the edge Case needed to tip the scales back in his favor.

"Old nigga had it coming," was Case's response.

"Maybe, maybe not. Right and wrong isn't the issue here. It's the dirt on your name that you should be concerned about," Jay told him.

"I ain't never gave a fuck about what niggas thought about me." Case was dismissive.

"Whatever you say, big dawg. Look, me and you have always had a good relationship. You're my guy. So, if you want I can go back and holla at my people. If we gotta scale your order back a bit then it ain't no thing."

"I ain't gotta scale shit back. Tell your people they'll get their money. I just need a little bit of time to scrape it together. Just have my hardware ready when I come calling for it."

"Fosho. And what about manpower? I know y'all not too long ago lost a man or two and your ranks are looking a little thin. If you need, I know a few capable guys I can reach out to. They've only been in the country a few weeks, so they're clean and ain't shy about blood," Jay offered.

"Thanks, but you know how I feel about working with outsiders," Case reminded him. He wasn't opposed to bringing in freelancers when a job called for more men than he had with him, but didn't like straying outside his unit. They were loyal to him, and not a payday.

"You might wanna rethink that, Case. As far as I can see, you only got two, maybe three solid dudes you can count on, and that's only if you include Lil Sorrow's troublesome ass. I got no illusions as to whether he's willing to bust his gun. In fact, he's probably too willing for something like this. I'd go five deep on this at minimum, just to be safe."

"Then we should be fine. Blackbird by himself is worth any two outlaws I can pay to ride on this," Case said proudly.

"Who? The jailhouse dude with the attitude problem?" Jay thumbed in the direction Pain had gone off in. "From what I've seen tonight, prison got that dude fried. I wouldn't bet my freedom on him."

"That's because you don't know him. When that cage finally pops open, that bird is gonna fly."

CHAPTER 13

"I'm so flyyyyy . . ." Passion sang along with the Lloyd Banks song, while doing a little dance in place. It was an older cut, but one that had grown on her over the years. This was thanks to Bo. On those occasions when she got dolled up and stepped out, it would be her theme song. She would roll all the windows down in her car and play it on blast. It was her message to all the younger girls who now felt like they were her competition, that she was still the baddest bitch! That's how Passion felt at that moment, like a *bad bitch*.

When Passion discovered that the spot Juju had planned for them to hang out was located in the backyard of a repair shop, she had expected some ghetto shit. Juju was her best friend in the world, but the girl had some serious hood rat tendencies. It showed in the company she kept and sometimes the places she chose to frequent. Whenever she was allowed to pick the spot it was hit or miss, with more misses than hits. To Passion's surprise, The Yard was not at all what she had expected. The garages they had seen when they were coming in was where the gambling went on. Inside the men sat around two card tables, both covered in piles of cash. Beyond that, through the waiting area and out the back door, was the actual Yard. It was a decent-size space with neatly trimmed grass with a fig tree planted on all four corners. A young cat with dreads sat under one of the trees in a lawn chair with his laptop across his lap. His fingers worked nimbly across the keyboard which controlled the music being broadcast through the Bluetooth speakers that were placed strategically throughout the yard. Small, solar-powered lights lined the outskirts of the big grass square. They provided enough illumination so that the party didn't have to stop once the sun went down. Their version of a bar was three folding tables pulled together in the shape of a horseshoe, manned by a girl who looked like she was younger than Passion. For as raggedy as the setup may have looked, Passion did spy some high-end booze behind their pieced-together bar. She couldn't front, the place was lit.

From the time the girls walked in, dudes were on them. Especially

Passion. She was still technically a kid, but she carried a grown woman's weight on her. The tight-ass pants she'd borrowed only made what she had stand out more. It seemed like every few steps some thirsty joker was trying to grab her hips. The attention was a bit much, but secretly it felt good. Passion always felt like she was moving through life over-looked, unless it was for the wrong reasons. Prior to Professor Higgins, the teachers in school didn't see her. The social workers didn't see her. Even when her parents were alive they couldn't seem to see what was right in front of them until the damage had already been done. Passion didn't fool herself into thinking that the guys pushing up on her didn't see her as more than just a piece of meat, but it still felt good to be the center of attention just once.

While Passion busied herself kung fu–blocking the hands pawing at her, Juju slid to the build-a-bar and grabbed them two drinks. Passion wasn't a big drinker because she didn't have the head for it. She knew how she could get when she was too faded, so she kept her intake limited to celebrations and funerals. When she expressed this to Juju, her friend replied, *"Bitch, we celebrating your liberation. Tonight is the night we start laying the foundation for your emancipation from Uncle Joe's plantation!"* Normally it would've taken heavier peer pressure for Passion to fold, but after the day she'd experienced, she deserved to let go. At least for a time.

The quick minute Juju had promised they would spend at the underground spot was now rolling into hour number two. Passion didn't mind so much. By that point she had a nice buzz going on. Likely from the few drinks she had let Juju gas her into having. She wasn't bent, just nice. This was thanks to the fact that she made sure to chug a bottle of water between drinks. Staying hydrated was a trick she had learned from Bo. Juju, on the other hand, was a little past nice. She wasn't quite drunk yet, but another drink or two might push her across the finish line. Passion watched her as she worked the room, being the social butterfly that she was. Juju was just one of those people that you could drop into any circle amongst any class of people and she could adapt. Despite the hood-chick persona that she projected, the girl was no dummy. For almost every hug or handshake she passed out, there was a weed sale attached to it. No matter how tipsy Juju was, her focus hadn't shifted from her paper.

While Juju did her thing, Passion went to find herself a seat. She lucked out when a dude who had been occupying one of the few folding chairs spread across the yard vacated his seat to speak to someone he knew. Passion didn't even wait to see if he was coming back before sliding into his spot. She wasn't really used to walking in heels of any kind, and Juju's shoes were giving her soles and ankles a workout. Nursing what she promised herself would be her last drink, she scrolled through her cell phone. She had two texts from Bo, and one from Uncle Joe. Both of them wanting to know where she was. Passion left them both unread. She'd get around to answering them at some point, but not then.

She continued scrolling through her phone. Still no texts from Birdie. She had hit her up twice to see if she was okay, and hadn't received an answer. Her first instinct was to ditch Juju and go back to the house to check on Birdie, but she decided against it. She thought about what Juju had said about not being able to help anyone until she helped herself. Birdie was probably still sleeping off her drunk, and Passion going home would've only succeeded in ensuring that she would be sitting in the house right along with Birdie and getting stressed out again. That wasn't something she wanted to deal with. She would probably hear Uncle Joe's or Bo's mouth when she got home anyway, so she figured since she was already out she might as well try to enjoy herself.

The drink started getting good to Passion, and she figured it'd be even better if she washed the last bit of it down with a cigarette. She removed one of her stash of loosies from the zippered part of her purse and placed it between her lips. She was in the process of fishing around for a lighter when she noticed a shadow cast over her. When she looked up, she found herself confronted with a tall drink, with rich brown skin and a fade so crisp that it looked like he got it touched up every day. He didn't wear a lot of jewelry, just a thick gold bracelet and two diamonds in his ears, but he had the serious eyes of a man who was about a dollar. He pulled up a foot or so short of Passion. She looked up at him with questioning eyes, waiting for him to state his business, but he only stared.

"Can I help you?" Passion asked, feeling uncomfortable under his gawking.

"You can't smoke that in here," the drink told her.

Passion looked around. There were people smoking either joints or blunts throughout the backyard. "I guess none of them got the memo, huh?"

"Bud is cool, but cigarettes gotta be smoked out front," he explained.

"Then I guess that's where I need to be." Passion made to excuse herself.

"Hold on," he stopped Passion when he touched her arm. She looked at his hand as if it had been dipped in shit. "My fault." He released her. "I was only gonna ask if we'd met before? You look so familiar."

"I don't think so," Passion said honestly. She was sure she would've remembered meeting someone as handsome as him.

"Maybe it was just in my dreams," he said.

"Is that the best line you got?"

"It's my only line," he replied. "I've found that the truth is the quickest route to the point you're trying to make."

"And your point?" Passion rolled her neck, tiring of him seeming to talk in circles.

"I . . . see . . . you . . ." he broke the words up as if Passion was slow. He followed by pointing to the roof of the garage.

Passion followed his finger and for the first time noticed the small camera pointed at the backyard. "What are you, some kind of voyeur?"

"No, I'm a gambler, but I'm also the one responsible for keeping people from doing shit they got no business doing in this joint. Such as you and your little friend. I've been watching the two of you pushing product since you walked in here." He gave her a knowing look.

"Bruh, I don't even know what you're talking about," Passion lied. She knew it had been a bad idea to come into a spot like this and try to freelance. She should've talked Juju out of it, but hadn't and now she was about to be in the middle of some shit.

"You're too pretty to lie. It's not becoming of a lady. I ain't pressed over them few twenty sacks. Just don't move any more, feel me?"

Passion didn't respond.

"Now that we've gotten that out of the way, what are you drinking?" He nodded at her now empty cup.

"So, you go from threatening me to offering to buy me a drink?" Passion gave him a *nigga, please* look.

"Drinks are free in The Yard, so the only thing it'll cost me is a walk to the bar. And for the record, I didn't threaten you. I just asked you to respect my place and not sell your shit in here without going through the proper channels. If I were threatening you, you'd know about it," he told her.

"Boy, go somewhere with that tough-guy stuff. You don't hardly look like no gangster." Passion waved him off. She had been around Uncle Joe and his people long enough to know a killer when she saw one and he wasn't that. He was too clean.

"That's because I'm not. I told you, I'm a gambler. I'd rather play the odds than play with my life," he said coolly.

Passion fought the hints of a smile that tried to touch her lips. He was witty, she gave him that. He also seemed to have a rebuttal to everything she said. That meant he was likely a capable liar; good at switching up on the fly. She knew the type because she was the type. Growing up as Passion had and going through some of the things she had gone through, taught her that sometimes a lie was more merciful than the truth.

"Dice."

"What?" Passion didn't understand.

"My name . . . it's Dice," he clarified. He waited for her to offer her name in return, but she didn't. "I hear that hot shit," he smirked. "I don't know why you trying to play all saditty while you're in here slumming right along with the rest of us."

"I'm not slumming, I'm celebrating," Passion told him.

"What's the occasion?"

"My liberation," Passion said with a tipsy chuckle, thinking back on Juju's earlier declaration.

Passion allowed Dice to keep shooting game at her, while she stirred the melting ice in her cup with a little straw. His words flowed like silk, but it was his mouth that she was focused on. His lips in particular. They looked suckable, for lack of a better word. They were a part of his enchantment and she was sure he knew it. Dice probably lured girls in nightly with the same sweet song that he was singing into her ears. Was he truly this suave lover that he was projecting, or was he just another foul nigga trying to fuck? The fact that he worked at an illegal watering hole in the middle of the hood probably put him in the latter. Dice would have liked nothing more than to take her to a cheap motel and punish her. What he didn't know is that she'd probably like it. She'd slip into that comforting oblivion of her mind, while he broke her body to the point where the pain brought her to a shameful orgasm. Maybe . . .

Passion had to shake herself out of her thoughts. When she realized how far down the rabbit hole she had just allowed herself to go, she dropped her cup. She'd had enough for the night.

"You good?" Juju walked up on them. She gave Dice a threatening once-over before coming to stand beside Passion defensively. Juju looked to her friend and saw that her eyes were a little glassy from the drinks. She was lit.

"We're great," Dice answered for her.

"Who you?" Juju questioned.

"The man who's been watching you sell weed in here all night," Dice informed her.

Juju looked from Dice to Passion with a confused look on her face.

"Long story," Passion said, and made a dismissive gesture. "This is Dice. He works here."

"Damn, you make it sound like I'm the janitor," Dice joked.

"My fault, he *runs the place*," Passion made air quotes with her fingers.

"I'm trying to get your girl to have a drink with me, but she acting like I'm out to drug her," Dice jokingly told Juju.

"For all we know, you just might be," Juju said seriously. She didn't know Dice, but she knew his type. The moment he spotted Passion under the influence and alone he probably swooped in for what he thought was going to be an easy kill.

"It ain't that serious, shorty." Dice didn't like what she was suggesting. He felt like he had been making progress with the thick lil chick, and then her cock-blocking friend showed up. Had it not been for Juju, Dice reasoned he could've had Passion somewhere with her legs in the wind by the end of the night. He imagined that her sweet young pussy tasted like honeysuckle, but her friend wasn't trying to let him sample the fruit. His attention was drawn from that situation to one across the yard when he heard a glass break. Near where the bar was set up he spied a crowd forming around two dudes who looked like they were into it. One of them he recognized. "Fucking Crows," he mumbled under his breath before going off to do his job. Postponing his quest to get into Passion's insides, Dice went off to do his duty.

"If he'd licked his lips one more time, I might've made a bad decision," Passion half-joked once Dice was gone.

"I know, which is why I came over here. You okay?" Juju asked.

"Yeah, he was just talking to me," Passion assured her. She didn't bother to mention her twisted fantasy from earlier.

"That's not what I mean." Juju looked her in the eyes, searching for signs that her friend was no longer herself.

Passion knew that Juju would likely be able to see through any veil she tried to hide behind, so she sprinkled her response with truth. "I'm okay, Juju. Just a little faded, that's all."

"A'ight." Juju left it at that. She knew that Passion was going through some heavy stuff at home, and had drunk more than she probably should've. Those two things never made for a good combination. When Passion was in that way she tended to be a little more reckless than normal, which is why Juju had been keeping an eye on her throughout the night. "It's probably best that we call it anyhow. I'm almost sold out," Juju lied. She still had enough weed left on her to pick up a few extra dollars, but she knew her friend well enough to know when she was standing on the ledge and thinking about jumping. She spotted her brother lingering on the fringes of the scuffle with a Black dude that she didn't recognize. "Let me go holla at big bro real quick and we can bounce."

Passion spared one last look at Dice, who was wading fearlessly into the unruly crowd in an attempt to restore order. Watching him toss people this way and that brought back the fantasy she'd had earlier about being broken by the gambler. Her face suddenly felt flushed, like someone had started a bonfire in the backyard. "I'll wait for you out front. It's getting a little hot in here."

CHAPTER 14

"It's getting hot in here . . . so take off all your clothes!" a girl in a too-short skirt sang along with the song at the top of her lungs, while twerking hard enough to break her own back. Several of her friends stood around cheering her on. When she tried to drop it low, her drunken knees gave out and she fell on her ass. Laughter erupted from those who had seen it, and the girl slunk off in embarrassment.

Pain watched it all from his position near the bar. It wasn't a real bar, just three long card tables in the shape of a horseshoe, lined with liquor bottles and plastic cups. Case was still across the room, huddled up with Tyriq and the kid Jay. Pain had a gut feeling about the nature of their conversation and wasn't sure how he felt about it. Pain and Case went back a long way, but he couldn't help but notice that something had changed since he'd been locked up. The whole vibe amongst their little crew felt off, at least where Pain was concerned. The funny glances between Case and Jay, Tyriq's slick remarks. None of it felt quite right. This made him question just how deep in he was willing to get with his old crew.

"What you need, baby?" The girl working the makeshift bar finally got around to taking Pain's order. She was a brown-skinned girl with long legs and a bright smile.

It had been so long since Pain had been out to a bar, real or fake, that he almost couldn't remember what he liked. "Henny," he requested more out of familiarity than actually wanting brown liquor.

"What you want to chase with that?" she asked.

"Chaser? I don't do all that," Pain chuckled.

"I hear you, gangster." The girl gave him a wink. A few seconds later she sat a plastic cup of Hennessey in front of him.

"What do I owe you, sweetie?" Pain pulled out the small bankroll he had collected from the homies throughout the day.

"You must be new to The Yard," she stated with a smile. "The only thing you pay for here is pussy and gambling. Everything else is courtesy of the owner."

"Must be a pretty generous man to be feeding and watering all these people." Pain looked out over the crowd that had gathered in the yard space.

"Domo is a lot of things, but I don't know if I'd call him generous," she joked. "The drinks are free, but we do accept tips."

"Say less." Pain was trying to peel off a ten, but accidentally dropped a twenty onto the tabletop, which the girl quickly snatched up and stuffed into the pocket of her tight jeans.

"Thanks, handsome. My name is Keisha, by the way."

"Pain," he replied.

"Pain? Do I want to know why they call you that?" Keisha asked.

"How about you come find me after you're done here and I can show you," Pain offered. He hadn't meant to come off so aggressive, but being back in his element gave him a confidence that he hadn't felt in some time. This made him a little cocky.

"I just might hold you to that," Keisha told him and went back to the other end of the table to fill more drink orders.

"Nice sneakers." A voice spoke behind Pain. He turned around and found himself looking up at a familiar face. It was Ms. Louis, aka Lolo.

"Thanks," Pain said in his coolest tone. He looked her up and down, from her designer jumpsuit to her expensive sandals. "You don't strike me as a sneaker head."

"I'm really not, but every so often something might catch my eye enough for me to take it home," Lolo said, in a tone that made Pain wonder if they were still talking about sneakers.

"If only I could be so fortunate," Pain capped back. He was amused at the fact that she hadn't even recognized him as the same dude she had tried to play to the left earlier. What a difference an outfit and hair change could make.

"And who says that coming home with me was fortunate? Misfortune comes in pretty packages, too." With that she gave him her back and turned to place her drink order with Keisha.

Pain found himself at a loss for words, a momentary lapse. Shorty had a slicker mouth than he had given her pretty ass credit for, but he could not be outdone. "I know a little bit of something about misfortune." He slid back into her line of view. "I got a story that'll tug at your heart strings."

"Hearts are for suckers, and that ain't what my mama raised. A sucker would get herself roped up in that sexy voice of yours. Or maybe those sad-ass eyes that makes a bitch wanna help fix whatever is broken inside of you, but I already told you that I ain't that."

"Then what are you?" Pain questioned.

"Too long in the tooth to get roped in by some short game," Lolo informed him. She was a woman about her business and didn't have time for the bullshit.

Keisha interrupted them when she slammed Lolo's drinks on the tabletop. She flashed Pain a dirty look, to which he responded with an amused look. She thought their sixty seconds of brief flirting meant they had come to an understanding, but as far as Pain was concerned the only thing it had done was open up the possibility. Keisha was so mad that she didn't even bother picking up the few singles Lolo had left on the bar for her.

"See what I mean? You've got something on your plate already and are still looking for the next meal. I'm good." Lolo scooped the two drinks and turned to leave, but Pain wasn't done.

Pain gently grabbed Lolo's arm. When she turned he asked, "Why you wanna cut me for, gal?" quoting the Muddy Waters line from the movie *Cadillac Records*. The fact that Lolo smiled said that she was familiar with the film.

"I'll give it to you, you ain't no quitter." Lolo shook her head in amusement.

"That ain't what my mama raised." Pain shot her earlier line back at her. "I ain't got no ill intentions. I'm just trying to get to know you. That's all."

"The one and most important thing you need to know about me is that I have a man," Lolo told him flat out.

"Good, then that means I don't have to do shit like take you out on dates. I'll leave that to the ol' boy and gladly take the rest of what comes with you."

"What comes with me is an issue that you aren't quite ready for," Lolo warned him. The young man was quite the charmer, and under different circumstances she might have let him chat her up to see where his head was at, but they were in the danger zone. She held no illusions about what was going to happen if he didn't fall back. Before she could give him the final push to be rid of him, her worse nightmare materialized before her eyes.

"What's popping?" Lolo's boyfriend Lee said. He was stocky but on the short side, only standing at about five-eight, maybe five-nine.

A heavy gold chain swung from his neck with the numbers 155, laced with diamonds, hanging from the end of it.

"Yeah, man. We were just talking sneakers." Pain pointed at his feet. He was attempting to defuse the situation before it kicked off, but it didn't do much to wipe the sour expression from Lee's face.

"I was just about to come back over with our drinks." Lolo held one of the cups out to Lee, but he didn't take it.

"Looks to me like you were over here bumping your gums," Lee said in a dangerous tone. His words were meant for Lolo, but his focus was on Pain.

Pain knew that look. Lee was the possessive type. He was one of those dudes who was willing to shed blood over a piece of pussy. If it went there, there was no doubt in Pain's mind that he would have to kill Lee. Lolo was fine, but hardly worth a murder charge. "Bro, I know what this probably looks like, but I didn't mean any disrespect."

"Homie, you couldn't disrespect me if you wanted to," Lee shot back. "You must be new around here and don't know who the fuck I am."

"You're right. I don't know you, and honestly, I don't care to. I just didn't come here tonight for no problems. Why don't you take your lady and the both of you enjoy the rest of your night?" Pain was trying to take the high road. He wasn't lying about not wanting any problems, but it wasn't for fear of Lee or anyone else. It was out of fear of what he might be pushed into doing.

"Baby, don't start," Lolo interjected. She had read Pain's eyes and her man didn't see what she did. She placed a calming hand on his chest in an effort to urge him in the other direction, but he slapped her hand away.

"What? You defending this nigga?" Lee asked angrily.

"Lee, you sound stupid. I don't even know this guy," Lolo said honestly.

"Fuck did you just call me?" Lee grabbed her by the arm roughly.

"Let me go!" Lolo squirmed as Lee dug his fingernails into her arm.

"Homie, that ain't even necessary," Pain said, against his better judgment. His good mind told him to mind his business and slide off while the couple sorted their shit out, but his sense of honor wouldn't allow him to stand by and watch a woman get beat on. Ms. Pearl had raised him better than that. More out of reflex than meaning to, Pain grabbed Lee's arm. The boyfriend turned to him with madness dancing in his eyes and the next thing Pain knew he was backpedaling from getting punched in the face. Lee had been drinking so his punch was sloppy and telegraphed. Had Pain been on point, instead of trying to play rescue hero, he could've easily dodged it, but he wasn't. Lee's punch hit square in the chin. He couldn't lie, the little dude put some power into it. Had Pain been a man with a weak chin, Lee probably would've knocked him out. Instead . . . he triggered him.

Pain's recovery was immediate. He swooped in on Lee and fired several quick blows, almost all of which peppered Lee's face. Lee threw a short hook, which found a home in Pain's rib cage. Pain ate the blow and headbutted Lee in the face. Blood splattered all over his new sweat suit and the bar/table. Lee's hands instinctively went to his broken nose, and that's when Pain launched another flurry. This time it was Lee's gut that got the seasoning. Pain was about to finish Lee when one of his boys caught Pain from the blind side. He had officially gone from the frying pan to the fire!

Tyriq had managed to gather up a small group of hood rats, which he brought over to entertain the group. Him and Jay were all over the broads, trying to force free liquor down their throats while playing stink finger up their short skirts. One of them had cozied up to Case. She was a nice-enough-looking girl, and normally he would've happily bought what they were selling, but he had more pressing business on his mind. Like how to get the money together for the guns he needed from Jay's people.

He was in a catch-22 of sorts. He needed money to get the guns, but he needed guns to get the money. Case wasn't broke, nor was he living as ghetto fabulous as he led people to believe. Robbing had always been his primary source of income, and he made nice money pushing pills and coke, but most of his flash came from scamming. With the credit card numbers they were snatching off the web, Case could walk into most stores and charge thousands of dollars up on someone else's credit line, but that was all digital and no cash. Still, Case was pulling in enough to where he should've been able to set himself up comfortably, but Case never wanted to be comfortable. He wanted to ball! He had allowed himself to become accustomed to a lifestyle that he really couldn't afford, and when his pockets started feeling the pinch and that lifestyle was threatened, it forced Case into a series of bad decisions. This was also a contributing factor as to why he was cash poor. The lick that he had spent almost a month trying to piece together would be a game changer for him, but he would need those guns.

"Bruh, why you sitting here looking like you got to take a shit when you got a fine-ass bitch over here practically begging to suck yo dick?" Tyriq ambled up to him. The girl who had been trying to get with Case had finally grown tired of being ignored so she had gone back to join her friends.

"I got heavier shit on my mind than getting my dick wet," Case told him.

"You still thinking about that shit with Jay? Dawg, don't worry about it. Between us and our niggas in the hood, we can pull together the guns to make this happen," Tyriq assured him. He was always the optimistic one of the group.

"No, this is too important to depend on a few dirty Glocks and maybe a MAC that's probably so old it don't shoot straight anymore. We need to step it up and I need those guns. I just have to figure out how to get up the paper they're asking for."

"We get it like we always do. We steal it," Tyriq said simply.

"That was the first method that popped into my head. The only thing is, shit is hot out there right now. When that free government money dried up, there were a lot of muthafuckas who had to take it back to the basics, including us. A lot of the spots we could've normally taken off for the amount of cash we need in the time we need it, are on point by now. They'll see us coming."

"They won't see him." Tyriq nodded in Pain's direction. He was at the bar chatting up the bartender.

"Shit, if Pain was back on the team a lot of these dudes would more willingly give over their shit than deny us. That boy was a beast in his day. I don't know what the fuck he is now," Case said disappointedly. He had been anticipating Pain coming home for months. That was the one man he knew who could help him right their sinking ship, or so he had hoped. Sadly, it wasn't to be. Pain was on a different type of vibe. Case had love for him still, but even he had to admit that Pain had come home a shell of the man he had been going in.

"Well, from as much as Pain claims to have changed, I see he still likes to play with fire," Tyriq laughed.

Case shook his head when he saw why Tyriq had made the remark.

Pain had traded in the bartender for Lolo. He was spitting heavy game at her and from as big as she was smiling it looked like she might be going for it. Case didn't know why he hadn't anticipated this happening when he saw Lolo was in the backyard. He thought that his warning to Pain about staying away from Lolo had been clear and his friend would've taken heed, but no. He was still the same old Pain. When he wanted something he went after it, whether it could likely get him killed or not. Lee must've peeped what was happening at the same time Case did because he was currently making a beeline toward the couple. From the twisted look on his face, Case knew what type of time he was on and so did Tyriq.

"Oh shit! It's up!" Tyriq was moving toward the altercation when Case stopped him.

"Fall back for a minute. I wanna see if that dog still has its teeth," Case said, and positioned himself to watch.

Unlike Lee, his friend hadn't been drinking, so his punch was well aimed and vicious. His fist connected with the side of Pain's head and he immediately heard the ringing in his ear. He'd barely had a chance to assess the new threat before another one of Lee's boys got into it. It was now a three-on-one situation. Pain tried to protect himself as best he could as the crew rained blows over him. His mind was snatched back to the brawl in the prison dayroom. It was no longer Lee and his team assaulting him, but Brute and the prison gang. It was then that Pain lost it. One of the men landed another shot, this one to Pain's jaw. He ate the punch and fired off one of his own. He knew the moment he felt a shift in the kid's jaw that he had knocked it off its hinges. When his buddy tried to help, Pain kicked him in the nuts, followed with an uppercut that deposited him on his back. Pain would've probably killed all three of them had it not been for the security team wrestling him away. They were trying to calm him down, but Pain was beyond the point of reasoning. He even bit into the arm of one of the men when he tried to yoke him up. The guys who worked security at those kinds of spots didn't play around, and would've likely worked Pain over had Chase not chosen that moment to step in.

"Fuck off, my man!" Case swooped in and shoved one of the security men. Tyriq was on his heels, ready to pop off. Even Jay stepped up, though he wasn't as eager to knuckle up over a dude who had tried to play him only moments prior. It became a shoving match between Pain, his friends, security, and whatever remained of Lee's people. The situation stank of something that was about to go so far left that it would probably make the local news, but thankfully the voice or reason finally spoke.

"Next nigga to throw a punch is going to be the last nigga to throw a punch." When Dice appeared, everything stopped. It wasn't because his presence was so grand that it commanded a pause in all activities, but the long .45 dangling at his side did. Dice waited until he was sure that he had everyone's attention before turning his irritated glare on Pain. "How did I know I would find a Crow in the middle of this shit? Turn him loose," he ordered his staff.

"Good to see you again too, Dice." Pain shook the wrinkles out of his clothes and went to stand with his people.

"I wish I could say the same." Dice tucked his gun.

"Wait . . . y'all know each other?" Case looked to Pain for an explanation.

Pain eyed Dice. He could see the discomfort in his eyes. Pain represented history, and that was never good for a man looking to reinvent himself. "Let's just say that the stories of our lives feature some of the same characters."

"Everybody good?" Dice shifted the conversation to Lee and his boys, who were licking their wounds.

"Nah, ain't shit good about this," Lee said in a menacing tone.

Dice knew Lee. Pain had hurt his pride. That wasn't something he would let go. "Ain't been enough blood spilled to make it a thing, Lee. This shit is light and I'm happy to turn a blind eye, but if it goes any further than this then the people I work for might feel in a way about it. I don't think that's something either of us want. I'm sure you'd agree?"

Lee didn't say anything right away. Dice was a gunslinger and a gambler, nothing Lee couldn't handle if it came to it, but the family he served was a different story. For as much as he wanted to put the hurt on Pain for embarrassing him, doing it there was not worth drawing the ire of the Stones. "Another time, my nigga," he said to Pain in a threatening tone.

"Rain checks are my favorite kind to cash," Pain taunted Lee. He was turned up by then and happy to go all the way with it.

"We'll see." Lee gave him a knowing nod. This was far from over. "Let's go." He snatched Lolo by her arm and pulled her behind him as he made his exit.

Pain watched as Lee manhandled Lolo, belittling her on his way out. She was probably going to get hands put on her at some point during that night, which wasn't Pain's problem. As Lee was pulling her outside, she cast a glance back at Pain. Something passed between them. It was like when Lot warned his wife not to look back lest she turn to salt, but she failed to listen. All it took was that last look for him to know that she hadn't totally closed the door on him. Earlier he had been on the fence about trying to fuck her, because he knew that Lee was going to be a headache, but now he planned on trying to fuck her for the very same reason. Taking Lee's life, if he'd chosen to, would've been easy, but taking his pride would be sweeter.

Dice waited until Lee and his crew were gone and the danger had passed before turning his attention back to Pain. "All these years later and King Crow is still leaving bloody messes in his wake."

"Says the man who turned down a set of wings of his own," Pain shot back. "I'd heard you hung up your hustle and started turning in the niggas you used to rob with."

"I'm providing a service. Whoever ends up on the wrong end of my expertise," he shrugged, "call it the luck of the draw."

The story of how Dice came into his new profession was one that was only known to a few. Dice was a professional gambler and part-time robber, and at the height of his criminal career he had been amongst the best in the city at both. Dice could make a truckload of televisions disappear with the same ease that he could sit down at a craps table and make the dice read pretty much any numbers he wanted. He also had a sleight of hand technique when dealing cards that was second to none. Dice was damn near the LeBron James of breaking the law, but his hall of fame career of stealing ended prematurely at what would be his last card game. He'd walked into a room with intentions on fleecing everyone at the table and left the lone survivor of a massacre. The killer had let him live on the condition that Dice deliver a message: "The bastard son has returned." It wouldn't be until days later when the bodies started dropping that the message would make sense.

"As I recall, you were the best at busting these joints out," Pain continued. "When the dust settled around here and everybody started picking sides, it wouldn't have been too hard to see you sitting at the head of your own poker table. You could've been a king."

"Maybe." Dice momentarily reflected on what might've been and then came back to his senses, "But I'd rather die old and unknown than young and notorious. You might do well to remember that while you're out here sniffing around what don't belong to you, Blackbird. Lee is a dangerous enemy to have."

"So am I," Pain assured him.

"So, what's up? We good here?" Tyriq asked. He was ready to keep the party going.

"As long as y'all niggas can keep your talons to yourself. Oh, and somebody gonna have to break bread over the shit y'all broke up," Dice told them.

"That's on me." Pain peeled off a few bills from his cash collection and tossed them down on what was left of the tabletop. "With my compliments." He patted Dice on the shoulder as he passed him. The Yard was starting to feel small and he needed a breather. He stopped short, turning to Dice with a question in his eyes. "That night . . . the one that they say changed you. What did you see at that card game that could make you pass on wearing a crown?"

Dice thought on it. Not because he didn't know the answer to the question, but because he was a careful man when it came to his words. "You wouldn't believe me if I told you."

CHAPTER 15

The night air felt good against Pain's face. It helped to cool the fire that was building in his gut. He couldn't believe that the young punks in the club had tried him. Had this been a few years earlier they'd have never tried that bullshit. Everybody who was anybody knew what time it was with Blackbird. Then he had to remind himself: He wasn't Blackbird anymore. The days of him putting people in the hurt locker were behind him. Now, he was just a man displaced in time and trying to figure out where he belonged.

"Got a light?" A feminine voice tickled his ear.

Pain spun, ready to tell whoever had dared invade his space to fuck off. He wasn't in the mood. Venomous words filled his mouth, but when his eyes landed on the girl with the cigarette dangling from her full lips, he found himself at a loss for words. She was tall. Not as tall as he was, but slightly above average height for a female. She was a pecan-colored beauty who had a shape that looked like it was giving the seams of those skin-tight jeans a run for their money. Long, neat dreads spilled from her head and touched her shoulders. There was something about her that struck him as familiar. He had seen her before, but it didn't hit him as to where until he looked into her eyes. He would know those eyes anywhere. It was the girl who had gotten her necklace snatched on the subway. Her face had been covered by a mask at their first meeting, but now that he could take in the whole of her he found her breathtaking!

"You got a light or nah?" the girl repeated her question.

"Sorry, I don't smoke cigarettes." Pain found his voice.

"Don't need to be a cigarette smoker to carry a lighter," the girl said. From the slight slur in her words he could tell that she had been drinking heavily.

Pain smiled. "You're right about that. Sorry I couldn't help." He was speaking about the incident on the subway, but she assumed he was talking about his not having a lighter.

"It's all good," she replied, digging through her purse in hopes that she could find some random matches. She spared a glance at him and noticed that he was giving her a curious look. He was likely wondering why she hadn't moved the hell on already after finding out he didn't have a light. She found herself studying him. He was handsome, to be sure, but it wasn't his face that held her attention. It was his eyes. They weren't anything special, just an average shade of brown, but there was something else there. It was sadness. They were the saddest eyes that she had ever seen on another human, with the exception of probably Birdie. His eyes made her want to reach out to him, but thankfully she caught herself before she did.

"You good, shorty?" Pain noticed the perplexed look on her face.

"My name isn't shorty, it's Passion," she replied, uncertain why she was so forthcoming.

"Passion," Pain repeated the name, letting it roll around in his mouth as if he could taste it. "That's pretty."

"You think? Most people I tell my name to think it's weird," Passion admitted. She was always teased in school about her name, or people thought it was an alias.

"You can find beauty in weird stuff too, Passion." He caught himself. "My name is Pain."

"Passion and Pain." She tapped her chin as if she was deep in thought. "Sounds like a song title," she joked.

"There is no doubt in my mind that we could make some beautiful music together." He hadn't meant to be so forward, but it was what was in his heart.

"So, you being named Pain the reason you're out here bleeding?" Passion motioned toward his bloodstained jacket.

Pain glanced down at himself. He hadn't even realized that he was wearing Lee's blood. "It ain't mine," he told her, slipping out of the sweat jacket, which had suffered the worst of it. There were splotches of blood on his T-shirt too, but they weren't too bad. The jacket was ruined. As he was balling the jacket up to discard it, he noticed that Passion was still staring at him quizzically. "So," he began awkwardly, "is this the part of the song where the two lovers exchange numbers with the promise of meeting again?"

"No, this is the chorus in the song when the lead singer talks about how she should've known better than to get caught up with a man covered in blood." Passion said in a tone that made it hard to figure out if she was joking or serious.

"You gonna let a little splatter deter you from making the best decision of your life?" Pain eyed her. He was like a cobra trying to hypnotize the curious mouse. She had an energy about her that Pain wasn't used to and he wanted to drink it in as much as he could.

"Instead of Pain they should've name you cocky." The drinks had added an edge to her tongue, and she was feeling a little cocky herself. She walked a tight circle around Pain, not close enough to touch, but close enough where he could take in her smell and her presence. "How many dizzy young broads you hit with them bedroom eyes and they fall into your lap? Nah, playa. You ain't gonna *Erykah Badu* me," she laughed.

"You got jokes."

"Nah, I got good sense," Passion capped with a wink. "Besides, it wouldn't make no sense to give you my number even if I wanted to."

"And why is that?" Pain wanted to know.

"Because I'm only here for a season, not a reason."

"Winter is coming." Pain quoted one of his favorite television shows.

"They say it'll be the longest winter in a hundred years." Passion matched his quote. She too was a fan of *Game of Thrones*.

"You House Stark or Lannister?" Pain asked, wanting to keep their banter over the shared show going.

"Neither, if I was around back then I'd be Khaleesi," Passion told him.

"Breaker of Chains?"

"No, conqueror of the world. My life is gonna stretch beyond these five boroughs and I plan to make an impact everywhere I touch," she said passionately.

"I'm still trying to figure out what all that has to do with you not wanting to give me your number?" Pain questioned. He was intrigued by the quirky girl.

"Because I'm probably not going to be in this city long enough for you to use it. I got a birthday coming up three weeks from today and I don't plan on celebrating it in New York. Chase another dream, handsome, because I ain't it," Passion said honestly.

"Spoken like a woman who is still trying to figure out her worth," Pain said.

"No, the problem is that I do know my worth and I'm sparing you the heartache that's gonna come with all this," she made a sweeping gesture over her curves.

Their flirting session was broken up by a low rumble approaching from the distance. It was faint at first, sending a soft vibration through the street. As it got closer the rumble grew into what was closer to a growl. Pain knew that sound and what was making it: a 1973 Harley-Davidson Panhead. Pain would know that sound against the rumbling of a dozen other engines and pick it out of the crowd every time. It was a sound that he had spent years of his life hearing day after day. For several months he even had the fortune of being amongst the pairs of hands that were entrusted to restore the old classic. No sooner than Pain had the thought did the Panhead come into view. It was black with gold trimming. Bringing up the rear were two more bikes. These were newer models, mostly made up of plastic and metal. Nice bikes, but they didn't deserve to share the same road as the Panhead. Traveling in the center of the triangle of bikes was a large black SUV. People gathered around to watch the motorcade, which happened to come to a stop right where Pain was standing.

"I wonder what this is all about?" Passion asked curiously. She had seen the bikes around town before, but never out in force like this. Something was going down.

"War," Pain whispered and abandoned their conversation.

After the scuffle, Case was able to smooth things over enough for Dice and his team not to ask them to leave. The night was young and Case wasn't about to let some bullshit fight cut it short. The two hundred dollars he had slipped into Dice's palm helped to make it all go away. Had it been anyone else, Dice would've had his team toss them out on their asses, but he knew Case. Letting him stay was the lesser of two evils. With Pain, you knew what you were getting. He would come at you head-on, but Case was sneaky. If Case ended up feeling some type of way over Dice doing his job, Dice would probably have to spend the next few weeks looking over his shoulder, until the petty muthafucka was ready to let it go.

Across the yard, Case watched Jay talking to a young girl in baggy clothes. If he recalled correctly it was his sister or niece. He couldn't remember, because Jay kept his family dynamics close to his chest. Case hadn't missed how Jay played the outskirts when Case finally did decide to step in on Pain's behalf. Jay wasn't soft, but he picked his battles based on which ones benefited him. Pain held no value. At least not yet. So why run the risk of souring potential business relationships with Lee, or Dice, over a nigga he barely knew? Case always thought that their relationship was tighter than that, but lately Jay had been feeling himself. Their conversation over the guns was further proof of that. Jay suggesting that Case couldn't handle his order in front of Tyriq could've been taken as a sign of disrespect. Case was a general and Jay had addressed him like a bum-ass nigga in front of one of his soldiers. Case wouldn't make a thing of it right then and there, but after he got what he needed he was going to remind Jay of his place in the pecking order.

"I'd say the dog still has its teeth, wouldn't you?" Tyriq nudged Case, pulling him from his scheming.

"I'm inclined to agree with that."

"I never had any doubt. I don't know why you did either? To keep it funky, I wasn't feeling that move. Having us fall back while Pain was scrapping," Tyriq told him. He was a proud and loyal young man, and not immediately coming to the aid of a comrade made him feel like a sucker.

"I was never worried about Pain getting hurt in that fight. If anything, I had my money on him killing one of those fools before it was said and done," Case said honestly. He knew what kind of monster Pain could be.

"Still, we should've popped off with him," Tyriq insisted.

"I know you would've handled it differently, lil bro, but this had to go down the way it did. I need Pain to remember who he is." Case was about to add to his statement when something caught his attention. He couldn't really tell over the music and people talking, but it sounded like motorcycle engines.

No sooner than the thought entered Case's head, he saw people spilling from the Yard and onto the street. Something was brewing. Case and Tyriq followed the crowd to see what was going on, and it didn't take long for them to figure out what it was. Case made it outside just as a man was pulling a beautiful black and gold motorcycle just short of Pain. When the rider removed his helmet, Case's mouth suddenly became very dry.

He was gone without another word, leaving Passion standing there feeling somewhere between rejected and confused. Pain's departure was abrupt and cold, leaving her to wonder what the hell was going on. She watched him curiously, approaching the rider who had just climbed from the black and gold bike. When he removed his gold helmet, she got a better look at the grizzled brown face beneath it. He was an older man, sporting a shaggy salt-and-pepper beard that was braided. His bushy hair spilled from a red, black, and green bandanna which was tied snugly around his head. Wearing dark glasses and a scowl, he looked every bit the outlaw biker. She could see Pain's shoulders tense when the biker moved in his direction. The crowd parted for them under the threat of violence, and Passion could feel her pulse quicken. She hadn't known Pain more than five minutes, if that, yet she felt vested in the outcome. Hopefully it went in his favor. A bubble of tension built between the two men, but before it could pop, someone grabbed Passion's arm and yanked her away.

"D'fuck?" Passion turned angrily, ready to bark on whoever had touched her uninvited. It was Juju's brother Jay. He had his little sister's arm in one hand and hers in the other.

"Time for little girls to get themselves out of harm's way," Jay said, pulling Passion by one arm and Juju by the other. There was an Uber waiting for them at the corner.

"Harm's way? I was just standing there. That fight didn't have anything to do with me!" Passion protested, half stumbling to keep up. Jay was in an awful hurry to get them off the block.

"That's how it usually happens. The bystanders catch the strays meant for somebody else. Not on my watch and not with my little sister," Jay said in a tone that let her know it wasn't up for debate. He snatched open the door to the Uber and motioned for the girls to get in. Passion was hesitant.

"Ju?" Passion gave Juju a questioning look. She felt like Jay was just tripping, but the nervous look on her friend's face said that it might've been more serious than she thought.

"Let's just go." Juju confirmed Passion's suspicions.

Passion rolled her eyes at Jay before sliding in next to Juju. Her leg had barely cleared the door before Jay slammed it behind her, patting the hood of the car for the driver to pull off. She turned around in her seat and peered through the back window to catch a last glimpse of Pain.

"Who was the dark-skinned cutie you were talking to?" Juju wanted to know.

With eyes still on Pain she replied, "Just another damaged soul."

CHAPTER 16

Pain stood there on the curb, arms folded and eyes defiant, watching the old-timer as he moved in his direction. The crowd parted like the Red Sea, with no one wanting to get in the way of the hard-looking biker. He stopped just shy of where Pain was standing, and glared up at him as he was shorter. Pain returned his glare, refusing to be punk'd.

"What up?" the biker finally spoke. His voice sounded like he had smoked thousands of cigarettes in his lifetime.

"I was hoping you could tell me, since you're the one who pulled up shooting daggers," Pain flexed.

"Slick as you talking, you must not know where you at," the biker said in a threatening tone.

Pain surveyed his surroundings. He had already spied three things that were lying within arm's reach which he could use as weapons. He felt a kinship with a broken umbrella that occupied the same trash bin as his discarded sweat jacket. "I don't. Why don't you show me?" he taunted, knowing he had his next three moves planned already.

That was it. The gauntlet had been laid and the only question that remained was, who would pick it up first? As it happened, it was the old biker who made the first move. His hand whipped into his jacket faster than you'd have expected of a man his age. Yet as fast as his hand moved, Pain's was faster. The biker had barely cleared whatever he was pulling from his jacket before Pain had one hand gripping the back of his head and the other on the broken umbrella, holding the point level with the biker's eye. "Man can't ride a fine machine like that one with one eye," he nodded toward the Panhead, "now, can he?"

"One-eyed man on a hog is about as useless as a stud with no dick in a whorehouse," the biker replied. With his eyes he motioned for Pain to look down. When he did, he saw the small .22 pointed at his nuts. "Prison has made you slow, boy."

"Bullshit, you pulled that peashooter way after I had the drop," Pain challenged. "Now stop fucking around and welcome me home properly." He spread his arms.

The old biker grabbed him in a bear hug and lifted him off his feet. For a man his size, he was far stronger than he looked. "Good to see you, Blackbird."

"You too, War. You too."

Warwick P. Jones, known to friends and enemies alike as War, was one of Pain's oldest friends, next to Case, and his mentor. He was one of the first dudes Pain had seen, besides on television, riding a chopper. There were other guys in the neighborhood who rode motorcycles, but not like the ones War fancied. He only fucked with Harley-Davidsons. The fiberglass numbers that most people rode around on he referred to as "crotch rockets" and wouldn't be caught dead on one.

Pain used to love to sit around and watch War ride through the hood on his metal steeds, robbing shit and raising hell like a modern-day Black cowboy. War's bikes always fascinated Pain, and he would steal a closer look whenever he could. When War would park his bike to go into one of the local gambling spots, or visit with one of the many young girls he was bedding in the hood, Pain would sit and stare at the machine for hours, imagining himself riding one on the open highway. One day War offered the curious boy a ride. From the moment Pain felt the powerful bike vibrating between his legs and the wind on his face, he was hooked. Most of the kids his age dreamed of riding around in Benzes or BMWs, but all Pain wanted was an Indian Scout.

When Pain got a little older, War started letting him hang around the Crow's Nest, a shabby repair shop where old bikers would hang out working on their bikes, drinking, and talking shit. Hanging around those old-timers, Pain got a better education about motor vehicles than he could've gotten at any trade school. Pain became the unofficial mascot of the Crow's Nest and a regular grease monkey. Working with the old-timers on their rides taught him the ins and outs of engines, and allowed him to make some cash on the side. Not only did Pain's time at the shop turn him into an ace mechanic, but it was there that he would meet the woman who would change his life.

"I see you're still running around with these hooligans," War said jokingly, nodding toward Case and Tyriq, who had just walked up.

"Crows always fly in a murder." Pain looped his thumbs and made the same bird-like shape that Jay had mimicked earlier.

"Some do at least," War said with a twisted smirk. "Sup wit y'all lil niggas? Can't speak?"

"What's going on, War?" Tyriq greeted him. He didn't know War as well as the rest, as he was the youngest of the group. What he did know was that he was a man of respect.

"Staying sucker-free," War replied. He then looked to Case, who was shooting him daggers. "You good, shorty?"

"I'm great, old head," Case replied in a cold tone.

"Let's see how long you stay that way. Cold world out there, man," War told him.

"Good thing I keep a heater," Case shot back.

Pain watched the awkward exchange between his best friend and his former mentor. Case and War had never had the same relationship that the old man had with Pain, but they all flew the same flag. From the way they were looking at each other you'd have thought that they were enemies. Pain got that feeling again. The same one he had gotten earlier when Case had hushed Tyriq before he could say whatever it was that he had been hinting at. If he wasn't sure earlier, he was absolutely sure now that there had been some kind of shift in the dynamics of their crew while he was away. Pain was trying to think of a subtle way of asking what the hell was going on.

"Let me introduce you to a couple of the boys." War took the attention away from the tension between him and Case. He motioned for the two riders who had brought up the rear. In almost military unison, they dismounted their bikes and came over. When they removed their helmets, Pain understood why they moved with such precision. They were twins. Both were brown-skinned, with large brown eyes and gaunt faces that gave them somewhat skeletal appearances. The only difference between them was that one bore a jagged scar that ran over his lip and stopped just short of his nostril. "These are Mike and Mick," he introduced scar-lip and the other twin.

"What up?" Pain greeted them. Mike, the twin with the scar, gave Pain a cold nod, but Mick was friendlier and extended his hand.

"Heard a lot about you, Blackbird. It's an honor to finally meet you," Mick told him.

"The twins been with us for a few months now. They ain't earned their wings yet, but they've got the makings of good young Crows," War said proudly.

"Good luck to you boys, and don't let this old fucker work you too hard. He can be a little intense sometimes," Pain joked.

"My intensity is what whipped your sorry ass into shape and

made you one of the greatest to ever sport them black wings," War reminded him.

Their playful moment was broken up when the door to the SUV slammed with such force that it was a wonder the windows hadn't shattered. From the driver's side stepped a man—at least he walked upright like one. The truth as to whether he had been spawned by a mother or a monster was still up for debate. He wore a beautifully tailored white suit, with a golden crow pinned to the lapel. The suit was where anything that could be considered *beautiful* about him ended. He easily stood six-four with long gangly arms and large hands, one of which was covered by a black glove. This was to hide the fact that he was missing two fingers. It was dark out, but his signature black sunglasses covered his eyes. His skin was completely devoid of pigment, a defect of his genetics. The only color on him came from the mural of tattoos that an artist had painted over almost every inch of his body, including his face. Six gold hoops dangled from his ears, and a large seraphim ring pierced his nose. He looked like something out of a freak show, and he prided himself on the effect his bizarre appearance had on people.

"Why are the two of you standing around like two fucking groupies instead of doing your jobs?" the tattooed albino barked at Mike and Mick. Mike opened his mouth to respond, but a nudge from his brother stayed his tongue.

"Good to meet you, and hope to share the road with you soon," Mick said to Pain.

"I wouldn't hold my breath on that one," Pain responded.

The two brothers moved to do as they were told, with Mike taking up a defensive position alongside the SUV and Mick speaking with someone through the partially cracked back window. This was all done under the watchful eyes of the albino. "Fucking idiots," he muttered.

"Why don't you take it easy, Prophet. We're amongst friends here," War told him.

"Says you, old man. Ain't no such things as friends; only Crows and carrion!" Prophet spat. He turned in Pain's direction, and though he couldn't see his eyes, he could feel them on him and it made his skin crawl. "If it isn't the fallen angel. I'd heard the rumors that you were out, but hoped that they weren't true."

"Hello to you too, Prophet." Pain wiggled his ring and pinky fingers at Prophet, taunting him for his missing digits. The two of them hadn't gotten along during the years they had been forced to share the road together, and absence from each other's company hadn't changed that. This was how it had always been between Pain and Prophet, and it probably wouldn't change.

His name was Prophet, but his purpose in life was chaos. This much had been certain from the time he came into the world. Prophet was born into a gypsy clan, and had the misfortune of being the only one amongst the troupe who suffered from this particular pigment defect. This made him an outcast amongst not only the other members of the traveling group, but his own family. They treated Prophet like a leper, and the only reason they hadn't murdered him as a child or left him on the doorstep of some church for the nuns to look after was because he had value. Prophet was born with what the elders called "the sight": the gift of being able to see the futures of others. This was why he always wore the dark glasses, to help ease the visions of other people's lives that constantly assaulted him. The troupe made him a part of their traveling act and exploited his abilities to line their pockets, but continued to treat the boy little better than a beast of burden. Prophet would find himself freed from bondage when a mysterious fire broke out at their camp, killing almost every member of the clan, including his entire family. No one could say for sure what had caused the fire, but some speculated that the albino had had a hand in it.

After being unceremoniously exiled, Prophet spent the next few years roaming throughout the South, breaking laws and bones in the name of survival. His life would change when a group of Crows passed through one of the towns he was then calling home. Their leader at the time had taken a liking to the pale boy and brought him into the murder. Prophet had been riding with the Crows long before Pain had come into the fold. At that time Prophet had been locked up in DC for drugs and assault. By the time he was paroled and returned to New York, Pain had already clawed his way up through the ranks and become the new favorite of the gang's leader. This put him on Prophet's shit list. He felt like Pain had stolen what rightfully belonged to him: the leader's favor. The few short years in which they shared the road after Prophet's release were spent trying not to kill each other.

"I see you still think you're the little comedian. How about I change the angle of that smile these women seem to love so much?" Prophet pushed back one side of his jacket and flashed the harness which held both a handgun and a hunting knife. He tapped a gloved finger on the hilt of the knife.

"You draw on me, you better be ready to go all the way," Pain warned.

"When am I not?" Prophet shot back. His fingers had moved from the knife to the handle of the gun. "Time we finished this game once and for all."

"Long overdue. Since you didn't learn from the first time, let's see what body part I'm going to take from you this go-round." Pain retrieved the broken umbrella that he had previously been threatening War with. It would be no match for whatever Prophet was toting, but it would have to do. The two combatants watched each other, neither wanting to be the first to draw blood and both wanting to be sure it was he who drew the last. Pain had decided since he was outgunned the first strike may as well be his. Just as his muscles coiled to attack with the umbrella, he heard something that stilled his heart. It was a song.

"*Your mama's name was Lonely, and your daddy's name is Pain,*" a familiar voice sang. The owner of the voice stepped into view and drew the attentions of all assembled. Her black thigh-high stiletto boots clicked across the pavement as she approached Pain. Black leather pants hugged her long legs and on top she wore a white blouse of pure silk. Her hair was bone-straight and dark, save for the lone white tuft that fell across her pecan-colored face. Eyes the color of caramel candy held Pain motionless as she reached up and cupped his face in her delicate hands. "*So, why you wanna fly? Blackbird . . . you ain't ever gonna fly.*" She ended the verse with a kiss to his forehead.

"My Queen," Pain whispered, burying his face in the nape of her neck.

In Pain's young life he had only loved three women. The first two were his grandmother and his mother; the third was the woman standing before him, the Outlaw Queen, Cassandra Savage. When he'd first met Cassandra he had been at a very low point in his life. His mother had been gone for a few years by then, but the pain of her passing still stabbed sharply at his heart. Ms. Pearl did as best she could to make sure he had a proper upbringing, but there wasn't much she could do with the angry young teen. Before she even realized it, Pain was off the porch and had no plans of coming back on. Back then he and Case were heist partners, but his two closest friends were Shadow and

Fresh. Outside of his grandmother they were the only real family that he had left. That was why he took it so hard when the trio split up over some bullshit that could've been avoided. Having suffered yet another loss of people close to him so early in life, Pain turned to the bottle to numb the ever-growing pain in his heart. The drinking took its toll, but it was nothing compared to when he started experimenting with harder substances.

When War finally brought Pain before the Queen, he was a far cry from the man he would become. He was a mess back then, and the Crows who were already in the murder made no secret of the fact that they didn't want Pain in the crew. An addict, even a budding one, was a liability in their line of work. Cassandra, however, saw something different in him. What she saw that had softened her heart toward the troubled teen he wouldn't learn until he had been with her for some years and had gained her trust. Over time, the rest of the Crows came to trust Pain as well, and embraced him as one of their own. They helped him clean up his act, and he made the transition from stickup kid to heist man. To the Crows, robbery was an art and Pain became their Picasso.

"It's about time that the state saw fit to return you to me. I can't tell you how much we've all missed you." Cassandra gave him a tight hug for emphasis.

"Not all of us," Prophet muttered.

"Prophet, you know that no one could ever take your place. Not even my Blackbird," Cassandra assured him. Her eyes then turned to Case. He was standing inconspicuously behind Pain, pretending not to see her. "What's up, Case? No love for the Queen?"

"Cassandra." Case gave a curt nod.

"Show some respect!" Prophet demanded.

"It's fine." Cassandra waved the albino away. "I only expect my birds to acknowledge my crown. Same rules don't apply to those who've had their wings clipped."

"Clipped?" Pain was caught off guard by the statement. When a Crow had its wings clipped that meant that they had been excommunicated from the murder. Outcast. He looked to Case for an answer, but it was Cassandra who would give him one.

A smile formed on Cassandra's black-painted lips. "You mean he hasn't told you, Pain?"

"This isn't the time or the place to have this conversation, Queen," Case told her.

"Why not? It's no secret to everybody else that you are no longer protected by the shadow of the Queen's wings. I'm not saying anything that you didn't make public when you spat in the hand that fed you for all those years," Cassandra said. There was no scorn in her voice, but her eyes burned.

"Say it ain't so?" Pain couldn't believe his ears. He had been the one who brought Case into the Crows and begged the Queen to accept him as one of theirs. Before Pain got locked up, Case had been flying the black wings, just as proudly as Pain had. This didn't make any sense. Pain waited for Case to tell him that it had all been a big misunderstanding, but the look on his best friend's face said what his mouth could not: Case was out.

"It's not as simple as that, Pain," Case told him.

"Yes, it is," Cassandra interjected. "You wanted to get out and do your own thing, and I let you. Albeit you were already knee-deep in your own thing while still taking your share of Crow prey. You can slap as much lipstick on a pig as you like, but it'll still be a pig. A dirty, greedy pig."

"I'm a pig for wanting to feed my people?" Case challenged.

"Not at all. What makes you a pig is the fact that you're messy as hell. You called yourself embarrassing me on your way out, by putting that bullshit out about how I'm running this operation, like I'm doing anything but making sure every soul who rests in the shadows of my wings is eating."

"Can't a man want a healthier serving?" Case questioned.

"No doubt, once he's earned it. Cutting corners, though." Cassandra shook her head sadly. "I guess I just expected more from my little birds."

"Well, since I ain't your little bird anymore, I got no reason to care about your expectations," Case capped.

"And that statement right there is why you and anyone who follows you will always find themselves left to pick over the scraps of their betters," she said.

"Cassandra, we got history, so even though you out here trying to style on me, I'm gonna hold my tongue out of respect," Case conceded. He wasn't feeling the way she was speaking to him, and he was only going to keep himself in check for so long before he did something crazy.

"You holding your tongue has less to do with respect than it does the fact that with a snap of my fingers I can have Prophet cut that cunt-licker out of your skull," Cassandra hissed.

"And a skilled tongue it is. Or so I hear from Shelly," Prophet taunted, dropping the name of one of Case's lady friends.

"Fuck that bitch!" Case barked. Prophet had him in his feelings by striking so close to home.

"You should've kept that same energy with them young boys from the Dog Pound. They clipped Charlie and y'all still ain't slid for him, but I digress," Cassandra added her two cents.

It was a low blow. Charlie had been a member of their misfit crew. He wasn't a Crow, but he ran with Case, Tyriq, and Lil Sorrow while Pain was away. From the story Pain had gotten while in prison, Charlie had taken on an ill-advised caper with some local knuckleheads. They carjacked a woman for her Benz and ended up sending her to the ER in the process. Little did any of them know, their jacking would have some unforeseen consequences that would rock their crew. They would later find out that the woman Charlie and his friends had robbed had been an acquaintance of a man who had come to be known as the Beast. His birth name was Cain, but only a select few still called him that, as what was left of his humanity had long ago been swallowed by the dark thing that now fueled his soul. Cain had only recently reached drinking age, but had a résumé of brutality that would one day put him in the serial killer hall of fame. When Cain was done with Charlie, there wasn't enough left of him for his mother to have an open casket funeral, and he had been the lucky one. Charlie had been fortunate enough to be allowed to die, but not his accomplices. Instead of death, Cain gifted them with his mark: melting half their faces off with a hot knife. For the rest of their days, all who laid eyes on the mutilated young men would know the consequences that came with running afoul of Cain. Not avenging Charlie's death was a hard pill for Case and the crew to swallow, but it beat the alternative, which would've been Cain and the Dog Pound slaughtering all their loved ones, including children, before allowing their victims to die. Only killing Charlie had been a rare act of mercy on the part of the Beast, so they grudgingly accepted it.

"Queen," Pain spoke her name. He saw where this was going. Case was a shiny pinball that was about to be slapped back and forth by the Queen's personal flippers, War and Prophet. Pain knew what

Cassandra was angling to turn this into, and he didn't want to find himself caught between his friend and his Queen.

Hearing Pain's voice softened Cassandra, and brought her back to why she had come in the first place. "Right, this isn't about a few stray pigeons. You and I have some things to discuss. Walk with me, Blackbird." She started down the street without looking back to see if he would follow or not. She didn't need to.

Pain fell in step with her, while Prophet trailed them by a few feet. He gave them their privacy, but stayed close enough that he could reach her in an instant if he needed to. They walked in silence for about half a block before Pain spoke. "I didn't know."

"I figured you didn't. Case has always been a man too proud to admit his mistakes. If his pride doesn't kill him, I'm certain his ego will."

"We don't speak death over those we love," Pain reminded her. It was one of the first things she had taught him: never to speak death or run the risk of inviting it.

"I know," was her response. "So, why is it that I had to hear through the grapevine that you're out of prison instead of from your lips?"

"It's only been a few hours. To be honest, I didn't want too many people to know that I was home just yet. I'm still trying to get my feet under me," Pain told her.

"How's that working for you?"

"Still too early to tell. I've only been gone a few years, but it feels like decades. I don't know, it's like everybody and everything is different now."

"Because they are. The older you get, the faster time moves. When you boys go away, time stands still for you behind the wall, but out here in the world the show is still going on. Don't rush yourself. Take your time with it and let things fall back into place naturally. In the meantime, War and some of the boys put together a little welcome-home package for you," Cassandra told him.

"You know how I feel about handouts. My hands still work." Pain curled his two index fingers and mimicked pulling the triggers of guns.

"I should hope so. Some people go into prison as one person and come out as another. Who are you? Percy or Blackbird?" Cassandra asked.

"I'm still trying to figure it out. I'd be lying if I said being locked up didn't give me some serious food for thought. Some of the shit that goes on in there . . ." he let his words trail off as the memories played back in his mind. "I can't see how some dudes treat it like a revolving door. I'm one and done on that jail shit."

"You don't have to tell me. I've been there and done that, so I understand what kind of hell it can be." Cassandra reflected on her own experiences being locked up in her home state of Louisiana. "You know, my heart ached for a long time while you were away. I always wished I could've done more for you."

"I mean, you dropped money on my books from time to time. You were one of the few who did, so I appreciate that," Pain said honestly. He used to look forward to the few dollars and occasional flicks she would send him.

"I'm not talking about money. What makes me a good queen is that I pride myself on being able to protect all my little birds. You're all men who are more than capable of defending yourselves, but the shadow of my wings spreads far and wide. During the first leg of your bid I was able to reach out to people loyal to me and make sure your issues were kept to a minimum. It was just shit luck that the last prison they moved you to was one of the few where there weren't any of our people. It was like someone blinded me and I couldn't see you anymore. By the time I could it was already too late," she said emotionally.

"What's understood doesn't need to be said." Pain could read between the lines. Cassandra always seemed to know his truth, whether he spoke it or not. "I'm in one piece and I'm alive. That's what's important."

"You always could find the light in even the darkest of things, including me." She smiled up at Pain before planting a kiss on his lips. They tasted of alcohol, and she fought the temptation to suck them until she was drunk. "So, now that the Blackbird has been freed from his cage, I assume you'll retake your place at my side?"

"You've got Prophet for that. He's much more qualified for the position than I am," Pain told her.

"Oh, so now you're leaving me, too?" Cassandra couldn't hide her surprise. For her, Pain being anywhere but at her side was unthinkable.

"No, it isn't like that. You and me have a connection that transcends the crew. We'll be linked forever, Queen. Never doubt that. It's just that prison gave me a lot of time to reflect on my life and some of the choices I made. I've seen where walking the path you're offering me leads, and right now I want to move in a different direction."

"And there it is." Cassandra gave a slow, theatrical clap. Her face was now tight and her lips twisted into a wicked smirk.

"What?"

"The grudge you're still holding against me for you getting arrested," Cassandra accused.

"Cassandra, you sound crazy! My bid was never on you. You didn't trick me into that car."

"No, but my nephew did," she countered.

And there it was. The elephant that had been lingering in the room ever since he set foot back in the old neighborhood. Pain had hoped to avoid this conversation, but he knew better. It was a part of all their shared histories. The night when the foundation of their *thing* crumbled.

FOUR YEARS PRIOR:

The night that would forever change Pain's life was a cool one, somewhere in the low seventies. The reason this detail stuck out to him was because it had been hot as hell all that week. Not regular hot, but the kind of heat where the temperature was still dancing around eighty at sunset. It was one of the worse heat waves in recent history, so the cool night was a welcome change and brought everyone outside, including Pain.

Earlier in the day, Pain, Case, and a Crow, who went by the name of Dre, had hit a nice lick for some jewelry and their fence had cashed them out. Case and Dre wanted to go to the strip club and blow a bag, but not Pain. He wasn't as eager as his friends were to give away the money he had just risked his ass for in exchange for some pussy. No, he would get his the old-fashioned way, with weed, liquor, and charm.

Pain had set up a rendezvous with a hood rat that he knew would get real nasty and was low-maintenance. She wasn't the most attractive broad he'd bedded, but she wouldn't ask for more than something to drink and something to smoke. He was coming out of the liquor store and about to try and flag down a taxi when he spotted a Crow named Ralphie. He was leaning against the whitest Mercedes that Pain had ever seen, chatting it up with two girls. Dripping in jewelry and with a confident swagger, Ralphie looked more like a rapper than a thief. He and Pain were more acquaintances than friends, but he was the Queen's nephew, so he didn't think twice before jumping in the whip when Ralphie offered him a ride to his destination. If he'd known then what he knew now, he'd had told Ralphie to fuck off and taken a cab.

The first red flag should've been the fact that Ralphie had been drinking. Pain knew dudes who could drive buzzed and not miss a beat, but Ralphie wasn't one of them. He was riding through the city in a sixty-thousand-dollar automobile with an open container on a Friday night. He was asking for trouble and would get it sooner than later. They were maybe five blocks from Pain's destination when Ralphie blew through a light that had just gone from yellow to red. A few seconds later they saw the flashing lights behind them. Pain wasn't strapped, so he wasn't worried about the police finding anything on him, and he doubted Ralphie was holding. Guns weren't his thing, which is why Cassandra primarily sent him as a driver on capers. He had no heart for steel. The worst that Pain expected to happen was maybe the police would smell the liquor on Ralphie and maybe hit him with a DUI. In that case, Pain would park the car somewhere for him, as he hadn't been drinking yet and had a valid license, and would notify their lawyer about what had happened to him.

The second red flag was the fact that Ralphie suddenly seemed to come down with a sudden case of the jitters. While they sat waiting for the cops to approach the car, he kept flexing his fingers around the steering wheel and his leg wouldn't stop shaking. Sweat had even broken out across his forehead. From the way Ralphie was acting you'd have thought they had just been stopped with a body in the trunk. The officers were now out of their car and making their way up opposite sides of the car. The next thing Pain knew, Ralphie had swung the driver's side door open and taken off running. Pain was left there, stuck on stupid and getting dragged from the car by the officers. He lay handcuffed on the ground as they tossed the car, and when one of them looked at his partner smiling, he knew why Ralphie had run. Under the passenger seat, where Pain had been sitting, was a plastic bag with cocaine in it. It wasn't more than an ounce or so, but with Pain's record and the fact that he was still on probation from a previous charge, the coke was more than enough to get him sent away for a few years. Pain would have several opportunities to tell the truth about who's coke it had been, but he didn't. Ralphie was an idiot, but he was still a Crow. More importantly he was the Queen's nephew. Out of loyalty to her, Pain ate the charge.

———————

"I always warned that fool nephew of mine about riding dirty," Cassandra continued. "If you have something in the car that you shouldn't, either have a place to conceal it or leave it at home. I drilled this into all of you, and my poor half-wit nephew let it go into one ear and out the other." She shook her head in disappointment. "No one would blame you if you were still in your feelings over his fuckup. It was months before I could even bring myself to look at him, let alone speak to him. His wings were clipped on the same night you got arrested. Had he not been my sister's son, there's no telling what kind of punishment I would've handed down. I just couldn't."

"I wouldn't expect you to. Ralphie did some dumb shit, but he's still your family," Pain said.

"But so are you!" her voice rose. "Percy, I know there's nothing I could offer that will replace the years that my nephew stole from you, but I want to make this right in any way that I can."

"Cassandra, I keep telling you that this isn't your mess to clean up. If anything, Ralphie's bitch ass should be the one out here apologizing. He wrote me a punk-ass letter and put a hundred dollars on my books twice when I first went upstate, but I didn't hear shit from him after that. At the very least, he could've come here with you and offered to buy me a drink."

"Ralphie's off the bottle. He has been since that night. He doesn't even smoke weed anymore. He got himself cleaned up and moved out to Queens with his girlfriend. He even has a daughter now." Cassandra pulled out her phone and showed Pain a picture of a cute little girl of about three or four.

"I'm glad one of us was able to have a shot at creating a life," Pain said sarcastically. "No disrespect, but why are you telling me this like I give a fuck about that boy?"

"To show you that he's a changed man. Ralphie has had no part of this life in years. He's a civilian now. A square. And therefore the rules we live by don't apply to him anymore."

"What? You think I'm planning on doing something to him?" Pain finally understood why she was pleading her nephew's case so hard.

"I know you, Pain. It was my hands that molded you into my

weapon of vengeance. You've done things to men for less, so why would I not expect my nephew to fall under the shadow of the Black-bird?" Cassandra asked seriously.

"Because that monster doesn't live here anymore." Pain placed his hand over his heart. "I'd be lying if I told you that in the beginning I didn't hold some hatred in my heart toward that dude. He took the one thing from me that I can never get back: time! The irony is that the same thing that he took from me is the thing that allowed me to finally get over it: time. I did a lot of soul-searching in prison, and I like to think I'm a better man for it. I'll never forgive him for what he did, but I don't hate him anymore. Your nephew has nothing to fear from me."

"Thank you." Cassandra cupped one of his hands in hers and kissed his scarred knuckle. "My biggest fear was being put in a position to have to choose between my heart and my blood."

"And what side would you have stood on?" Pain asked curiously.

"My last name is Savage. From the Bayou to Boston, everybody knows how my clan feels about family," she said seriously. "Enough about blood and death. You are home and this is cause for celebration. Let me take you out for dinner. We can grab a nightcap afterwards like we used to?" she suggested.

"Maybe another time. I've got an early day tomorrow, so I should probably take it down for the night," Pain respectfully declined. Memories of having this beautiful old broad splayed on her stomach while he pushed himself into her soaking wet pussy made his dick hard, but he couldn't give her that type of control over him again. Not just yet.

"Another time then." She gave him a knowing smirk. "Well, should you change your mind, all you have to do is reach out. There will always be a place for you at my side and in my heart."

"Thank you, my Queen." He kissed her on both cheeks. Pain made to rejoin his waiting friends, but Cassandra had some parting words for him.

"The pages of this story are about to turn." She cast a glance at Case, who was still watching them. "When the book is closed, don't let misplaced loyalties land you on the wrong side of history."

"So, you just gonna sit there on some mad shit for the rest of the night?" Case broke the silence that had been lingering in the car for the past ten blocks. He was behind the wheel with Pain in the passenger seat. Tyriq was in the back seat, drunk off his ass and still going. He'd made them stop by a liquor store to grab himself a pint before they dropped Pain off.

"I ain't mad, Case. Just disappointed that you would keep something this big from me," Pain told him. There was no judgment in his tone. He was simply starting how he felt about it.

"I wasn't keeping it from you, dawg. I just knew that based on your relationship with the Queen, it would've been hard for you to hear, so I had to wait until the right moment presented itself to break it to you."

"We been together at least ten hours off and on since you pulled up on me in the hood this morning. You mean to tell me you couldn't find no time in between to tell me you've decided to go rogue?" Pain asked.

"Ain't nobody rogue. I just ain't jacking that Crow shit no more. To her credit, Queen gave us a play coming up, but we grown-ass men now. We supposed to live off that broad's mercies forever? Kicking her up a taste off everything we hit, all for what?"

"Because she's the Queen!" Pain countered.

"Of *thieves*," Case corrected him. "That's one crown out of the five which now govern this city. Respect to Cassandra for helping us get our feet wet, but her vision is shortsighted. All we'll ever be is thieves and stickup men under her, but why limit ourselves? Since we freed ourselves from those feathered shackles, we've been able to expand our operations. We still doing heists, but we're also moving drugs, protection, and pussy. We're running the whole gambit out here now." Case broke it down. "I know you're in your feelings because of how close you and Cassandra are, but I need you to see the bigger picture. What I did was for the benefit of all the homies."

"If you say so, Case," Pain replied. He understood where Case was coming from, he truly did, but the fact that Case had kept the split from him made it feel shady, and Pain didn't do shade. After the revelation, he couldn't help but wonder what else his friend might've been hiding. The car had barely made it to a full stop on Pain's block before he was swinging the door open and stepping out. Tyriq managed to pull himself from the back seat to take Pain's place in the front. He drunkenly tried to hand the bottle he had been swigging from to

Pain. Pain shoved it away. "I've had enough for the night and from the stench coming out your pores, so have you."

"Nigga, I'm just getting warmed up. I'm about to pull up on a bitch and hit her with the Hennessey dick tonight!" Tyriq made thrusting motions with his hips.

"You shot out, man," Pain laughed.

"It's still early, my nigga. Let's keep the party going; get some bitches and some more drink. We ain't even gave you your welcome-home gift yet." Tyriq was trying to convince Pain not to turn it in. The last time Tyriq and Pain had hung out he'd still been a kid, so he was eager to show his big homie the kind of clout he carried as a young man.

"Give it to me tomorrow." Pain gave Tyriq dap, then a hug. He walked around to the driver's side and leaned into the window. He and Case stared at each other for a long beat, before Pain held up his fist. "Still my nigga."

"That ain't never gonna change." Case bumped his fist. "You gonna think about what we discussed earlier?"

"Yeah, I'll weigh it up," Pain said, still not quite ready to go there.

"One and done, baby. Easy work," Case assured him.

"It's always easy work to the ones who ain't doing the heavy lifting." Pain slapped his palm against the top of the car twice. "I'm gone."

"Boy moving like he big mad," Tyriq said as they watched Pain disappear into his building.

"Nah, he ain't mad. Just uncertain," Case assured him.

"Maybe if he'd seen his present it would've swayed him. Showed him that we're the ones with his best interests at heart and not Queen Crow," Tyriq suggested.

"Or made this whole situation ten times worse. You saw how he acted around her. That old whore still got his nose wide-open. Gonna take a steady hand to pry him loose from her teat without doing any major damage."

"So, since you ain't trying to give it to him, what are we supposed to do with it?" Tyriq wanted to know. The high point of this night was supposed to be seeing how Pain's eyes would light up when he saw how big they had did it for his coming home.

Case shrugged. "No refunds and no exchanges."

"Say less. I got it."

"Nah, I got a better idea," Case told him before pulling out his phone.

Alexander Jenkins, also known as Lil Sorrow, sat behind the wheel of the lime green Audi, bumping his head to Lil Baby's "Sum 2 Prove" as it pounded through the speakers. As usual, a black bandanna was tied snugly around his braids, pulled down so far that you almost couldn't see his eyes. From somewhere in his mouth he produced a razor, which he ran along the side of a cigar, gutting it like a freshly killed stag. He replaced the tobacco he had just dumped out the window with a healthy amount of sticky green buds, before taking his time to break it down between his thumb and index finger. He had just sealed the blunt and was about to light it when his phone vibrated. When Lil Sorrow saw the name flashing on the screen he felt his heart quicken. He'd been waiting for this call all night and only hoped the conversation went as he had imagined.

"Talk about it," Lil Sorrow answered. He listed as the person on the other end of the phone spoke, nodding occasionally. "You know you ain't even gotta ask me twice," he said smiling into the phone. He was about to end the call but the person on the other end wasn't done. "What? Tell that nigga ain't nobody smoking in his bitch's whip," he lied, sparking the blunt. He knew that the owner of the car hated people smoking, but they should've considered that before having him babysit for the last couple of hours.

After ending the call, Lil Sorrow got out of the car, burning blunt pinched between his lips. He was sixteen, but had the swagger of a grown man as he ambled toward the trunk of the car, dark jeans hanging off his ass, butt of his .380 slightly visible in his back pocket. He gave a casual look around before popping the trunk. Inside it, bound, gagged, and wedged between a case of water and a gallon jug of motor oil, was Pain's welcome-home present: Cassandra's nephew Ralphie. Case had had Sorrow and Tyriq snatch him while he took Pain shopping. Lil Sorrow had just been waiting for the word that would decide his fate. He took a deep pull from his blunt before flicking the ashes on Ralphie. "Last stop, fuck nigga. Everybody off the train."

PART III
DUSK

CHAPTER 17

It took a couple of weeks, but things had finally managed to go back to normal at Uncle Joe's place. Well, *normal* wasn't quite accurate. Things were never normal in that place. It was just less fucked-up as usual. After the incident with Birdie and Ted, Passion noticed some changes around the house. Passion wasn't sure what Bo had said to Uncle Joe after they had gotten into it, but whatever it was brought about some changes in him as well as their lifestyle. Uncle Joe was less of an asshole, not jumping down the girls' throats for every little thing. He was still no walk in the park, but he became slightly easier to deal with. After the time with Ted, he never touched Birdie again. In fact, he treated her like his new favorite, not tripping when she slacked on chores and coming in with little gifts for her from time to time. Some might've said that his new treatment of her was out of guilt, but Passion knew that guilt didn't live anywhere in that black heart of his. If anything, he was probably afraid of what would happen if word ever got out that he'd developed a taste for children. Joe fucking young girls was nothing new, but Birdie was practically a baby.

Probably the biggest change was that Uncle Joe no longer allowed tricks to come to the house to spend money. Everything was outcalls. Zeta and a steady rotation of new girls handled most of those. Sometimes Claire would go out with them, but not too often. Joe kept her and the younger girls in the house, busy helping him with his new primary hustle, which was now drugs.

Uncle Joe had his hands in a few different income streams, from extortion to running girls. They all brought in money, but his bread and butter had always been whores. He sold drugs through his young boys, but not on a large scale. It was just a few ounces here and there. He'd always claimed that the business of drugs was too risky to go all-in, but somewhere along the line he must've changed his mind, because now he was moving weight. No one was quite sure what had made him take on a bigger role in the drug business. One day he had come home and dropped a duffle bag full of coke on the table and announced that the family was expanding their operation. He had Bo teach Passion and the other girls how to cut the drugs, while she handled his street distribution. Joe was handling so much coke that sometimes they would be up all night, mixing and packaging the stuff.

While the other girls were happy to be seeing the extra money, Passion was still leery. You didn't go from selling a few ounces here and there to becoming the Snowman overnight. How had Joe gotten his hands on such a big bag seemingly out of nowhere? Passion didn't trust Uncle Joe, or his magic bag of snow, any further than she could throw either one of them, but she wasn't dumb enough to turn down the money he was paying his little helpers. Joe was the devil, but that money would be her angel of mercy. Between what she was stacking working for him, and the income tax check she had gotten in the mail from working at the diner, she would have enough to follow through with Juju's plan. If it worked, then she would finally be able to put Uncle Joe and his little shop of horrors behind her.

Her daydreaming took her back to the backyard party and the guy she had met. Pain, that had been his name. He had been on her mind quite a bit lately. More out of curiosity than anything else. From the few minutes she kicked it with him, he appeared to be smart, warm, and funny as hell. Those were all the qualities a woman could ask for, but she knew from watching Uncle Joe that men always showed you what you wanted to see before revealing what you had actually signed up for. She had heard too many stories of women getting roped in to be broken down to bite just because the bait was enticing.

The man who called himself Pain was a gangster, to be sure. Not even for the fact that he had been splashed with another man's blood at the time of their meeting, but the fact that he had managed to inflict harm on someone in a spot like that and not get bounced out on his ass, or worse. He was obviously someone of note in the ever-rotating circle of thieves, killers, and no-goodniks, but there was something about him that just didn't fit. He was the perfectly sculpted and polished circle trying not to stand out in a room full of jagged edges. Passion felt it from their first word exchange. His power . . . his grace. Pain was a king who had yet to don his crown, and in a perfect world she might've entertained him and allowed herself to see what it felt like for a man to love her properly, but the world she lived in was anything but perfect. It would've been easy to give in to what he was after and risk dulling his light with her bullshit, but instead Passion let him go so that one day he might shine. She wasn't worthy and he didn't deserve it.

"Girl, you gonna sit there daydreaming or finish putting them packages together? I told you I got somebody waiting on them." Bo brought Passion out of her moment of self-deprecation.

"Sorry," Passion offered and went back to what she was doing. On the table in front of her was a Tupperware bowl full of Ecstasy pills, which she had been sorting and putting into smaller plastic baggies for the last twenty minutes. The E-pills were something else Joe had been selling along with the coke. Those were more popular with the kids her age.

"You okay?" Bo asked.

"Yeah, why?"

"Because usually when I get on you for dragging your feet you give me some lip behind it," Bo said.

"Nah, just lost in my own head." Passion downplayed it.

"That's a dangerous place to be, stuck in your own head, that is."

"Seems like that's the only place I can find my peace," Passion replied. She finished bagging the pills then dropped the smaller bags into a ziplock before handing them to Bo. "If y'all don't need nothing else from me, I'm gonna head out for a while."

"Where you off to?" Bo questioned.

"Nowhere, just to hang out with Juju."

"Oh, I thought you might've been heading across town to cash your income tax check," Bo said, much to Passion's surprise. She had been extra careful when she got the check, meeting the mailman in the lobby when it came so that nobody knew she had it. The last thing she needed was Uncle Joe trying to confiscate her money. "Girl, don't look so surprised. You know that I know everything that comes in and out of this house. Don't worry, I ain't gonna tell your Uncle Joe. That's your money. You earned it, so spend it how you see fit. Just make sure you put something up for a rainy day."

"I will," Passion assured her.

"You seen Birdie? I asked her to clean the bathroom and it never got done."

"She was in the bedroom lying down the last I checked. She came home from school early. Said she wasn't feeling too good," Passion explained.

"That girl has been dragging ass around here for the last few weeks. I don't know what's gotten into Birdie lately. Seems like when she ain't sleeping or smoking weed she spends all her time chasing behind that boy. She think I ain't hip to her creeping out of here in the wee hours to meet up with him. She better not bring her ass in here pregnant, because we can barely feed the mouths we got here now, let alone add another one to it."

"Birdie is too smart for that. Besides, I always make sure she has condoms," Passion told Bo. Passion always kept a supply of condoms, which she got from the clinic every week or so. She wasn't getting much action so she mostly gave them out to Birdie and the other girls to make sure were always strapped while they were turning tricks. Zeta was the only one who saw fit to thumb her nose at the generic condoms, claiming that her pussy was allergic to certain types of latex. That probably contributed to why Zeta had caught at least two STDs that Passion was aware of.

"I hope so, Passion," Bo continued. "I've seen plenty of smart girls become fools for good dick."

"She wouldn't be the only fool for love living under this roof," Passion said under her breath.

"Best watch that mouth of yours before you let it walk you into a wall, young lady," Bo warned. In response, Passion rolled her eyes. Bo dropped the bag Passion had handed her onto the table and leaned in so that she and Passion were almost nose to nose. "Roll them eyes at me again and bet I snatch them out your head."

Passion looked down at the table.

"That's what I thought." Bo sat back up. "Passion, I know you're still in your feelings about what happened to Birdie, but how long are we gonna drag this out? I done got on Joe and he gave me his word that nothing like that will ever happen again."

"And you trust Uncle Joe's word?" Passion asked.

"No, but I trust the fact that he's too afraid of me cutting his throat in his sleep. That's what I promised him if he ever jumped that far out of character again with one of the young women in this house."

"Uncle Joe makes a lot of promises, but doesn't always keep them," Passion replied.

"This one he will. I know you were mad at me for letting it go down, and in truth I was mad at myself. I should've never allowed them to put Birdie in that position. That's something I'm going to have to carry. I can't change what was, but I can do something about what will be."

"I hear you," Passion said disbelievingly. She finished packaging the drugs and began cleaning off the table. She had just enough time to take a quick shower and change before heading out to meet Juju. She was about to head to the bedroom when Bo stopped her.

"You're better than this," Bo declared.

Passion measured the declaration before responding. "You're right. I'm just disappointed in myself that it took me this long to realize it."

When Passion entered the bedroom, she found Birdie lying on her little daybed with the blankets pulled up to her chin. She appeared to be sleeping, but from the fluttering of her eyelids Passion knew that she was only pretending. "It's only me."

Birdie's lids slowly opened and she gave Passion a lazy smile. "Hey, Passion, I wasn't sleeping. Just dozing. Can't get no proper sleep with Claire's ass running in and out all day, or Bo tasking me to do chores all damn day."

"You need to have your ass up doing something instead of waiting out the days," Passion said sharper than she'd meant to.

Birdie sat up. "Did I do something to piss you off?"

Passion looked to Birdie. Her eyes were wide with concern, water dancing in the corners and threatening to fall at the slightest hint that she had run afoul of Passion. Birdie could be overly sensitive when it came to her, and Passion often had to remind herself to measure her words when chastising her when she did something wrong. That day, she just didn't have the time, so she fed it to her straight. "No, Birdie, I'm not pissed at you. Just a little disappointed. Since when did you abandon your dreams of getting out of this place?"

"I haven't, Passion; I'm still working on them. I want to finish school and escape just like we always talk about," Birdie said.

"Kinda hard to do when you'd rather lay on your ass getting high, instead of focusing on your future."

Birdie lowered her eyes in shame. "You know I ain't been feeling good lately. Been real tired and ain't got no energy."

"Maybe because those pills you've started popping are keeping you up all night. It's kind of hard to fall asleep when you're always rolling off Molly," Passion said, much to Birdie's surprise. The younger girl opened her mouth to reply, but Passion knew that whatever would come out next would be a lie, so she waved her silent. "Please don't make me think less of you by trying to spin me some bullshit, and respect me enough to keep it one hundred."

Birdie looked up at her shamefully, lie pursed on her lips even after she had been warned. She could lie to anyone without thinking twice except Passion. "What gave it away?"

"You did, just this second." Passion sat on the bed beside her. "I started suspecting when I noticed you sleeping less and hardly eating anymore. Always running around swigging orange juice like you got a vitamin-C deficiency or something. I tried to tell myself that maybe you're under some stress, but stress don't do that to your pupils." She tipped Birdie's chin and looked into her eyes. The blacks were like little pinpoints in a sea of brown.

"It ain't that deep." Birdie pulled her face away. "I clip a few pills whenever we package them up for Uncle Joe. I drop once in a while when I'm feeling down or need a quick pick-me-up. Most times me and Junior split the pills, if Claire don't want some, but I hardly ever do a whole one by myself."

Passion shook her head sadly. "Damn, am I the only one in this bitch who ain't getting high off the supply? I knew from the minute Uncle Joe walked in here with that magic bag that it would bring as much trouble as it did profit. From here on out, that shit stops. You hear me?"

"Yeah," Birdie said unconvincingly. She went to get back under the blanket, but Passion took hold of her arm and gave her a little shake.

"I ain't playing with you, Birdie. I'll crack your head wide-open if it'll keep your ass from turning into a zombie like them kids we see on Lexington by the train station. Promise me, no more pills!"

"Okay, I promise! Now turn me loose!" Birdie winced. Passion released her grip. Birdie examined her arm where Passion had grabbed her and a bruise was already starting to form.

"I'm sorry," Passion said, seeing that she had hurt her friend. "Birdie, I know it ain't easy living in this hellhole, and sometimes we all need a little something to numb us. Lord knows I'm guilty of drowning my sorrows with cheap liquor sometimes, but I don't need you crawling so far down the rabbit hole that I can't reach you to pull you back out. You and me are all we got in this world, feel me?"

Birdie nodded.

"Well, not that it makes it any better, but I'm glad to know that it's the pills that got you laying around like a wet log. Bo thought you might be pregnant," Passion laughed. Birdie did not. "Birdie? I know damn well you weren't stupid enough to let Junior knock your ass up."

"Calm down, Passion. I just ain't been feeling too good. I think I'm coming down with something. My stomach's been sour and certain things I eat I can't keep down. I know for sure I ain't knocked up though, because I got two pregnancy tests from the corner store and they both came back negative."

"The same corner store that sells old meat at a discount? Ain't nothing in that store credible, especially no pregnancy test. Why would you even need to take one? What happened to all the condoms I gave you?" Passion pressed her.

"Me and Junior always use them when we do it, but . . ." Birdie's words trailed off.

"But what? Did y'all slipup?" Passion pressed her.

"No, me and Junior were always real careful because neither of us want no babies before we're done with school. I think something might've happened that day with Uncle Joe and Teddy," Birdie confessed.

"You let one of them old niggas run up in you raw?" Passion couldn't believe what she was hearing.

"I didn't let anybody do anything. I mean we had condoms. I know for sure, because I grabbed some from your stash. I was drunk so some of what happened is a little fuzzy. I remember Uncle Joe had me bent over and when he got done I was wetter than normal down there. When I used the bathroom I thought I saw a piece of the rubber in the toilet, but it could've been tissue. I asked Uncle Joe if maybe it broke on him and he swears that he was strapped up the whole time," Birdie recounted.

"No, no, no . . ." Passion said over and over with her head in her hands. A thousand different scenarios played out in her mind and none of them were good.

"I'm not pregnant, Passion. I'm sure it's just the flu or something, like I said. I'm gonna quit the pills, and rest for a few days. I'll be fine. I promise." She rubbed Passion's back as if she was the one who now needed consoling.

Passion raised her head and looked into Birdie's eyes. Even after all she had been through there was still so much innocence in them.

If it was the last thing she did she would try and help Birdie salvage whatever was left of her childhood. "I gotta get you to a doctor."

"For what? I told you I already . . ."

"I know, took two of those bootleg-ass corner store pregnancy tests," Passion cut her off. "Not good enough. You need to see a real doctor and let them administer a test and give you a full STD workup. They should still be able to get you in at the free clinic downtown. They don't close until 6 PM."

"Passion, don't you think you're overreacting?" Birdie couldn't understand why Passion was acting like the world was coming to an end over a little slipup.

"Me overreacting would be stealing Bo's gun out of her purse and blowing that old pervert Joe's head off for touching you. Before it's all said and done I still may revisit that plan, but I'll cross that bridge when I come to it. For now, you need to get your ass to the clinic."

CHAPTER 18

One and done . . . the words danced across Pain's mind as he blew smoke rings at the ceiling. He was lounging in a king-size hotel bed, enjoying the softness of the high-thread-count sheets. They were far nicer on the skin than the Dollar Tree spreads he had on his twin bed back in the projects. The flat-screen television was turned to the twenty-four-hour news station, but the sound was muted. On the screen an anchor was soundlessly reporting on the goings-on in and around the city. On the nightstand behind him sat an empty bottle of Moët, and beside it a pint of Hennessey that had long been drained of its contents. Beside those sat two abandoned glasses, one smeared with plum lipstick. The sight brought back memories of the events that had landed him in the hotel the night before and a smile crossed his lips.

Careful not to wake his sleeping companion, Pain reached over and grabbed his glass. There were still remnants of the Henny and champagne concoction he had been sipping on, which he downed. The glass had been sitting out half the night, so its contents were piss-warm, but Pain didn't care. He was feeling like himself . . . his true self, for the first time in a long time, and he just wanted to bask in it for as long as he could. "One and done," he repeated the promise he had made to himself with a chuckle. One job and he was out, or so had been the plan. From the first time Pain had felt the weight of a gun in his hand after so many years, he knew that it would be a promise hard kept. The thing Pain had forgotten about the heist was, it was very much like a gourmet potato chip, you couldn't stop at just one.

To Pain's credit, he had genuinely intended to keep the promise he had made to himself and his grandmother. He was a changed man now, walking the straight and narrow, but that was before he found himself at a fork in the road. The first domino to fall happened the morning after his little scrap with Lee. He could remember waking up sour as hell that day. His knuckles were scuffed, swollen, and his chin was bruised from the sucker punch. The last time he had been in a scuffle had been in prison when he poked Brute up, and the rest of his bid had been smooth sailing, so he had almost forgotten what the aftermath of battle felt like. Thankfully, none of his injuries were so severe that they couldn't be taken care of with a hot shower and some rest.

That day was to be a big one for Pain. He was meeting his new PO for the first time, and from there he had to check in at the re-entry program that was supposed to hook him up with a job. Pain wasn't looking forward to either, but he would suck it up and do what he had to do. Ms. Pearl had insisted on cooking him breakfast that morning. He told her that she didn't have to, but she insisted. "I ain't never sent you off to the first day of school without a hot meal, so I fosho ain't about to send you off to your first day of work with an empty belly," had been her words. He didn't really have the time or appetite, but to refuse her would surely hurt the old woman's feelings. Reluctantly, Pain agreed.

Ms. Pearl's fridge was on life support, so Pain had to run to the store and grab a few things. She offered her EBT card, but he refused. He still had a few dollars in his pocket from the day before. It wasn't much, but buying a dozen eggs and a pack of bacon wasn't going to break his bankroll. He took his time strolling up the avenue to the supermarket. He saw some heads that he recognized from the neighborhood, but for the most part the faces that now occupied the strip on which he had gained and lost over the years were foreign to him. Cats that didn't even know what the other side of the porch looked like were now all the way off it, and Pain felt somewhat the outsider.

He'd stopped briefly to chop it up with a guy who he used to buy his bootleg DVDs from, and spent fifteen minutes listening to him gripe about how streaming services were taking food off his table. Pain was half listening to the old hustler because his eyes were focused on the woman walking past him. She was a curvy young thing with neatly twisted locks. Pain knew the bounce of that ass when it was in motion. He'd seen it when Passion was walking toward the Uber that day. If it was indeed her and the universe saw fit to give him a second chance at something special, he didn't plan to squander it. This in mind, he fell in step beside the girl and touched her arm gently. When she turned to him he found himself confronting not the object of his thoughts over the past few days, but a close facsimile. She wasn't her.

He continued on his way to the local supermarket. The store, now called Bravo, had been in the neighborhood almost as long as Pain had. The awning out front had sported several different names over the past couple of years, but for the most part the people who worked there remained the same.

As soon as he stepped into the store he was greeted by a familiar face: Lewis Rudd. Lewis was older than Pain, but not quite as old as Goodie or his mom had been. He was a product of the generation somewhere in between. He played around in the streets a little, but never too heavy. Lewis was a working stud and never tried to paint himself as anything else, which is why the street dudes respected him. Pain could remember back when Lewis stocked shelves in the supermarket for five bucks an hour, but he now sported a name tag highlighted with the words REGIONAL MANAGER.

"Percy, been a long time! How you?" He greeted Pain with a warm smile and a firm handshake.

Pain offered a shrug. "I've been better, and I've been worse. Never complained either way. I see you're moving up in the world, huh?" He playfully plucked Lewis's name tag.

"Yeah, they got me managing this location as well as three other ones around the city," Lewis said proudly.

"That's good shit, man. Good shit." Pain gave him dap. He meant it, too. He was glad to see that Lewis was doing well for himself and hadn't fallen into the bullshit.

"So, what brings you over this way so early? Your grandmother send you?" Lewis asked.

"Yeah, I gotta grab a few things for her. She insists on making me breakfast like I'm still thirteen and off to middle school," Pain joked.

"Oh, I thought she sent you for . . . never mind. Go ahead and do your shopping. I'll chat with you later," Lewis told him. There was obviously something else on his mind.

"What?" Pain noticed the shift in his face.

"It's nothing. Really." Lewis downplayed it.

"Must be something if you brought it up. Spit it out, man. You know I don't do the guessing games," Pain told him.

"Well . . . it's just that, I thought your grandmother had sent you around to settle her tab," Lewis said with a hint of embarrassment. "Your grandma gets her stamps every month, but the state barely gives these elders enough to feed themselves for an entire month, so I let her pull up and grab what she wants when things get tight and pay it back whenever she can. Thing is, unbeknownst to me, when these new people took over this franchise they installed a new system that accounts for every dollar coming and going. Been in place for a few months now. The receipts not matching up with the inventory has raised some questions and there's only so much I can blame on shoplifters, since this is the only location taking the hits. Percy, if it was just about me I wouldn't care. I love Ms. Pearl, you know that. It's just . . ."

"Say less," Pain cut him off. "How much my grandmother into you for?" He pulled out his bankroll and started flipping through it.

"Four hundred for this month and last," Lewis informed him.

"Nigga, what?" Pain stopped his counting. "My grandmother is about a hundred and ten pounds and you trying to tell me she ate up four hundred dollar's worth of food in two months, outside of what she spent in stamps? Why I feel like you trying to play me like I won't run up in yo shit?"

"Pain, you know I would never. I love my life too much to try and bullshit you." Lewis held his hands up in surrender. "Quiet as kept, it ain't Ms. Pearl's appetite that ran that bill up, but her big heart."

"What you mean?"

"Well, I ain't trying to get up in Ms. Pearl's business, but you know she's got a soft spot for every joker with a sob story. One of my cashiers told me she was in here the other day with crackhead Larry, buying food for him and them kids he don't half take care of no way. Knowing him, he probably ain't did nothing but went up on the ave and sold whatever she blessed him with to get a blast."

Pain shook his head in frustration. Ever since he could remember, his grandmother was always taking care of grown folks who didn't deserve her kindness, including him. He peeled off four hundred dollars from the six or seven he had left, and shoved the money into Lewis's hand. "I'll take care of Larry's thirsty ass when I catch up with him. As far as my grandma, no more credit. I got her from here."

"You're a good dude, Percy. I hate to even come at you with it, but I need this gig. You know how it is, right?" Lewis held out his hand to give Pain dap.

"Whatever, nigga." Pain bumped past him and went into the supermarket.

Pain grabbed the items he needed from the store and headed back to the apartment. His grandmother chatted him up while she prepared his breakfast. Pain offered muttered responses here and there, but his mind was elsewhere. It took everything in him not to get on her about her letting Larry take advantage, but he knew it wouldn't do much outside aggravating him further. Ms. Pearl's heart was a rest haven for the downtrodden, overlooked, and lazy alike. Your stamps didn't come yet and you needed a little something extra to tide you over until the first? Ms. Pearl got you. You need some carfare to get to that job interview? Go knock on Ms. Pearl's door. Even if she knew you were running game and just wanted to get high or indulge in some other vice, she'd still give you a few dollars just so you wouldn't be out stealing for it. Ms. Pearl was one of the last of a dying breed, the Big Mamas.

Ms. Pearl slapped together a breakfast consisting of eggs, bacon, and pancakes made from scratch. They took longer that way, but Ms. Pearl didn't believe in pancake mix, or any other kind of mix that couldn't be made with just a little flour and some love. It was not only the best breakfast, but the best meal Pain had had in years. It was a far cry from powdered eggs and bologna fried on a hot plate. He was so full when he got up from the table that all he wanted to do was lie down and take a nap, but he had things to do.

When Pain came out of his building he was both full and irritated. His bankroll was dwindling, he didn't have anything lined up to replenish it just yet, and his granny's bills were still hanging over his head like an executioner's blade. He needed some wreck to relieve some of that frustration. He needed to hit something or someone. In a perfect world he'd have run into Larry's bum ass and thrown him a beating for taking advantage of his grandmother, but it wasn't to be. However, he did run into another familiar face on his way to the subway station.

A local who went by the name of Ron was coming through the projects with a young girl. Ron was at least a year or two older than Pain, but the girl he was walking with was only about sixteen. For as long as Pain had known Ron he'd always had a thing for young girls, which is why he didn't fuck with him like that. Pain kept his head down, pretending not to see Ron, but of course Ron went out of his way to speak.

"Oh, shit! Is that my nigga, Pain?" Ron shouted, and greeted him with a toothy grin. He made a big production of his greeting, doing a two-step in place before trying to lean in for a hug. Pain kept him at arm's length.

"Sup?" Pain greeted him flatly.

"You, sometimes me," Ron replied. "How long you been home?"

"A min," Pain said in a tone that most people would've taken as a cue that he wasn't in the mood to talk, but not Ron.

"About time we got some real niggas moving around the hood again," Ron continued. "I was just telling my shorty the other day how these young niggas who running around doing their thing now ain't built like we were. We the last of a dying breed, ya heard?"

"Yeah, I hear you," Pain said. He just wanted to make his appointment and didn't have time for Ron's bullshit. He was about to brush Ron off and keep it moving, when he noticed the chain hanging from the young girl's neck: white gold with two hearts hanging from the end. It was the same necklace that had been snatched from Passion's neck on the subway. "That's a nice piece of jewelry, shorty. Where'd you get it?"

"Oh, Ron copped this for me to celebrate our one-year anniversary. It's real gold, too," the girl said proudly.

"Is that right? I got a special lady friend that I'm trying to get something nice for, too. You mind telling me where you copped, Ron?" Pain gave him a knowing look.

"Oh . . . um . . . I got a connect on Canal Street that gave me a good deal. If you want, I can plug you in," Ron offered.

"That'd be cool, but I got a better idea. How about I give you two hundred bucks for that one?" Pain pointed to the lockets.

"C'mon, Pain. How am I gonna sell you something that I had custom made for my lady? That wouldn't be player on my part," Ron said nervously. He'd really purchased the necklace from some young dudes who were hawking hot items on 125th Street, but he couldn't tell her that.

"Player?" Pain laughed. "I hear you talking, my nigga, and I'm gonna let you have that. You wanna negotiate? I'm with that." He draped his arm around Ron's neck and led him out of earshot of the girl. "Now, your little friend might believe you gave enough of a shit about her to truly invest on something heartfelt, but you and I both know that necklace is as hot as a firecracker."

"Pain, I—"

"Let me stop you before you let that baby-licking mouth of yours turn this into something this ain't gotta be," Pain cut him off. "Where you buy your slum to trick these young girls into giving your depraved ass some pussy ain't my concern. Today, you just happen to have the misfortune of baiting your twisted-ass hook with something that belongs to a friend of mine. That being said, you can take this money and save face or I can take your face." He dangled the two hundred dollars.

"Take it off," Ron told the girl in a shaky voice.

"What? No! You bought this for me!" the girl protested. She had already been flexing with the small necklace on Instagram.

"Bitch, I said take it off!" Ron snapped.

For the first time since she had been dealing with Ron, she saw something in his eyes that she hadn't ever before: fear. It was at that moment she realized the seriousness of the situation. Without saying another word, she undid the chain and handed it to Pain.

"Thank you." Pain accepted the necklace. "Y'all enjoy the rest of your day." He tossed the money in Ron's face, leaving him standing there embarrassed.

Pain continued his walk to the train station, grinning. What had started out as a not-so-good day was looking to turn around. A part of him felt bad about muscling the necklace from the girl, but she'd get over it. If she didn't? It wasn't his problem. He turned the lockets over in his hand, examining them. On the backs were inscribed two names: GEORGE and EDNA. Who were they? And what did they mean to Passion? This was a question he would ask when he returned the piece to the girl. His only dilemma now was how? He knew nothing about her and didn't have anything to go on other than her name. But it was a start.

Pain ended up arriving forty minutes late for his scheduled appointment with his new parole officer. This was due to a homeless person who decided he wanted to light a cigarette on the train, and got aggressive when someone suggested he put it out. The police were there to greet him at the next stop, and that turned into an incident. Seems that there was more than tobacco in whatever he was smoking and he turned into a barbarian when the police tried to arrest him. To the homeless guy's credit, he gave the first two cops on the scene straight hell. He even managed to wrest the nightstick from one of them. When their backup arrived they put a good whipping on the man, which caused a delay with the subway service while they sorted it out. This forced Pain to take the bus the rest of the way downtown, and he swore that the driver was purposely getting caught at every other red light.

Pain finally made it to the sixth floor of the Department of Parole. He had run all the way from the bus stop as he didn't want to be any later than he already was. Thankfully it wasn't that crowded. The way he'd heard it, the building had only recently started receiving parolees in person again since the pandemic had everything shut down. During the outbreak they had to resort to Zoom calls or phone-ins for those who didn't have access to the internet. The officers weren't even allowed to make home visits during those times. Pain wished that he'd come home just a few months sooner so he could've been in that number that didn't have to deal with the bullshit of reporting in.

He ended up waiting about an hour before his name was called. Not because there were so many people ahead of him, but because the staff seemed more interested in doing everything but their jobs. There was more socializing between the employees than anything else. His new parole officer, Ms. Day, was hardly what he had imagined. Back when Pain had been on juvenile probation, most of the officers who worked in the building were older ladies, bookish looking, hard, or somewhere in between. Ms. Day was none of the above. She was young—older than Pain, but not by much—and attractive. A pretty brown-skinned girl who wore her hair in a short cut. Her face was made up, not heavily, just a bit of lipstick and some eyeliner. She was chewing a piece of gum and when she blew out a small bubble, Pain couldn't help but to zero in on her lips. They were full and soft. He wondered to himself what they would taste like if she let him suck on them.

For as sweet as Ms. Day looked on the outside, her insides were all sour. When she spoke to Pain, her words were short and to the point. "I'm gonna make this short and sweet because I got a hair appointment in an hour, so I'm trying to get y'all out my face as soon as possible. I need to see you twice a month and I expect you to be on time."

"My fault. There was a situation on the train and—"

"Your excuses don't concern me. You playing with my time does. You're late, you get kicked to the back of the line and stay there until I say otherwise. Now, from your records," she flipped through the folder on her desk, which contained both Pain's juvenile and adult mug shots, "this isn't your first time at the rodeo, but I play a little different. You miss a check-in, I'm violating you. You piss dirty, I'm violating you. I ain't no babysitter, so what you do in your spare time doesn't concern me so long as you don't get caught and cause me to have to fill out a bunch of paperwork. You wanna trick yourself back into prison—"

"I know, you're gonna violate me." Pain finished her sentence with a playful smile.

Ms. Day scowled. "Don't get cute, Mr. Wells. That pretty smile might work on the hood rats in whatever slum you crawled out of, but it'll get you nowhere with me. Get it?"

"My bad. Just trying to lighten the mood," Pain said apologetically. Ms. Day was proving to be a real bitch.

She eyeballed him for a beat longer to make sure her message had been received, before pulling a sticky-note loose from a pink pad and scribbling a name and address on it. "Go to this address and ask for Mr. Carson. He runs the job program and should be able to help you with gainful employment. You got a résumé, Mr. Wells?"

"Never really had use for one," Pain said honestly. The closest thing he ever had to a job was the brief time he worked at the butcher shop and that had been a hook up, not a situation where he had to apply.

"Of course not. You've probably been in the streets all your life and never had a job outside of stressing your mother out," Ms. Day said accusingly. "Doesn't matter. I'm sure Mr. Carson can find something for you to do. What? I don't know, nor care, so long as you're gainfully employed. Do you have any questions?"

"Nah, you've showed me everything I need to know," Pain said, not bothering to hide his growing dislike for Ms. Day. He wasn't sure how he was going to make it through the length of his parole term under Ms. Day before she provoked him to do or say something that would likely get him sent back to prison.

"Good, then that means you and I should get along just fine." Ms. Day matched his tone, letting him know that the feeling was mutual. She reached into one of her drawers and pulled out a small plastic container. "Drop some piss, bring it back, and be about your way," she dismissed him.

After leaving Ms. Day's office, Pain found himself back on the subway. This time he was headed north. The address she had given him was deep in the Bronx, near the Hunts Point area. At one time that had been one of his favorite hunting grounds. The section was lousy and filled with strip clubs and pockets of stray prostitutes, which meant that there was always cash around. Pain would play the strip clubs, laying in the cut and watching to see who was spending what or had the flashiest jewelry. He was always able to catch one of them slipping. At some point he didn't have to go inside the clubs anymore. He'd just bless one of the dancers with a few dollars and they would tip him off as to who was holding the biggest bag that night. Once they came out of the spot tipsy and horny they'd be greeted by the barrel of Pain's 9mm. Pain feasted on all the strip clubs and their patrons. Sometimes he would even hit the same spots two or three times in one night. He was brazen like that. When the clubs started getting hip and things got hot for Pain, he turned his predatory sights to the prostitutes and their Johns. Robbing the tricks never yielded as big a bag as the strip club licks, but if he hit enough people a night the money started to add up.

The re-entry program Ms. Day sent him to was run out of an old trailer that sat at the rear of a junkyard. Pain looked around in disgust as he navigated the heaps of trash and broken-down cars. The place smelled like the graveyard, which it probably was if the area was still anything like Pain had remembered. It wasn't unheard of for bodies in various states of decay to be found hidden inside old junkers, or buried in shallow graves on the properties. It was sometimes weeks or more before some of the victims were discovered. By then, between being out in the elements and the rats, there usually wasn't enough left of them for police to trace back to the killer. Pain knew this from first-hand experience.

The inside of the shed smelled nearly as bad as the outside. The smell of mold filled the air, coupled with that of food left sitting out. He found Mr. Carson sitting in the back office, which was only slightly larger than a bathroom. Mr. Carson was hands down the fattest white man Pain had ever laid eyes on. He weighed at least four hundred pounds, with a sack of loose pink skin that hung from his jaws down the front of his shirt. It made him look like a pelican. He sat behind a desk with part of his belly hanging over the top, chomping on a jumbo-size bacon cheeseburger that looked to be more bacon that burger. He was just taking another bite, ketchup dripping down his chin and grease squirting from the burger onto some papers on the desk, when he noticed Pain standing in the doorway. He cast his beady eyes on Pain and swallowed the burger without bothering to chew. "Help you?"

"Percy Wells. Ms. Day sent me over," Pain introduced himself. He considered extending his hand to shake, but decided against it.

"Right," Mr. Carson said with a nod. He reluctantly placed his burger down before wiping his hands on the blue coveralls he was wearing. While Pain waited, he shuffled through one of the drawers in the desk until he came up with the one containing Pain's file. He thumbed through it briefly, getting grease on it but not seeming to care. "I see you just did time for drugs. Let me tell you straight off the bat that if you get caught with any of that shit on my yard I'll call the police on you."

"That won't be a problem, sir," Pain assured him.

"Good," Mr. Carson said before flipping through Pain's file again. "I don't see any résumé or job skills listed. What do you know how to do?"

"Anything that'll put a few dollars in my pocket and keep me off Ms. Day's shit list," Pain said honestly.

Mr. Carson studied Pain for a few seconds, before letting a smile form on his thin lips, exposing the tobacco-stained teeth behind them. "That's exactly what I wanted to hear. You'll fit right in around here."

If by "fit right in" Mr. Carson meant that Pain would work like a slave for long hours, doing backbreaking work for low wages, he had hit the nail right on the head. He started Pain off where he started most new parolees, sorting trash. Pain was placed with a group of young men who would receive the trucks when they came in with junk. The cargo was emptied onto the lot and it was up to Pain to separate the junk accordingly: metal, wood, copper, etc. Everything went from the dumped pile into a separate pile of its like. The work was hard, disgusting, and in his onion, demeaning, but it kept him out of jail, so he suffered through it. His days started at 6 AM and ended at 6 PM. By the time Pain made it back to his grandmother's house most nights, he was too tired to eat, so he just crashed. Slave, sleep, repeat. That became his routine.

After being there for about a week, Mr. Carson discovered that Pain knew his way around an engine, so he pulled him off the sort pile and put him in the garage. That wasn't so bad. Pain mostly helped keep the yard's vehicles maintained, but he'd occasionally find himself performing repairs that Mr. Carson brought in after-hours. These repairs became his side hustle, amongst other things.

For the most part, Pain kept to himself. The other parolees and misfits weren't quite his cup of tea. There was one dude he became somewhat friendly with. They called him Sauce. He was a lanky kid who hailed from North Carolina, but had done time in New York for burglary. He had been working for Mr. Carson longer than any of them, so he knew the ins and outs better than most. Upon picking his brain, Pain discovered that Sauce was a genius at hacking alarm systems. He had gone to school to be an electrician, but got sidetracked by the need to put food on the table for his mother and little sisters back home. Sauce had been part of a team of heist men who tried to take off a jewelry store, but ended up being caught when the lookout got caught slipping and let one of the police get the drop on them. Pain knew all about going to prison over someone else's fuckup, so they bonded over that. It was from Sauce that Pain learned the junkyard was a front for a chop shop that Mr. Carson was running. He had a crew of amateur car thieves who would bring in stolen vehicles during the wee hours of the night, which the mechanics and body guys would strip down for parts to be shipped off to God knows where. Sauce claimed to make decent money on the side helping flip the stolen cars, and even offered to put a good word in for Pain, but he declined. Pain was just there to work his hours and present his PO with a check stub. Nothing extra.

Into his second week of working for Mr. Carson came the day Pain had been waiting for: payday! Through all the slaving, slick, borderline racist remarks from Mr. Carson, and treatment that certainly violated every labor law imaginable, Pain had managed to hold his head and not crash out. His reward was finally at hand. When the girl who worked for Mr. Carson came around handing out the envelopes containing the paychecks, Pain was hyped. His hands trembled with excitement when she made it to him. Pain found himself a private corner where he could savor the milestone accomplishment of his first paycheck. The fact that it came from doing something honest filled his chest with pride. He hadn't expected it to be much, because it was barely a minimum-wage job, but it was his. At the very least he'd be able to buy himself a couple of pairs of pants, maybe some shirts, and put some food in his granny's fridge. These were small things, but at the time they meant a great deal to him.

When Pain slid his paycheck out and his eyes landed on the dollar amount, all the joy and happiness he had been feeling immediately melted away. He scanned the check a second and third time before turning the envelope upside down to see if there had maybe been something else in it? There wasn't. Pain wasn't the sharpest knife in the drawer, but he knew math better than most and his check wasn't adding up. His first instinct had been to flip. One thing Pain didn't play about with was his paper. He had laid cats for less, and just as serious as he was about his money in the streets, it would be so in the working world. Then he thought about it. That wasn't how things worked. If he wanted to function in this new system of being a square, he had to play by its rules. If anything, it had probably been a clerical error because he was new and a conversation with Mr. Carson would get it sorted out.

Pain was hopeful when he stepped into Mr. Carson's office. The fat man was sitting back, sipping a tall can of beer with a straw, and watching something on his phone. Porn likely. When he saw Pain, he put the phone down and gave him his attention. "What's up, Wells?"

"Hey, Mr. Carson. I got my first paycheck." Pain held up the envelope. "Thanks."

"No problem, Wells. You're a hard worker, and I appreciate that. If we have five more like you then I'd be running a well-oiled company instead of a revolving door for felons and fuckups. No offense," Mr. Carson said apologetically.

"None taken," Pain assured him. "So, I was looking at my check and these numbers seem off. I've been working five days at twelve hours per day, sometimes more, at eight bucks an hour. I've worked here nearly two weeks, but there's only four hundred dollars here."

"And?" Mr. Carson asked, as if he still wasn't sure what Pain was getting at.

"Well, I'm about five hundred dollars short."

"You sure? Let me see that." Mr. Carson took the paycheck from Pain's hand and examined it. He pulled out a brown plastic calculator and started punching numbers with his pudgy fingers. He stared at the figure in contemplation as if finally realizing his mistake. "You know what, Wells? You're right. These numbers are off. I actually paid you thirty bucks too much. Since you're such a good worker, don't even sweat it. Think of it as sort of a bonus for having such a good first week." He handed the check back to him.

"Bruh, if this is your idea of a joke, I'm having a hard time finding it funny," Pain said, feeling his patience slip. It was short money, but it was his and he needed it.

"Nah, bruh," Mr. Carson mocked him. "This ain't no joke. Obviously ain't nobody explained to you the finer points of how this here arrangement works. See, employing boys like you comes with its fair share of risks. No risks are without their necessary rewards. We take a small taste off the top for our troubles. Think of them as taxes. The first bite always stings the worse, but from here on out it'll only be a nibble. You'll hardly miss it."

Pain just stood there glaring at the man in disbelief. He was running a line of bullshit down to Pain and expecting him to smile and accept it. "Fat man, I ain't never been extorted a day in my life and we ain't about to start now. You got me fucked up." He started toward Mr. Carson, but froze when he produced a gun.

"Let's not turn a mountain into a molehill." Mr. Carson waved the .22 at Pain. "I'll bust a cap in your ass and claim you tried to rob the joint. Who you think they gonna believe?"

"This is some bullshit!" Pain fumed.

"No, this is the game. I didn't make the rules, but I'll be damned if I don't cash in on them. Now you can get this money like it's coming to you, or quit and run the risk of your PO sending you back to the can over this shit."

"I don't think quitting a janky-ass job counts as a violation of my parole," Pain challenged. Ms. Day was a bitch, but even she couldn't hold him accountable on this one.

"It might when your PO is also getting a cut," Mr. Carson said, much to Pain's surprise. "Like I said, Mr. Wells. I didn't make the rules, I'm just cashing in on them."

Pain left Mr. Carson's office feeling like a sucker. The fat white man had pretty much told him to his face that he was getting extorted and dared him to do something about it. Blackbird would've probably shot the man for his show of disrespect, or at the very least broken his jaw, but all Percy could do was swallow his pride and leave the office with his tail between his legs and his check still short.

Going out like that made Pain physically ill. So much to the point where he barely made it out of the subway station before throwing up all over the sidewalk. People gawked as they passed him, hunched over with hands breached on his knees as he continued to dry heave. He could only imagine what he must've looked like, but in truth he didn't care. Mr. Carson had stripped away the last bit of pride he had brought home with him from prison. After a time, Pain was able to compose himself enough to stand with the confidence that there was nothing left in his stomach to expel. He turned and caught a glimpse of himself in the reflection of a store window. It was like seeing himself for the first time, and he couldn't say that he was happy with what stared back at him. On the outside, he was still Pain . . . still that dude. But on the inside, there was something missing. He couldn't see the part of himself that made him who he was, if that makes sense? Trying to navigate the new world he had chosen to explore was weighing on him. Pain was trying to do everything right, but it felt like he was the only one playing fair. From his crooked-ass parole officer to the crackheads still gaming his grandma, everyone had an angle. He was not opposed to change, but at what cost? One thing that became clear to him that day was, the life he was trying to create for himself couldn't be achieved without some help from the life he had left behind. Pain took his four-hundred-dollar paycheck and gave it one last look before crumpling it up and tossing it into the nearest trash can.

When Pain reported for his shift the next morning, he found the place in an uproar. Mr. Carson was waddling back and forth between his office and the junkyard, raging about something. It was the most Pain had ever seen the man move since he had been working there. He found Sauce standing off to the side with a few of the other mechanics, watching Mr. Carson's meltdown.

"Sup with the fat man?" Pain asked, taking up a position next to Sauce.

"Shit, man. It's all bad," Sauce said in his drawl. "Somebody broke in here and rode off with some shit that was already paid for, feel me?"

"Damn, any ideas on who did it? I know he got cameras all over this muthafucka."

Sauce shrugged. "I ain't fosho, but I know ol' boy been giving muthafuckas the pink slip all morning over it. Only reason my ass ain't on the block is because I happened to be in Brooklyn handling something else for him at the time. I'm happy for that, because I need this little bullshit job to satisfy my PO."

"You ain't never lied." Pain gave him dap and then headed in Mr. Carson's direction.

Mr. Carson was in the middle of a profanity-laced tirade the likes of which Pain hadn't seen before. "What?" he snapped when he noticed Pain. The vein in his forehead was so far popped out that it looked like it would bust at any second. He was clearly having a terrible morning, and little did he know that Pain was about to make it worse.

"Ain't nothing, boss. I'm good, but you stomping around like somebody stole your girlfriend." Pain faked concern.

"Worse, they stole my product. Couple of guys crept in here last night and snatched two cars that I was supposed to be holding onto for somebody. Little fuckers think they're slick, but I got them on camera. They think because they were wearing masks, I won't find out who they are, but they got video experts for this kind of shit. I'm gonna spare no expense to find out who did this!" Mr. Carson vowed.

"Well, maybe I can save you a few coins. I was one of them," Pain revealed.

Mr. Carson's face froze as his brain made sure that it was correctly processing what Pain had just said to him. "You took my shit."

"I sure did," Pain confessed. "You got a good thing going on here, Carson. Could be better, though. That being said, me and a few of my guys decided to help start the process of making improvements by doing a little housecleaning."

"You ungrateful, piece of shit little nigger! I give you a job and you repay me by stealing? I'm gonna kick your ass and then have Ms. Day throw your ass back in a fucking cage, just where you belong!" If Mr. Carson had been angry before seeing Pain, he was ballistic after. His figure loomed imposingly over the smaller Pain, like some great beast about to devour a lamb. But then something unexpected happened.

Pain's response to Mr. Carson's threat was an open-hand slap. It wasn't just a regular slap, but one he put his hips into and which empowered his palm with all the rage that had been mounting in him since coming home from prison. Mr. Carson blinked twice before collapsing over his desk, knocking it over and spilling the contents onto the floor. "Who the fuck you think you're talking to?" He stood over Mr. Carson and drew his hand back as if he were going to hit him again, causing the man to cringe. Pain now had his attention and his heart.

"Boy, have you lost your damn mind?" Mr. Carson held his jaw and stared up at Pain fearfully.

"Nah, man. I've actually found it," Pain said with a sneer.

Mr. Carson scuttled to the overturned desk and snatched one of the drawers open. His hand searched frantically inside for something that wasn't there.

"You looking for this?" Pain produced the .22 Mr. Carson had threatened him with the day before and pointed it at him. "I took this too when we came in here and robbed you."

"Don't kill me!" Mr. Carson raised his hand fearfully.

"I'd thought about greasing your ass just for playing with me and my bread, but then I got to thinking. You're worth more to me alive than dead. At least right this second."

"What do you want?" Mr. Carson asked, uncertain that he wanted the answer.

"Let's start with a little respect." Pain lowered the gun. "And we can end with a piece of the action. Like I said, you got a decent little thing going on, and with my help we can really pull a few dollars out of this dump. I got a crew of young niggas who can run more cars through here faster than your guys can hack them up. And I'm not talking about the bullshit you've got sixteen-year-olds snatching off random street corners. I'm talking about some high-end whips. The best part is, this little arrangement is just between us. No need to cut your partner, Ms. Day, in on what we got going on. Let her keep eating off that saucer. I'm offering you a plate."

This got Mr. Carson's attention. The cars that came through his yard weren't always the highest-end, but it was all profit to him. He made enough money to keep his head above water from the current inventory they bought in, but he could be making a lot more with the kind of cars Pain would bring in. Still, what if this was all bullshit and Pain was just trying to get back at him for taking his money? "Bull-shit, Wells," he said. "For all I know you're just some ex-con trying to run a game on me, or worse, a snitch trying to jam me up." For all he knew this could've been a plan orchestrated by Ms. Day to see if he would be willing to cross her or not. It wouldn't be the first time she tried to send one of her snitches at him. The greedy bitch was always testing him.

"Blackbird," Pain corrected him. At first Mr. Carson didn't understand, but then a light of recognition went off in his head. "Your face tells me you've heard the name. You're a thief, and there isn't a thief in this city who isn't familiar with the right hand of the Outlaw Queen. If you know my name then you know my pedigree. I'm good at two things: turning a profit off shit that don't belong to me, and punishing my enemies. So, have I made an enemy this morning or a partner?" He extended his hand.

Mr. Carson studied Pain's hand for a long moment as if he thought it may have been a trick. He was indeed familiar with Blackbird. They had never met personally before this, but he knew enough of the man to know that he wasn't someone who bluffed. Mr. Carson looked from the extended hand to his office window, which gave him a view of the rest of the yard. He could see the men he employed trying to pretend that they weren't watching. He desperately tried to establish eye contact with at least one of them in hopes that they'd come to his rescue, but he would find no heroes amongst that lot. He'd had his foot on their necks for far too long. With little other choice, Mr. Carson shook his hand.

And just like that, Pain was back in the game.

As a part of Pain's new partnership with Mr. Carson, he would continue providing Pain with paystubs and kickbacks to Ms. Day. This would keep her out of Pain's hair and away from their new side business. He was eating again.

Because Pain had never been one to dine alone, he invited Tyriq and Lil Sorrow to the table. They were the ones who had helped him snatch the cars in the first place, so it was only right that he allow them to eat from the score. They were in charge of supplying Mr. Carson with the cars he needed, and in exchange Pain would split whatever he collected on his end, fifty-fifty. Of course, Case balked at Pain's generosity, pointing out that he could get the two youngsters to do the job for less than that, which was true, but Pain kept it at fifty-fifty. Part of the reason for this was because if he made the young men feel like they were vested in something instead of just hired help, they would work that much harder to protect their own interests. He was teaching them to be young bosses. Case didn't get that, which is why Pain had always been the leader of their group and not him. Besides, it had never been about the money for Pain. For as long his trigger fingers worked, money would come. Pain's hostile takeover of the chop shop had been about power.

"What you thinking so hard about, baby?" the female who had been sleeping next to Pain asked in a sleepy voice.

"The irony of life, love. That's all," Pain replied.

Lolo sat up, propping herself up on one elbow, and gave Pain a quizzical look. "Why do I feel like you always talk in riddles?"

"Nah, baby. I always say exactly what I mean. It only sounds like I'm speaking in riddles to those who don't know how to read between the lines," Pain told her. The look on her face said that she still didn't get it, which was no surprise. Lolo was bad as hell, but that was about as deep as that well went.

Pain had lusted after Lolo from the moment he laid eyes on her in the sneaker store that day. Even after she had dismissed him like a common beggar, it hadn't quenched the fire that burned in his crotch for her. Lolo tried to act like she was out of his league, but Pain knew better. There wasn't a woman in the world that he didn't believe he could bag, and she was no exception. She had been on his radar since he came home from prison, and if he wanted to get at her he would have to make it onto hers.

After the hostile takeover of the chop shop, there was no way Pain was going back to the life of a square. He had sampled that meal and found it too hard to digest. It was like Sonny had said in *A Bronx Tale:* "The working man is a sucker." He jumped headfirst back into his old tricks with Case and the gang. He hated to admit it, but he was way more comfortable with a gun in his hand than a time card. Being back on the wrong side of the law made him feel alive again. He had rediscovered his passion for the heist.

Getting back in the game with Case felt good, but it wasn't without its drawbacks. One thing that Pain learned was that time hadn't made Case any less sloppy. He was still moving reckless in the way he broke the law. His crew was small and spread out all over the place, with their hands in a little bit of everything, so it made it hard for them to focus on one hustle. Pain changed that. The shooters he kept close; they rode out with them on armed robberies and heavy capers. Those who didn't have the stomach for bloodshed he delegated to B&E jobs, boosting, or put them under Tyriq and Lil Sorrow with the carjacking operation. The drugs he entrusted to the few females who were loyal to them. Of course Case scoffed at this new arrangement. He was used to being hands-on in every aspect of the business so that he could watch everyone and count every dollar. It took some convincing, but Pain was finally able to get him to see the bigger picture. Dividing the crew up into groups according to their specialties allowed them each to focus on specific tasks, which brought in more money. In the few weeks since Pain had been back in the fold, the crew's profits had noticeably increased. Everyone was eating. Better days were in their futures thanks to the changes Pain was making, and for the most part the soldiers were happy. But not everyone was as receptive to change. Pain would learn this sooner than later.

It didn't take long for word to start getting out that the Blackbird was back. Wherever he went in the neighborhood, people shouted him out or tried to take up his time to get a bit of conversation. Even before going to prison Pain had been a respected man, but this time around it felt different. He wasn't the Queen's feared Blackbird and prince of the Crows. He was getting to it on his own, and on his own terms. When word of his exploits started getting around, Cassandra reached out. She wanted her Blackbird back. Being back in the fold and with his Queen was tempting, but Pain respectfully declined. Serving under Cassandra was in his past and Pain was trying to build a future. A part of him missed some of the perks that came with flying the open road with the Crows, especially those intimate moments he had spent with the Queen, but he learned that he far more enjoyed living the life of a true outlaw. One without restrictions. One day he might revisit returning to the nest, but that would be a conversation for a different time. Until then, he would keep the Queen and her Crows at arm's length.

Pain's name was ringing again and it wouldn't be long before Lolo would hear the bells, too. Being that Pain was back associating with the criminal element, it would only be a matter of time before their paths crossed again. He and Case could often be found in local hotspots that catered to men who danced on the wrong side of the law. He had seen her in a few spots, but almost every time Lee had been with her. He and

Pain would exchange dirty looks from opposite sides of the room, but to that point it hadn't gone beyond that. At least not yet. Pain could see that the two black eyes he'd given Lee when he broke his nose hadn't healed yet, and it would probably be a slow road to recovery. Lee was a respected man in the streets and Pain had marked him. That wasn't something he was likely to let go easily. Pain knew he wouldn't. It would only be a matter of time before they clashed again, but that was a bridge he would cross when he came to it and crush Lee once and for all. But currently he was plotting on crushing something else.

Lee hadn't been the only one watching Pain. Lolo had taken notice of him. He could feel her eyes on him whenever they happened to occupy the same spaces. Those were the nights when Pain sensed a little something extra in the air. Normally Pain was the quiet one, content to play the shadows and let Case and Tyriq have the spotlights, but on nights when he knew that Lolo was in the building, he was right there with them popping bottles and talking big. This was out of character for Pain to those who knew him, but there was a method to his madness. He was putting himself on her radar. See, Pain didn't know Lolo, but he knew her type. Women like her were like moths, attracted to whoever's light shone brighter. So, Pain tried to blind her every chance he got. The hook had been baited and eventually she would bite.

The night it finally happened had been a low-key one, and she hadn't been who he'd had his sights on. Case had been telling Pain about this huge score that he had been plotting for months, and the time was almost at hand to execute it. They had a ritual that dated back to when they were still young men sticking up weed spots. The night before a big heist, the Crows would go out and celebrate. It was like manifesting the success of a job before even undertaking it. This was also just in case one of them happened to fall while on the job, so if this was to be their last night as free—or living—men, they'd at least have some great memories.

A small group of them had rolled to a spot that Tyriq had put them onto. It was in the Bronx, right across the 145th Street bridge. It was a cool little spot where the drinks were strong, the DJ was rocking, and a hundred dollars slipped to the doorman allowed Lil Sorrow to enter. Case had to give his word that Lil Sorrow wouldn't drink in order for the doorman to go for it, for fear of him getting caught and costing the spot their liquor license. Lil Sorrow didn't like it, but it beat the alternative, which was him being left on the block while the rest of them partied. Pain had been on the fence about Lil Sorrow when they first met. He was a new face, but more importantly he was way too young to be caught up in the type of games that Case was playing. But all suspicions he'd had about Lil Sorrow were squashed once he had seen the boy in action.

Lil Sorrow could break into a car and be gone with it in under a minute, and he drove like a stock car driver. In addition to being a talented car thief, the boy had a heart bigger than most. Lil Sorrow hadn't met a foe that he wouldn't square up with, and it didn't matter how big or small they were. One night when they had been on the block drinking, Lil Sorrow had gotten into a heated exchange with another member of their crew that everyone called Hook, because of his vicious right hook. In another life Hook had been an amateur boxer. Words turned into fists flying, and of course Lil Sorrow got knocked on his ass. Hook had caught him with a nasty blow, one that would've sat men twice his size down for good, but Lil Sorrow got back up and came at him again. Hook knocked Sorrow down at least three or four times, but the boy wouldn't stop coming. Even when his eye was black and swollen closed, Lil Sorrow kept attacking. Hook would've probably beaten him to death had Pain not stepped in. Lil Sorrow had not only proved himself to be solid, but loyal as well. With the proper guidance, Lil Sorrow was sure to become a ghetto superstar, provided he didn't get himself killed first. From then on Pain made it a point to keep the runt close to him, as he had once done with Tyriq.

The minute Pain and his gang walked into the Bronx spot, people took notice. Since mostly locals hung out there, when new faces entered the building they stuck out like sore thumbs. Pain was dressed in loose-fitting jeans, wheat-colored Timbs, and a cream sweater. Swinging from his neck were two chains: the Blackbird pendant that Tyriq had gifted him and a slightly larger chain. It was a Cuban link that hung slightly longer than the Blackbird chain. Dangling from the end of it was a circular medallion, trimmed in small diamonds. In the center of it was a picture of his departed mother. For the most part, Pain spent almost every dollar he pulled in from the streets on getting his grandmother out of debt. He had to be slick about paying off her medical bills because he didn't want to have to explain to her where the extra money was coming from. For all she knew, he was still working the shitty job at the junkyard that his parole officer had hooked him up with. The chain was the first and only major purchase Pain had made for himself.

They didn't roll too deep that night. Only the homies who would participate in the heist. Pain and Case led the entourage, as always, looking like two handsome movie stars. Lil Sorrow moved quietly in their shadows. His oversized hoodie was pulled up over his head, hands shoved deep in the pockets. From beneath its folds his small eyes watched everyone who wasn't a part of their crew and some who were. Not far behind was Tyriq, with his confident swagger and reckless eyeballing of every female they passed. He was looking to see which one of them were trying to get chosen to be his plaything for the night. The only time his mind wasn't on pussy was when it was on stealing. Bringing up the rear were Hook, and Pain's buddy from the junkyard, Sauce. Sauce had been keeping time with Pain and his friends since the takeover of the chop shop. He had proven to be more valuable to them than he ever was to Mr. Carson. It had been Sauce who helped them disable the alarm system on an appliance store they had broken into earlier in the week. They made off with at least fifteen grand worth of toasters, microwaves, and other goods. That had been the biggest score they'd taken off since Pain had rejoined the crew, but the one Case was planning for them next was said to be even bigger.

You would've thought that Pain and his gang were rappers the way they turned heads while crossing the room. Even the DJ acknowledged them. "Shout out to Blackbird and the crew! Welcome home, Pain!" he announced over the microphone.

"Damn, bruh. You didn't tell me that you were a celebrity," Sauce joked, falling in step beside Pain.

"Shit, I ain't nobody special," Pain told him humbly.

"You got that right," Hook mumbled.

"What you say?" Pain stopped and turned to him. Hook had been talking slick since the night Pain stopped him from beating up on Lil Sorrow. Pain had chosen to ignore him to that point, but he was starting to work his nerves.

"What he means is, no one man above the team, right?" Case tried to clean it up.

"Yeah, man. That's what I meant," Hook said unconvincingly.

"A'ight." Pain looked him up and down distastefully and walked off. Had he bothered to turn around he would've caught the grimy look that Hook was giving him. He missed it, but Lil Sorrow didn't.

Because the crew had dropped extra money at the door for bottles, they were given a private section in the back. It was more like a bench and two chairs set around a small wooden table, but they made the best of it. Tyriq rounded up a few girls who looked thirsty, literally and figuratively, and invited them to join the group. There were four of them, all different shades of brown. Case had his sights on the butterscotch cutie with green eyes, but she jumped on Pain before he could stake his claim. Pain wasn't really interested. He just made small talk with her so as not to be rude. The whole time she was chattering, his eyes were sweeping the room. That was when he spotted her. Lolo was posted up near the bar with a few of her homegirls. Pain looked around for her ever-present shadow, Lee, but to his surprise he wasn't with her.

"Pardon me for a minute. I need to hit the bar," Pain excused himself from the girl who was trying to attach herself.

"What you going to the bar for if we got bottles?" Tyriq threw his hands up in confusion, but Pain was already moving across the room.

"Tender dick nigga," Hook grumbled once Pain was out of earshot.

"Blackbird been a pussy hound for as long as I can remember. You could learn a thing from him," Tyriq teased.

"I'd rather chase a bag than a bitch," Hook replied.

"Says the broke nigga with no chicks," Lil Sorrow commented, drawing a laugh from the crew.

"You sound like somebody trying to get his head knocked off," Hook growled.

"And you sound like a hater," Lil Sorrow countered.

"I see that ass whipping I gave you hasn't taught you how to keep that big mouth closed," Hook said, standing.

"I'm a slow learner. That's why I had to repeat the third grade." Lil Sorrow rose, and stood toe to toe with Hook. The man was almost a foot taller than him, but Sorrow didn't back down.

"Y'all knock it the fuck off," Case commanded.

The two men eyeballed each other for a few seconds longer, Hook with his fist balled, and Lil Sorrow flipping the razor around in his mouth that he had snuck in under his tongue. He was ready to get to it, and everyone knew it, including Hook. It was Hook who broke his stare first. "Fuck this." He sat back down and grabbed one of the bottles from the table.

"What's up with you, homie? You been on some real sour shit lately." Case leaned in to speak with Hook.

"My problem is ya man Pain," Hook told him.

"You still holding a grudge about him getting between you and that business with Lil Sorrow? He did what he was supposed to do, and protected a member of this crew," Case told him. He had actually been impressed that Pain stepped in on Lil Sorrow's behalf, as he didn't know him that well. That was confirmation for Case that Pain was all in and dedicated to the crew.

"Fuck that midget terrorist!" Hook spat, looking in Lil Sorrow's direction. He found the young man watching him intently from behind his sunglasses. "I could give a damn about all that. I'm just not feeling this new pecking order."

"Pecking order?"

"Bro, we been out here putting in the work all this time with you leading the charge. Then ya man comes home from prison and they're treating him like some kind of fucking war hero." He was glaring at Pain, watching people go out of their way to show him respect as he made his way across the room. "They act like he's the one running this show instead of you."

"You know I ain't never gave a fuck about what other people thought," Case reminded him.

"I ain't talking about other people." Hook looked to Tyriq and Sauce, who were enjoying the company of two girls. They were laughing together like two old friends instead of a couple of guys who had only recently met. Pain had brought them together, as he had with other members of their crew, new and old. He had an uncanny ability to bring strangers together for a common cause. Another testament to his leadership abilities and the willingness of men to follow him. "You need to watch that pretty muthafucka, Case. One day you might look up and find you ain't the one calling the shots anymore."

Case didn't reply to Hook's warning, but he received it.

Pain tried to move with stealth, but it was hard considering that someone seemed to stop him every few feet. Some of the people he knew in passing from the streets, and others were just trying to get a few ticks with the notorious Blackbird in hopes that they would get put on. It was one of the drawbacks of street fame.

Lolo and her crew were currently in the middle of a full-court press by a group of dudes rocking a lot of floss, big jewels, and cold bottles. She caught a glimpse of Pain when he neared them. Her eyes lit up hopefully as he drew nearer, thinking he was about to approach, but instead he walked by her like he hadn't even seen her. He perched himself on a stool three down from Lolo and her group and gave his order to the bartender. Pain didn't have to turn around to know that she was looking at him because he could feel the heat on the back of his neck. About the same time the bartender placed a vodka and cranberry in front of him, Pain felt a presence at his back. He still didn't turn.

"Drink on you, handsome?" Lolo got his attention.

Pain gave a half turn, glanced at her, and sipped his vodka. "I don't buy drinks for women who belong to someone else," he told her in a tone that said he didn't have time.

"Oh, so you on that now?" Lolo moved to position herself in his line of vision. "That day in the backyard you were trying to make it your business to get to know me."

"And the day I tried to get at you in the sneaker store on 145th you acted like I wasn't worth your time," Pain reminded her.

Lolo studied his face. When she'd seen him in the backyard he felt familiar to her but she couldn't place him. Now that he mentioned it, she remembered where she'd seen him for the first time, but all clean-shaven and shining he looked like a totally different person. "That was you?"

"Should it matter?"

"Blame it on my head and not my heart. I was going through something at the time." Lolo invited herself to the stool next to Pain. "How about I buy you a drink instead? To make up for me being rude to you and all."

"I've got a better idea."

"And what would that be?" Lolo asked curiously.

Pain took a sip of his drink before answering. "How about we cut the bullshit and get straight to what's this really is. Tell your friends you'll catch them later and let's get out of here."

"I'm no whore!" Lolo said defensively.

"Relax, baby. I ain't said all that. You just ain't been fucked properly in a while and I aim to change that," Pain said coolly.

"And what makes you think that?" She folded her arms.

"The fact that you've entertained me for this long without walking away or slapping my face for talking to you like that," Pain replied.

"You know I got a man, right?" Lolo reminded him.

"Yet you're still over here up in my face, letting me tickle your ears. It ain't that serious, shorty. That nigga can have you back when I'm done. I ain't trying to keep you, just borrow you." Pain downed the rest of his drink. "I'm going to flag down a cab. Don't take too long making up your mind." He slid from the stool and made his way to the exit. The way he had played it was a long shot at best, but he felt good about his odds. If Lee's hold on Lolo was as tight as he thought, then Lolo would remain loyal and Pain would be riding away alone and feeling like a fool. But if she was any bit the ambitious bitch he thought, she was getting her ass cracked that night. She chose ambition over loyalty.

———

Lolo's lips were still moving, but Pain couldn't hear a word that she was saying. He had learned how to tune her out throughout the night. Lolo was fine, and fucked and sucked him like he had never been fucked and sucked before, but that was the extent of her value. Beneath the beauty and fancy clothes was a grade-A hood rat. All she talked about during the night they had spent together was neighborhood gossip, designers, and what was going on in the blogs. Her mouth seemed to go nonstop and the only time she was quiet was when Pain threw his dick in it. He had put so much into chasing her, and now that he had her he couldn't wait to be rid of her.

His cell phone vibrating saved him from whatever mindless bullshit she was talking about. When he saw the number that flashed across the screen he excused himself to the bathroom to answer it. "What's good?"

"Time to make the doughnuts," the voice on the other end responded.

"Say less," Pain replied and ended the call. He went back into the room where he found Lolo propped against a pillow, rolling up some weed.

"Everything cool, baby?" Lolo asked, noticing the seriousness in his expression.

"Nothing for you to worry yourself over. I'm gonna have to cut our little morning short, though. I gotta go to work. You can go ahead and enjoy the room until checkout, though."

"I was thinking maybe we could keep the room for one more night.

Then after you get done handling your business we can go out for dinner and drinks?"

"And why would you think that?" Pain asked, sitting on the bed and pulling his pants on.

Lolo eased behind him and began running her hands over his chest. "Well, since you were in here fucking me and eating ass like you loved me—"

"I fucked you like a nigga who just got out of prison." Pain removed her hands and stood to pull his sweater over his head. "Don't mistake a good time for anything other than that."

"Damn, it's like that?" she asked, not able to hide the hurt in her voice. Lolo was usually the one dismissing men, not the other way around. This was new to her.

"It ain't like nothing other than what I told you last night. I don't want to keep you, just borrow you." He tossed a few dollars on the bed. "That should be enough to cover dinner for one and your ride home. Never let it be said that the Blackbird wasn't a gentleman."

"Fuck you, Pain! I should've never gave your jailbird ass no pussy!" Lolo spat furiously.

"And yet you did," he shot back.

"You're gonna regret treating me like this," Lolo threatened.

"What you gonna do? Tell your boyfriend how you came in here, fucked another nigga, and then got mad when he didn't want anything else to do with it?" Pain asked. Lolo was silent. "That's what I thought. See you around, shorty." He saluted her and left the room.

Lolo waited until Pain was gone to let the first of the tears she had been holding back roll down her cheeks. She couldn't believe that Pain had played her like that. Granted, when he was still running around broke she wouldn't give him the time of day, but now that he was starting to get his weight up she saw the potential in him. She even enjoyed being around him, which was more than she could say about Lee. He had just been someone to sponsor her lifestyle and give her status. With Pain it was supposed to be different. In the end, he turned out to be just as much of an asshole as the rest of them. It was okay, though. He didn't know it, but this little stunt had started some shit that she was going to be the one to finish. No one embarrassed Yolanda Gooden and got away with it.

While Lolo sat plotting her revenge, another anchor had replaced the one who had previously been on the television screen, with a breaking news report. It was brief, no more than thirty seconds to touch on the story of a Queens man who had been found shot to death and dumped in the Hudson River. It was just one of several murders that had taken place over one night. The difference with this one was that it would alter the course of several unsuspecting lives.

CHAPTER 19

It had taken Passion about twenty minutes to shower and start getting herself ready. By the time she came out of the bathroom, Birdie was no longer in the bed. According to Claire, she had borrowed twenty dollars from her for a taxi because she had something to do downtown. Passion hoped that something included taking her ass to the clinic. Passion wondered why Birdie hadn't just waited for her to get out of the shower to get the twenty bucks, but she reasoned that she might still be in her feelings from the conversation they'd had earlier. Passion had been very direct with Birdie, because she needed her to understand where she was coming from. She was worried about her adopted little sister. Ever since that morning with Uncle Joe and Teddy, something had changed in Birdie. It wasn't a significant enough change to be obvious to the casual observer, but Passion knew Birdie better than her own mother. She had practically been raising her over the last couple of years, so it didn't matter if it was her hairstyle or her cycle, Passion would notice. She'd been playing in a dark corner lately. Part of it was probably due to the drugs, but Passion knew that a lot of it was due to the emotional scars left behind from the ordeal. She had been violated in ways that Passion couldn't even begin to imagine. She was too young to be carrying all that weight, and it would only be a matter of time before her shoulders collapsed beneath it.

After a last-minute mental check to make sure she hadn't forgotten anything, Passion grabbed her knapsack and left the bedroom. Her luck held up and she didn't bump into Uncle Joe on her way out. He had been gone since that morning, doing whatever it was that he did. However, she did bump into Zeta's miserable ass. She was sitting on the couch, blunt pinched between her painted nails. She was watching a reality TV show on the big screen that sat against the wall in their living room. From the tight green dress she wore and the fact that her hair was freshly done, Passion knew that she was working that night. Her sitting there dressed meant that Joe would probably be there soon to pick her up. This added urgency to Passion's need to get out of the apartment.

"Where you off to?" Zeta asked over her shoulder, eyes still locked on the TV show.

"Nowhere special. Just to hang with Juju," Passion replied.

"Since when you need an overnight bag to hang out with that bitch?" Zeta turned and eyed her suspiciously.

"Why are you all up in my business, Zeta? I don't press you about where you're going or who you're doing, so do me the same." Passion didn't have time for her bullshit.

"Listen to you, sounding like you be outside like that," Zeta said with a chuckle. "You think you're so slick, Passion, but I see through your bullshit."

"And what the fuck is that supposed to mean?" Passion didn't really have time to entertain Zeta, but she was getting tired of the slick talk and was ready to address it.

"It means, I can see through your mask." Zeta took another pull from her joint before flicking the ash onto the carpet. "Since I chose Joe as my man and moved in here with the rest of y'all, I been feeling the shade coming my way. From Bo, because I'm younger and finer. From Claire because she's a gutter ho who don't have half my flash or polish, and from Birdie because . . ." she thought about it briefly. "She's a weak bitch who's gonna go with the majority rule and hate me because everybody else does. That girl can't wipe her ass without somebody telling her to and how. You, you're a different case. You don't like me because I see you: Joe's fake baby niece who is too good to go out and sweat under a nigga to keep these lights on like the rest of us. Bo, Uncle Joe . . . they all think you're some type of golden child, but I know better. I know what you are."

"And what's that, Zeta? What am I?" Passion asked, genuinely curious as to what her answer would be.

"A siren," Zeta answered, much to Passion's surprise. She wasn't even aware that the girl knew the word. "I read about creatures like you back when I was in school. Beautiful women who lured unsuspecting sailors to their doom. That's the same thing you do, only you ain't crashing boats. You're crashing people's lives."

"You don't know what you're talking about," Passion dismissed her.

"Don't I?" Zeta raised an eyebrow. "See, the one thing about being on the streets twenty-four seven is, my ear stays to the ground. You'd be surprised what you hear when you're keeping time in the slums. That was a nice piece of work you put in to get back at Jason's baby mama for putting hands on you."

"You bugging. I didn't have nothing to do with what went on between them. That was some domestic shit," Passion said defensively.

"Yup, a crime of passion that was started by that girl finding another bitch's panties in his bedroom. I wonder how they got there?" Zeta gave Passion an accusatory look.

"I wouldn't know," Passion said in an unconvincing tone.

"Singing that sweet siren song yet again, but I can't hear it. I'm deaf to your bullshit, Passion." Zeta laughed mockingly.

"Fuck you, Zeta."

"No, fuck you, lil bitch. I keep telling Uncle Joe to kick your ass to the curb before you lead to his downfall too, but you got his nose open so wide that I could drive a truck up it. His simple ass ain't gonna be satisfied until you put him in an early grave like you did your parents."

"Watch your mouth, bitch!" Passion snapped. "My parents died in a car accident."

"That you caused," Zeta countered. "It was you that they were arguing over that night when your daddy lost control, weren't they?"

"Shut up, Zeta," Passion growled. She could feel her heartbeat quicken and her face begin to flush. Zeta ignored her warning and kept going.

"You whispered that sweet siren's song in your daddy's ear about your mother's extracurricular activities. Broke that poor man's heart." Zeta's voice was almost compassionate. "He confronted your mom about it that night y'all were riding home from church. Things got nasty between them while daddy was driving and the next thing you know you're an orphan. Saddest story I ever heard. You been tricking people into early graves since you were little."

Passion was too stunned to speak. Zeta's words hit her like a combination thrown by a professional boxer. There were only three people who knew the circumstances surrounding the accident that killed her parents, and two of them were dead. What she had done that night was one of her life's greatest regrets and the reason why she'd always felt responsible for her parents' deaths. It was a secret that had been weighing her down for years and now here was Zeta throwing it in her face. How could she know? Passion felt the coolness in her stomach. The darkness was coming. This time she didn't fight it. She welcomed it. Icy fingers crawled from her gut through her limbs and fingertips. The first tears began to fall as the cold traveled up her neck, and sucked her into its frigid nothingness.

Passion couldn't be sure what happened next, or how long she'd been out of it. It was like waking up from a nap that she had taken on a bed of ice. She was aware of two things: the coldness still lingering throughout her body and a set of hands tugging at her. It was Bo.

"Girl, have you lost your fool mind? You're going to kill her!" Bo was shouting.

Her? Who the hell was *her*? Then Passion remembered Zeta. She found her lying on the floor at her feet, between the coffee table and what was left of the television, which was now lying on its side with the screen cracked. Zeta's face was bloodied, and her lip split and swollen. Her head lolled back and forth as she mumbled incoherently. Passion looked from her red, swollen fists back to Zeta. She wanted to feel something, but she felt nothing.

"Uncle Joe is gonna kill y'all behind this TV," Bo said, still in shock at what had transpired.

"Fuck Joe!" Passion said, before collecting her things and leaving.

———

Passion could remember something that her mother used to always say: "Speak the devil's name and he shall appear." That was exactly what happened. No sooner did she exit her building, she ran into Uncle Joe. He was leaning against his white Suburban talking to an associate of his. This man was tall, light-skinned, and at one time had probably been handsome but now looked like he had been through some things in his life. Passion had seen him in the neighborhood a few times but had never been introduced, which was fine by her. The way his hazel eyes followed her whenever she saw him in passing gave Passion the creeps.

When Uncle Joe noticed something distracting his associate, he turned to see what he was looking at. That's when he noticed Passion. "Sup, baby girl?" he greeted her. Joe leaned in to hug her, but Passion didn't return the gesture. She was never really warm toward him, but that day she seemed extra cold. "What's wrong? What happened to your face?" He noticed the scratch on her cheek. It was nothing major.

"Must've scratched myself when I was washing my face," Passion lied. She knew that he would eventually find out about the fight between her and Zeta, but she didn't feel like dealing with it right that second.

"Put some cocoa butter on it. That way you don't have to worry about it leaving a scar on that pretty face of yours," Joe's associate suggested. He was trying to give her his best bedroom eyes. To her he looked like a washed-up version of the singer Christopher Williams.

"I don't recall nobody inviting you into this conversation!" Uncle Joe said angrily. He was fiercely protective of Passion when it came to other men, especially ones that he did business with.

"My fault, Uncle Joe. I was just trying to give the young lady a compliment." The associate raised his hands in surrender.

"Probably followed by a yard of dick. I know how you get down, nigga. So, don't try it," Uncle Joe told him before turning his attention back to Passion. "Where you off to with the book bag?"

"Going to meet up with Juju. I promised her I'd let her borrow an outfit." Passion patted the bag.

"You and that girl ain't nowhere near the same size." Uncle Joe eyed her suspiciously.

"You know Juju likes to wear her clothes extra baggy," Passion reminded him.

Uncle Joe shook his head. "I don't know why a young girl so fine would go out of her way to hide it by dressing like a boy. I saw her a few minutes ago in front of the store with them drunk niggas."

Passion looked at the time on her phone. "Thanks, let me go so I can catch up with her."

"A'ight, you be safe out here, baby girl. A lot of crazy shit going on in the world," Uncle Joe told her.

"Tell me something I don't know." Passion started to walk off, but stopped short. "Uncle Joe, can I ask you something?"

"Sure, what's up?"

Passion paused, searching for the words. "The night my parents were killed. Do you know anything about it?"

Uncle Joe shrugged. "Only what the police report says, that your dad lost control of the car and ended up in oncoming traffic. Why? You okay?"

"Yeah, I was just curious. Thanks." She walked off.

Uncle Joe stood there watching her, and wondering what had made her ask about her parents' deaths again after all these years.

"You straight?" the associate asked.

"Yeah, man. I'm good," Uncle Joe assured him. He noticed that his associate's eyes had drifted back to Passion again. "What the fuck did I just tell you?"

"I ain't speaking, I'm peeking. Ain't nothing wrong with looking, right?" the associate smirked. "And why you out here still stressing over whore money when I just opened the pipeline for your old surly ass? What's the matter? Drug money ain't good enough for you?"

"All money is good, and she ain't no whore," Uncle Joe told him.

"Oh, now I get it. I know you liked them young, Joe, but she looks young enough to still be in high school," the associate pointed out.

"Nah, Passion ain't no little girl. That's for sure," Uncle Joe said with his eyes taking on a look like he had just been transported to some imaginary place. "So, we gonna keep shooting the shit about my tastes in women or we gonna discuss this paper? The pills are moving like hotcakes. When do you think you'll be able to lay some more on me?"

"Shouldn't be but a day or so. I gotta be mindful of how I'm moving so as not to arouse suspicion," the associate told him.

"And how's our little fish doing these days?" Uncle Joe asked.

"Still running around like he's the sharpest knife in the drawer," the associate laughed.

"A butter knife," Uncle Joe chuckled. "I was actually surprised at how easy it was to line him up. You said that he was smart."

"Oh, he's quite smart. He's also quite greedy, and that's how I was able to make him my personal bitch," the associate said.

"So, you gonna keep playing with your food or eventually eat it?" Uncle Joe asked.

"Neither, I'm going to forgive his debt."

Uncle Joe gave him a look. "Since when did you grow a heart?"

"I didn't. In exchange for his life he's going to give me something that's worth more to me than money." The associate rubbed his hands together in anticipation.

Passion reflected while she walked, not on Uncle Joe's response to her question about her parents, but his delivery. He didn't miss a beat when he parroted the police report about what had happened. There was no emotion in his eyes, which was his tell whenever he was lying or omitting the truth. Uncle Joe was someone who spoke with either passion, anger, or conviction when it came to everything. Even when he told Bo what he wanted for breakfast, you could see how hungry he was by his eyes. The only time his eyes were that flat was when he was feeding one of the girls a line of bullshit. She had seen him do it enough times to know. Zeta knowing the intimate details behind how her parents had died unnerved Passion. She was fairly certain that Zeta wasn't a clairvoyant, so that meant someone had to have told her. The question was, who, and how did they know? For reasons that Passion couldn't understand, her mind kept going back to Uncle Joe. She was certain that he knew more than he was telling, but just what she had no way to be sure.

She found Juju just where Uncle Joe had said she would be. Passion's bestie was huddled up with Ed, Paul, and Mud. She was smoking a joint while the other three passed around a bottle of something in a brown paper bag. When Juju saw her, she rolled her eyes and tapped her watch indicating that Passion was late. "Tell me something I don't know," Passion offered in way of a greeting. "My fault, girl. I was dealing with some shit upstairs."

"You good?" Juju asked with concern, noticing the scratch on Passion's cheek.

"Some hood rat bullshit. Nothing to stress over. You ready?" Passion was ready to get in motion.

"Yeah, let me just finish this." Juju held up the joint before hitting it. She took a deep pull and handed it to her girl. Passion took the joint and inhaled so deep that Juju feared her lungs would cave in. "Damn, girl! You sure you're okay?"

"This too shall pass," was Passion's response, as she exhaled a thick plume of smoke.

"You smelling real good over there, Ms. Lady. I'm glad the smell from all that bacon grease ain't rub off on you." Mud swigged from his bottle, eyes locked on Uncle Joe and his associate, who were still visible on the ave.

"If you feeling some type of way, why don't you go and express it to Uncle Joe," Passion said sharply, not in the mood for Mud's shit.

"I ain't talking about Joe. I'm talking about the fake pretty light-skinned nigga he's with. That boy is the police," Mud informed her.

"Mud, you think everybody is five-oh," Ed said, taking the bottle from him and sipping.

"I'm telling you what I know! That chump locked me up like six or seven years ago. I was getting money out this spot with my man Ish. That's back when I was a young punk still out here trying to move five-dollar rocks," Mud insisted.

"And you still out here moving five-dollar rocks," Juju joked. This made even Passion laugh.

"Laugh now and cry when he got them folks running up in Uncle Joe's crib and got all y'all in bracelets."

"The police running up in the crib is the last thing Uncle Joe is worried about. He's got that covered," Passion assured him. Of all the things she feared in Uncle Joe's apartment, the police busting in wasn't one of them. Uncle Joe was connected in ways that people like Mud wouldn't understand, even if she tried to break it down to him.

"That's the same thing Ish said," Mud remarked before taking his bottle back from Ed. He took a swig and extended it to Passion, who looked at him as if he had just asked her to put her mouth on a dead squirrel. "I forgot. You got champagne dreams."

"To match this champagne life we about to have," Juju offered, which got her a look from Passion.

"Come on, Ju. We got shit to do." Passion grabbed her by the arm and pulled her away.

Mud watched Passion's round ass switch away until it disappeared around the corner. "One day, lil bitch. One day," he said to no one in particular. He then turned his attention back to Uncle Joe and his new friend.

CHAPTER 20

"Friend, you is really killing them tonight. I mean that shit," Juju said just above a whisper into Passion's ear.

Passion simply smiled, because she knew that her friend wasn't lying. She had shed the streetwear she had been rocking earlier and was now wearing a sleek black dress that hugged her just the right way about the hips. The dress showed enough thigh to be sexy, but not enough to be trashy. It was just enough to keep people looking. It was a struggle walking in the heels, but the definition they gave her oiled, toned legs was worth the price of admission. So, yes. She was killing it. What really made the outfit pop were the jade earrings she was wearing. Juju had borrowed them from her mom. Passion had initially refused to take responsibility for the expensive earrings, but Juju insisted. If they were going to pull off their little caper, they had to look like money. Like they belonged. Juju was already rocking a diamond necklace and matching earrings, so it wouldn't look right if Passion went in plain-Jane. Reluctantly, she agreed, but found herself conscious of losing the earrings the entire night.

Juju was looking pretty good herself in her white hanbok, which had been hand-painted with delicate images of roses that started at her neck and disappeared under her left arm. Her hair was pulled high on top of her head and held in place with two silver hair chopsticks. At least a foot had been added to her true height, thanks to the open-toe white block sandals. Juju was really playing up the Asian bit. But at the end of the day, that's what they were there for: to make a good showing of it and get paid. So far, they had made good on the showing. It was the getting paid part that still had them both on edge.

Passion had been skeptical, to say the least, at Juju's plan when she first presented it. According to her, she had overheard her brother talking about a gambling spot where once a month they hosted a high-stakes poker game in a private room. It was to be held at a secret location and invite-only. Juju claimed to have a hookup with some kids she knew that could get her and Passion in as their guests.

She suggested that Passion use her income tax check, and Juju put up some of the money she had saved from hustling, to get in on the game. Passion immediately shot the idea down. She wasn't a gambler, and furthermore there was no way in the hell that she was going to risk everything she had on a wager. This was when Juju hit her with the sweetener: One of the games would be rigged. An understanding had been established between an associate of Juju's dad and one of the dealers that would allow them to skim off the game. Flat-out busting them out would be too dangerous, but there would be a nice chunk of bread skimmed off the top. The more money in the pot, the bigger the skim. All Passion and Juju would have to do was watch the Korean and bet as he did.

After about an hour of Juju trying to convince her and the promise of giving Passion at least half her money back if things went south, Passion agreed. And this is where the plot twist came in. Apparently, Juju's connect to get them in wasn't who they said they were. So in order to get them in, she and Passion would have to pose as prostitutes and possibly give out a hand job or two to sell the story. This is where Passion drew the line. Juju wasn't the only one who had connections.

It had been a long shot when Passion reached out to Dice. He had been on her that first night, but that had been nearly a month ago, and outside of the occasional texts back and forth, she hadn't been buying whatever he was selling. Her responses were always cute and cordial. Enough to keep hope alive, but never commit. Much to her surprise and pleasure, Dice was still checking for her as heavy as he had been the night they met. He tried to front like he wasn't, but Passion saw through his bullshit. He was all too willing to let her and Juju roll to the game as his guests on the condition that Passion let him take her to breakfast the next morning. She could read between the lines, but still she agreed because she needed this play to go down. He offered to pick them up, but Passion told him they would meet him there and to just shoot the address over. Which he did. Juju called the move Passion had pulled off "luck," but Passion called it "paying attention to detail." Dice was a well-known gambler, so it was only natural he would be tapped into a card game of that magnitude. Now that Passion had secured their entry, it was time for Juju to work that hustler's magic she had become so famous for.

They both agreed that they would have to spend money to make money, so that's what they did. Juju secured them a hotel room that was three blocks from where the house that would host the game was located. That would be their staging point, where they would lay out their plan and put it into motion. Earlier in the week, Juju had hooked them in with some boosters who agreed to front them some clothes for the evening, with the promise of points on top of the regular prices once they got right. Next, she hit up a cousin of hers who was dead nice with nails and makeup to come beat their faces. By the time Passion and Juju stepped out of their hotel room, they looked like they had been made over by an entire glam squad instead of a crew they had put together on the fly.

Dice was waiting for them out in front of the spot when the luxury SUV transporting the girls pulled up. A handsome Spanish cat in a nice black suit got from behind the wheel and walked around to hold the back door open for Passion and Juju. From the way people were watching them, they obviously thought the Asian and the Black girl were handling. They had no clue that it was an UberXL. Passion and Juju didn't mind spending the sixty dollars the Uber charged to take them a few blocks, so long as they looked good getting out of it.

"You look amazing," Dice greeted Passion when she exited the ride.

"You're not looking too bad yourself." She admired his outfit: a nice black suit with a shirt, no tie, and black shoes polished to a high shine. Dice looked quite nice indeed.

For all the secrecy and hoops they'd had to jump through, Passion expected more when she walked into the spot. In her mind, she pictured it being like a scene from an old mobster movie, with a smoke-filled hotel room playing host to a half dozen wiseguys sitting around a card table betting dirty cash. It was not. The space which hosted the game was a renovated home on a quiet block in Brooklyn. They were greeted by a doorman who scanned the invitations of the guests with a small LED device. Once he validated the invitation, he used a swipe card, which was attached to a cord on his belt, to open the door that would allow them into the foyer. This is where they came to a second door, manned by two more guards. They were both armed with wands and wearing gloves. They separated the people by sex and lined them up on opposite sides to be checked. Once they were sure that no one was carrying a weapon, Passion and Juju were allowed inside.

Dice led the way for the girls, with Passion on one arm and Juju on the other. From the way people stopped him every few feet to shake hands or bend his ear for a few moments, you would've thought that

Dice was the crown prince of gamblers. He took it all in stride and with grace. This was a different side of Dice than the one Passion had seen when she thought he was just security for the backyard. No, Dice was far more than that and she found herself intrigued.

After the initial pleasantries, it was time to get down to business. There were several rooms dedicated to different games of chance, where people drank while they wagered. They had everything going on, from spades to dice games. She even spied a room that was lined with chessboards where men and women squared off in pairs. It just went to show that people would gamble on anything. One of the chess players, to Passion's surprise, Juju identified as the Korean. He was a bookish-looking man of slight build, with a receding hairline and wearing wire-rimmed glasses. He looked right at home huddled over the chessboard, but far from the master card shark that Juju had made him out to be. And what the hell was he doing playing chess in a room full of men playing poker? Passion suddenly had a very bad feeling about the situation.

From the few glimpses Passion was able to catch of the insides of the rooms, there was quite a bit of money being gambled, but that all paled in comparison to the poker game. This was held in a room at the back of the main floor of the brownstone, which looked like it may have once been a den or family room. One armed guard manned the outside of the door while another was just inside. Seated at a large poker table there were just under a dozen men, engaged in a game that was already underway. There was no cash on the table, but chips that carried value. From as high as some of the men's stacks were, Passion could tell that there was big money being passed around. Money that would never make it into their pockets because Juju's ace in the hole was in the wrong damn room. She was about to question her about it when Dice spoke up.

"This way, ladies," he said, motioning for them to follow as he crossed the room.

"Aren't you going to play?" Passion asked when she caught up to him. They were heading away from the table to an adjoining room.

"In a minute. First I have to get you guys situated," Dice told them. He shook hands with another man who was standing outside the door of the adjoining room.

Passion peered over his shoulder to get a better look. It was a smaller room buzzing with people. Mostly women and a few dudes mixed in. Some were drinking, while others smoked or noshed. The one thing that did stand out was that every eye in the room seemed to be locked on something just outside Passion's line of vision. They would look from whatever was on the wall, back to small handheld devices that several people were carrying. Passion was confused as hell and it showed.

"The big room is for players only," Dice answered the question on her face. "Entourages kick it in here where you can watch the game." He pointed up. It was then that Passion saw what had everyone's attention. There were flat-screens on the walls where guests could watch a live feed of the poker game in the next room.

"Oh, I see. I was under the impression that we'd be able to gamble a little." Passion glanced back hopefully at the poker table.

"The buy-in for the game is ten grand. You rolling that heavy?" Dice asked.

"Nah, that's too rich for my blood." Passion gave an embarrassed giggle.

"Take it easy, Passion. I'm only messing with you." Dice touched her arm reassuringly. He whispered something to the man he had shaken hands with. The man nodded and produced one of the hand-held devices, which he handed to Dice. "Everybody's money is good in here, not just the ballers. You can place side wagers on the game using this." He placed the device in Passion's hand. It looked like an old smartphone.

"But how . . ." Passion began, but was cut off.

"Dice, you playing cards or getting laid?" Someone shouted from the other room. It was one of the players seated at the card table, a gray-haired Italian who looked like he had fallen asleep in a tanning booth.

"Be right there!" Dice called back. "Listen, I gotta handle my business. I'll check on you ladies in an hour or so. Until then, if you need something just ask somebody and they'll bring it to you," he told them, and went to join the game.

Passion and Juju sat there looking like two dumb-ass fish, staring up at the screens with everyone else, pretending they knew what was going on. Passion had never played poker a day in her life. Hell, she had only recently learned how to play spades, and that was only be-cause she was tired of being teased about being Black and not knowing how to play. Gambling had never been her thing. This awkwardness went on for about a half hour before Passion finally got up the nerve to quiz one of the men in the room as to how to place bets.

The way it worked was that you gave your cash to the house woman, who was an attractive lady sitting in a smaller room beyond the one they were in, working a laptop. Your cash went into a safe and she used the laptop to preload your deposited dollar amount onto the handheld device. Once you had cash on it, the screen lit up. There were initials highlighted by a designated color, each representing a player at the game. It didn't allow you to actually wager money in the game, but to make side bets on the fortunes of each player: who would fold, who would win, etc. It was an odd system, but Passion managed to catch on enough to not look like a complete idiot. The minimum bet you could wager was one hundred dollars. Passion dropped a hundred on Dice, as he was the only player she knew. Luckily for her, he won that hand, but then lost the following two she wagered on him. She would have to place her next few wagers sparingly and wisely. She had only come in with two grand, and a little over four hundred of that was gone already. She just hoped that the Korean worked whatever magic he was going to work before she went broke.

The universe must've heard Passion, because not twenty seconds after she'd had the thought, the Korean walked into view of the camera. He was carrying a glass of champagne in one hand and a clear plastic container full of chips in the other. He had obviously won his chess match. He paused to study the game that was currently underway. When the player who'd been in the seat marked green on the handheld got up and left, the Korean took his place. Now it was time for the magic to happen. She bet two hundred on the Korean, a hand he lost, and then another hundred. He lost that, too. Passion was damn near halfway through everything she'd walked in with, and was ready to call it and cash out, but Juju pleaded with her to be patient. "It's a part of the finesse," she told her. And she wasn't lying. The sly Korean won the next four hands in succession. Within an hour, Passion not only won back the money she'd lost between the bets on the Korean and Dice, but she had turned her two grand into five grand and climbing.

"What the fuck are you two doing here?" Passion heard an angry voice and looked up to find Juju's brother standing over them. She had been so engrossed in watching the Korean flip her money that she hadn't noticed him approach. Jay looked good in his pinstripe suit and white shirt. Standing in his shadow was his date: a shapely brown-skinned girl with an ass so big Passion wondered if it had been purchased.

"Umm . . ." Passion began, then looked to Juju, uncertain what to say. Juju looked shaken.

"Don't just look at each other all stupid, answer my question!" Jay demanded. Juju just looked at the floor, so Passion spoke up.

"Trying to get lucky like everyone else in here," Passion told him.

"Are you freaking insane? Do you know what type of place this is?" Jay was firing off questions faster than they could answer.

"Listen," Juju finally found her voice. "We just came in to score some quick cash. We're not drinking and we're not bothering anybody. So why are you tripping?"

"Tripping?" Jay ran his hands over his face in frustration. "You two dizzy-ass broads have no idea what kind of shit being in a place like this can invite into your life. As a matter of fact, how did the two of you even get in here?"

"They're my guests. What's the problem?" Dice appeared. He had taken a break from the game and came to check on Passion. Apparently, he had arrived just in time.

"The problem is that you walked two underage girls into this joint like you don't know what we do here, Dice! Especially when one of them is my baby sister!" Jay was hot.

Dice's eyes went to Passion for an explanation.

"I'm eighteen," Passion half lied. She hadn't crossed that milestone yet.

Dice just shook his head. He figured that Passion was young, but not that young. Then again, he never came out and asked, so he really had no one to blame but himself. "Yo, Jay. I didn't know."

"Man, y'all gotta roll." Jay grabbed Juju up and then reached for Passion, who jerked her arm away.

"I ain't going nowhere. I got money on the table," Passion told him defiantly. By her count, her winnings were now approaching seven grand.

"Passion, please. I'll collect the money for you and bring it by your place later. You got my word on that. I just need you and my sister to go. Now!" Jay insisted.

At first, Passion thought that Jay was just being overly protective of his sister, but she quickly realized that it was more than that. Jay was scared. In all the years she had known that family, Jay had been tough as nails. The only two people he feared, to her knowledge, were God and his dad. So what had him so nervous that he was trying to force her to leave without collecting her winnings? She would find out when one of the monitors showing the live feed of the game glitched and then went black.

CHAPTER 21

Pain was quiet, as he often was before a job. He was riding in a van with Lil Sorrow and Case, with Case behind the wheel. The other members of the crew who were to participate in this caper were in another vehicle with instructions to rendezvous with them at the spot and not to be late. Everybody being on time would determine not only the success or failure of the mission, but whether everyone who went in would be able to walk out.

Case and Lil Sorrow were chatting it up about something. A few times they tried to engage Pain in conversation, but his answers were short if he responded at all. He could give two shits what they were talking about. His mind was on the mission and the bag that would come with it. To keep himself from overthinking and getting into his own head, Pain occupied himself watching the passing scenery of the different neighborhoods they rode through. He happened to catch a glimpse of a police car that had pulled up alongside them at a red light. One thing the Queen had always taught him about dealing with police in traffic was to never make eye contact with them. It made them feel like you were challenging them and could bring unwanted heat. It was too late. The eyes of the cop driving the patrol car contacted Pain's. The staring contest only lasted a few seconds, but to Pain it felt like an hour had passed. Pain's finger looped around the trigger of the automatic weapon on his lap. No way he was going back to prison. Not then, not ever. Something in his gaze must've relayed his thoughts because when the light turned green the patrol car eased through it and the cop didn't spare Pain a second look.

"You good?" Case asked, noticing how tense Pain was.

"I'm great," Pain replied confidently. In truth, his stomach was in knots. He wouldn't say that what he was feeling was fear. No, this was more like the jitters you might experience after getting behind the wheel for the first time after a long time of not driving. You still remembered how to operate a vehicle, but were afraid that your reflexes might've gotten dull from lack of use. This wasn't his first robbery since he had returned home. In addition to the chop shop, he had been on the streets with Case real heavy, robbing anything they could get their hands on. This time was different, though. What they were about to pull wasn't an ordinary robbery; this was a heist.

When they were a few blocks from the spot, Case pulled over and addressed the other occupants of the van. "A'ight, everybody know what to do?"

"Fo sho." Lil Sorrow adjusted the ski mask that sat cocked on his head, then chambered a round into his gun. He was clearly excited to be finally putting in some real work.

"Don't pop that thang unless it's absolutely necessary, get me?" Pain pressed Lil Sorrow.

"I got you, big homie. Only bang out if shit gets thick and I gotta cover your exit," Lil Sorrow repeated what Pain had made him promise before they left for the mission.

"Right on." Pain gave him dap before sliding from the van. Lil Sorrow followed closely behind. "Case, let's not forget our agreement, either."

"C'mon, P. It's almost showtime and you still on that?" Case sucked his teeth.

"Say it nigga, or I'm gone," Pain insisted.

Case looked at him for a time to see if he was serious. Indeed, he was. "A'ight," he sighed. "We go in for the dirty money, nothing else, and no civilian casualties," he repeated the oath Pain had forced him to take. "Why do you even give a fuck, P? Everything is profit."

"I give a fuck because half the muthafuckas in there gambling will have faces that look just like ours and come from places just like the ones we do. They're just trying to change their fortunes so they can keep from starving. Same as us." Pain slammed the car door and went around to the back of the van where Lil Sorrow was waiting for him.

———

Once all of the guests were settled in the house and the games were in full swing, the block was relatively quiet again. To the casual passerby, it didn't look like there was anything going on outside of an intimate gathering. For all intents and purposes, it now looked like any other house on the block. One of the golden rules of the spot on the nights they hosted the exclusive poker games was that there was no parking in front of the house or hanging out. You either took a rideshare or had somebody drop you off and keep it pushing. They needed to have that street clear at all times so as not to block the flow of traffic. Hiding in plain sight was how the spot had been able to keep the games going for so long.

Now that there was no one else coming in for the night, security found themselves with pockets of free time. Some of them rotated in and out of the house in shifts for things like bathroom breaks and to make sure everything was good inside. It was Sean's turn to man the front. He wasn't happy about his number being called in the rotation because he had been in the house most of the night ogling the women. Still, everybody had to do their part. He was leaning against the fence, putting flame to the tip of a cigarette, when he saw a man approaching. He was thick, wearing jeans and a black leather jacket. Sporting jewelry and designer sunglasses, he didn't look like a robber, but Sean was still on point. He tossed his cigarette and moved to intercept the man.

"Can I help you, my man?" Sean stood between the thick man and the house.

"Yeah, I'm here for the card game," the man replied. There was a bit of a slur to his voice. He wasn't quite drunk, but another drink or two would push him there.

"Ain't no card game going on here, fam," Sean told him.

The guy in the shades looked up at the house. Though you couldn't see who was inside, you could tell that there were people milling about. "C'mon, man. Quit playing. I'm already late." He tried to slide past, but Sean grabbed him by the arm.

"Fuck is you doing? You know where the fuck you at?" Sean barked.

"Yeah, I know where I'm at and that's what I keep trying to tell you! I'm here for the card game. Here, let me show you my invitation." The man in the shades reached into his inside pocket.

At the mention of him having an invitation, Sean relaxed a bit. Only the guests knew about the method of entry, so it was possible that the man had been telling the truth about running late. His willingness to give the man the benefit of the doubt would cost him his job and his chin. Sean had been in plenty of fights as a kid and even as an adult, but he could not remember being hit as hard as he was that night. He didn't even see the punch coming until it was inches from his chin and it was too late to do anything about it. The first blow hit him with so much force that he felt his lower teeth connect with his top, breaking several of them. The second blow landed on his temple, and the last thing Sean would remember seeing is the ground coming up at him as he fell.

"Dumb muthafuckas," Hook said as he removed the designer glasses to admire his handiwork. He knelt and searched over the man's person until he found what he was looking for. He then took out his cell phone, turned on the flashlight, and waved it over his head three times before putting it away. A few seconds later, Sauce and Tyriq pulled up in a van identical to the one Case was driving. They double-parked the van, with the ass of it sticking out just enough to prevent cars from easily passing. To the casual observer, it appeared to be just another case of someone not knowing how to park, but this was intentional. They wanted to back traffic up so that if police or reinforcements were to show up they'd be slowed down.

"You laid that boy smooth out!" Tyriq whistled as he passed the unconscious Sean. He was wearing painter's coveralls and a ski mask. An AK-47 was cradled in his arm, locked and loaded. He hadn't come to play.

"That's what I do. Knock niggas the fuck out," Hook boasted, cracking his knuckles menacingly.

"Whatever." Tyriq made a dismissive gesture. "You got that?"

Hook held up the key card and smiled triumphantly. "Right where he said it would be."

"Money well spent."

"We gotta get to the money before we can spend it. Where my strap?" Hook asked.

"Right here." Sauce joined them on the curb. He too was wearing painter's coveralls and a ski mask. Slung over one shoulder was a black shoulder bag and cradled in his arms was the biggest assault rifle he had ever seen, a P415. He passed it to Hook and watched him handle it with one hand like a child's toy.

"This is what the fuck I'm talking about." Hook stroked the gun lovingly.

"Put some shade on that shit, my nigga. We don't want the neighbors to see and get spooked. Or worse—these niggas spot it on one of their cameras and be waiting on us when we walk in," Tyriq warned.

"That's a problem we ain't likely to have," Sauce said proudly, and flipped the shoulder bag open. Inside was what looked like a toaster oven with a bunch of blinking lights on it. "Got me one of them Wi-Fi jammers from eBay and made my own upgrades. Once I turn it on, any radio signal within two hundred feet of this thing will be compromised."

"Then you lead the way." Hook pressed the key card into Sauce's chest.

Sauce snatched the card and walked grudgingly up to the door. "Can't stand this fool," he mumbled before pressing the card against the lock. It blinked red twice. He tried it again. This time it flipped green, but almost immediately flashed red again.

"What are you doing? Jerking your dick?" Hook whispered, looking around nervously. He was itching to get inside.

"Shit ain't working. Maybe the jammer is interfering," Sauce reasoned, continuing to swipe the lock with the same results.

"Man, fuck this!" Hook stormed toward the door.

"Don't do it!" Tyriq warned as Hook stomped past him. He was about to fuck up Case's carefully laid plan, forcing them to have to improvise and putting their lives at risk. He moved to stop Hook, but the minute he raised his foot to kick the door in, it swung open.

"Damn, Sean. How many times do I have to show your stupid ass how to use that card?" A well-built man wearing all black snatched the door open. He expected to find the new guy he had been assigned to work with that night, but instead he found death.

The three robbers and the man who had opened the door were caught off guard, but it was the robbers who reacted first. Sauce moved with the grace of an alley cat, dropping the jammer and drawing a knife from his coveralls. With one hand he covered the man's mouth, and with the other he drove the knife into his ribs several times. He was dead before he could even summon a scream. Sauce held him there until he was certain that the man was dead, before laying him on the ground tenderly.

"Thought you specialized in electronics?" Tyriq asked, staring down at the dead body.

"I specialize in survival." Sauce wiped his blade on the man's jacket and retrieved his jammer box. He gave it a quick once-over to make sure that it wasn't damaged.

Tyriq stood in the doorway of the house with a cylindrical object in his hand. The grenade had been a specialty order from Case's shopping list, just as Hook's P415 and Pain's peculiar request for the battering ram had been. He still couldn't figure out what the Blackbird had wanted with it, and it was above his pay grade to bust his brain over it. It was time to get paid. "Let's announce ourselves," he said before pulling the pin and tossing the concussion grenade inside.

———————

Passion was amongst the many who were trying to figure out what the heck was going on. One minute they were trying to determine what happened to the power, then there was an explosion from somewhere near the front of the house, and then came the chaos. Gamblers, hangers-on, and security all seemed to bolt in different directions in response. It was a stampede in the small space. Passion immediately looked for Juju. She spied her friend being pulled toward an exit by Jay. The whole time Juju kept looking back at Passion and trying to fight to get to her, but Jay had a tight grip on her. Passion's head whipped this way and that, trying to find a route for her own escape. In every direction there was furniture being overturned. One of the televisions had fallen off the wall, cracking someone in the head in the process. Passion stood like a deer in headlights, trying her best not to get swept up in the tide of people who were running for their lives.

She turned just in time to see a burly man screaming like a woman and running at top speed in her direction. He would've surely bowled her over had it not been for a pair of soft hands taking her about the waist and spinning her out of harm's way at the last second. It was Dice. He twirled her with the grace of a dancer and pulled her to a safe corner of the floor.

"What's going on?" Passion shouted frantically, hands covering her head as glass and feet fell round her. Were those gunshots she heard from the other room?

"The place is being robbed," Dice informed her, using his body to shield the girl.

Robbed? Was he fucking serious? Didn't places like that have protection against those kinds of things? Why did this have to happen on the night that she was there and had wagered her life's savings on a long shot? So many questions filtered through her brain, but she was too busy trying to keep from getting trampled or shot to add voice to them.

From where she and Dice were crouching, Passion could see into the room where the men had been playing poker. The Italian who had called out to Dice about the game was now on his feet, barking instructions to his security team. Passion now knew who ran the spot. Three men dressed in black rushed out the door that led to the front of the house where Passion had first heard the loud bang. They were a tough-looking lot, probably ex-cops or hired guns. Surely, they would get things back under control. Not long after they had cleared the door, Passion heard what she was now certain was gunfire, followed by screams. Several seconds later the tough guys who had run out were being ushered back into the room. Three of them had gone out, but only two came back. The blood splatter on the side of one of their faces told Passion exactly what had happened to him. Behind them were two men, both armed. One was wearing painter's coveralls and a ski mask, while the other had on a leather jacket. His eyes were covered by sunglasses. The one with the glasses cradled the biggest machine gun Passion had ever laid eyes on, sweeping it back and forth over everyone in the room. She guessed that he had been the one responsible for thinning security's numbers. There was something about his scowl that told her what evil lurked in his heart. All Passion was trying to do was make a little money to pull herself out of the hell that she had been living in, but instead she'd crawled into a hell that was far worse. A hell that she was starting to doubt she would live to tell about. Just when she thought that her night couldn't get any worse, the entire building shook.

———

Maggie, the woman who'd been in charge of exchanging the cash for preloaded credits, had been in the streets for a long time. She had risen from running to the store to put her granny's daily numbers in, to being one of the most respected bookkeepers in the underworld. She'd always had a thing for numbers, and was one of the few honest players in the game. Maggie's primary source of income came from her bookkeeping business that serviced mostly criminal organizations. Maggie worked seven days a week for three weeks out of each month, year-round. The only days she took off were when the monthly card games rolled around. The gig paid well for only a few hours of work, so she was always up for it. Handling money for the gangsters and killers who frequented the card games never bothered her. They all came from the same thing. Maggie had been in the streets all her life, so she had a level of street smarts that either escaped or was underappreciated by the average woman. It was these smarts that kicked in at the moment she realized that the place was being robbed.

Before security could even process what was going on, Maggie was already in motion. The first thing she did was grab her pistol from the drawer of the small desk she sat behind and make sure there was a round in the chamber. Next, she removed the small flash drive from the laptop she had been working on and stuffed it into her lady parts. She then smashed the laptop against the floor before dropping it into a mop bucket full of water and bleach. She kept it close by for just such occasions. There was some loose cash on the desk that hadn't made it into the safe, which she swept into her shoulder bag. Whatever was in the safe wasn't her concern, but the cash would be her severance. She could hear shots coming from the front of the house, which was good. That meant the back would be clear. There was a small closet in the office that had been a part of the renovations. What most didn't know though was that the back wall of the closet was false. It was a door that opened to the outside. This was how Maggie had planned to make her escape. Sadly, her plan was dashed when the entire wall of the renovated office came crashing in, burying her under a pile of plaster and Sheetrock.

"We gonna crash out!" Lil Sorrow shouted into Pain's ear. The roar of the bike in such closed quarters was deafening and the exhaust fumes threatened to choke them.

"No, we're not. Now stop speaking failure over this mission!" Pain shot back over his shoulder. His hands gripped the handlebars of the bike, giving and taking power from the throttle. He wouldn't say it aloud, but he shared in Lil Sorrow's apprehension. When he'd sat down with Case to go over his plan to rip off the poker game, he'd found it flawed. The biggest hole in his plot had been their method of entry, with them all going in through the front and betting on the element of surprise. That was leaving too much to chance, so Pain tweaked the plan. What he'd come up with had been creative, as they would never see it coming, but it was also very dangerous. Well, he was committed to it now. No turning back.

"You ready?" Pain was speaking to himself, but Lil Sorrow took it upon himself to answer.

"Hell no, but fuck it."

Pain sank down into the seat, leaned over the handlebars, and dug his heels in. He could feel Lil Sorrow's grip tighten around him, rattling the chains that were coiled between them. There was a tense moment when Pain thought about calling the whole thing off and figuring out another way. Then he thought about his grandmother and dying broke. When Case threw the back doors of the van open, Pain pulled back on the throttle and shot out like a bullet.

———————

Passion, as well as damn near everybody else in the room, cried out in shock as the rear office of the house was leveled. Two men riding on a motor bike with some type of battering ram mounted on it smashed through the wall of the office, burying the lone woman who worked back there beneath a pile of rubble. The guard who was assigned to that area rushed to attend to her. His efforts were thwarted when the man who had been steering the bike slid off of it to meet him. He was like a ninja with a clean dismount, drawing a sawed-off shotgun from somewhere at his back. He gave the guard both barrels, sending him flying back into the sitting room, landing next to where Passion and Dice were. He wriggled around on the ground in pain, but was still alive. From his wounds it looked like he had been hit with buckshot. The night was getting more insane by the minute and Passion cursed Juju for walking her into this action movie.

———————

"You think she dead?" Lil Sorrow asked, looking from where he was sitting on the bike to the woman lying in the floor. Pain was kneeling beside her, checking her pulse.

"Nah, but she's fucked up. Not our problem." Pain jogged back to the bike. He was relieved that he hadn't killed her. The guard he'd blasted with buckshot was fair game, but he had a thing about hurting women. Pain grabbed the length of chain, which had been rolled up on the seat between him and Lil Sorrow, and uncoiled it. At the end were two large hooks. He secured the safe with one end and the other was fastened to the bike. "Now." He gave Lil Sorrow the signal.

The boy slid into the seat Pain had vacated and cranked the bike. "You, know something? You're a genius, Blackbird. Don't let nobody tell you different."

"Ride, fool!" Pain slapped the ass of the bike as if it was a horse.

Lil Sorrow swung the bike expertly in the tight space and shot out through the hole they'd created in the wall. The chain tensed before the safe came flying loose from the floor and clanged along behind the bike. Pain didn't dare breathe until he spied Lil Sorrow and Case loading the safe into the back of the van. When Pain had come up with the plan, the whole crew called him crazy, but it had been successfully executed and no civilians had to die for them to get what they wanted.

No one had wanted to go along with Pain's alteration of the heist when he originally laid it out. "This is some James Bond–level shit and it ain't gonna work," Hook had complained when Pain put in the request for the battering ram. Pain could see where his plan looked shaky to the crew, because they hadn't done the footwork like he had. Case had provided them with a blueprint of the spot, but when Pain visited the building personally he discovered that the blueprint hadn't included the office in the back. That wasn't a part of the original design. It had been an add-on during the building's renovations. He gambled on the fact that the materials they used would have been of a cheaper quality than they had been forty years prior, when the brownstone had been built. The office wall would be the sweet spot. Thankfully, the gamble had paid off. While Hook, Tyriq, and Sauce raised hell in the front, Pain and Case would creep in from the back.

"A'ight," Case began, stepping through the rubble where the wall used to be. "Y'all know what this is, so no need for the speech. Give it up, and we'll let you get out of here and back to your families."

"Get cute, and it's Halloween!" Hook let off a burst from his silenced machine gun, blowing holes in the ceiling.

"You boys are making a mistake! Do you know whose game you're robbing?" The Italian sprang to his feet.

Case gave Hook a nod, and the boxer slammed the butt of his assault rifle into the Italian's face and laid him out.

"Now, if there are no more interruptions?" Case scanned the room. "Good, let's get this over with."

The robbers gathered everyone in the sitting room, where Passion and Juju had been watching the feed of the poker game. Hook, Sauce, and Tyriq went about the task of collecting the cash, which they stuffed into plastic garbage bags, while Pain and Case kept everyone covered. Between the murdered guard in the other room and seeing the Italian get his teeth knocked out, nobody else wanted to play hero. They cooperated with the robbers in hopes of escaping with their lives.

"Man, I ain't never had a lick this sweet!" Hook beamed, carrying a trash bag full of money, which he dropped at Case's feet. "Gotta be at least twenty or thirty large, and that ain't even counting whatever we find in the safe and the jewelry. Some of these niggas was in here real heavy." He kicked a man sitting on the ground who he had snatched a chain from. "You done brought us Christmas early, boss!"

"I can't take all the credit." Case looked to Pain. "You know, I have to admit that we were a little bit skeptical about your improvements to my plan. What's a robbery without a little bloodshed? In the end, your way worked better."

"Of course it did. You know nobody plans a robbery better than your boy," Pain boasted.

"I'm gonna help the boys carry this cash out. You and the homie cover our exits," Case ordered, grabbing two bags of cash. Tyriq and Sauce also grabbed two. Case went out the hole Pain had created in the back while the other two robbers went through the front, back to where they had left the van.

"Them bags better not be light either when it's time to count up!" Hook called after them. He waited until everyone was gone, except for Pain, to help himself to a little something extra. He started digging into the pockets of some of the men for cash, and taking jewelry off the ladies.

"What the fuck are you doing?" Pain asked. They had just hit what could've possibly been one of the biggest scores of any of their careers and had enough cash to choke a horse, and he was digging in pockets like a common thief.

"Getting mine. What does it look like?" Hook replied, yanking a ring off the pinky of one of the men they were holding hostage. The man glared at Hook hatefully, trying to commit what little bit of his face he could see to memory in case their paths should cross again.

"This wasn't a part of the plan. We ain't got time for that petty shit," Pain said, looking around cautiously. They had already been inside longer than they were supposed to be.

"Who you think you talking to?" Hook came to stand in front of Pain and gave him a defiant look. "You think because you had some input on this caper that makes you some kind of shot-caller?"

"Nah, man. I'm just a nigga trying to get paid. Same as you," Pain said, trying to defuse the situation.

"We ain't the same by a long shot. The minute you forget, I'm gonna remind you," Hook threatened.

"Man, what the fuck is your problem?" Pain had finally tired of Hook and his bullshit. It seemed like every time they were in each other's company he had something slick to say.

"My problem is that I don't trust you. I don't give a shit how much history you and ol' boy are supposed to have, you're still a new nigga to me."

"Whatever, nigga. We're done and I'm gone." Pain started for the hole-in-the-wall. His eyes happened to land on a familiar face and it gave him pause.

Passion had never been so terrified in her life. Her dress and her hair were covered in debris from the wall that had just come crashing in. When she saw the Italian get his teeth knocked in she knew that they were going to die, but then one of the men who had come through the wall restored order. She was actually relieved when all of the gamblers were herded together into the sitting room and their wrists zip-tied.

She spied Juju and Jay sitting on the floor across from her. They hadn't made it out, caught by the men who had come in through the front. Juju looked at her with frightened eyes. The same couldn't be said for Jay. She looked to Dice, hoping she would find some comfort in the man she had come to the spot with, but didn't. He was in what appeared to be a trance, staring blankly at the wall and rocking back and forth like a mental patient. Passion nudged his leg to try and get his attention but it was no use. *"The bastard . . . the bastard son . . ."* he kept repeating, as if he was having some type of psychotic break. Passion knew she would get no help from him. She was on her own. She watched as three of the robbers made their way around the room collecting cash. They had managed to fill six trash bags and there was still cash scattered on tables and on the floor. She remained as quiet and as still as she could, hoping not to draw unwanted attention to herself.

Passion's eyes rested on one of the robbers, a tall man wearing a ski mask. There was something about his posture that rang familiar to her, but at the moment she was too frightened to put the pieces together. She was too worried about dying to focus on anything else. After collecting the money, the men made their exit, leaving two behind to cover their backs. Unfortunately, one of them was the big one with the glasses, who seemed to be the cruelest of the group. She was hoping that now that they had the money they would leave, but it wasn't to be. The big man wasn't done. She watched him dig into pockets, taking cash and snatching jewelry from the necks of women. It was then she remembered the jade earrings in her ears. There was no way she could let them get Juju's mother's jewelry, but with her hands bound she couldn't move to take them off. While she was trying to solve her dilemma one of the robbers walked past her, moving up and down the line of hostages making sure everyone was secured. He paused when he reached Passion and gave her a look of recognition. It was ever so brief, but she caught it and he knew she had.

If it wasn't for bad luck, Pain wouldn't have any. Of all the joints they could've planned on robbing, it had to be the one she was in. Wearing a gown and with her face all painted up she looked older, but Pain was still able to recognize her. What were the odds that the universe would have their paths cross three different times under three different sets of circumstances? By that time he was convinced that it was no longer a set of coincidences, but kismet.

"What have we here?" Hook came to stand between Pain and Passion. He reached for her, and she recoiled in terror. "I'm a thief, not a rapist, shorty. Run them earrings."

"I can't," Passion said with shaky voice.

"That wasn't a request," Hook said in a stern tone.

"But you don't understand—" she began, but was cut off when Hook roughly snatched one from her ear, ripping the lobe. Passion shrieked, her ear beginning to bleed.

"You still got one lobe left. Give it up, bitch, or rock clip-ons the rest of your days," Hook threatened.

"Homie, you out of pocket. We said we ain't off this kind of shit," Pain interjected. He was speaking to Hook, but his eyes were on Passion. He wanted to go to her and comfort her, but he checked himself. This was about business, not fantasies.

"We ain't said shit!" Hook barked back. "I don't know what kind of pussy-ass arrangement you and Case came to, but I'm a thief. I'm here for it all," he told Pain before turning his attention back to Passion.

Passion waited until Hook reached in to snatch her second earring before firing her head forward. Her forehead slammed into Hook's lower lip, drawing blood, but she damn near knocked herself out in the process. She was jarred back to her senses when Hook slapped her across the face. It was only a slap, but she might as well have been hit by a lead pipe. Passion flew backwards, bounced off the wall, and landed on the floor in a daze.

"Bitch, is you crazy?" Hook kicked her. "You ready to die over some jewelry?" He drew his foot back to kick her a second time, but paused when he felt the familiar press of a gun barrel at the back of his head.

"Go ahead. Kick her again. I dare you," Pain said in a hiss. He had his gun to Hook's head and his finger curled around the trigger, prepared to squeeze.

"You gonna draw down on me over a bitch?" Hook growled. "You smelled like a tender dick nigga from the moment I met you. I knew you wasn't right for this crew."

"I can agree with you on that. I ain't right for no crew that's members get their kicks from beating on women. I also ain't a nigga who bluffs. Now, we can leave here and go see about splitting this money up, or you can try me and die here. At this point, I'm hoping you feel like trying me."

Hook weighed his options. "A'ight, you got it." He began backing away from Passion. When he was no longer standing close enough to hit her again, he felt Pain relax a bit and that's when he made his move. He spun on Pain and slammed the assault rifle into his face with so much force that Pain lost his grip on the pistol. Hook was relentless, hitting him over and over again, eventually dropping Pain to the ground. He then braced the machine gun against his hip and pointed it at Pain. "The last nigga to draw on me was the last nigga to draw on me. Night-night, tender dick."

What happened next unfolded in slow motion for Pain. He saw Hook take aim and lock his finger around the trigger. From the cold look in Hook's eyes, Pain knew with certainty that he was about to die. He thought of his grandmother and her constant fears over him dying in the streets. Pain had always dismissed her fears, but as it turned out, she had been right. He wouldn't close his eyes to meet his end. He would go out like a soldier, staring his killer in the eyes before he left this world. He heard shots, but they hadn't come from Hook's gun.

Hook howled in pain as his shoulder exploded, causing him to accidentally fire off the machine gun. Bullets narrowly missed Pain as they perforated the ground mere inches from him. There was another shot. This one took out Hook's knee and put him on his back. The eyes of everyone in the room turned to the hole in the wall, where Lil Sorrow stood holding a smoking pistol.

"You good, big homie?" Lil Sorrow asked Pain while keeping his eyes and his gun trained on Hook, who was writhing on the ground in pain.

"I'm straight." Pain climbed to his feet.

"I did like you said and didn't let this thang bang unless it got crazy. I think this counts as crazy," Lil Sorrow said proudly.

"Indeed, it does."

"I can't believe this little muthafucka shot me! I'm gonna kill the both of you!" Hook vowed.

"You ain't gonna do shit but bleed!" Lil Sorrow stomped on Hook's ruined knee. He pointed the gun at the boxer's head. "Say the word, big bro, and it's the end of the world for this pussy!"

Pain thought about it. Having Lil Sorrow end Hook would've brought him untold joy, but it would be yet another stain on his already soiled soul. No, he had a far more sinister end for Hook in mind. "Nah, he ain't worth the bullet." Then he stood over Hook and said, "In light of this being a gambling spot, let's make a little wager. Who do you think will get here first? The cops or the muscle behind this operation you just helped us rob? Either way, it's a safe bet that your run on these streets is over."

"Fuck you! You're gonna regret not killing me. If it's the last thing I do, I'm gonna watch your punk-ass burn!" Hook vowed.

"Shoot your shot, homie," Pain told him and started for the exit hole in the wall. As an afterthought, he picked up the earring Hook had snatched from Passion's ear and tossed it at her feet. "You should pick less dangerous spots to hang out at," he said, before disappearing through the hole and into the night.

CHAPTER 22

Mercy . . . that's what Pain told Case he had shown Hook by leaving him to the dogs instead of killing him. Case was hot when Pain and Lil Sorrow showed up back at the van minus Hook. Pain had given him the rundown on how things went left when Hook got greedy and put the crew and the mission at risk, opting to leave out the part about Passion. Lil Sorrow backed his story. Hook was a liability and had to go.

"No one man above the team!" Case had ranted. He and Hook were crime partners and had pulled off many jobs while Pain was away. Pain had not only cost him a close friend, but his muscle. With the kind of problems he had hanging over his head, he needed all the available shooters he could get, especially ones with Hook's kind of blind loyalty.

"It was either him or me and I chose him," Pain said flatly. He didn't give a shit how Case felt about losing his flunky. In hindsight, he probably should've let Lil Sorrow wax him and be done with it, but the choice was no longer in his hands.

As luck would have it, the police got to Hook before the Italians who ran the gambling spot did. He managed to hobble out of the brownstone and make it half a block before collapsing due to loss of blood. When he woke up he was in the hospital and under arrest, but not for the robbery. Hook had been on the run for a prior drug charge and he had skipped bail, so his days on the streets were numbered either way.

"I don't know, man. Who's to say that ol' boy ain't feeling some type of way about Pain crossing him and catch a case of loose lips?" Sauce questioned. He didn't know Hook well enough to care about him being cut out. Pain was the one who had brought him into the crew, but Hook now represented a loose end that could hang them all.

"Nah, Hook is solid. He ain't gonna talk," Case assured him. "When things cool off a bit, I'll pay him a visit and see if I can smooth things over. Whatever lawyer fees that need to be paid are coming out of your end, Pain."

Once that was settled they moved onto the important business: the money. In total they had relieved the gambling spot of over one hundred thousand dollars, not including the jewels that still needed to be fenced. Even split six ways, they all made out with a nice piece of change. Pain's end was enough to finally wipe out his grandmother's debt and still have enough money to hold him down until he figured out what he was going to do with his life. The incident at the robbery had left a bad taste in his mouth, and he decided that he was going to fall back from running with Case and the crew for a while.

The next week or so was quiet for Pain. He kept it close to home and spent time with his grandmother, watching game shows together and eating. It felt good to hang out with the old woman, and it was a reminder to Pain of what he had been missing all the years he was away. Case had hit him up a few times about jobs, but Pain always made up an excuse not to take part. He still had a few dollars left over from the poker heist and was still pulling in money from the chop shop. He wasn't rich yet, but he wasn't hurting. He'd also gotten word that the Queen had been trying to reach him. She didn't have his new number, as he had only gotten his cell phone on the day he got out. She knew where he lived, but her popping up wasn't likely. Ms. Pearl had never made her dislike of the Outlaw Queen a secret. She always blamed Cassandra for Pain's troubles. What did she want that hadn't been said on the day he'd seen her? He started to reach out, but decided against it. There was only one thing that Cassandra could've wanted from him: the services of the Blackbird, and he wasn't in the Crow business anymore. Case was easy enough to turn down, but Cassandra not so much. He didn't need her screwing with his head while he was still trying to get things sorted out. So he avoided her.

Someone who had been seriously invading his thoughts was Passion. Seeing her at the robbery had been both unexpected and fortuitous. The connection he felt between them was too strong for him to believe that these were some random meetings. "I'm only here for a season, not a reason," Passion had told him when they met. He hadn't agreed then and he certainly didn't agree now. They were in each other's lives for a reason, though what that was he was still uncertain of. Circumstances aside, she was looking good enough to eat that night. All traces of the robbery victim and the tipsy girl at The Yard had been washed away, and she pulled up on some real grown-woman shit in her black gown and jewels.

Seeing Passion become one of the victims at the robbery had changed the dynamics of it. If Pain was being honest, he wished that he had handled the situation with Hook differently. He was out of line for getting into it with him, especially in the middle of a job, but he felt like he had a personal stake in Passion, and seeing Hook draw blood from her made him react without thinking it through. Whenever he saw the girl it reminded him of stories he had heard crackheads tell about hitting the drug for the first time and constantly chasing that initial high. Passion was like a drug to Pain, and in his line of work, he couldn't afford any types of habits. He needed to go cold turkey from her, and the first step would be to return her necklace.

Getting the information he needed to find Passion proved to be easy enough. He was the Blackbird, after all. When Pain was still the right hand of the Queen he had access to dozens of little birds: spies who carried information like dry leaves on the wind. Most of his old contacts were gone, dead, in prison, or out of the information business, but he was able to luck up and find someone he used to ride with called Sparrow. Like Pain, Sparrow was no longer a part of the Queen's murder, but still in the business of information. It took a day or so, but he was able to give Pain a rundown on the girl.

From Sparrow he learned that Passion lived in Harlem. She shared an apartment with a pimp they called Uncle Joe and several of his whores. According to Sparrow, Passion didn't sell pussy. At least not yet. From what he was able to uncover, she was a decent-enough girl trapped in a bad situation. Armed with Sparrow's information, Pain began shadowing Passion. He would post up outside her building and watch her comings and goings. She mostly went to work, school, or the store, but didn't hang out on the block with the other hood rats.

There were a few nights when Pain had posted up across the street from the diner where she worked, off Broadway, and just observed her. He had more than a few opportunities to approach her there, return the necklace, and be done with torturing himself, but he could never find the strength to do so. Giving the jewelry back would mean the end of his surveillance of Passion, and he wasn't sure if he was ready for that just yet. Why he couldn't simply let this girl go was a question that Pain wouldn't find the answer to until he asked, and so against his better judgment, he did.

———————

The days leading up to her birthday were rough for Passion. All the money she had been saving had been lost in the robbery. She'd had a bad feeling about it from the start and should've followed her first instincts, but she was desperate. Each day she was forced to stay with Uncle Joe passed by like a month. It had already been a powder keg waiting to blow, but the fight with Zeta made things worse. Of course, she had run straight to Uncle Joe. Passion hadn't been there, but Birdie had told her the whole story. Zeta painted a picture of Passion having jumped on her, but Joe busted her ass in the lie. What only a few knew, and Passion herself had just discovered, was that Uncle Joe had cameras in the house. Birdie heard him yelling that that's how he knew she was lying. Passion was mortified to hear this. She had been living with Uncle Joe all that time and had no clue. Had he been watching her? All of them in their most intimate moments? Bo had assured them that there were no cameras in the bathrooms or bedrooms, only the common areas, but Passion didn't believe her. It seemed like with each passing day she discovered a new level to Uncle Joe's depravity. From then on, she made sure that she was always fully covered, even in her bedroom. She would change her clothes under the bed sheets, and when she showered it was always in the dark. Something else had transpired between Uncle Joe and Zeta, too. Birdie wasn't sure what, because Uncle Joe had dragged Zeta into the bedroom and when she came out she was holding her face and crying. The next morning, she woke to find all her shit packed and was shipped off to work at one of Uncle Joe's spots in Philadelphia.

Having Zeta out of the apartment didn't ease the tensions that lived there. In fact, they had increased. Uncle Joe went through the roof when he saw Passion the day after the robbery and spotted her swollen and bruised cheek. The guy at the card game had clocked her pretty good, even loosening one of her back teeth. He demanded to know who had done it so that he could deal with it. Passion told him that she had no idea who the man was, which was the truth. She just told him that she was out with Juju and some dudes tried to rip them off at the weed spot. He forbade Passion from hanging out with Juju so much, blaming her for putting her in harm's way. Her seeing a lot of Juju anymore wasn't going to be a problem. After her brother Jay snitched to her parents about her being in the gambling spot, they put Juju's ass on lockdown. She couldn't even go to the pharmacy to buy pads without one of her father's or brother's people with her. Juju beefed about it, but Passion sensed that secretly she didn't mind being put on time-out from the streets. That robbery had been a terrifying experience for both girls, but for Juju it hit different. She confided to Passion that this was the first time she had ever really thought about dying. Passion thought about death every day.

Since the robbery, Uncle Joe had been playing Passion closer than usual. He was always checking on her to see if she needed anything, and wanted to know where she was at all times. Uncle Joe had always been overly protective with Passion, but lately he had been treating her like she was made of glass. He was constantly prodding her about how she was feeling and her mental well-being. He'd even broached the subject of her parents' deaths again by asking her what she remembered from that night. "Nothing except waking up in the hospital," she told him, which was the same story she had been repeating since the accident. However, that was no longer entirely true. Zeta's verbal attack had stirred broken memories of that long-forgotten night.

Passion was getting frustrated, and desperate. She was broke and out of options. Her mind went back to Birdie's drunken confession about Uncle Joe's secret stash. Joe's sudden influx of cash when he announced that they were getting into the drug business was as unexpected as it was suspicious. Pimping his girls out had kept Joe out of the poorhouse, but those hustles weren't enough to bring in the amount of drugs they had started out with. The more she thought about it, the less far-fetched Birdie's story was starting to sound.

"Passion, what the hell are you doing back here, sleeping?" Gus coming up behind her startled her out of her daze. Gus was a burly Black man with a salt-and-pepper beard and beady eyes. He was wearing a chef's hat, white pants, and a white T-shirt that hugged his big belly. He was the lead chef and owner of the diner where Passion worked part-time.

"Sorry, Gus. I got a lot on my mind," Passion said apologetically.

"Well, get out of your head and to them tables. A lot of hungry people out there," Gus told her.

"I'll get to it," Passion said, tying on her apron.

"Be quick about it and don't let me have to tell you again. There are plenty of girls I could bring in here to do your job," Gus warned, as he always did when he was trying to spook the girls who worked for him.

"Yeah right," Passion said under her breath.

"Don't sass me, gal. You're the one who begged for extra shifts. You think because it's your birthday you're gonna get some special treatment?"

"Don't remind me," Passion sighed. In addition to everything else that was going wrong in her life, she found herself having to pick up a shift on her birthday. Working at the greasy spoon was the last place she wanted to be. She should've been landing in California by then, watching the sunrise light up the ocean on her special day, but that dream had died when she lost all her money. She was flat broke and back to where she started. The utter sadness of her situation brought tears to her eyes.

"Hey, hey now. I was only giving you a hard time like I always do. No need to cry about it," Gus said sympathetically.

"It's not you, Gus. I'm just stressed out." Passion wiped her eyes with the corner of her apron.

"Whatever is going on with you will pass. I'm sure of it." Gus draped his arm around her comfortingly. "How about this. Since it's your birthday and all, maybe we'll have us a little celebration. We can close this place early tonight, I'll cook your favorite meal, and maybe pop a bottle of wine or something. Then maybe after that," he let his hand travel down her arm.

"Don't!" Passion pulled away.

"Oh, you too good for ol' Gus to touch you now?" His demeanor switched and he was angry now. "I can remember wasn't that long ago when I had your ass bent over a box of burger patties and you were screaming my name. Now you're on some new shit, huh?" He was in her face. Passion's back was to the wall with Gus's hands pressed on either side of her.

Sadly, what Gus was saying was true. He had had the fortune of catching her during one of her episodes. She and Uncle Joe had gotten into a nasty argument and he'd said some things to Passion that cut deep. Against her better judgment, she had decided to have a little bit to drink before she started her shift. She didn't care if Gus smelled it on her and fired her because she was feeling self-destructive. Joe had made her feel worthless and she needed someone to make her feel wanted and it didn't matter who it was. It had only happened the once, but that was all it took to keep Gus sniffing around her to try and get a second helping. He would do things like press himself against her when they passed each other in the kitchen, or pinch her ass when he thought no one was watching. It seemed like each attempt Gus made to get back in her pants became more aggressive than the last. It was to the point where she was afraid to work until closing unless one of the other girls was there with her. She didn't trust Gus, but she needed the job too bad to quit.

"You know it ain't like that, Gus. It's just that time of the month, ya know?" Passion said, trying to calm him.

"If a horse can go through mud, then best believe Gus can go through blood," he rhymed. There was a very, very hungry look in his eyes. The only thing that saved Passion from whatever Gus was thinking was when a waitress named Heather came in the back and interrupted them. She was an older white woman and had been working with Gus since he opened the place.

"Gus, you got them steaks ready for me yet? The people at table eight are . . ." Heather's words trailed off when she saw Gus and Passion in a compromising position. "Everything okay?"

"Yeah, everything is fine," Gus answered.

"I wasn't talking to you," Heather informed him. "Passion, you okay?"

"I'm fine, Heather," Passion told her, but Heather didn't believe her.

"Passion, we need you on the floor. There's a guy at table two. Why don't you go and take his order?" Heather told her.

"Don't you see us talking?" Gus snapped.

"This conversation is over," Heather matched his tone. She was the one person Gus knew better than to fuck with. "Passion, take care of table two. Gus, go get those steaks out."

Passion slid from under Gus's arms and rushed for the doors leading to the dining room. "Thank you," she whispered to Heather as she passed. Passion breathed a sigh of relief once she was away from Gus. Had it not been for Heather there was no telling what Gus's perverted ass would've tried. It was bad enough that she had to sleep with one eye open at home, but the predators were circling at the job, too. She wasn't sure how long she would be able to go on like this.

Passion took a few beats to compose herself before making her way over to table two. There was only one person sitting there, a man. He had his face buried in the menu trying to figure out what he wanted to order. Whatever he decided, she hoped that it wasn't something that would require her to go back into that kitchen. "Sorry to keep you waiting. My name is Passion and I'll be your server. What can I get for you, sir?"

"How about a light?" he said from behind the menu. When he lowered it, Passion found herself staring into a pair of familiar eyes. Eyes filled with great sadness.

"Pain?" Passion gasped.

"You remembered my name. Guess that means I made a good first impression," Pain smiled.

"What are you doing here?"

"I just came to wish the most beautiful girl in the world a happy birthday." Pain gestured to something on the table in front of him that she hadn't initially noticed. It was a cupcake with a small birthday candle in it, like the ones you get from the Dollar Store.

Passion looked from the cupcake to Pain. "How did you know it was my birthday?"

"Three weeks," Pain announced. "That's what you told me when we met. You had a birthday coming in three weeks."

Well, he got points for being attentive. Most men couldn't remember what a woman said three minutes before, let alone three weeks. Passion was very impressed. She was about to tell him as much and then something occurred to her. "Wait, how did you know where I worked?"

Pain didn't answer right away. "I . . . um, I was in here getting a takeout order about a week or so ago and I saw you in here. You guys were swamped with the dinner crowd and you looked busy or else I'd have spoken," he lied. It was a small lie, but it beat telling her the truth about how he had been stalking her. "Blow out your candle and make a wish."

Passion thought about it, closed her eyes, and blew out the candle.

"What did you wish for?" Pain asked.

"If I told you then it probably wouldn't come true," Passion replied.

Pain pondered her response. "You might be onto something with that. Me? I've been of the thinking of wishing for what I need versus what I want." Pain pulled a jewelry box from his pocket and slid it across the table to Passion.

She eyed the box suspiciously. "What is this?"

Pain shrugged.

Passion opened the box and when she saw what was inside her breath caught in her throat. It was her lockets. Her eyes filled with tears and for a minute she couldn't compose herself enough to speak. "How?"

"Please, don't ask me questions that I won't be able to give you an honest answer to. Just know that I didn't have anything to do with it being taken. I'm only grateful that I was able to return it to its rightful owner."

Passion was overcome with emotions. She had thought she would never see the lockets again. The last thing in the world she treasured had been snatched away from her violently, just as her parents had been. Losing it had put her in a dark place, but Pain had turned the light back on. Uncle Joe always said that there was no such thing as the kindness of strangers, but the man sitting in front of her had proven him wrong.

"I'm sorry. I didn't mean to upset you," Pain said. Tears were freely streaming down Passion's face.

"It's fine. And thank you. You have no idea how much this means to me." Passion wiped her eyes with her apron.

"So, what happened to that trip you told me you were taking? I thought you would be long gone by now." Pain changed the subject to a lighter topic.

"It's a long story," she said, lowering her eyes.

"I'm a good listener."

This made Passion smile a bit. He was a good-looking man, thoughtful, and he knew all the right things to say. So far, he had all the makings of a prize catch, which meant that he wasn't for her. Nothing good ever manifested in her life. It would be just her luck that she ended up entertaining this man and he turned out to be a grade-A asshole or worse, an ass-whipper. Life already had its foot buried knee-deep in her ass, so there was no room for anyone else's.

"Passion, what the hell are you doing? I ain't paying your ass to stand around!" Gus shouted across the restaurant, causing everyone to look her way. It was embarrassing.

"What a fucking asshole," Pain said, glaring at Gus who was glaring right back at him.

"My life is full of them," Passion mumbled. "Look, you got to order something or I'm gonna get in trouble."

"Okay." Pain picked up the menu and began scanning it. "What do you suggest?"

"Honestly, I wouldn't eat a damn thing on that menu. The pie is safe, though. We get those from Walmart. Gus don't make them."

"Okay, let me get a slice of apple pie."

"A true-blue American, huh?" Passion teased him.

"No, I just like apple pie."

"Let me go and get your pie." She collected his menu.

Pain watched Passion walk away, admiring her curves. Even in the plain black slacks she wore under her apron you could tell that she was holding. When she made it to the counter where the pie displays sat, she was greeted by Gus and he didn't look happy. They exchanged heated words, which Pain was sitting too far away to hear, but their body language told the tale. Passion was trying to explain herself, but Gus didn't want to hear it. He barked something at her and she stomped off into the back, out of Pain's line of vision. Gus said something to one of the other waitresses and then followed Passion into the back. Something was afoot.

The waitress Gus had been speaking to came over to Pain's table. She tried to hide her nervousness, but did a poor job of it.

"What happened to Passion? She was supposed to bring me my slice of pie," Pain said before she could open her mouth.

"She . . . umm . . ." she stammered. "I'm sorry, but I'm going to have to ask you to leave."

"Why? What's the problem?" Pain already suspected the answer to that question but asked it anyway.

"It's my boss. He has a strict policy about no outside food in the diner." She pointed to the sign in the window near the entrance that said NO OUTSIDE FOOD, and then gestured at the cupcake.

"So, I guess that booze doesn't count." Pain nodded to a table where a group of young men were not-so-discreetly spiking their iced teas with a bottle of liquor.

"Mister, I don't want any trouble. I'm just doing what I was asked," the waitress said nervously.

"No worries, love. I'm a man who believes in carrying his own water. Your boss wants me gone? I'll let him tell me himself." Pain got up from the table and walked toward where he had seen Passion and Gus disappear.

"Wait . . . you can't go back there!" the waitress called after him, but Pain never broke his stride.

The double doors he passed through led him into a storage room.

Canned goods and pantry items were hastily stacked on shelves that looked like they had seen better days. From somewhere in the recesses of the room he could hear raised voices. One of them he identified as Passion's.

"C'mon, Gus. Why are you even acting like that? I wasn't doing nothing but being nice to a customer like you always tell us to do," he could hear Passion saying.

"Bullshit!" Gus snapped. "I saw you out there batting your eyes and shaking your ass like the little tramp you are. You all up in that nigga's face and I can't get the time of day!"

"You don't have to be talking to me that way."

"This is my joint, and I'll talk to you any damn way I please. You don't like it, get your shit and get the fuck out. As a matter of fact, you're done here. Leave your apron and name tag at the front with Heather."

"Gus, don't do me like that. I need this job!" Passion pleaded. She was to the point of tears by then. This part-time job was her only source of income. Without it she would never have a shot at escaping Uncle Joe.

"How bad do you need it?" Gus asked sinisterly. He reached out and touched her face. This time she didn't pull away. Gus wiped a tear from her cheek with one of his fat fingers then stuck it in his mouth. He closed his eyes, savoring the saltiness. "Damn, you taste good, girl." He ran his hand down the front of her blouse and cupped one of her breasts. "See, this ain't so bad, right?"

Passion closed her eyes and tried to shut out the world around her. She knew what Gus was attempting to do was wrong, but the twisted part of her brain told her that she deserved it. If she had only done her job instead of cozying up to Pain this wouldn't be happening. She was the one in the wrong. She tried to call up the darkness, but it was taking its time. All she had to do was give Gus what he wanted and things would go back to normal. She would be able to keep her job and save for her great escape. She just prayed that it would be over quickly. "What the fuck are you doing back here?" Passion heard Gus ask someone, followed by a loud crashing. When she opened her eyes, she found Gus sprawled on the floor with Pain standing over him.

"Low down, dirty dog nigga. What, you think you was about to take that girl's pussy? Not on my watch," Pain hissed.

"Now wait a minute. You got it all wrong. Me and Passion got an understanding, don't we?" Gus looked to Passion, who said nothing. She was too embarrassed to speak.

"You know, I was in prison with guys like you. Sick fucking perverts who liked to have their way with young girls who ain't got nobody to protect them. You're a predator, and would you like to know what we did to predators in prison?" Pain asked. He grabbed a loose knife from one of the shelves and tested the sharpness of its point against his index finger. "We castrated them. Real slow like." He flung the knife and it embedded itself in the floor between Gus's legs, narrowly missing his penis.

"Wait . . . wait . . . wait. This was all a mix-up. If you want the bitch you can have her. She's all yours!" Gus told him. This only made Pain angrier.

Pain drew his foot back and kicked Gus in the nuts. "Creep-ass nigga. She ain't property to be bartered. She's a person . . . a fucking human being!"

"Whatever you say, man. I just want you and this nutty broad out of my spot. You're done here, Passion," Gus told her.

"I've been done, I'm just mad I keep having to go through shit like this to realize it," Passion said. She had nearly let Gus defile her for eight dollars an hour. That was a new low and it didn't feel good.

"You straight?" Pain asked, checking her for injures. She was shaken up but otherwise unharmed. Passion nodded her head. "C'mon, we're getting you out of here." He draped his arm around her. As he was walking her out, he had some parting words for Gus. "This one here," he hugged Passion tighter, "she ain't your victim no more. She ain't nobody's victim."

When Passion and Pain emerged from the storeroom they found that an audience had gathered. Waitstaff and patrons alike had their eyes glued to the double doors, eager to sip the tea as to whatever was going on back there. Passion had expected that with all the racket someone would have called the police, but they hadn't. She looked to Heather, who was leaning against the wall where the diner's phone was mounted. She's was likely the reason no one had called. When she gave Passion a nod of approval, that confirmed it. She was free, at least of one monster.

They were passing the counter when Pain told her, "Hold tight for a second." She watched in amusement as he slid across the counter, popped the cash register open, and helped himself to whatever cash was inside. When he made it back to Passion, Pain held the money up and winked at her. "Severance pay."

That was the first time Passion had laughed in a very long time.

CHAPTER 23

"*All my momma gots to do now is collect it and smile . . .*" Case sang along with the Scarface classic featuring the late Tupac. Whenever he was in a mood he bumped either Pac or Face, depending on how he was feeling. That particular song provided him with a dose of both, so it was his go-to when he was trying to sort through a particularly sticky situation, which was what he was doing at that moment.

While Pain might've taken a sabbatical from the heist, it was still business as usual for Case and the gang, especially Case. He was out robbing and stealing like a man possessed, and with good reason. He was a marked man and would be so until he cleared his debt. However, the price of clearing this debt had become too high. Money was no longer on the table. The man he owed was asking for blood. He had managed to lie his way to a temporary stay of execution. Case had always been a good talker. He could sell water to a whale, but this was no whale he was dealing with. It was a barracuda. So far, he had been able to stay one step ahead of his karma, but the footfalls were getting closer.

When Pain touched down and decided to throw his hat back in the ring, it made Case hopeful. That was his ride or die and someone who he knew would pursue the bag with him full throttle. He just knew that once he filled Pain in on the jam he found himself in, his childhood friend would be able to get him out of it. Then when the situation with Hook came about it changed the dynamics of their relationship. Pain was a legend in the streets, but Hook was a respected member of the team. Some had considered the way Pain had left him for dead to be sucker shit, and they weren't wrong. Though Case understood why Pain handled it the way he did, it didn't make it any less wrong. He had sacrificed one of their own, which brought his pedigree into question. Pain fucking Hook over, for whatever the reason was, hadn't gained him any brownie points in the streets or amongst the crew. The fact that Case as their leader had let it slide only made things tenser. Hook had been one of them, and Pain had betrayed him, but so far there had been no consequences for his actions. Case had instilled the mantra of *"no one man above the team"* in all of his soldiers, but the fact that he was willing to turn a blind eye to what Pain had done called his leadership into question. This he could not have, so he did damage control as best he could.

Case picked up the glass on the bar top in front of him and sipped from it. As a second thought, he downed it and motioned for the bartender to bring him another one. Case was known to turn up, but he was mostly a social drinker. You never caught him at a function too drunk, or out in the streets off his square. *"Be aware and be prepared,"* is what Pain used to tell him when they first started going out on heists together. Those were words Case had carried with him into any room he planned to leave with more than he walked in with, and they had always carried him home safely. But that day the lessons his best friend had taught him didn't hold as much weight.

"You got something for me?" JK-47 slipped onto the barstool next to Case.

"What happened to 'hello'?" Case asked without bothering to look in Jay's direction. The bartender had just brought him another drink and that currently had his attention.

"Pleasantries between us went out the window when your folks' bullshit put my people in harm's way. My little sister could've been hurt!" Jay said sternly. "You rolled in shorthanded and the job played out sloppy, like I told you it would," Jay said. His tone was condescending.

Case glanced up from his glass at Jay. He understood that Jay was upset because his little sister had unexpectedly been caught up in the robbery, but at the end of the day, what was a girl her age doing in a den of killers in the first place? Case was okay with being empathetic, but not a scapegoat. "It ain't my job to keep track of your sister's comings and goings. That's on you." Case took an envelope from his pocket and slid it across the bar to Jay. He watched as Jay took his time counting through the money, before adding, "Five grand for your providing the inside track, and the rest of what I owed your people for the toys." It was Jay who had given them the intel about the rotating security shifts and the swipe cards that allowed entry into the house. "Thanks, by the way, for speaking with them and getting them to show me a little love on the down payment. I know that wasn't easy for you to swing."

"That's an understatement. I had to use my personal guarantee that you would make good on what you owed. And with these guys your life is used as collateral for these kinds of guarantees. Had you fucked them over we'd both be dead," Jay told him.

"Well, I didn't and we're both very much alive."

"You know, I admit that it struck me as a little odd when you added the battering ram and concussion grenade to your shopping list. My people thought maybe you were on some terrorist shit and were a little skeptical about it. Local heat is easy enough for those guys to deal with, but terrorism is federal territory."

"That was Pain's idea," Case admitted. He too had been skeptical when his friend had requested those items. Even when Pain tried to explain to him what he planned to use them for, Case was still on the fence. He thought Pain had a better chance at killing himself in the attempt than he actually did at making it through the wall. Once again, his friend had proven him wrong.

"I'm big enough to admit when I'm wrong, and I was definitely wrong about your buddy Blackbird. Seeing him in action, I can understand why he was so well-respected back in his day. That cat is like a freaking action hero."

"I tried to tell you young punks that, Blackbird was the truth!" Case bragged.

"Yeah, you did and he is. Though I think Hook probably feels differently. I heard he's looking at an asshole full of time and doesn't plan on taking it lying down. He's in the city jail's infirmary talking real crazy. One of my people's wife works there as a nurse. You better watch yourself, man," Jay warned.

"Hook ain't no snitch," Case dismissed Jay's warning. "Besides, he'd never turn on the crew."

"Why not, when the crew turned on him?" Jay questioned.

"That wasn't a decision made by the crew. That's all on Blackbird." Case had tried to express this same sentiment to Hook when he'd called him a few days ago, but Hook didn't want to hear it. If whatever Case had to say didn't start and end with Pain's death then Hook was deaf to it. *"You owe this to me,"* had been Hook's exact words, and technically he wasn't wrong. Hook had been Case's right hand when Pain was gone. He knew where all the bodies were buried, figuratively and literally. If he wanted, he could burn the whole crew down. Case doubted that he would go there, but the only way to ensure it would be to have Hook murdered in prison or do something to appease him.

"Yeah, I was there. I know," Jay continued. "I wouldn't wish prison on my worst enemy, but your boy was out of line for putting his hands on that little girl."

"What little girl?" Case asked, confused.

"The chick Passion that my sister hangs around with. Hook roughed her up over some earrings, even ripped one of the girl's earlobes over them. Pain took it personal. Shit went left from there." Jay filled in the blanks.

Case tried to hide his utter shock at this piece of news. Pain and Lil Sorrow had told him that Pain and Hook's fight had been over Hook taking unnecessary chances and pulling a gun on Pain. Neither of them had mentioned a girl being involved. He had been lied to, but why? If only one of them had told the lie, he still wouldn't like it but could understand, but the fact that both of them were telling the same story meant that they had conspired to come up with it. This made Case wonder what else the two of them were in cahoots about. He then thought back to Hook's warning about Pain usurping leadership of the crew. At the time it had been laughable, but in light of this new information it wasn't so funny anymore.

"So, what you about to get into? I'm gonna slide uptown and get some bud from my guys. They just got some new shit in from Denver that's supposed to be bomb as fuck. Roll with me and I'll throw you an ounce on the strength," Jay offered.

"Thanks, but I got somewhere else that I need to be." Case slid off the barstool and hit the exit.

The bombshell Jay had just dropped on Case had killed his buzz and he was completely sober when he left the bar. After all he had done for Pain since he'd come home from prison, and this was how he repaid him? Case had not only put Pain back on his feet, but he had been his veil of protection. There were some who would've liked to see the Blackbird fried, and it had been Case who was standing between Pain and those who wished him harm. Case was tempted to step to the side and let the chips fall, but couldn't bring himself to do it. At least not yet.

The logical part of him said to just confront Pain and see what he had to say about it, but his bruised ego told him otherwise. Pain was a master manipulator and all he would do was try to spin it and have Case feeling like he was being paranoid, while he continued to plot on snatching his crew out from under him. Case didn't even know why he was surprised. Pain had always been an overly ambitious son of a bitch. Since they were kids, Pain always had to be the one to outside every-body else. When they became Crows it remained the same, especially with that bitch Cassandra always feeding his ego. Pain had always been the Queen's favorite. Even when Case was the one to bring the licks to the table, somehow Pain got the credit. Everything had to be about Blackbird. Pain soaked that shit up like he was a movie star and every-one else just spectators at his films. This decision Case had finally come to hadn't been an easy one to make, but he felt like his hand had been forced. The law of the jungle was survival of the fittest. He had hoped that prison would've humbled Pain, but since it hadn't he'd have to be the one to do it.

———————

Hook sat in the infirmary of Rikers Island city lockup, which was to be his home for the next few months while he fought his case. His leg and shoulder were still killing him, and the generic meds they had been pumping him full of did nothing to help. In the time he had been there, all he'd had to occupy himself were his pain and his rage.

He had spoken to Case a few times, and of course Case had tried his best to quell the boxer's rage. He had promised Hook that all of his legal expenses would be covered and his share of the heist would go to his family. "Don't worry about it. I'm going to take care of everything. You got my word," Case had promised. But the last Hook had heard, Pain was still alive and living it up, so Case's word didn't count for shit. He was tired of waiting around for the situation to be corrected, so he decided to be proactive.

The nurse who administered the meds to the inmates on that floor came walking into the room. She was a shapely light-skinned chick of about twenty-five. Whenever she was on the floor the thirsty men in the infirmary would always try to get with her, but none of them would ever taste her goodies. The same couldn't be said for Hook.

"Sup wit you, Nancy?" Hook greeted her by name. The two of them had known each other from the streets, back before she had squared up and had a kid. It was sheer luck that he happened to be placed in the unit where she was working.

"Another day, another dollar," Nancy said, pausing to give an inmate two beds over his medication. After taking care of him she moved over to Hook's bed. "How you feeling? You good?"

"Yeah, but I'll be better if you tell me you got what I asked you for," Hook said in a low voice.

Nancy gave a cautious look around to make sure the guard on duty wasn't paying attention. He was more interested in the book he was reading than what she was up to. Nancy removed a cell phone from the pocket of her scrubs and slid it to Hook. "Be quick. I don't wanna fuck around and get fired for messing with you."

"Don't worry, baby. It took God seven days to create the world, but it's only going to take me thirty seconds to burn it down," Hook said sinisterly, while punching in a number. The person he was calling picked up on the second ring. "Yeah, is this Prophet?" The caller said something to which Hook replied, "Who I am isn't important, but what I have to say is. I got some information for Queen Crow. It's about her nephew."

CHAPTER 24

The liberation of Passion from her job had been an unexpected twist to Pain's day. He hadn't planned on it, it was something that just happened. Pain had always made it a practice of steering clear of other people's problems, especially those of the domestic nature. He'd heard enough of their conversation to know that whatever was going on between Passion and Gus wasn't new, and by right it was none of Pain's business. There was just something about watching Gus attempt to force himself on her that pushed him to the edge. She looked so fragile and weak. As he thought more on it, she had reminded him of his mother and the shell of a woman she had become toward the end of her life. That's what made him snap.

After the adrenaline from what he'd pulled wore off, the realization of how stupid it was set in. He had gone into a man's place of business, a civilian at that, laid hands on him, and then robbed the joint. All without wearing a mask and in front of at least a dozen witnesses. There was a chance that Gus, or maybe one of his employees, would go to the police after he had gone, but he doubted it. Gus was a deviant and probably into way more than just forcing himself on young girls. Men like that shied away from any kind of attention that would shine a light on whatever sick shit they were into. Gus wouldn't go to the law, or at least Pain hoped. He had acted without thinking, which was further evidence of how deep he had allowed Passion to burrow into his head.

"You good?" Pain asked once they were away from the diner. She had been very quiet. Probably still shaken up.

"I'll be fine," she told him. "Thanks for what you did."

"You don't owe me no thanks. It was the right thing to do. Homie was out of pocket. I'm surprised that you got involved with a guy like that. He doesn't strike me as your type."

"He's not, and we weren't involved. We just . . ." her words trailed off. She was too embarrassed to even speak of how she had played herself by sleeping with Gus.

"Look, it ain't my business and I ain't no one to judge. I just think that somebody like you deserves so much more. You're too good for that."

"That goes to show how little you know about me. I ain't shit." Passion gave a sad chuckle.

"Don't say stuff like that."

"Why, when it's the truth? Every fucked-up thing in life that's been happening to me, I brought it on myself," Passion said emotionally. Tears began to fall. They weren't tears of sadness, but frustration.

"C'mon, ma. Stop that." Pain wiped away her tears with his thumbs. "Life is unkind, especially when it comes to people like us."

"And what kind of people are we?"

"The broken," Pain replied. "We are the kids that the world has cast aside. We ain't supposed to be shit, which is why it's such a sweet sensation when we rise above the odds and become everything that society says we aren't supposed to be. The key to that is, we have to believe even when no one else does. That's the only way we can ever rise above this shit."

"You sound like one of those street corner preachers," Passion teased him.

"I ain't preaching, baby. I'm just speaking my truth."

"So, have you managed to rise above this shit yet?" she asked.

"Nah, but I'm working on it. I'm not where I want to be yet, but I sure as hell ain't where I was." Pain reflected on those cold nights in his prison cell. "It's getting late. I should get you home."

"No, you don't have to do that!" Passion said a little too quickly for Pain's liking. "I mean, you've already done enough. Besides, I don't feel like going home. Not now." She hugged herself.

"Well, I don't know how comfortable I am about you just wandering the streets by yourself after what you've just gone through."

"Don't worry about me. I'll be fine. And you've already put yourself out enough for me. I don't want to take up any more of your time."

"I got no plans, and since you obviously don't have to be at work, you don't either. Might as well blow the rest of the day with me," Pain suggested.

"Boy, look at me." Passion motioned to her work uniform and black nonslip shoes. "Where am I going dressed like this?"

"Some place where it won't matter. I got this," Pain assured her.

"I don't know." Passion was hesitant.

"Do you trust me?" Pain asked, extending his hand.

Passion looked into his eyes, those sad eyes that had drawn her in from the first time they met. They didn't know each other, but that hadn't stopped Pain from putting himself at risk for her. It was the first time that any man since her father had ever tried to do anything besides exploit her. She was afraid at what would happen if she allowed this man, this angel of mercy, into her chaotic life. Would she poison his existence like she had done to everyone who had ever tried to love her? Against her better judgment, she stepped out on faith and took his hand. That was the first time they felt the sparks.

Pain had proved to be Passion's knight in gold chains and Timberlands, but it wasn't a chariot that he whisked her away on, but a No. 2 train. It took them about forty minutes to make it from Manhattan into Brooklyn. The subway car was hot, as the air-conditioning was out, and far too crowded. Passion had to stand up for almost the entire ride due to lack of seating. It was a miserable undertaking, but when they arrived at their destination it was all worth it.

Passion had lived in New York for her entire life, but had never been to the Brooklyn Botanical Gardens. New Yorkers tended to take for granted things that tourists traveled miles to see. It was close to closing time when they arrived, so Passion and Pain pretty much had the run of the place. They walked through the gardens and talked, getting to know each other better. Pain was honest with her about not having been out of prison too long. He expected that it would spook her off, but Passion was quite understanding. She told him about her dreams of fleeing New York to start her life over in California, and how the robbery had snatched that dream away from her. This seemed to deeply sadden Pain.

They explored the gardens, occasionally stopping to touch or smell the flowers. The place was so beautiful that Passion was mad at herself for not having come sooner. Little did she know the best was yet to come. When they arrived at the reason why Pain had brought her to the Botanical Gardens, Passion's breath was stolen. She stood in awe at the trees that stretched to the heavens with blooms of beautiful cherry blossoms. They almost didn't look real.

"They only bloom at a certain time of year. Usually in April," Pain explained. "I used to come every year, but haven't been able to see them in a while. I used to think that they were the most beautiful things in this rotten-ass city, but my opinion on that has recently changed." He brushed the back of Passion's hand with his finger.

"Boy, you got more game than a little bit," Passion blushed.

"One thing you'll learn about me is that I don't do games. You'll figure it out, though." Pain winked.

"Who says that I'm going to be around that long?" Passion questioned.

"You think after searching for you my whole life I'm gonna let you get away that easy?"

"There's that game again. So, how did you discover these cherry blossoms?" Passion changed the subject.

"My mom used to bring me here every year as a kid. When she passed I just kept coming."

"I'm sorry to hear that," Passion said sincerely.

"Thanks. She's been gone for some years now, but the pain still feels fresh."

"I know the feeling. I lost both my parents a few years back. Sometimes I dream that they're still here, and when I wake up and realize that they aren't it's like somebody pulling my heart out all over again," Passion confided in him. Thinking about her parents made her emotional, and her eyes misted. She felt Pain's arm drape around her, and nestled herself against him. For the first time in a long time, she felt truly safe. In the short time Passion had known Pain, he had made her feel things that no man had to that point. He had been kind to her, so she decided to repay his kindness with the only thing she had to offer: honesty. "Pain, I have to tell you something and I'm not sure how you're going to take it."

Pain removed his arm from her and took a cautious step back. "Here we go. I knew the other shoe was about to drop. What? You got a man and this can never go anywhere, right?"

"No, no . . . it's nothing like that. It's just that . . ." she began, but paused while she searched for the words. There was no pretty packaging she could wrap this in, so she just got straight to it. "I know that today wasn't the first time you saved me from a monster. You were there the night this happened." She pointed to her bandaged earlobe.

"What are you talking about? You said you fell." Pain played dumb.

"You and I both know that's not what happened. I know you were one of the guys who robbed the gambling spot. You got into it with the big dude who hit me," Passion insisted.

"Shorty, I didn't rob shit. I don't know what you're taking about," Pain lied. That night when they had noticed each other something had passed between them. Something familiar. But it was impossible for her to make a positive ID because he had been wearing a mask.

"Your eyes," Passion said, as if reading his mind. "From the first time I saw them, those beautifully sad eyes, I knew that I would never forget them. I never wanted to forget them."

Pain thought about continuing his lie, but it was pointless. She now knew who and what he was, and he wasn't upset. He was relieved. "What now? You thinking maybe you can get some type of reward for turning me in?" he tested her.

"I would never! After all you've done for me, the last thing I could do is bring myself to cause you harm. You're my savior," she took his face in her hands and stared into his eyes, "my angel of mercy."

"Blackbird," he whispered softly. Their lips were so close that Pain could taste her breath and she his. "That's what they call me. The slayer of your monsters . . . Blackbird."

Passion let the name roll around in her head. It fit this chocolate king as perfectly as a glove. "My Blackbird," she said before kissing him deeply.

Neither of them was sure how it happened, but they ended up in a thicket of grass behind some tall bushes. The bushes hid them from view of the few people who were still exploring the Botanical Gardens, but had they seen them the couple still wouldn't have cared. As far as they were concerned, they were the only two people in the world.

Passion pushed him onto his back and pulled his shirt over his head. She took a minute to marvel at his well-defined chest and flat stomach. He had obviously taken care of his body while he was in prison. On his chest there was a tattoo of a blackbird with its wings spread, with the word *Loyalty* under it. She ran her fingers down his stomach and played with the hairs just above his beltline. When she went to undo the belt, Pain stopped her.

"You don't have to," he said, eyeing her hopefully.

"I want to." Passion kissed him. She removed her shirt, showing full breasts held up by a satin bra. There was a hungry look in her eyes that she fixed on Pain. She could feel the cold spread through her body as the darkness made its presence known. It sent icy chills that caused her nipples to harden under her bra. Slowly, it crawled up her body and spread through her face, but there was something different about it this time. Normally, she was a spectator riding the wave of darkness while it took control of her body, but not today. No, for the first time she and the darkness occupied the same space. It hadn't swallowed her, but draped her in something she could only describe as a feeling of power and confidence. They would be partners in the conquest of this man.

Pain lay like a man in a trance, while Passion hovered over him. Every time she leaned in to kiss him, her dreads swiped across his chest, tickling him. Every so often he would force her head up just so he could stare at her face. "You are so beautiful," he said, breathlessly kissing her full lips. His eyes drifted to her arm and that's when he noticed the scars on her inner wrists and forearms. Some were old and healed, while others looked fresh. When she saw Pain staring, Passion attempted to pull away. "Don't," he stopped her, taking one of her wrists in his hand. "You're perfect." He kissed her scars.

Feeling his lips on her skin sent shockwaves of bliss through Passion's body. The way he was making her feel frightened Passion. There was no way that a man so flawed could be so damn perfect. She wiggled out of her work pants and then began helping him get his jeans down over his hips. She wanted to cry tears of sweet joy when she finally pulled his dick from his pants and found that she needed two hands to accomplish the feat. She thought to herself that they should've called him Black Stallion instead of Blackbird. Keeping his throbbing dick pressed between them, she worked herself up and down his body. She could feel him swelling and growing with each pass. She wanted him inside her more than she had ever wanted anything in her life.

Pain looked down at the top of Passion's head while her lips explored him: chest, neck, face, and back again. His whole body felt like it was on fire and Passion's love cave was the only thing that could put the flames out. She lifted herself so that his dick was aligned with her pussy. She was so wet that he didn't even need to use his hands to guide himself inside. Pain's dick swelled at the feeling of her walls closing in on him. The warmth of her was so intense that he let out a soft moan. He felt like a stone-cold bitch from the sounds that he was making, but he didn't care.

Passion let out a little yelp when she felt the tip of Pain's spear stab her insides. She had to adjust herself until she found a comfortable position to ride him, but it was no easy task. She started slowly, rocking back and forth and picking up speed as she began to get comfortable on him. She knew it was getting good for Pain, too, when he grabbed her by the hips. His brow creased and his lips drew back into a sneer as her pussy juices slathered his stomach and thighs, and soaked the grass beneath them. She began to buck wilder and wilder, while his fingers dug deeper into her sides.

Pain was trying to keep his cool, but it was no easy task. Passion was riding him like she was trying to win first place in a rodeo. They finally established a rhythm and Pain started putting his hips into it. The harder he threw it into her, the harder Passion bucked. They were battling each other for supremacy. Pain dug his heels into the earth, propped his hips up, and started going in. He held Passion by the shoulders so that she couldn't move and jammed into her faster and faster. When she yelled, he thought he might've hurt her, so he attempted to stop and check on her. This is when he saw a side of Passion that he didn't know lived there.

"Don't you dare fucking stop!" Passion said in a guttural tone. "You better keep drilling this pussy! Stop trying to make love and fuck me like a nigga who just came home from prison!" If that's how she wanted to play it, Pain was happy to oblige, so he pounded into her harder, which turned her on even more. "That's right . . . fuck this pussy, you twenty-three-and-one, locked-down, yard-spinning, grilled-cheese-on-the-radiator-making, nasty, big-dick nigga! Welcome home, baby . . . welcome the fuck home!"

Pain stared up at Passion with a nervous expression on his face. Her eyes were wild and spittle from her mouth rained down on his face and chest while she hurled obscenities at him. He wasn't sure what to make of the switch that had flipped in Passion's head. The sweet and timid girl he had only hours earlier saved from being raped was replaced by a demon. Passion had clearly gotten out of the car and he had no clue who was now in the driver's seat. He tried to motion for her that he wanted to switch positions, but Passion wasn't having it.

"Don't-you-fucking-move!" she snarled at him, leaning in to bite at his lip. Pain didn't know it, but he had just wandered into uncharted territory in her pussy. There was no way she was going to risk letting him ruin the moment. If Pain removed his dick from her, even for a second, she just knew that she would fall over and die. His dick was like life support! "I need you inside me forever . . . I need you inside me forever . . ." she ranted like a mad woman. "Right there." She started throwing her hips in a circle. She looked down at him from under hooded eyes and saw that his face was twisted like he had just smelled something foul. "Give it to me, my Blackbird. Spread your wings and fly!"

It took all of Pain's strength to get Passion off of him a split second before he exploded. His seed sprayed from the tip of his dick, spewing hot, sticky jizz all over his stomach and Passion's inner thigh. Pain looked up at Passion, still stunned over what he had just experienced. She sat straddling his stomach, smiling down at him like a mad hatter.

"Next time." Passion planted a kiss on Pain's sweaty forehead before rolling off him.

Pain sat there on the grass, watching Passion as she cleaned herself up with some wipes that she'd had in her purse. Every so often she would flash him a smile, and he would smile back. In Passion, Pain saw everything he had ever dreamed of in a woman; beauty, intelligence, ambition, but beneath it there was something else that gave him food for thought . . . instability.

"Shit!" Passion cursed.

"What's the matter?" Pain moved to join her. When he looked over her shoulder she was holding the lockets. The chain had popped.

"Must've happened during our . . . you know," Passion blushed. "I just got it back and almost lost it again."

Pain plucked the necklace from her hands and examined it. "This is an easy fix. We can take it to my guy uptown. He'll solder the pieces back together. Shouldn't take long at all." From somewhere in the grass, Pain's cell phone rang. It must've fallen out of his pocket during their romp. He finally found it, resting near the trunk of one of the bushes. Passion had shot out a random joke about him being on all fours, at which he laughed, but the smile was snatched from his lips when he saw who was calling. "Ms. Loretta? Is everything okay?" Ms. Loretta had been Ms. Pearl's down-the-hall neighbor for years, and one of the few people who checked in on her. Pain had given her his cell number in case of emergencies, and knew Ms. Loretta wouldn't be calling unless it was an emergency.

The sudden change in Pain's demeanor when he answered his cell didn't go unnoticed by Passion. She could see in his eyes that the more he spoke to whoever was on the phone, the further he slipped away from Pain and the closer he came to Blackbird. By the time he ended the call, the man who had just made beautiful love to her in a public garden was gone, and only the Blackbird remained. "Everything good?"

When Pain turned to her you'd have thought he was just seeing Passion for the first time in his life. "No, somebody is about to die."

PART IV
SUNSET

Pain was eerily silent for the whole ride back uptown. It wasn't the contemplative quiet of a man who had something heavy on his mind, but the still focus of a Roman gladiator who was about to step into the arena. Passion tried to chat him up. She knew he didn't want to talk, but she needed to hear her own voice against the backdrop of him going mute. He offered to drop her off home while he handled his business, but Passion had declined and opted to thug it out at his side. Pain had already put himself out for her so much that the least she could do was be a shoulder if he needed to lean or an ear if he needed to speak. Passion wanted nothing more than to be the calm to his storm.

The taxi had barely pulled to a full stop before Pain was shoving a wad of bills into the payment slot and sliding out of the backseat. Passion followed at a respectable distance. She was close enough to be there if he needed her, but not close enough to crowd his space. She was familiar with the look in his eyes. It was the same one she saw every time she looked in a mirror while the darkness was on her. There were dark forces at work in the heart of the man she had come to know as the Blackbird, and the smart thing would've been to leave things where they were, but she couldn't. Passion had tasted the love buried under all that sadness and found it intoxicating. In him she had found what years of therapy could never accomplish: a cure to her madness.

He shot through the doors of the emergency room of St. Luke's Hospital so fast that he startled the security guard manning the front desk. The fact that Pain's presence had surprised the guard was apparent to everyone who had seen it. His ego must've gotten bruised in the process because he decided that he would get up and come around his desk and stand between Pain and where he needed to be. "Where you off to, my man?" The guard raised his arm like he was trying to stop traffic.

"Look out, lil bro. My people in this joint and I'm just trying to see her. Pearl Wells, yo," Pain said impatiently. He hadn't meant to be short with the man, but the phone call he'd received had him in a different state of mind. Ms. Loretta had called to tell him that his grandmother had been hurt and was in the hospital. He didn't hear anything beyond that, he just moved.

"I hear you big dawg, but you still gotta respect the rules. You in here flaring up ain't gonna work. Step over to the desk so we can come to an understanding," the security guard told him. His tone wasn't disrespectful, but it carried enough weight so that Pain would know they were both from the same place. Pain didn't take it that way.

"My nigga, do I look like I give a fuck about protocol when my granny . . . the only person to ever love me the right way, is laying up in a hospital bed in a bad way?" Pain was pacing back and forth, fists flexing and eyes locked in on the security guard. He was working himself into a small rage that was built on guilt and the unknown. The security guard saw that Pain was past the point of reasoning with, and there was only one language that the two of them would be able to speak. With this in mind, his hand drifted to the flimsy wooden nightstick that was hooked onto his belt. This was absolutely about to go bad. Or at least it would've had it not been for Passion.

Quietly, Passion moved to stand between Pain and the security guard. Pain wouldn't look at her. He was too afraid of what she might've seen in his eyes at that point, but she didn't have to. Passion laid one of her hands on his chest and whispered, "Be still." Pain glared down at her, nostrils flaring. The fire still burned in his eyes, but not as high. Passion took the security guard and had a sidebar conversation with hm. By the end of it, she had Ms. Pearl's room number and two passes for them to get upstairs to visit with her.

When they arrived at Ms. Pearl's room, Passion had expected the worst. Based on the way Pain had reacted, she had thought something terrible had befallen Ms. Pearl, but thankfully things hadn't turned out quite so severe. Ms. Pearl sat propped up on two pillows in one of the hospital beds. She was spooning yogurt into her mouth while watching a rerun of *Law & Order* on the wall-mounted television. There was a small Band-Aid across her withered forehead, and a bandage around one of her dainty wrists. She had clearly been in some type of altercation, but wasn't too bad off. Ms. Loretta sat in a chair at Ms. Pearl's bedside, watching the show with her over the rim of her glasses. She was the first to notice Pain and Passion enter the room.

"Granny, you okay? Are you hurt?" Pain was at her bedside, covering her cheeks and forehead in kisses while checking her for injuries.

"I was until you came in here and started flipping me back and forth!" Ms. Pearl swatted him away. Her bandaged wrist hit her bedrail and caused her to wince. Pain tried to comfort her, but she pushed him away. "I'm fine. I've been hit in the head by tougher men than them who tried robbing my place."

"Tried *robbing* your place? What do you mean?" Pain questioned. His grandmother had been living in that housing project for nearly half a century. It was home to a who's who of killers, thieves, and everything in between, but the one thing Pain never had to worry about was someone hurting his grandmother in that hood. It was an unspoken thing that the elders were sacred.

Ms. Pearl hesitated, then looked to Ms. Loretta. "Baby, can you go to the vending machine and get me a soda with some real caffeine in it?"

Ms. Loretta had known Ms. Pearl and her family long enough to where she could read between the lines. "Sure thing." She stood and moved for the exit. She gave Pain a welcoming hug before letting her eyes come to settle on Passion. "She's cute, Percy." Ms. Loretta winked and headed out.

"Percy?" Passion asked with an amused smirk.

Pain shook his head, embarrassed, and turned his attention back to his grandmother. "What happened?" He waited for his grandmother to fill him in, but her attention was somewhere else. She was looking at Passion, who was leaning against the wall near the television. "Don't worry, she knows how to keep a secret."

"The last woman you said that about contributed to you going to prison," Ms. Pearl reminded him. If Passion had taken offense at Ms. Pearl's remark, her face didn't show it. Ms. Pearl let her eyes linger on Passion before turning her attention back to Pain. "I was in the house watching my shows," she said to Pain, "when I hear somebody knock on the door. It was a little on the late side for it to be the post office, but I know sometimes UPS can drag ass and I had some dishes that I ordered coming in. Anyhow, I get to the peephole and the next thing I know the door done hit me in the forehead and I'm lying on the kitchen floor."

"Did they take anything?" Pain asked.

"That's the thing. They kept asking me where it was at? I gave them the money I keep in the sugar bowl, but that still wasn't enough for them. They were looking for something. They finally stopped tearing my place up when they found that old speaker you keep in the back of your closet."

There was a delayed reaction when Pain heard what she'd just said. "My speaker?"

"They acted like that's what they had been looking for the whole time. Percy, I hope you didn't stash no drugs in my house. I told you I wasn't going for that! What was in that speaker, Percy?"

"Everything," Pain said with a sigh and flopped onto the foot of Ms. Pearl's bed. Inside that busted old speaker was where Pain had stashed every dime he had been saving since he touched down from prison. Besides the money he had in his pocket and the few dollars owed to him on the street, that speaker contained all he had in the world. Now that it was gone, he was sick.

"Who would do such a thing, Percy? Why would they do that to us?" Ms. Pearl questioned him. She wasn't pointing the finger at Pain directly, but it sure felt like someone was jabbing a knife into him with every question.

Pain sat there silent and numb while his grandmother continued. *How could his have happened?* was the question that kept exploding in his head. But he knew the answer. This was his doing. It had been Pain and his evil deeds that had brought this down on his grandmother. He'd thought that he was slick, and moving too low-key through the underworld to attract attention, but the streets were always watching. With tears in his eyes, he leaned in and hugged Ms. Pearl. "I'm sorry, and I promise I'm going to make this right." He could count on one hand the number of people who knew what he was into, and that number was even smaller when it came to who knew what kind of paper he was handling. This wasn't some random act. This violation had been intentional, and so would be his vengeance.

———————

Passion excused herself and let Pain have his time with his grand-mother. She told them that she was going to use the restroom, but Passion really needed a cigarette. Pain was in an extremely vulnerable place and she wanted to do him the honor of her not seeing him in that state. He was hurting, and she couldn't say that she blamed him. She could only imagine what she would feel like if someone she loved as much as Pain loved his grandmother had been beaten and robbed in such a way. She knew that Pain was in a bad way, and as much as she wanted to go to him and hold him, as he had done for her when she threatened to go to pieces, the best she could do for him at that point was give him space.

She was walking down the hall, trying to retrace her steps to the elevator that would take her back to the ground floor. She figured she would burn a cigarette or two before coming back up to check on him. It didn't take her long to find it. As she arrived at the elevator the doors were just sliding open. There were two orderlies wheeling off a girl on a hospital bed. She didn't appear to be in very good shape, with a heavy cast on her arm and a bandage wrapped around her head. One of her eyes was swollen shut and her jaw stuck out at an odd angle. She was thrashing back and forth, but the leather strap that held her good arm to the bed kept her from moving. Passion turned her head away, not wanting to witness whatever kind of psychotic episode the girl was having. She would've passed and kept going without a second look had the girl on the hospital bed not whimpered her name.

"Passion . . ." The sound was garbled, due to her broken jaw.

It took for her to hear her name twice before realizing that the girl on the gurney was talking to her. Passion studied the patient, trying to figure out how they knew each other. The girl's face being as swollen as it was, Passion didn't recognize her at first. It wasn't until she saw the rhinestones decorating her electric blue nails that she realized who she was looking at. "Birdie?" she asked in shock. Without waiting for an answer, she rushed to her side.

"Don't let them take me, Passion. Please don't let them take me!" Birdie mumbled frantically. She was in a great deal of pain and looked to be on the verge of a full meltdown.

"What are y'all doing? Where are you taking her?" Passion asked, blocking their path.

"Up to surgery, and I'm going to need you to get out of the way so we can do our jobs," the female orderly said. She was holding Birdie down with one hand and trying to steer the rolling bed with the other.

"Surgery? Somebody tell me what's going on and why she's being restrained!"

"Because she tried to throw herself in front of a moving train," the other orderly informed her. He was less sympathetic than his partner.

"What?" Passion went numb. She had just seen Birdie that morning and she seemed anything but suicidal.

"Passion . . ." Birdie cried out. Her head whipped back and forth like she was trying to shake the bandages off.

"Please, that's my sister Ruth Tolbert. Can I talk to her? Just for a minute?" Passion threw herself on the mercy of the orderlies.

The female orderly looked at the chart on the patient's bed. Her name had indeed been Ruth Tolbert. "Look, I'll give you thirty seconds and then I gotta get this girl into the OR."

Passion nodded in thanks and went to Birdie. She looped her fingers in Birdie's, the ones that weren't in a cast, and gave her a little squeeze. "Talk to me, Birdie. Why would you try and hurt yourself?"

"They killed me, Passion! They killed me!" Birdie shot up from the bed, yanking her hand from Passion's and using it to grab her behind the neck and pull her closer. She began whispering frantically in Passion's ear. The orderlies were quick with their responses, but by the time they pulled them apart, Birdie had already told Passion more than she ever wanted to hear.

CHAPTER 26

Cassandra sat in the parlor of her Staten Island home, chain-smoking cigarettes. Back in the day she had been a heavy smoker, but had quit a year prior. Her quality of life had improved since giving them up and she promised herself she would never go back, but with all that she had going on at the time she would indulge in whatever vices she chose. She had several missed calls on her phone. Mostly from people back home in Louisiana. She had been expected to show up for her nephew's homegoing service, as was tradition in her family, but couldn't bring herself to do it. Of course, some of the elders were upset that she had ignored the call, but she didn't care. Only sons of the Savage clan were bound to the call. She was a daughter.

There was a soft knock on the door. Cassandra ignored it. She continued sitting there, staring into the mirror at her red, swollen eyes. She had been crying off and on since she had received the news a few weeks prior. She was upset at the death of her nephew, but the alleged circumstances surrounding his death were what had broken her heart.

"Queen?" Prophet stuck his head in the door. Under normal circumstances he wouldn't have entered her parlor without her telling him to come in, but these were anything but normal circumstances.

Cassandra looked at Prophet but said nothing.

"I'm sorry to disturb you, but War is back from his errand," Prophet informed her.

"And?" Cassandra asked hopefully.

Prophet's face was grim. "Maybe it's best if he tells you himself."

Prophet stepped aside so that War could enter the parlor. Instead of his usual jeans and leather, he was wearing a suit. It had been a part of his disguise that day. "Madam, Queen. How you be this evening?"

"Cut this bullshit and please just get to it," she commanded.

"Well, I did like you said and went up to the jail to see the guy who called Prophet. Real piece of shit, that kid Hook. I know who he is from the streets and he would walk over his mother for a dollar,"

War said. He didn't care for Hook, and he cared for what he had to say even less.

"So, he's asking for money in exchange for this information?" Cassandra asked. It hadn't been the first time someone had tried to barter information for cash from her. If that was the case then she could likely punch holes all in his story. He was probably just another desperate crook who was trying to scam his way into some lawyer money.

"That's what I thought it was gonna be when I went up there, but apparently he doesn't want anything. He said to consider it a personal favor to you and maybe one day down the line you'll remember he did it."

"That doesn't make sense. Why would he bring this down on his crew and not ask for anything in return?" Cassandra couldn't figure it out.

"Because he's probably the only person on the planet who hates Blackbird more than ol' Prophet." War tried to make a joke to lighten the mood, but it fell flat.

"What did he say?" Prophet pressed.

"He fingers our former brothers as being behind what happened to your nephew," War said sadly.

"I told you! On life, you should've let me exterminate those roaches years ago," Prophet said heatedly.

"Prophet, please!" Cassandra silenced him. "War, what exactly did he say? Did he say that Pain was directly involved or was this Case's doing?"

"I'm sorry, Queen. He puts this one all on Pain. Case gave the order, but it was Pain who pulled the trigger."

Cassandra deflated in her chair. She had hoped that when War came back he would say anything but that. Case and his gang she could have wiped out without giving it a second thought, but her Blackbird? "This doesn't make sense. He gave me his word."

"And then he broke it," Prophet chimed in. "Queen, I know that the Blackbird holds a special place in your heart, so this is a sensitive matter for you, but he's shown you that the love is one-sided. He looked you in your face and flat-out lied. He has to answer for this. Him and his whole dusty gaggle. You let this slide and it's going to send the wrong message to the young Crows who now fly with our murder. If word gets out that you not only let them break off from the organization, but then sat and did nothing, it will plant the seeds of revolt. I will respect your decision either way, but that doesn't mean everyone else will. Make your choice."

Cassandra stood and went to the window. She looked out into the night absently, weighing the information and her choices. She had sent War to speak with Hook instead of Prophet because she knew that he would be honest with her. This wasn't to say that Prophet wouldn't have been truthful, but he might've also let his hatred for Pain distort the facts. Her heart was heavy. Heavier than it had ever been during the time sitting on the throne. She wanted to go to Pain and have him look her in the face and tell her that he hadn't been the one who touched her nephew, but they had been down that road already and Pain had lied. Pain was her heart, but Ralphie had been her blood. "Do it," she said softly.

"As you command." Prophet gave a half bow. He had been waiting for years for this day to come. He was finally going to clip the wings of his Queen's precious Blackbird.

"I'm not touching this one," War said, much to everyone's surprise.

"You would deny a direct command from your Queen?" Prophet inquired.

"Never, Cassandra knows where my loyalty lies. It's just that . . . this isn't sitting right with me. Pain has dropped his share of bodies over the years, but those were all about business. It was never personal with him. Even if he did decide that he was going to go back on his word and touch the Queen's nephew, why would he do it in front of witnesses? Pain is a lot of things, but sloppy isn't one of him. This was a mess and not his style."

"Fuck his style. If the Queen says he goes, he goes. What? You plan on jumping in front of a gun for a traitor? Where are your loyalties these days?" Prophet questioned.

War gave Prophet a serious look. "Son, you ever question where my heart is again and me and you gonna have to go outside and dance. I'm not jumping in front of a gun for nobody, but I'm making the choice not to stand behind one either. Not for this. You don't like it, do what the fuck you gotta do," he told Prophet and walked out.

"Old man is out of touch. Maybe he's getting too old for the open road," Prophet said after War had gone.

"No, he's probably more in touch than any of us," Cassandra said, thinking about his words.

"So, what are we going to do about your wayward birds? War get you to change your mind?"

"No, they're still getting their wings clipped. Do the lot of them. I want a total Murder of Crows." Cassandra had passed the death sentence. Anyone who had once borne her mark or eaten from her table who now stood with her former protégé was meat.

"I was hoping you felt that way, because I've had Mike and Mick on Case and his boys since Hook called. They'll take care of Case and his gang. I'll tend to Pain personally." Prophet started for the door, but Cassandra wasn't done.

"Alive." Her voice shook with the weight of what she had just put into motion. "Bring the traitor to me so he can tell me to my face why it was so easy for him to break my heart."

CHAPTER 27

There were at least a half dozen men sitting around in the project apartment, including Case and three of his henchmen. Only one of the men in the room was a member of Case's original robbery crew, and that was Lil Sorrow. The rest were guys who were part of their gang, but usually stayed on the outskirts. They weren't a part of his inner circle. At least they hadn't been before now.

After leaving the bar, Case had decided then and there that he was going to clean house. There was no telling who else from their inner circle Pain had managed to sway, so Case needed fresh eyes and fresh shooters around him. Men who had no loyalty to the Blackbird. Those who he had to question he planned to get rid of at his earliest convenience. The only reason Lil Sorrow was there was because, next to Blackbird, he was probably the most dangerous of the traitors. He knew that as soon as it popped off he would likely have to lay him down first, so he was keeping him close.

"I can fuck with a nigga like you. I ain't never been paid up-front to do shit," Ruben said, counting through the bills Case had given them. Each of the men assembled had been given an advance of three thousand dollars against their profits from the next job Case was lining up.

"They'll be plenty more where that came from. I'm a man who believes loyalty should be rewarded."

"For this kinda cash I'll be as loyal as a dog," Butch added. He was the oldest of the group, recently home from a prison bid. Case had worked with him in the past so he knew that as long as he kept Butch paid he would do whatever was asked of him. It wasn't as good as having Blackbird or even Hook guarding his back, but he would make do.

"Man, Riq and Sauce gonna be mad they missed out on this lick," Lil Sorrow said, counting his money. He was happy to have been pulled off the bench, and was ready to do whatever it took to stay in the game. He was a loyal and true soldier, but to Case he belonged to the Blackbird.

"Which is why I told y'all to keep this quiet," Case reminded him.

"Riq and Sauce are good soldiers, and there'll be plenty more jobs for them, but this is for the new blood. I been seeing all you guys grinding and doing what you gotta do to climb up through the ranks. Me laying this out exclusive for y'all is my way of saying I see you. Especially you, Sorrow."

"Me?" Lil Sorrow was surprised to be singled out.

"Yeah, man. Time and again you come through for the crew. I didn't forget about that piece of business you handled for me the other night. I got big plans for you, man. All I need you to do is stay true."

"Say less, big homie. I appreciate you letting me feed myself. I'll never forget what you've done for me. For that I'll be forever loyal," Lil Sorrow vowed.

"I'm sure you will," Case said. In the back of his mind he was thinking how Lil Sorrow had probably hit Pain with the same speech. "Sorrow, do me a solid. Run to the store and grab us some roll-up and a six pack."

"Man, why I gotta be the nigga still making the store runs? I thought I was down with the team now?" Lil Sorrow pouted.

Case leaned in and looked at him. "This coming from the dude who just got finished giving me a speech about loyalty? Fuck it, I'll do it myself." He made to stand.

"I got it." Lil Sorrow was on his feet. "At least give me the money."

"Take it out of that three grand I just gave your little cheap ass. Now get!" Case fake kicked at him. He waited until Lil Sorrow was out of the apartment before addressing the others. "A'ight, so everybody straight on what they need to be doing?"

"Yeah, as we're walking into the spot I creep up behind the lil nigga and put his brains on the curb," Butch said as if it was nothing. He had been killing cats for years, so for him this was just another day at the office.

"Yeah, and make sure it's quick and clean. I kinda like the dude, so no need to make him suffer unnecessarily. We can save that slow death for his big homie."

"It's still crazy for me to see what this has come to. You and Blackbird used to be like brothers, and now y'all about to go to war?" Ruben said, shaking his head. He was from the neighborhood. He knew Blackbird by reputation, but not personally. Back in the day, he and Case had been inseparable and now he was scheming on killing him.

"Can't call it a war if the other side doesn't have a chance to fight back," Case snickered. His new team was amped up, ready to gun it out in the streets over what Case had claimed was his own. They were motivated, and that was a good thing. They would have to save their bullets for another time, though. What nobody other than Case knew was, he planned to end the war between him and Pain without having to fire one shot.

The elevators were broken, as usual, so Lil Sorrow took the stairs. He wanted to hurry and get back from the store so that he didn't miss any of the planning for the job they were about to pull. He was so excited to finally be allowed to play in the big leagues that he didn't know what to do with himself. He knew Case could be a dick sometimes, but he had made up for some of his past antics when he started letting Lil Sorrow run with them. Under Case and Blackbird, he was finally starting to see some real money.

Lil Sorrow liked Case because he was feeding him, but he fucked with Pain heavy because he was a real nigga. Their relationship was based on his respect for the legend and not how much money he could put in his pocket. It made him sad when he discovered the tension between Pain and Case. Though neither one of them ever came out and said anything about it directly, Lil Sorrow could tell there was something going on. Pain hadn't been on a job with them in a while, and whenever he would ask Case about it the subject would always get changed. He had texted Pain a few times just to check in on him, but the responses were always short. After a while he just left it alone. He respected Pain, but he was no one's dick rider.

The boy's train of thought was interrupted when the stairwell door he was passing swung open and someone snatched him into the hallway. He reached for the gun that he kept in his waistband, but before he could get to it something cracked him upside the head and the lights in the hallway began to dance. He feared he would pass out, but a vicious slap across his face kept him conscious. When his head stopped ringing and his vision cleared he couldn't believe who it was that had snatched him. "Pain?"

"Were you in on it?" Pain growled, pointing a gun at Lil Sorrow's face. With his free hand he removed the gun that Sorrow had been reaching for and put it in his back pocket. It was a .380.

"Huh?" Lil Sorrow was confused. Pain slapped him again.

"Stop playing with me, Sorrow. I asked you a fucking question. Were you in on it?" Pain repeated.

"Pain, I don't know what's going on or what you talking about, but I'm gonna need you to get that gun out of my face," Lil Sorrow said, trying to keep his voice steady. He wasn't afraid, but he didn't want to die, either.

Pain studied Lil Sorrow's face, searching for signs that he was lying, but found none. The boy was telling the truth and he really didn't know what had happened. A part of Pain was relieved that he didn't have to add Lil Sorrow's name to the list of souls he had collected. He lowered his gun, but kept it in his hand. "Get the fuck out of here, Sorrow. I don't care where you go. Just don't go back to that apartment."

"Pain, just tell me what's going on. If somebody did something to you, tell me. We can get at them together. We family!" Lil Sorrow said sincerely. He would've followed Pain into hell if he had asked.

"After tonight, we won't be anymore. Go home, lil bro. Go home." Pain faded into the stairwell.

Case never bothered to look up from the line he was snorting when he heard the door open. It was a vice that he indulged in every so often. Everyone in the crew except Pain knew that he dabbled, but they all turned a blind eye. That was another reason why some of the members had been so happy when Pain came home. Case was a good dude and a solid leader, but between him chasing women and getting high he was starting to slip. The crew had been treading water up until Pain came home, and now they were swimming. Case inhaled deep, letting the coke singe his nose and drip into the back of his throat. "What the fuck?" he heard someone shout before blood and brains splattered on his pile of white powder. When he looked up his blood ran cold, and it wasn't from the cocaine.

Pain swept into the apartment like the angel of death. He paused only briefly to take in the faces of every soul that he was about to collect. There were no words from him. No grand speeches about betrayal or questions as to why it had happened. He just started dumping.

Two poor slobs who Pain had never seen a day in his life caught the first wave of his wrath. "What the fuck?" one screamed in surprise before Pain put a bullet in his mouth that came out the back of his head. His buddy tried to make his escape by bounding over the couch, and caught two in the ass, before Pain hit him again in the kidney. If it wasn't over for him he'd wish that it was. One of the faces Pain did recognize was that of the old-timer, Butch. Butch was a killer same as he was. Butch managed to draw his gun and let off, but Pain was already moving low across the living room so he missed. He slid right up on Butch and shot him through the chin, putting his brains on the ceiling. Ruben took that opportunity to bolt for the door. If Pain wanted, he could've gunned him down, but he decided to let him go. He wanted him to spread the word and let the hood know that it was the Blackbird who had paid a call on that house.

Case sat on the couch too stoned and too stunned to immediately react to what was taking place. There was a look of utter shock on his face, but it only stayed there briefly before his survival instincts kicked in. His eyes reflexively went to something on the other side of the room. Pain followed his line of vision and spied the gun on the dining room table. They lunged for it at the same time.

Pain had the angle, so he got there before Case. He tackled his friend, sending him crashing into the wall. Case landed on his knees and Pain was on him immediately. "Where you going, huh? Where you going?" He whacked Case on the side of the head with one of the pistols. "You're supposed to be my brother and you gonna do some foul shit like this?" He slapped him with the gun again, drawing blood from Case's mouth. "How could you turn on me like this?"

"Turn on you? Nigga, all I ever did was try and help you!" Case shot back. "From the moment you came home from that bid, I showed you love. I let you eat when you was out here starving, but a slice of the pie wasn't enough for you. Like always, you wanted the whole thing! Coming around with your big ideas and that Hollywood personality of yours, trying to take over what I built!"

"Take over? Dumb muthafucka, all I ever tried to do was make sure that we got fat and grew old together. The only thing I ever wanted was to eat with my family, and you're trying to tell me I'm wrong for that?" There was sadness in Pain's voice. "Fuck you, Case. I know you took my shit and I want it."

"This is the shit I be talking about," Case laughed sadly. "You always think somebody wants something you got. You been like that since we were both two stupid niggas begging for a pat on the head from Queen Crow. It ain't always about you, P. Your ego is what's brought us to this point. I've been living in your shadow since we were kids, and I just wanted to have a little sunshine of my own."

"I would've given you my last, Case," Pain said emotionally. He wasn't sure when it had happened, but at some point, his gun had found its way to his best friend's forehead.

"And I could never truly be free so long as you were giving me anything. I needed to get it on my own. Do what the fuck you gonna do, my nigga." Case rose to his feet and stared Pain down.

"I love you, my nigga," Pain said with tears in the corners of his eyes. He felt like his whole body was trembling, yet his trigger finger was still.

"I love you too, my nigga." Case moved the barrel of Pain's gun from his head to his heart. "In case anybody cares enough to give me a send-off, at least leave enough of me to have an open casket. At least let me get that."

Pain nodded, and wiped the tears from his eyes. A few seconds later the sound of thunder could be heard bouncing off the apartment walls.

Twenty minutes after Pain had left the apartment, Mick and Mike stood with a few dozen spectators just outside the crime scene. A half dozen police officers stood out in front of the project building, keeping anyone from entering or exiting. Residents of the building complained about being kept from their homes, but their complaints fell on deaf ears. The paramedics wheeled three gurneys through the lobby, all covered in white sheets that were soaked with blood. Detectives canvased the neighborhood asking if anyone had seen or heard anything, but they would find no help in that community. You didn't talk to cops, that was the unspoken law in the hood. They did happen across a crackhead who had been in the stairwell freebasing at the time of the murders. According to him, this was done by one man. When they asked the crackhead if he had gotten a good look at his face the man laughed and replied, "The angel of death ain't got no face. And that was who done these boys in." The detectives dismissed the drug addict and his account of what he'd seen, but Mick and Mike didn't. When they'd heard enough they slipped from the crowd and went back to where they'd left their bikes parked.

"Looks like somebody beat us to the punch," Mick said to his brother.

"Give you three guesses who it was and the first two don't count," Mike said. "He must have taken his best friend running up in his grandma's place personal."

"Wouldn't you?" Mick asked. "I know if somebody pulled that shit with our nana, we'd kill them and anybody they ever cared about."

"I agree," Mike nodded. "The difference between us and him is, at least we'd have killed the right man. Only thing worse than having to kill your best friend for crossing you is finding out that he didn't have anything to do with it."

"You think the Queen is gonna be mad that Prophet sent us at Pain before she officially gave us the order?" Mick asked.

"No, because she's never going to find out. As far as anyone is concerned the story stays as is; it was a simple robbery," Mike said before slipping on his helmet. The twins hopped on their bikes and went to meet up with Prophet to tell him of their findings.

CHAPTER 28

Passion felt like she was walking through a dream when she left the hospital. She was so blown away by what Birdie had told her that she had dashed out without bothering to tell Pain she was leaving. He had called her, but she didn't answer. It's not that she didn't want to. She just couldn't. She didn't trust herself enough to speak without breaking down. She felt bad about ghosting him like that, but she needed time alone to process what she had just learned. She would call him later to let him know that she was good and to see how his grandmother was doing, that would have to wait until her head was a little clearer. The story she had gotten from Birdie was so sickening that she had to stop and throw up. How could God let this happen to someone so innocent? She was a child with so much life, but that life would now be cut short.

She walked eighteen blocks from the hospital back to her block. It was late and there weren't very many people outside, which was a good thing. This way she could weep in peace without anyone seeing her. By the time she'd reached her neighborhood, Passion's tears had dried. She was all cried out. Seeing her building looming, she felt her sadness turn into white-hot rage. Mud and a few other jokers were in their usual spot, hanging out and drinking in the walkway on the side of her building. Mud said something slick as she passed. Normally Passion would've cursed him out, but that night she didn't give him a second look. It's like he wasn't there. Only one person existed in Passion's mind at that moment.

When she stepped off the elevator on her floor, she could hear the soft sounds of the Stylistics coming from her apartment. As she drew closer she could also smell weed. That meant that Uncle Joe was home, because he was the only one allowed to smoke bud in the house. She took a deep breath to compose herself before going inside. She wanted to tear through the house like a tornado, but she knew that she couldn't. Her next moves would have to be calculated. Inside the lights were dim, and aside from the music the house was quiet. When she stepped into the living room she found Uncle Joe sitting on the couch, joint in one hand and a glass of scotch in the other. The old-school lava lamp that sat on the coffee table illuminated his face. His head was bowed and his eyes were closed as if he had a lot on his mind. He must've felt her standing there, because his eyes suddenly flickered open and landed on her.

"Hey, baby girl. How long you been standing there?" Uncle Joe asked, sipping his drink.

"Not long," Passion replied. "Where's everybody else at?"

"Bo had to work late. Something about some kids she has to remove from the house of the man abusing them. I told her to let somebody else handle it, but you know Bo don't play when it comes to her job," Uncle Joe told her.

"That's a laugh," Passion said. It always baffled her how Child Protective Services let a woman who moonlighted as a bottom-bitch for a pimp work for them. To her credit, Bo did her job well enough when it came to keeping those kids safe. Passion just wished she had kept that same energy when it came to the children being abused under her own roof. Bo had the power to stop Uncle Joe, she just chose not to use it.

"What was that?"

"I asked where the girls are," Passion lied.

Uncle Joe shrugged. "Claire went down to the bus station to meet one of the new girls who will be staying with us. Gotta have someone to make up for the money Zeta was pulling in now that she isn't here. I got no clue where Birdie is, but that ain't nothing new. Lately she comes and goes as she pleases. Looks like it's just us for the next few hours," he smiled. His eyes were glassy. He had a good buzz going on from the weed and liquor. He noticed her staring at the bottle and held it up. "You want a taste?" Passion shook her head in the negative. "C'mon, it's your birthday. Have a taste with your Uncle Joe."

Passion sat on the couch with him, keeping a safe distance. Uncle Joe poured her two fingers of scotch into a plastic cup from a pack that was on the table and handed it to her. She was glad that it was dark, so he couldn't see the murderous look she was giving him. If she had a knife she would've stuck it through his heart. On the way there she had gone over the things that she would do and say when she saw Uncle Joe, but now that she was in his presence all she could do was glare and loathe him.

"Happy birthday." Uncle Joe raised his glass. Passion wordlessly toasted him. Joe threw his drink back, but Passion sipped hers. A silence lingered between them. Uncle Joe stared at Passion like he had something to say, but couldn't find the words. "I know it ain't been easy on you, living here amongst all this craziness. I thought when you came to stay with me after your parents were killed that my life had no place for an impressionable young girl."

"Then why take me in?" Passion asked. The question caught Uncle Joe off guard and he didn't answer right away.

"Because I loved your mother," Uncle Joe finally said. "Jessie was always there for me when we were growing up. Whether I was right or wrong, she always had my back when nobody else did. I didn't always do right by her, so I saw you as my chance to make up for it."

"That's what you call the way I've been forced to live? Making up for it?" Passion asked coldly.

"Hey, I know these aren't the most ideal living conditions, but I did as best I could with what I had to work with. I always made sure you had nice clothes, you never went to bed hungry, and never had to earn your keep like the other girls."

"You mean sell my pussy?" she shot back.

When Uncle Joe looked at her there was hurt in his eyes. "Baby girl, I ain't no saint, but I ain't put a gun to nobody's head to make them do what they do. My girls get to the money of their own free will."

"Even Birdie? Is that what I should tell her when she gets out of the hospital? That you and your nasty friend gangbanging her was of her own free will?" Passion asked heatedly.

"Hospital? What is Birdie in the hospital for?" Uncle Joe seemed genuinely concerned.

"Because she tried to kill herself!" Passion shouted.

"What? Why would that girl go and do a fool thing like that?"

"Because she's HIV positive!" Passion roared. "She had been complaining about not feeling well so I made her go to the clinic for a checkup. When the results came back she found out that she had been infected. She tried to throw herself in front of a moving train because she couldn't bear to live with herself after what you did. The only reason she's still alive is because someone grabbed her when she stepped off the platform. She's came out of it with a broken leg for her troubles, and I thought I heard one of them say something about a concussion? That was about all I could tell from what I saw. Won't know more until someone speaks with the doctors, but I don't need a medical degree to know that girl was fucked up."

"God. No . . ." Uncle Joe fell back on the couch, head in his hands. He'd made it a point to get himself tested every six months because he slept with whores and didn't always use protection. It was more than likely Teddy who had given her the bug, but they had both run in her and his condom had broken. Was he now infected, too? "I'm sorry," he whispered.

"You destroyed that girl's whole life and the best you got is 'sorry'? Joe, you're fucking pathetic!"

"Passion, let me explain." He reached for her, but Passion jumped up and out of his reach.

"Don't touch me, you diseased pervert. I can't even stand the sight of you right now!" Passion threw her glass of scotch in his face.

Uncle Joe leapt to his feet and his hand instinctively drew back to slap her. If he expected Passion to cower, or even flinch, he was disappointed. She stood there defiantly with murder in her eyes. Joe calmed himself and took a step back. "I guess I deserved that."

"Don't even get me started on what you deserve, Uncle Joe. I fucking hate you!"

Uncle Joe's eyes misted. Her words cut into him like a knife. "Don't say that, Passion. Please, I know you think I'm an evil man, but everything I've ever done for you has been out of love." He moved closer to her.

"Nigga, you sound crazy! You don't love me. I'd have rather have gone into foster care than to have suffered through this bullshit over the last couple of years." Passion was crying freely. All of her anger and frustration were in those tears. Joe wrapped his arms around her and pulled her into a hug. She tried to push him away, but he held fast. "Leave me alone!"

"I can't, Passion. Can't you see that? It's like with you I have a second chance. To do the things for you that I failed to do for your mother. I love you, child," Uncle Joe said passionately, and then quite unexpectedly tried to kiss her.

"What the fuck?" Passion shoved him away, causing Joe to fall on the couch. "What kind of sick shit you on? You trying to fuck your sister's kid?" she asked in disgust.

"Stepsister," Uncle Joe said to her shock. "Me and your mom don't share blood. My daddy got involved with her mother, so we came up around each other. I loved your mother from the first day my dad introduced me to her and your grandma, and she loved me, too."

"What are you saying to me, Joe?" Passion's head felt like it was spinning.

"I'm giving you my truth. We never intended to be together in that way. It's just something that kind of happened. We were able to keep our relationship a secret for years, and by the time it came out into the open we were both old enough to where nobody could stop us. I got into some shit and had to get out of New York for a while, and by the time I came back your mom was already with your dad and they had you. Your daddy was a good dude, but even he knew that deep down her heart belonged to me and mine to her."

"You're lying. I know you are." Passion shook her head from side to side. What Uncle Joe was trying to tell her was impossible, or was it? Then she remembered what Zeta had said. "It was you who told Zeta about the argument, wasn't it? You were the man I found out my mother was creeping with, and that's how you knew her secret was out."

"I was so lost when your mother was killed. I carried a lot of guilt behind it, because I knew I had been partially to blame. I should've just left her alone, but I was like a bee drawn to her honey. It was a cruel trick that God had played on me, making me fall so in love with your mother and then taking her away, but he made up for it when he sent me you. You've grown up to look so much like her. Even the way your eyes go all wild when you're mad. In you, my one true love has been returned to me." Uncle Joe stumbled toward her. She could smell the liquor coming off him.

"You are drunk and out of your mind." Passion shoved him back.

"Don't reject me, Passion. I couldn't live with being denied love twice in a lifetime." Uncle Joe pulled her close. His grip on her arms was like steel. "You're eighteen now, so we can be together, and there is nothing anyone can say or do about it. Be with me."

Passion looked Uncle Joe in the eyes. There was a hint of madness dancing in them. He truly believed what he was saying. He wanted her with more than just his body. His soul craved hers. This is why she took such joy in her response. "Sick-ass old man, I wouldn't piss on you if you were on fire. The only thing I wish for in this world is that one of these dope men you're dealing with finds out who your two-faced ass really is and takes your life like you took my parents'," she said venomously before spitting in his face. She wanted to hurt him as much as he had hurt her, and she did.

Uncle Joe stood there wearing the expression of a child who had just found out that there was no such thing as Santa Claus. Her spit ran down his face, mingling with his tears. He wiped his cheek with the back of his hand, and when he next looked at her there was no compassion in his eyes, only madness and hate. Before Passion could get out of the way, Uncle Joe hauled off and slapped the fire out of her. She flipped over the coffee table and landed in the same spot she had deposited Zeta during their fight.

"You ungrateful little bitch!" Uncle Joe was standing over her and shouting like a madman. "I try to give you a good life, keep you off the streets, and show you how it feels to have nice shit, and this is how you repay me?" He grabbed a fistful of her dreads and dragged her to the couch, which he tossed her onto roughly. "Is it another nigga? You don't want me because you've found someone else like your mother did?"

"Uncle Joe, you better fall back. Put your hands on me again and I'm going the police," Passion threatened.

Uncle Joe threw his head back and laughed like it was the funniest thing he had ever heard. "You go right ahead. What do you think they're going to say when they find out who you're trying to get locked up? Bitch, there's nobody short of God who you can call on that can keep me from you. I wanted our first time to be special, but I see you wanna play it different."

Passion tried to get off the couch, but Uncle Joe was on her. He forced her down and began snatching at her clothes. "Get off me!" she yelled, but Uncle Joe had tuned her out. He ripped the font of her shirt, exposing one of her breasts that had popped from her bra. She wanted to die when she felt Uncle Joe's dry lips clamp down on it and start suckling.

"You taste even sweeter than she did," Uncle Joe gasped. He pinned both her hands over her head in one of his and began roughly yanking her pants down. "Stop fighting me, Passion. Your mom was a little rigid at first too, but she learned to love the way I throw dick. Just like you will."

Passion continued to struggle, but Joe was far stronger than she was and the fact that he was drunk didn't help. Joe attacked her like a wild animal. He had managed to work her uniform slacks down to her hips by then. Her only saving grace was that she was thick and lying on her back, so he was having trouble getting them all the way down. She knew that once those pants cleared her hips it would be over for her. Not even the darkness would be able to wash this stain from her mind. Her strength was failing her, so she used her brain. "Okay, baby, okay," she said, relaxing herself. "I'll admit. I'm into you, Uncle Joe. I know you see me watching you pimp on the girls when they're acting up. That shit turns me on, but I never wanted to embarrass myself by saying anything. I just knew there was nothing you would see in a young square bitch like me."

Joe's eyes lit up. "Baby, girl. Ain't you been listening to nothing I've said? You are my gift from God. I'd cut all these whores off today and run away with you if that's what you wanted. I'd do anything for you, Passion. Just give me a chance to prove it."

"I will, Joe. We can do something. Just try not to be so rough. I don't want my pussy all beat up for my birthday," Passion cooed.

"Okay, I'll be gentle. I promise." Uncle Joe released her arms so he could take his shirt off and that was her window of opportunity.

Passion grabbed the lava lamp from the coffee table and cracked Joe with it. The glass didn't break on the first hit, but it did on the second. Colorful paraffin wax splashed all over the living room. Uncle Joe rolled off of Passion and was crawling away, clutching his bleeding head. She had neutralized the threat and was out of harm's way, but Passion was no longer in control of her body. The darkness had her and she was a helpless surfer on the wave. "Where you going, baby? Don't you wanna see what my goodies taste like no more?" She kicked Joe in his ass and sent him sprawling onto his stomach. Passion climbed on his back. "Dirty dick nigga! I hate you . . . I hate you!" She hit him several more times while ranting. By the time the darkness had finally released its hold on Passion, Joe was lying on the living room floor with his head busted open and she was covered in his blood.

"Dear God, what have I done?" Passion's hands flew to her mouth. She scurried as far away from Uncle Joe's body as she could, but couldn't tear her eyes from it. She had envisioned killing Uncle Joe hundreds of times in her head, but she never imagined she would actually go through with it. Life as she knew it was now over. All her hopes and dreams of finishing college and the life she wanted to build for herself on the West Coast had died with Joe. Bo would kill her, if the police didn't get to her first and lock her up until the end of her days. Neither option seemed appealing. If she had any hopes of getting out of this, she would need a miracle. No sooner than she had the thought, she heard someone knocking on the door.

CHAPTER 29

It was raining by the time Pain exited the building. He welcomed it. He lifted his face to the heavens and let the water wash away the tears that were rolling down his cheeks. It had been a long time since Pain had cried. The last time was after the death of his mother, if he recalled correctly. That had been the most devastating loss he had ever suffered, but what he had been forced to do in that apartment came in at a close second.

Pain looked down at his hands—hands that had just slaughtered an apartment full of people. He had killed before, in the heat of battle or when his life had been put at risk, but this had been an execution. Pain didn't know most of the men in that house, and as far as he knew they had never wronged him. Their only crime was being in Case's company when death came calling. Case's betrayal inflicted a type of pain on him that he wouldn't have wished on his worst enemy, let alone a friend. He had done everything right, been loyal to the crew, fair with soldiers, and honorable. Yet it wasn't enough. For all he had given there were still those wishing on his downfall. That was to be expected. Haters were a part of the game, but when it came from someone who he considered a brother it just didn't make sense. Had this hatred been living in Case's heart all along and Pain was blind to it? Or had it been as his friend had accused, and Pain had brought this upon himself because of his ambitious nature? These were questions which Pain would never have the answers to. He had brought about the end of a once-great era.

For the next hour or so, Pain wandered aimlessly. He felt so lost. Normally when something was weighing that heavily on him he could've taken it to Case, but that door was closed to him forever. He was tempted to call Tyriq, but decided against it. If Case had been conspiring against Pain, then there was a good chance that Tyriq had been in on it, too. It was doubtful, because he and Tyriq had always been solid, but time and absence changes a man. There was a very good chance that Case had managed to turn the entire crew against him. He was their leader, after all. The one they had been getting money with all these years. Pain was just a guy fresh home from prison trying to figure out where he belonged. One thing that he was certain about was that he didn't belong in that life anymore. He could no longer live in a world where the price of admission was his soul. As soon as his grandmother was well enough to travel, he was going to scrape up whatever money he could on the streets and get out of New York for a while.

The rain had caused the temperature to drop and there was a chill to the air. Pain didn't have on a jacket, so he shoved his hands into his pockets for warmth. That's when he felt something odd. When he pulled his hand back out, he was holding Passion's necklace. With all that had gone on, he had forgotten to give it back to her. The situation with Passion was something else that he needed to figure out. Before getting the call about his grandmother, they had been having a beautiful afternoon together. Probably one of the best Pain had ever had. He thought that the two of them had had a real connection, right up until she had gotten ghost on him. He tried calling her a few times, but she didn't answer. She did send him a text letting him know that she was okay and they'd talk later, but that had been several hours ago. Maybe she just wasn't as into Pain as he was into her, and their lovemaking session in the garden had just been a fuck? He wasn't mad at her, though. From what he could tell, that girl's life was fucked up enough without him bringing his craziness into it. No, he would leave the relationship between him and Passion where it was. When he looked up at the street sign, he realized that he wasn't too far from the building she lived in. Against his better judgment, he decided to drop by so that he could drop the necklace off to her. Unlike Passion, who snuck off like a thief in the night, Pain would say his farewells in person.

Passion almost shit herself when she heard someone knocking on the door. She tried to be as quiet as possible, even holding her breath. Mere feet away from her lay the dead body of her guardian, and her mother's former lover. She didn't know what to do. Should she run? Should she call the police? She couldn't think and whoever was knocking on the damn door wasn't helping.

Finally, the knocking stopped. Almost immediately after, her phone started ringing, scaring the daylights out of her. She looked over to her purse, which held her phone. It was lying on the floor next to Uncle Joe's body. She dared not go anywhere near it, but then something occurred to her. What if Bo or one of the girls was calling to say that they were on their way home? Passion would have a hard time explaining why she was half naked and covered in a dead man's blood. Sweet Jesus, the ringing phone had caused whoever was at the door to resume their knocking. She was sure they'd heard the ringing, so they knew someone was inside. This time the knocking was more urgent. Whoever it was, it was obvious that they weren't going away. Gathering her nerve, she crept to the door as quietly as she could. As she neared it, she thought she heard somebody call her name. Uncle Joe's peephole was a two-way mirror, so she didn't have to worry about whoever was on the other side seeing her. When she peeked out, her breath caught in her throat. God had heard her prayers.

Pain stood outside Passion's door thinking to himself how terrible of an idea this had been. He could've just mailed the damn necklace to her. It wasn't like he hadn't gotten her full address from Sparrow. There was no reason that he had to come up there in the rain other than the fact that he just needed to see her. Even if it would be for the last time.

He knocked on the door and waited. Nothing. He pressed his ear to the door and thought he heard music playing but couldn't be sure. He knocked again and still nothing. He had decided that she either wasn't home or didn't want to be bothered, so he turned to leave. While waiting for the elevator he figured he'd call her just to let her know that he had come by to return her necklace. At the same time the phone started ringing in his ear, he could hear it ringing in the apartment. That meant she was home, but if so, why not answer the door? Even if it were just to tell him to fuck off and stop stalking her, at least come to the door. Then he recalled how reluctant she had been to go home earlier and found himself filling with a sense of dread. Something was definitely going on in that house and there was a chance that she hadn't come to the door because she couldn't.

Pain went back to the door and knocked again. This time he

knocked with more authority. "Passion?" he called out, listening in at the door. He was about to knock again when he heard the locks being hastily undone on the other side. Pain waited impatiently. He wasn't sure what kind of reception he could expect from Passion. Would she be angry at him for popping up? Happy to see him? Of all the ways he thought she might greet him, half naked and covered in blood wasn't one of them.

"Pain!" Passion threw herself into his arms and immediately began sobbing.

"Wha . . . what's going on? Are you okay?" Pain pried her loose from his neck and held her at arm's length. She had scratches on her wrists and throat, and one of her breasts was out of her bra and exposed through her ripped shirt. She was nicked up, but he didn't think it was her blood.

"I did a thing, and I'm so fucked now. My whole life is fucked! But it isn't my fault," Passion began babbling.

"Slow up. First off, let's get out of the hallway." Pain looked around to make sure no one was watching before slipping into the apartment. He locked the door after he was inside, taking extra care to cover his fingers with his shirt so as to not leave prints behind. He didn't yet know what he was walking into, but when he entered the living room he was glad that he had taken the extra precautions. "My God," was all he could say when his eyes landed on the dead man. "Did you do this?"

"He . . . he tried to . . ." Passion broke down in tears again.

Pain didn't need her to say it to know what had happened. He could tell from the ripped clothes and the bruises. Someone else had tried to make her a victim and caught a bad decision. "I got you, shorty. First thing, is there anyone else in the house?"

"No, everyone is out but they'll be back. I just don't know when," Passion told him.

"Then that means we have to move fast." Pain went and knelt beside Joe's body, careful not to get any of his blood on him. Joe's head was busted open pretty bad and he'd lost a lot of blood. Upon closer inspection he noticed that he had several wounds to his head and back. This meant that she had hit him more than once and from behind. "Damn, girl. You fucked him up pretty good."

"I didn't mean to. He attacked me and it just happened. I was fighting for my life," Passion said.

"And that's what we need to tell the police when they get here," Pain said, much to Passion's surprise.

"No . . . no police!"

"We have to call them. Look, this was clearly a case of self-defense. Big man like him attacks a teenage girl. They ain't even gonna book you for this," Pain told her. He didn't know what Passion had expected, but there was no way in hell that he planned on getting caught up in whatever happened in that apartment. What he had done to Gus at the diner was light. A dead man carried way heavier consequences. Pain didn't believe in talking to cops, but in a situation like that, going to the authorities and pleading her case was her best course of action.

"I can't go to the police," Passion told him.

"And why the hell not? If you—" His words were cut short when a pain exploded in his side. He pitched forward on his hands and knees. He glanced back and was shocked at what he saw. From the condition Pain had found Uncle Joe in, he had assumed the man was dead. There was no way he could've survived what Passion had done to him. Yet here he was, face covered in blood and armed with one of the glass shards from the broken lava lamp. That's what he'd stabbed Pain with.

"You trying to take from me, too!" Uncle Joe accused in what sounded like a wet gurgle coming from his mouth. One side of his head looked dented and it seemed like he was having trouble finding his balance, so he came at Pain in a stumble.

"Nigga, I'm trying to help you!" Pain shouted, clutching his ribs and cursing himself for not dropping the damn necklace in the mail.

"Uncle Joe, stop it!" Passion yelled, which drew her uncle's attention to her. His eyes went soft, but only briefly as he remembered what she had done.

"Funky bitch! I'm gonna kill you!" Uncle Joe hobbled in her direction, swinging his glass shard awkwardly back and forth. Before he could reach her, Pain jumped on his back. The two of them began to tussle and fell to the floor.

When they hit the ground, Uncle Joe ended up on top of Pain. He was trying to stick him again with the glass, but Pain was able to hold him off. Just beyond Joe he could see Passion huddled in the corner trembling. "Fuck is you doing? Help me!" he shouted. Passion snapped out of her panic and ran into the bedroom. His attention was pulled from her when he felt a pain in his forearm. Joe had bitten him. His mouth was latched onto Pain's arm like a pit bull and he wasn't letting go. "Get the fuck off me!" He clubbed his fist into the side of Joe's ruined head over and over. He sacrificed a bit of his skin to finally pry Joe's teeth from him. No sooner had his head lifted and cleared Pain's body than it exploded, depositing brain matter on Pain's face. Using his shirt, he wiped the blood free of his eyes and blinked. Behind where he and Uncle Joe lay, still in a heap, was Passion.

"He was going to kill you," Passion said softly, lowering the gun she had just used to shoot Uncle Joe. It was one of his. At her feet lay the lockbox that he kept it in.

Keeping his eyes on Passion the entire time, Pain carefully slid from beneath what was left of Uncle Joe. Slowly, he moved toward Passion. "It's okay," he kept repeating softly as he got closer and reached for the gun. He had seen her check out before and wasn't sure how deep that rabbit hole went.

"I couldn't let him kill you," Passion told Pain.

"I know, baby. You saved my life," Pain said, and gently plucked the gun from her hand. He looked from the frightened girl to the dead man and finally at himself holding the strange gun and thought that this situation couldn't get any worse. He would soon find out that it could. "We gotta call the police, ma. We gotta tell them what happened."

"Haven't you been listening to anything I've been trying to tell you?" Passion snapped at him. She grabbed the lockbox from the floor and pulled out the item that had shared its confines with the gun. It was a detective's badge. "We can't go to the fucking police, because Uncle Joe *is* the police! He's vice."

Pain's legs turned into noodles. If it had not been for him bracing himself against the wall, he would've likely fallen down right next to Uncle Joe. Accidentally killing a regular civilian would've been bad, but still easy enough to fight in court. But killing a cop? And a detective at that. Passion might be able to get out of this with a few years or parole with the right attorney, but Pain? Technically, he hadn't done anything. He had just been a spectator. But with his record and the fact that he was on parole, even being in the room when it happened was enough to send him back. He would need a million-dollar lawyer just to have a snowball's chance in hell at fighting this.

"We gotta run," Passion said quite unexpectedly. She began pacing the living room and rubbing her hands together like a nervous tic. "I can't let you go down for this shit, when you've done nothing but rescue me time and again."

"Passion, you just killed a cop and now I'm tied up in this, too. Where the hell are we gonna run where they won't come looking for us? We don't need to run, we need a lawyer."

"I got one!" Passion said excitedly as soon as the thought hit her. "He's a friend of my parents' based out of California."

"Call him! You got a number?" Pain asked hopefully.

"No, but I know where he lives. I haven't seen him since my parents' funeral, but I'm sure if we go to him with this he'll help us. He won't turn us away."

Pain looked at Passion as if she had three heads. What she was suggesting was the craziest thing Pain had ever heard. After killing a cop, she now wanted him to run off with her to California to throw themselves at the mercy of a lawyer who Pain wasn't sure was even qualified to take this type of case on. But she seemed so certain. In Passion's mind there was no doubt that this would work. "Girl, are you crazy?" he finally addressed the elephant in the room. He cared about Passion, but there was definitely an imbalance within her.

"So I've been hearing all my life," Passion responded. She moved to Pain and cupped his face in her hands, drinking in those sad eyes that she loved so much. "Sweet baby, know with everything that's been going on I look like nothing but a messy bitch with more problems than she knows what to do with, and I absolutely am everything they say I am. You can go your way and I'd never mention your name, but this is something I'm going to have to deal with at some point. Right now, this guy in California is my best shot, even though it's a long one. I'd rather die free and running than caged and waiting on the end. How about you?" She extended her hand, same as he had done when he'd asked her to trust him.

After some contemplation, Pain took her hand. "I ain't never going back in anybody's cage. I see your vision, but I'm still unclear on the execution. We can't even get out of the city, let alone to California, with no car and no money."

Passion thought on this dilemma for a time and then it hit her. It was a long shot, but it was all she had. "What if I told you that I had a way to get both? We may just have to get our hands a little dirty."

CHAPTER 30

"I have to admit. I was surprised to get your call," Jay said, opening the door for his guest. He was in one of his low-key stash apartments where he conducted his illegal business. He'd been getting ready to close a deal on some pills that he had lined up when he received the SOS.

"If I'd had any other choice I wouldn't have pulled you into this," Case said, stepping into the apartment. He was a man who took pride in his appearance, but that night he looked like shit. His clothes were dirty and bloody. There was a bandage covering his face from his lower jaw to just above his left ear, and it was soaked in blood due to the fact that he hadn't had a chance to get someone to stitch his wounds properly, only wrap them as best they could.

"Damn, he did all that to you?" Jay was speaking of Case's injuries. His face was heavily bandaged, but the exposed skin he could see was all black and blue.

"I did this to myself." Case flopped on the couch, thinking about his failed attempt to double-cross his best friend. One whole side of his face was beaten to hell, but his ear had taken the brunt of the damage. Pain could've taken his life, and he wouldn't have been wrong in doing so. Instead he opted to scar Case, pistol-whipping him severely, and for good measure he'd laid the barrel of his gun against the side of Case's face and pulled the trigger repeatedly. He'd suffered burns from the barrel, had part of his ear blown off, and could no longer hear on that side. Still, he was allowed to keep his life. It had been a rare act of mercy on the part of the Blackbird.

"Whatever, man. I don't know what's going on between you and your man Blackbird, but I'm hearing y'all crew has been thrown into some type of civil war over your differences. You really rough Pain's grandmother up?" Jay asked.

"Jay, you know better than that. Niggas are just making a mountain out of a molehill." He and Pain were at odds, but Case would never let it touch Ms. Pearl. She had been better to him than his own mother had been.

"I'm just telling you what's out there, bro. That's some scandalous shit, but I ain't here to judge. All me and mine care about is our bottom line and whether or not you'll be able to continue to meet it in light of all this shit you got going on," Jay said honestly.

"Don't worry. As soon as I get sorted out, everything is going to go back to normal," Case assured him. He paused when he heard a knock at the door, and gave Jay a suspicious look. "You expecting somebody?"

"Relax, man. I ordered some food before you called. Sit tight, I'll be right back." Jay went to the door.

Case flopped down on the couch. He was both mentally and physically exhausted. He needed to regroup and plan his next move. The fact that Jay knew what was going on meant that word was already starting to spread. That wasn't good. He'd planned to have Pain out of the way, and he had an airtight story to feed the crew before anyone knew what was happening. This complicated things. He knew his soldiers. They were loyal to him, but there were more than a few who had love for Pain. This would cause a rift and people would start picking sides. He heard Jay speaking to someone and they sure as hell didn't sound like a delivery person. He sprang to his feet, but it was already too late.

"There's my little bitch." Goodie rounded the corner, gun drawn and aimed at Case.

"Jay, you crossed me?" Case asked in disbelief.

Jay shrugged. "It ain't personal. I told you all I cared about was my bottom line. The dumb shit you did could have some adverse effects on that."

"Don't blame Jay. I could've laid my hands on you any time I wanted. I was just giving you enough rope to hang yourself, and from what I'm hearing you did just that," Goodie said with a smirk.

"Goodie, man, we can fix this. I've put a lot of money in your pocket and done everything you asked of me, whether I wanted to or not."

"Yeah, you did everything except the one thing that would convince me to let you keep breathing." Goodie pointed his gun at Case's face. "You promised me a bird, yet my cage is still empty. Where is Pain?"

SEVERAL DAYS LATER:

The 32nd Precinct in Harlem had been abuzz all morning. Everyone was talking about the suits who were currently in one of the conference rooms with Lieutenant Wolf and Captain Connors. From their drab clothing, silent stares, and near-mechanical movements, you could tell off the back that they were from the government. The question had been which branch. Even the desk sergeant had been kept in the dark and given instructions to provide their guests with anything they might need without question. Whatever was going on in that room had to be major.

Inside the room the blinds were closed so that no one on the outside could see who or what was going on. This meeting and what was discussed during it would be on a need-to-know basis. A large whiteboard had been erected on one side of the room. Pinned to it were pictures of several men and women, with notes scribbled on stickies. At the top of the pyramid was a face that most in the room were familiar with.

Lieutenant James Wolf sat quietly in a chair with his hands folded on the table. He stood out amongst the clean-cut men and women, with his cornrows and baggy sweat suit, but it had been his day off when he got the call. He hadn't expected to be called in, especially for something of that magnitude. He had been listening for twenty minutes and still wasn't sure why he was there. The only other person of color in the room was an older Black woman. She was wearing an olive green business suit and glasses. She would look up every so often from the legal pad she had been taking notes on, but outside of that she hadn't said a word. She looked just as out of place in the room as Wolf.

"So, really quickly, let's just go over what we already know," Captain Connors was saying. "At ten hundred hours Thursday night, vice detective Joe Brown was found murdered in his apartment. In addition to being a fifteen-year veteran of the department, he had also been working as a confidential informant in an ongoing investigation involving police corruption."

"The irony of that," Wolf said under his breath. He knew Uncle Joe. The man was a piece of trash who used his badge to do all kinds of crooked shit, but Wolf had been no choirboy in his days as a young detective. The brass looked the other way on Uncle Joe, so he did, too. Now he understood why.

"When Joe started out, we had been looking into what we thought were some local cops running drugs. But thanks to Joe we figured out that it went way higher up the food chain than just some locals making a few extra bucks. This is why our friends from the federal government have so graciously volunteered to give us an assist on this one. The man we are after is one of theirs." He pointed to the top picture. It was of a light-skinned man with a sharp chin. "Marshall Gooden, a rogue US Marshal who's been running his own little pharmacy from New York, to some say as far as Indianapolis. He's been using his position to pinch drugs from state and local seizures and redistribute them in the streets. Joe had given us almost everything we needed to bring him and his organization down until his untimely death."

"You think he's the one who clipped Uncle Joe?" Wolf asked. The wheels in his brain had already began whirling and examining the case from several different angles.

"Not his style. Gooden isn't one who likes to get his hands dirty. His thing is manipulating other people to get what he needs," a red-headed man in a gray suit answered. From his tone it was clear that he didn't care for Gooden. Wolf would learn later that this was Agent Fredericks. He was a big shot at the FBI.

"Which brings us to yet another plot twist in this already crazy story," Captain Connors continued. "During the autopsy the medical examiner was able to lift a second DNA sample from Joe's mouth. Apparently, he bit whoever was behind his murder. I had the lab put a rush on it. We came up with a hit, and it pointed us to this man," he indicated at another photo in the pyramid. This one sat lower that most of the others. "Percy Wells, known as Pain or the Blackbird. He was recently released from prison after doing time on a drug charge. Before his little vacation he was the right hand and sometimes en-forcer to the Queen of Thieves, Cassandra Savage."

"How does he connect to Joe?" Wolf asked.

"He doesn't, at least not directly. As it turns out, Wells and Gooden are from the same neighborhood. From what I'm told, Gooden also had a relationship of some sort with Wells's mother years ago."

"So, it stands to reason that Gooden got this Wells kid to kill Joe, doesn't it?" the Black woman who had been taking notes asked.

"All signs point to it, which is why this matter has been escalated to urgent status." Captain Connors looked to Fredericks to pick up.

"Gooden is a lot of things, but sloppy isn't one of them," Fredericks continued. "If he did use Wells to kill Joe, that means he knows we're on to him. Gooden is going to track this Wells kid down and kill him and then get ghost. We figure if we can get to Wells before Gooden does we may be able to flip him. All we need is Wells to admit that a US Marshal contracted him to kill a cop, and we don't even need the drug charges anymore to fry him. Wells has now become the key to this investigation and the top priority of this precinct."

"And the girl?" the woman with the notepad asked. On the board, between Blackbird and Uncle Joe, was a picture of a young girl with a question mark under it.

"Joe Brown's ward, Passion," Connor said. "She was last seen going into their building not long before Joe's murder. Since then, nobody has been able to find her. Not even the other women she lives with know where she is, and her cell phone was found in the elevator shaft of the apartment building. We think she may be Wells's hostage."

"Or an accomplice," Wolf thought out loud.

"How about we get the facts before we condemn this girl," the woman with the notepad challenged.

"Detective Wolf, this is Special Agent Lauren Higgins," Captain Connors made the introduction. "She's been working undercover on this since the beginning. She's been posing as a professor at the community college that Passion attends. The two of them have gotten very close during the course of this investigation. She knows this girl better than anybody."

"Which is why none of this is sitting right with me," Agent Higgins spoke up. "Look, Passion has got some very deep issues, but she's no cold-blooded killer. Even if the victim is a flesh-peddling demon. I knew Joe before the badge, and what I think is that something happened in that apartment that got out of hand, and this Wells kid just happened to be in the middle of it."

"Well, we can figure out whose theory was right and whose was wrong when the two of you bring them in." Fredericks looked from Higgins to Wolf.

"Say again?" Wolf wanted to make sure he'd heard correctly.

"A joint effort between the NYPD and the FBI to bring down a multimillion-dollar drug operation and put a dirty government agent down as a sweetener," Captain Connors said. He looked at Wolf. "I told Agent Fredericks that you're the best tracker in this department. There's nobody I'd be more confident in to catch these kids."

"That's a high compliment coming from you, Captain," Wolf said.

"And Detective Wolf, so you don't run into any red tape over jurisdiction while you're on this case, I am authorized to deputize you as a federal agent for the duration of this manhunt," Fredericks announced. "I don't care how far you and Agent Higgins have to go or what you have to do, but we want these kids."

Wolf looked to Agent Higgins, who was staring at him coldly. She was not looking forward to this undertaking. He then turned back to Agent Fredericks and nodded, letting him know that he was in. "Any ideas on where we should start looking?"

EPILOGUE

Ted was having himself a grand old time. Since someone had punched Uncle Joe's ticket to the hereafter, Ted figured the money he had been holding on to became his by default. With Joe gone, Bo was the only other person who could contest his claim, and she was clueless about the nest egg Joe had been building. Ted wished that he could see the sour old bitch's face when Joe sprang it on her that he was running off with Passion. Joe was like a fool over that young girl, and from what the streets were saying she had something to do with ending him. Ted could see the vicious little harpy, waving that sweet young pussy under Joe's nose until she got him to let his guard down. Ted was glad that he hadn't gotten a chance to sample her pussy that morning, because he might've found himself half crazy and dead like Uncle Joe. Thankfully, he was very much alive and enjoying the fruits of Joe's labor.

To celebrate his windfall, he had hit the club and popped a few bottles. Ted never really cared for champagne. He was more of a whiskey man, but the expensive bubbles were a magnet for thirsty young girls. As proof of that, he managed to leave the club that night with two of them, and for the last hour or so, they had been in the private room he kept at the back of his dealership getting real freaky. He was on his knees with his face buried in the pussy of one of the girls while the other one was running her tongue through his ass. Ted was a freak like that. Her tongue was getting good to him when she suddenly stopped.

"Damn girl, why'd you quit? You were hitting my spot," Ted said over his shoulder. When she didn't answer, he looked back to see what was going on.

There were two more people in the room with them. They were cloaked in the shadows so he couldn't get a good look, but he could see very clearly that the taller of the two was pointing a gun at him. Foolishly, Ted lunged for something on the floor. He heard the shot and pain exploded in one of his ass cheeks. "Damn, I was only reaching for my pants!"

"Can never be too careful," the taller of the two said.

They stepped into view so that Ted could get a better look at them. They were both wearing all black and had bandannas covering their faces, one black and one pink. The eyes of the person behind the pink bandanna rang familiar to Ted. "What is this?" he asked.

Passion thought back to her conversation with Birdie, and how they would run up in the spot. She slipped her mask down so that Ted could see exactly who was doing this to him before responding, "A muthafuckin stickup."

ABOUT THE AUTHOR

K'WAN is the No. 1 *Essence* bestselling author of *Welfare Wifeys, Section 8, Gutter, Still Hood, Hood Rat*, and others. He wrote his first novel, *Gangsta*, as a therapeutic release, and it went on to become an *Essence* bestseller and a part of urban-lit history. In 2008, K'wan received the Black Author of the Year Award from Black Press Radio. He has been featured in *Time, KING, New York Press*, and on MTV and BET. Besides an author, K'wan is also a motivational speaker, a mentor to at-risk children, and the CEO of Black Dawn, Inc. and Write 2 Eat Concepts, LLC. He lives in New Jersey.